PRAISE FOR KATHLEEN NANCE!

THE TRICKSTER

"Kathleen Nance has weaved a story unlike anything I have read before and for that I applaud her. She is a true genius."

—*Scribesworld.com*

"Kathleen Nance spins a unique and clever tale. *The Trickster* is warm, funny and tender."

—*Romantic Times*

"There's almost nothing I didn't like about this book. . . . It's the perfect pick-me-up."

—*All About Romance*

MORE THAN MAGIC

"*More Than Magic* is an undeniable treasure trove of pleasure, bursting with magnetic characters and a bewitching plot that's sure to capture the imagination of fantasy and romance readers alike."

—*Rendezvous*

"Another winner. Ms. Nance has a very special touch!"

—*Romantic Times*

"An astonishingly original story in a world which contains far too few paranormal romances, *More Than Magic* is more than satisfying."

—*Affaire de Coeur*

WISHES COME TRUE

"Kathleen Nance has penned a supremely enticing tale with laughter, intrigue, the paranormal and, of course, a passionate steamy love that comes across in spades. . . . Put *Wishes Come True* on your list for a tangy must read."

—*Rendezvous*

"A story of magic, wishes, fantasy, and . . . a lot of spice. Ms. Nance is wonderful in her debut novel. Fantastic! 5 Bells!"

—*Bell, Book and Candle*

PACKING HEAT

The pounding of his heart echoed the rhythm of hers. It was good to know that he wanted this as much as she did. Her fingers teased playfully down the front of his shorts. Yes, he definitely wanted her.

Armond grabbed her hand. "Not so fast."

Callie pushed on his shoulders, urging him down to the bed. He resisted, and she was powerless to move him. "Next time we can be slow," she offered.

"It's a deal."

Then he caressed her again, kissed her, and her warrior claimed her with a frantic, rising need that spiraled between them. He was intense, untamed, and he roused primitive instincts in Callie, wild feelings that both thrilled and frightened her.

Her hands wrapped around his waist.

She felt the hard gun at his back.

THE WARRIOR

KATHLEEN NANCE

LOVE SPELL   NEW YORK CITY

For Pat, who shows what courage truly means.
I am blessed and privileged to call you sister.

A LOVE SPELL BOOK®

June 2001

Published by

Dorchester Publishing Co., Inc.
276 Fifth Avenue
New York, NY 10001

ISBN 0-505-52417-1

The name "Love Spell" and its logo are trademarks of Dorchester Publishing Co., Inc.

Printed in the United States of America.

Visit us on the web at www.dorchesterpub.com.

ACKNOWLEDGMENTS

With many thanks to:

Bob Core, for taking the time to show me the beauty of Traverse City. I wish I could have included it all.

Les and EJ Williams, for their generosity and their cabin on the lake that introduced me to the area.

Robert and Nadine Begin, proprietors, and Mark Johnson, vintner, of Chateau Chantel for their hospitality and answers to my questions. Any mistakes made and liberties taken are mine alone.

The many people of the wineries and vineyards on Old Mission and Leelanau peninsulas, who answered questions, let me taste the wines, and made research a true pleasure.

THE WARRIOR

The Myth of Callisto

Zeus spied the nymph Callisto running through the woods, serene and fluid as the wind, and his heart beat with wildness in his chest. He enticed her, seduced her from her innocence, and brought her to his bed. In time, she bore him a son.

Hera, furious at Zeus's continued infidelity, turned Callisto into a she-bear. The quiet nymph's hands grew round, with crooked claws, and her cool voice a mere growl with which she bemoaned her fate. Clumsily, she fled in terror from hunters and other bears alike.

One day, a hunter came into the woods, and Hera sent him before Callisto, who knew him as her grown son. When she rose to hug him, he prepared to kill her, not recognizing her. Zeus intervened to prevent the tragedy and Callisto was set among the stars along with her son. Hera, her thirst for revenge still strong, bade that the stars would never be allowed in the ocean. To this day, the Great Bear and the Little Bear twirl the night sky without setting.

Thus was written the legend of Callisto.

Legends can be wrong.

Prologue

Guilt, the guilt of others, tasted astringent, like a wine spoiled by excess tannins. It was a familiar taste.

Special Agent Armond Marceaux popped a stick of cinnamon gum into his mouth as he stepped from the 8th District New Orleans Police Station into the French Quarter at two A.M., relieved to escape the pervasive undercurrents from the criminals who filled the halls. Their guilt plucked at him, jarring dangerous instincts he'd long ago forced himself to master but could never ignore.

Tonight's work was satisfying: a criminal finally brought to justice and two lives saved from a deadly fire, including one of the few men Armond deemed a friend.

Justice was an exacting mistress, though. Armond was bone tired and his face itched from stubble and ash. The suffocating humidity stuck his clothes to his skin, and the acrid scent of burnt straw clung to him like an irritating burr. How much dry cleaning would it take to get out that smell?

Small prices to pay. His inner need to bring evil to justice, to hunt and do battle, was a relentless siren, as inevitable as the beating of his heart. Tonight, he'd prevailed.

Tonight, for once, it wasn't enough.

Rain misted the streets to a slick shine under the harsh lights. He combed a hand through his dark hair, drew in a breath filled with dampness, and then strode through the quieting streets of the Quarter. An odd restlessness and a simmering hunger accompanied him, and he knew at once the reason why.

Callie Gabriel.

She'd helped him nail this last case, but it wasn't gratitude that drove his footsteps now. He'd thought it was over between them. Armond's lips twisted. Eight months since he'd left for DC, left her, but his reaction to her was as potent as the first time they'd met. Clearly it wasn't over, at least for him.

Something in him tonight felt raw and exposed. Perhaps it was how close he had come to losing a friend. There weren't that many people he trusted like he trusted Mark. They had shared a lot in their youth— the troubles that boys without guidance find, the skill to watch each other's back. Perhaps it was being back in New Orleans, a city that cherished the past.

Whatever it was, he didn't want to be alone right now. He wanted life, and not the seedy kind he usually dealt with. He wanted sunshine and sweetness and a few hours respite.

He wanted Callie.

He passed a tiny liquor store, an unprepossessing hole in the vibrant Quarter. Abruptly, he reversed direction and went in, spitting out his gum in a nearby trash receptacle. " 'Lo, Danny Bob," he greeted the man, who wiped the counter with a white rag.

"Detective Marceaux! You been a stranger too many months. You back in town to stay?"

"Only a few days. And it's Special Agent Marceaux now."

"That's right, you left the po-lice. Took some other job."

Job. Lifelong dream. Undercover assignment. Take your pick. Armond nodded. "With the FBI. I'm based in Atlanta."

Danny Bob sniffed and rubbed a hand across his bald head. "Bet Atlanta don't got an okra gumbo like you always wanting."

"No, and the crawfish . . ." Armond shook his head in regret. "Thought I might take back a special bottle of wine." The public part of the shop was ordinary liquor, but to those who knew, Danny Bob's favorite stock was hidden away in a climate-controlled wine cellar. "Would you have a Cabernet Sauvignon? Nineteen-ninety-eight. Rochon Estates." Armond had tasted it before and found it silky, lush, and concentrated sweet currant.

"One of the Old Mission Peninsula wineries? Let me check." Danny Bob disappeared for a moment. When he returned he handed Armond a bottle. "Here you go. You know, I never would have thought to try these Michigan wines if you hadn't ordered them, but I've enjoyed them."

"Thanks. I thought you might. How much?"

In minutes, Armond had his wine and found himself walking the dark streets again. Occasionally when a passerby brushed against him a whisper of knowledge, a sure feeling of their *guilt,* slid across his skin, tightening the fine hairs on his arm and puckering the

15

back of his tongue. Idly, he'd wonder what they had done.

He'd learned from an early age to mostly ignore the odd sensation, except when he needed it for a case—to do otherwise was madness. He'd also learned the very painful lesson that to act on it without thought or control was a dangerous path to vigilantism and violence.

The edginess, the foreign knowledge, however, stirred other instincts, ones primal and basic to any man.

Automatically, inevitably, he found himself outside Greenwood, Callie Gabriel's vegetarian restaurant. A light shone from the back. As he suspected, she was still at work. As owner-chef, her workload demanded tremendous dedication and hours. It was one of the things that attracted him to her, thinking she would understand the demands of his work.

The first thing he'd noticed about her, though, was her smile.

Callie was always smiling.

The door was locked, and he knocked. No answer, even to a second knock. He made short work of the lock—one of several unconventional skills he'd picked up over the years—and headed inside.

The restaurant was quiet, the bustle of preparing hundreds of meals done for the day, but the aromas of spices, tomato, hot chiles, and sesame oil lingered. The door behind him shut with a soft thud, closing out the chaos of the city, and he locked it.

Inside was peace.

Desire flared through his chest, then lower. It was as though, by shutting out all the irritating gusts of emotions surrounding him, this one clear need was free to burn bright.

"Is someone there?" Callie's voice called.

"It's me. Armond."

"Armond?" The breathy catch told him what he needed to know.

He had not misread the signals. Things between them were not as settled as they'd thought.

Callie appeared in the doorway of her office. Her brown hair was pulled down from the knot she wore when she worked, and a yellow glow backlit her, giving the shoulder-length tresses the smooth sheen of a fine sherry. She wore loose jeans, a shirt of brilliant red over a tight knit tank top, and a chunky necklace made of primary-hued cubes of acrylic.

Her eyes widened, taking in his dishevelment. "What's wrong?" she asked.

He lifted the wine bottle. "Would you share a glass of wine with me? I arrested Guy Centurion tonight."

"So, it's over."

"Yes." It wasn't. Centurion's tentacles went wider than the smuggling ring he'd broken up, but Callie didn't need to know that. "Are you going to invite me in?"

"Ah, sure." She motioned him into her office. "I could use a break from the accounts. Let me get a corkscrew and glasses."

Armond hung up his jacket on the coat tree, then splashed water on his face and washed his hands in the small corner sink. Drying off with a paper towel, he glanced around her office, curious to see whether she'd made changes since he'd left eight months ago. He'd been here twice when they were dating. Tonight, he couldn't see the tiny garden out the window, but he expected it was still there as Callie used fresh herbs in her cooking. File cabinets, lumpy sofa and cracked leather chair, huge desk strewn with papers, all were familiar. He snapped off the overhead light, replacing it with the narrow beam of the desk light, then picked up a melon from the row lining the edge of her desk and sniffed it. Near ripe and sweet.

Callie returned, two wineglasses in one hand, a corkscrew and a plate of biscotti in the other. "I thought these might go well with the Cabernet."

"They will." Deftly, Armond opened the bottle and poured two glasses of the deep red wine. He sat on the sofa, holding both glasses. When Callie sat next to him, he handed her one glass.

The wine was as good as he remembered.

They savored it in silence, until Callie asked, "What happened tonight?"

Armond shook his head. "I don't want to talk about it, don't want to think about it." He stretched a hand along the top of the sofa, until the tips of his fingers touched the back of her neck and the silky strands of hair. "Ask me tomorrow, not tonight."

"All right." Callie tucked her stockinged feet beneath her and chatted in a stream of conversation that was so Callie.

The wine infused him with a pleasant glow. Armond lightly stroked her neck, listening to the sound of her voice rather than her words. Her hair and skin were soft and of a texture both feminine and unique to Callie. He felt himself growing hard with the touch and scent of her.

She stirred under the light caress, not moving away from him, but uneasy. Like a wild animal wary of a strange scent or sound, yet not alarmed to the danger. She clutched her wine as a glass barrier between them.

She'd never seen this part of him, this street warrior from his youth that tonight craved release. He'd let very few people even know of it, and none of them were women. And it was making her uneasy. With difficulty he replaced the cultivated veneer that had become second nature to him.

Beneath, however, the desire for her still thrummed with urgent demand, making him taut and ready.

"Do you want me to leave, Callie?" he asked mildly, gentling her with feathery strokes at the top of her spine. She was so soft, so sweet, so *honest;* she grabbed at his every sense. How could he feel both peace and excitement when he touched her? "I will if you ask."

"Why did you come here tonight?"

"I needed to be with someone."

"Anyone would do?"

He shook his head. "Only you."

"Is this wise?"

"I think there are things still unsettled between us, Callie."

"We broke up eight months ago. When you left New Orleans Police for the FBI."

"We broke up because eight months ago I asked you to my fishing cabin, but you never came. I'm not here to ask why," he murmured. "Not tonight."

Eight months ago they'd been ready to move beyond dating to intimacy. To sex. Eight months ago he'd been tempted by this special woman into believing he could share his solitary life, share his secrets. He'd asked her to his cabin in the swamp, given her directions to a place he'd never told anyone else about.

They'd both known what the invitation meant.

She'd promised to come.

She hadn't. Hadn't sent word, hadn't called. Nothing.

At first, he'd been frantic with worry, thinking she was hurt. When he found out she was fine, worry was replaced by the bitter taste of betrayal. Or so it had seemed at the time.

Armond thrust the thoughts away. Now he was back and it was tonight that mattered. He struggled for control of the heat bursting inside. He'd almost lost his closest friend tonight. He couldn't accept that he'd lost Callie, too.

Running a finger down her cheek, he was pleased to see a shudder of desire catch her.

"Tell me to go," he told her, "and that will settle it one way. Tell me to stay, and it will be settled another."

Callie stilled, and every atom inside him stopped with her, expectant. She laid a hand on his chest, branding him with a touch, both strong and feminine, that jump-started his heart. "Do you mean it? You'll stay?"

"Yes." Couldn't she feel her effect on his blood? Couldn't she see it? Didn't the need reach out to her?

Her uptilted lips curved into a smile.

It was the only invitation he needed. He finished the wine with a single gulp, set both glasses aside, and then kissed her. Her lips were soft and eager, her mouth warm almond, her neck smooth and spicy scented. Armond drowned in the maelstrom of sensation as he lowered her to the sofa.

She didn't seem to mind his weight; her arms embraced him. Her curves beneath him, ah, those he didn't mind at all. Desire spun through him like a whirling, shining blade, dangerous and impossible to ignore. With an uncharacteristic clumsy urgency, he opened the vibrant red blouse, shoved up the knit undershirt. No bra, as he'd suspected. Her breasts, the skin above her heart, her belly were open to his fingers and his mouth.

"Callie, you have a ring in your navel," he said with

bemusement, rubbing the tiny silver circlet; then he kissed the two silver studs she wore in each ear. "Any other piercings I should know about?"

"That's the lot. You have any?"

"Ah, no."

"Didn't think so."

He ran his tongue around the silver ring and around her navel, then slowly kissed his way upward to her breasts, where he took full plunder.

Callie's hands gripped his hair, holding him close. "Oh, Armond, I never imagined . . ."

"I did." And he took his time, savoring the taste of her, committing to memory each texture and moan. Imagination had left out a lot.

He fumbled with his shirt, but she stopped him with trembling hands. "Let me."

Slowly, too slowly, she undid each button. Armond held himself in rigid check, exerting every honed ounce of control over his body to let her finish. As soon as she had it open, however, he gathered her in, pressing her to him, imprinting the feel of each inch of bared skin.

"I want it all, Callie. I want all of you."

"I want you, too."

Hands flew over confining clothes, releasing just enough in their speed. Strokes, suckles, nips, caresses followed until they were both naked and aroused. Armond settled onto her.

"Wait," Callie whispered, "wait."

Armond groaned. "Callie, you aren't going to say no, now?"

"Would you stop if I did?"

Could he? "Yes. But I wouldn't like it."

She smiled into his shoulder. "No, I'm not stopping. It's . . . protection," she whispered.

He should have been the one to think about that,

but something about Callie Gabriel had always set logic in a spin. "I have—"

"Let me." She slid beneath him, then walked to the desk. By the pink tint of her delectable skin, he knew she was embarrassed to walk naked in front of him, and it delighted him to know that she blushed everywhere.

She rummaged in the desk. "Where—? Ah, here." Triumphantly, she returned, holding up a strip of foil squares; then she slipped back to her place beneath him. "I never thought I'd get the chance to use this. Will you let me put it on?"

Armond only nodded, unable to talk with the dizziness at feeling her trembling hands on him. Her fingertips were slightly cold as she rolled the condom over him. Armond feared he might come right then, right in her hands, but he forced himself to hold on. The interlude had only stoked him higher, not cooled him, but it would not be over so soon.

She swore once before she finished.

"Is something wrong?" he asked.

"Oh, nothing. I've just never done this before."

Armond reared back. "The condom? Or the sex? Are you a virgin, Callie?"

"Would it make a difference?"

"In the outcome? No. In the speed we took there? Yes."

She grinned at him. "I meant the condom."

"Good."

Swiftly he rolled over her, settling home between her thighs. With one stroke he was inside her, the primitive warrior claiming his woman. She welcomed him with a wet heat.

He kissed her—neck, shoulder, earlobe, the length of her arm—while he stroked deep inside. She held him tight and returned each caress. Armond slowed.

Now that he was seated where he'd wanted to be, he took his time, calling on every fragment of control to bring her shuddering in his arms.

"Armond," she breathed. "Could you *hurry up!*"

They whirled and spun, while inside him was the glistening of the rising sun. Armond vaguely heard rain start up again, its tattooing a counterpoint to the pounding of his heart. Higher, tighter, faster until—

The inner explosion, matched by Callie's breathless wail. A keen release surged through him, leaving behind exquisite exhaustion and peace. Armond slumped down, just to the side of Callie, anchoring her to him with hand and arm. She gave a soft sigh of contented pleasure. The ebb after explosive sex warmed him slowly.

How long they would have stayed in that contentment, Armond didn't know. Suddenly the rain beat against the window and it flung open, letting in a driving summer storm and soaking them.

"What the hell!" Armond sprang to his feet and struggled over to the window. He slammed it shut.

Callie burst out laughing. "So much for the glow of aftermath," she giggled. "At least our clothes didn't get wet. Let me get a couple of dish cloths from the kitchen."

She was back in a moment with the squares of cotton. They dried as best they could, then dressed. Armond ran a hand through his damp hair. "That wasn't how I would have chosen to end it."

"Does that end it?" she asked softly. "What next, Armond?"

He stroked back her tangled hair. "I have to be gone a while—"

"A while? How long? Where? Why?"

"I can't tell you that, Callie. But when I come back—"

"—you've been assigned to New Orleans?"

He stared at her. "No."

She pulled away from him. "No? You said you'd stay."

"Stay tonight. I'm assigned to the Atlanta field office."

"What is this, then? A one-night stand?"

"No!" Armond ran a hand through his hair. "I needed you tonight, yes, but I thought—" *Merde,* he hadn't thought, he'd only needed. "We can figure out something."

"Like, I'm supposed to just pick up and follow you? What about this 'a while'? Undercover, right? And what am I supposed to do in the interim? You didn't even think about refusing, did you?"

"Of course not. Where did you get a pea-brained idea like that? I'm LE, Callie. Law enforcement. I can't change that."

"Can't? You mean won't."

"I mean can't."

"Always a cop at heart," she said bitterly. "I can't—I thought your coming here meant you'd understood what went wrong before. Last time you never even called to say you were leaving for DC."

"Why the hell should I have? You were the one who broke it off. You never came to meet me; you never even picked up the phone."

She gazed at him stubbornly. "I need to know you're always going to be there for me. How can I trust you when you leave me alone?"

"And I need to know I've got your understanding and trust, Callie. I need your utter loyalty. I guess I've got my answer to settling things between us."

They stood in silence. Rain beat against the windows. A driving rain with no lightning, no thunder, just howling winds that echoed the silent howling inside.

She turned away. "Please go, Armond."

Peace and contentment turned to hard knots inside him. He'd always known he was destined to be alone, but until this moment he'd never truly accepted it.

And never known how badly emptiness could hurt.

Armond locked his jaw and returned military stiffness to his spine. He shrugged on his jacket, straightened the sleeves an inch below, then pulled his tie from his pocket and carefully knotted it. He smoothed a hand across his hair. He spared one final glance at Callie.

They both knew it was over for good. He would not forget this night. This moment.

"Good-bye, Callie," he said, then walked out into the rain.

Chapter One

Two months later

Hera sent the book of mythology careening across her Chicago office with one flick of her peacock-eye–painted fingernails.

"Wrong! Always wrong! You'd think at least one chronicler would have tried a different slant." She thrust to her feet and paced to the bank of windows that lined the Peacock Cosmetics presidential suite.

Beneath her, streetlights winked out and downtown Chicago awoke. Beyond lay Grant Park, a strip of shadow in the pink dawning morning, and farther out rolled the endless waves from vast Lake Michigan. The lake was steel-blue, a testament that autumn would soon be winter. It was beautiful and majestic, a treasure in its own way, yet so different from the mountains and hot springs of her home world.

Which was precisely why she had chosen this city for her headquarters. She would not live among mountains again unless they were the mountains of her first home.

Reflected in the glass, the discarded book caught her eye and reminded her of her frustration. Always she was painted as cold, bitter, jealous, vengeful.

Hera didn't see it that way; but then, a couple of millennia of distortions did tend to color one's view. Tartarus, but she hated to admit it had been that long! She had only three, maybe four centuries left.

"Try hurt, disappointed, frightened the next time you write of me," she muttered at the book. "Be original." She laid her palm to the cool glass, covering the reflected volume, and rubbed the clouded ring on her middle finger. Outside the windows, clouds gathered in a roiling mass while a blue shimmer spread across her hand to the reflected image. Behind her the book's pages ripped and spun in furious tornado, then collapsed to a shredded heap. The clouds vanished.

Hera gave a satisfied nod. Her husband Zeus might control the sound and the lightning, but she commanded the powers of rain and wind.

After one last look at the brilliant sunrise, she returned to her desk and the problem at hand. Once known as queen of the gods, she was now known as Harriet Juneau, queen of cleansers and blushers. Her cosmetics made women feel pretty, confident. She was wealthy, respected, had a realm of friends and companions, and she was proud of what she had earned.

Yet . . . she wanted to go home.

When Zeus had been banished to Earth with his band of followers, she had been caught in the punishment from the Titanic Oracle, the ruling council of her world. Ancient Earth had seemed a paradise to the exiles, lush and green and bountiful. The skills, powers, and equipment they possessed had made them the gods of old, until man stopped worshiping them and technology usurped their mystique. For a short time, though, they had reveled in the glory—and none more than Zeus.

She had come, out of duty and love, leaving behind all that was familiar for an alien world, and discovered a distasteful emotion unknown on her world—jealousy. In that the male myth writers were accurate, although so much else they wrote was wrong. She had never harmed another woman or a child.

Except once.

A low whistled tune from her outer office distracted her from her flirtation with unpleasant memories. Hera, recognizing it, waited. Seconds later, Zeus strolled in.

He looked fit, as always, with trimmed salt-and-pepper hair and a tidy mustache as befit Zeke Jupiter, successful owner of Jupiter Fireworks. She'd heard others mistake him for a popular Scottish actor, though personally she'd never seen the resemblance, except perhaps in the resonant voice.

"Been reading the myths again?" Zeus tilted his head toward the heap of tattered paper.

Unwilling to admit aloud her petty irritation, Hera shrugged. "You smell like a dog."

"While you are elegant as usual, my dear." He bestowed a light kiss to her cheek. "I took Cerberus for his walk, though the tri-headed beast saw fit to run away."

"He'll come back when he needs us," Hera answered, unconcerned. Cerberus, the dog who guarded the gates of Hades, was quite capable of looking out for himself and getting others to do his bidding.

Zeus aimed his next kiss to her lips.

Hera shifted away, ignoring the excitement he always fanned inside her. Too many hurts and disappointments, too many years apart to be overcome in a few short months. She smoothed her jacket. "Behave yourself."

"Behave *myself,* love?" He burst out laughing, then settled himself into a chair. "You are as incorrigible as me."

"We have work to do."

Two months ago, when she had first relocated her husband, she had thought him engaged in his old trick of seducing innocent earth women. Instead, he had gotten the foolishly sweet idea that he could atone for his past misdeeds to the women he had wronged by uniting their descendants with a true love, thus breaking the unexpected legacy he had left in their family lines. Love, the deep and long-abiding kind, had eluded these women, who fell in love with the wrong men, or chose unwisely, or listened to the drum of practicality instead of the flute of desire. They did not trust in the magic that was love.

She had helped him, discovering the cycle could only be broken by uniting the women with a son of Olympus, a man descended from the gods. Their first attempt had been a success, uniting a woman of Io— Joy Taylor—with Mark Hennessy, a descendant of Hermes.

"So, who will be the next woman who receives our help?" Zeus seemed eager for another foray.

So was she, Hera admitted. It had been fun, and as she had told him yesterday, passion and amusement had been sadly lacking in her life of late. Life with Zeus was never dull.

"Callie Gabriel," Hera answered promptly. They had

met Callie once, very briefly, during their last adventure.

Zeus stared at her. "Callie Gabriel? The woman descended from Callisto?"

"Yes."

"No! You are never rational on matters of Callisto, my dear."

"Which is precisely why it must be she."

Despite the myth chroniclers, Callisto was the only one of Zeus's lovers to pay a permanent price for Hera's jealousy. Serene, composed, graceful Callisto—Hera had truly feared the nymph would turn Zeus's affection away permanently, so the goddess had turned her into a she-bear, as the myths stated.

There, the story diverged from fact, however. That bit about the Great Bear and the Little Bear circling the skies was sheer fancy. In truth, Callisto's child had been a girl, not a boy. To taunt Callisto once more before she allowed the nymph to return to human form, Hera brought the child before her mother. Callisto rushed forward in joy, but the child, not recognizing her mother in the form of a bear, screamed. A nearby hunter, fearing attack, killed the bear.

To this day, Hera felt the horror of what she had done. She knew she would have to make reparation to a descendant of Callisto.

The Oracle would not allow her to return home without it.

Hera perched on the edge of her desk. "You said the woman would be my choice."

Zeus gave a suffering sigh. "Then let's see what she's doing."

He rose and locked the door, then stood beside her while Hera pulled a blue geode into the center of her desk. It would not do for humans to see the powers of the gods.

Hera sprinkled a white powder into the crystal center of the geode, then added a folded paper bearing the name of Callie Gabriel. Zeus held his hand above paper and powder. Sparks surrounded his palm, and the powder ignited with a flash. Cedar-scented, far-see smoke wafted up in a thin line, then spread, like the tail of a peacock, into a fragrant screen.

The wavering form of Callie Gabriel—shoulder-length hair, round figure, average female height, dressed in shorts—appeared in the smoke. Scratching a bite on her bare leg—it must be warmer in Louisiana than it was today in Chicago—she trudged beneath a tunnel of leaves formed by a dense stand of live oak and cypress. She looked determined.

She did not look happy.

Especially when she ran into a spiderweb.

"I wonder why she goes there?" Hera waved her hand and expanded the View of the far-see smoke to a weathered gray house on stilts with an aluminum boat beached from the bayou beside it. In the dense greenery beside the house, a man became alert to the sound of Callie's approach. A man of dark hair and aura, of masculine strength, of poetic motion.

He spun around, and Hera sucked in a breath. Zeus uttered a pithy curse.

Ares. The god of war.

Not the actual Ares, of course, but Armond Marceaux, one of his seed. The power of the gods was as strong, or stronger, in this one as it had been in Armond's friend Mark.

Ares. Also portrayed so incorrectly in the myths. The warrior. The dispenser of justice. The defender. Virile, suave, seductive, Ares was all that was masculine.

"He cannot be the son of Olympus destined for her," Zeus said in a low voice.

"Agreed," Hera breathed as the smoke faded.

Ares, the warrior, knew nothing of the gentle arts of love. He could not break the legacy; he could only bring more heartache.

When the spiderweb caught in her hair, Callie Gabriel remembered one reason she hadn't accepted Armond's invitation to his fishing cabin. Wildness, in man or nature, sat firmly in the category of things she avoided.

The sticky fibers clung to her neck, tightening her spine and chest. While she drew in a labored breath, her world narrowed to cypress and live oak trees, the lingering October heat and Louisiana humidity, and the rising beat of the music in her headphones. This place was too untamed.

For a moment she was tempted to turn around, but she was past halfway. And she needed to find Armond.

Gingerly, Callie brushed away the web, afraid the spider at its center would crawl down her arm if she disturbed it further. The motion dislodged her small black earpiece and she quickly replaced it, grateful for the synthesized techno sound of *Ooh, Ahh . . . Just a Little Bit* from her portable CD player.

A blue heron soared elegantly overhead, while a squirrel chattered at her for disturbing his fall duty of nut collecting. Intellectually, even viscerally, she treasured the beauty of this place. Some people would write poems about it, rhapsodize over it.

Some people didn't suffer from an odd phobia over nature.

Yet here she was, in the bayou with only a heron, a squirrel, and spiders for company.

Callie focused on the music. The music had gotten her this far.

Her foot caught in a vine. The disturbance startled a sunning lizard, which took off . . . right up her leg. Callie screeched and brushed it away, then stood, panting, until she was sure the lizard was gone.

Likely she was on a fool's errand. Her mother had warned her, suggesting, calmly, that Callie be in no hurry to find Armond, and insisting, serenely, that later was soon enough. Lillian Gabriel, in serene and calm mode, was not a person easily ignored.

Some days it wasn't easy being the daughter of the modern-day equivalent of the village witch.

If that weren't discouraging enough, the person who answered Armond's office phone number claimed he was fishing and didn't know when he would be back. The rare people whom Armond deemed as friends hadn't seen him either, not more recently than she had, anyway.

Armond disappearing was not unusual. Finding him would be.

Yet find him she must, to tell him before he heard the news from someone else. She owed him that much, and she had to do it now, before she lost her courage and heeded her mother's advice.

She trudged forward. The cabin was the only other place she knew to look. No one else knew it existed, much less how to get to it, but he'd given her directions last winter.

Park below the levee, walk back one mile. Twenty minutes, that's all it will take. The path will narrow, then disappear, but don't give up, Callie. I'll be waiting.

Armond, who never asked a favor, had asked her to come, and she had promised she would. She never had, more the coward she, but the instructions were etched deep in her mind.

Above the low synthesizer from the CD, an acorn crunched under her foot. Callie's nerves stung and her stomach lurched, bringing her back to the wildness surrounding her. Leaves rustled behind the cypress trees, a whispery sound that flicked across her edgy senses. She turned up the music volume.

Right now, she'd give two dozen Portobello mushrooms and her best chopping knife to be back in her car.

The thick-boled trees narrowed down on her; this must be the part about the path disappearing. A big part of her had hoped Armond had been joking. She should have known better.

Callie glanced at her watch. Fifteen long minutes she'd been on this path. She could grit out five more. Armond would be at the cabin. He was fishing; this was his fishing cabin, he had to be here.

Branches brushed against her arms and neck and dry, wind-tossed leaves stalked her down the vanishing path. More than once she stumbled over live oak roots and cypress knees.

Damn nerves made her so clumsy outside.

"He'd better not have lied about that twenty minutes," she grumbled, gripping the smooth metal of the CD player.

One last stumble almost landed her face-first in the dirt since she was also trying to avoid another spiderweb. Swearing, Callie righted herself, then broke through the final barrier of green bars into a tiny clearing. She halted, staring in dismay.

She'd hoped *fishing cabin* was a euphemism for "isolated, elegant chalet," which fit her image of Armond.

Obviously she had a few things to learn about the man.

A shaft of sunlight took advantage of the break in the trees to shine down on the gray, weathered shack before her. Lopsided porch, vines encroaching, no flowers or sign of cultivation like a garden, a kerosene lamp on a hook beside the door. No electricity, she'd bet.

An aluminum boat pulled up from the bayou was the only sign someone might be here. "Hello?" She turned off the CD, pulled the earphones from her ears, and hung them around her neck. From the silence, even the squirrel had deserted her.

She was alone. Callie turned the CD on, shoving back the edge of panic with music from the dangling head-phones.

"Armond?" she called again, scrambling up the steps to the porch. The only reply was the rustle of the leaves.

Callie peered into the curtainless, screened window. The interior of the simple cabin with its hand-carved furniture and large brick fireplace didn't match her expectations either, although it did look comfortable. It was a very masculine room, like the man who owned it. Shelves next to the fireplace held pots and pans and a few tins of food.

"Don't tell me you cook in a fireplace," she groaned.

This was worse than she'd dreamt. Worse because it was empty. Desolate even.

A single door led out the back. To the outdoors? A bedroom? She could see no bed, but for all she knew, Armond slept on the floor or sofa here. A bathroom? This didn't look like a place with indoor plumbing.

"Note to self," she muttered. "Don't drink anything."

A two-foot block of wood—half carved, no fresh shavings—sat on a small table, but other than that the room was barren. No toiletries. No magazines. Not a trace of recent habitation.

Armond wasn't here. She was alone, without an-other soul close enough to hear her voice. Her insides contracted into a hard knot. Breathing became a chore.

Callie turned the music up, realizing just how much she had counted on Armond being here. She turned around and faced the wall of green blocking her way back. Cypress trees blended to a blur. Mother of Mary, she couldn't even find the path!

She couldn't stay.

She couldn't leave.

Her harsh, shallow gasps echoed in her ears.

An indeterminate sound from the back cut through the rising wave of hysteria. Someone was behind the cabin! Right now she didn't care if it was Jack the Ripper. It was a living body.

Callie raced around to the back of the cabin. "Armond," she shouted, then skidded to halt at the edge of the still, black bayou, looking around.

No one was back here. Oh, mother, maybe it was an animal she'd heard. An alligator. An alligator, fifteen feet long, coming out of the depths of the bayou to bite her leg. Or a rabid squirrel. Or a snake. What kind of poisonous snakes did Louisiana have? No, it was the feral hog she'd read about during her fourth-grade field trip to Bayou Sauvage.

Certain she was about to meet a gory demise, Callie froze. Panic scrambled her nerves, leaving her unable to move or think or defend. There was no shadow, no sound that gave her warning, but in one second she sensed someone behind her and in the next she found herself surrounded by a pair of strong, warm, masculine arms.

"Looking for someone?" asked a low voice close to her ear.

Recognition was instantaneous. *Armond!* She wasn't alone. Callie sagged in the embrace, panic receding behind the flood of relief. "Mother of Mary, Armond, you scared me."

For one endless, grateful moment, she reveled in

the remembered pleasure of his arms around her.

Until reality returned.

She squirmed to free herself, but his grasp didn't lessen. His unyielding strength braced the full length of her. The pressure of their joined bodies generated sweat and heat, while a curling in her belly reminded her that her reaction to him had never been bland. "Let me go! What kind of game are you playing?"

Instead of answering, he ran his hands intimately and thoroughly across her torso and hips. A caress, or was he checking her for weapons? With ever-cautious Armond, she'd say the latter, except he knew the idea of her with a weapon was ludicrous. Yet he'd never been the kind for a quick feel.

Her shirt had hiked up, and for a brief hesitation his hand lay against the sensitive skin below her breasts. That curling in her stomach tightened to a hard knot and her breath quickened. Not panic. Sheer, unadulterated lust.

No, she wouldn't travel that road again. Once had left her with plenty of problems.

"You're frisking me?" she demanded, turning residual fear and frustration to temper. "This is me, Callie. Remember? The vegetarian pacifist. What the hell's the matter with you?"

"Nothing. You startled me . . . Callie." Abruptly he let her go and shifted away.

She stumbled backward, her body protesting the loss of his support. "Right," she snapped, catching her balance and turning around. "You mean you didn't hear me coming? You didn't recognize me? I'd have . . ."

Thought trailed off as she gaped at him.

Often, in the deepest night, her unruly dreams taunted her with those too brief moments of passion with Armond. She found now her imaginative remembrance was a mere shadow of reality.

He wasn't quite naked; he had on a pair of soccer shorts. But they didn't conceal much and he was near enough to naked for her libido to burst like heat from a bite into a Thai pepper.

Her breath stuck in her throat, and that curling, knotting excitement spread through her, lower body first, then up to jump-start her heart. Time and distance had done nothing to lessen his impact on her, damn it.

She'd always suspected a wildness below the surface Armond had let her see, below the precise haircut, the business suits or casual clothes he wore with elegant ease, and the by-the-book attitude. It was one of the reasons she'd backed off at first.

Today, it was there in toe-curling force.

He was magnificent and untamed. The dark hair was still short, but rougher, like he hadn't had a cut since she last saw him, and he had several days' growth of beard. Hard planes, supple muscles, and the most perfect pair of arms.

She was a sucker for a man with great arms.

Despite her best efforts to shift it, her gaze drifted down and lingered on the black shorts that left little to the imagination. Not even when he stirred in reaction to her frank admiration.

Shoot, this was going to be tough.

"Why *are* you here, Callie?"

She pulled her gaze upward again, to see him frowning at her, his arms folded across his chest. Knowing any physical reaction from him was simply the response of a virile male for a woman shooting out pheromones was enough to douse said pheromone shower.

Unable to meet his eyes, Callie ran a shaking hand

across her hair, tucking one strand above her ear. "I'm sorry I barged in here without an invitation. I know it's over between us, except . . . well, there's something I think you deserve to know. Let me say my piece, then I'll be on my way." She looked up at him then. And followed it with a closer, second look.

Something wasn't right. He was magnificent, still, yet he was also suspicious. Or wary. There wasn't a shaft, um, particle of recognition or pleasure in his gray eyes.

They hadn't parted on the best of terms, but this detachment went beyond that. Callie frowned. Beneath a wayward strand of hair, an ugly gash and bruise mottled his forehead. Now that she looked, she could see bruises formed part of the beard shadow, too, and discolorations from other scrapes and injuries marred his skin. Was it pain that fueled his caution? A sympathetic ache tightened her skin.

She shifted closer, and he watched her warily. He reminded her of an injured tiger—cautious, yet needing help.

Something about his responses bothered her. It was like seeing a mirror image where the picture doesn't look right, but you can't put your finger on what's wrong.

Maybe it was seeing that uncivilized core he'd kept hidden.

"What happened to you?" she whispered, then brushed away the concealing lock of his hair, wishing, not for the first time, that she had inherited her mother's and sisters' healing talents. "Does this hurt?"

His gray eyes bored into her, as though her words held something of vital importance, and an unreadable emotion went across his face. Then he shifted from her touch, arms still crossed. "I'm fine. Just tell me why you're here."

She might have lost out on the family talent for intuition, but even she could read body language like that. Callie's fingers closed around air, and she lowered her hand. She'd invaded his privacy; he had a right to tell her to go to hell. At least he was willing to listen.

"Armond," she said, "I'm pregnant."

Chapter Two

My name is Armond.

Hers was Callie.

It would be nice to know surnames, but he would take whatever bits of memory were given to him by this woman who—

"Pregnant?" Armond repeated.

"Yes."

"You're sure?"

She nodded.

Was it his? He might not have a memory, but he knew enough not to ask *that* question.

"I just thought you should know," Callie continued. "I don't expect—Ouch!" She brushed a mosquito off her arm.

Its bold companion buzzed Armond's head. He waved it away, and the motion exposed the large bruise in the crook of his arm. From blood drawn or drugs given, he didn't know yet, but he suspected the answer was integral to his loss of memory.

Quickly he refolded his arms. "Come inside. We'll talk about it there." And maybe he would get a clue to what the hell was going on.

"Really, it isn't necessary; I've got everything under control. Gabriel women are like that—in control. I'll be leaving now—" She stopped backing away and glanced around uncertainly. "If I can find the path . . . Are there feral hogs in these woods?"

"Lots," he answered drily, not knowing one way or the other. "I'll show you the way back . . . later."

She scowled. "I need to go."

Let this woman, who seemed to know him so well, disappear? Not a chance. "You can spare fifteen minutes." Gently but implacably, Armond steered her toward the cabin. Inside, he excused himself and went into the bedroom to put on a long-sleeved shirt. Fortunately, there had been clothes left here, for the ones he'd arrived in were in no condition to be worn. They were torn, bloody, soaked with strange smells. And a hideous plaid.

Armond rubbed the bridge of his nose. *Merde,* he didn't even know how he'd found the path to this cabin. Instinct, he supposed.

Nor was he sure how long he'd been here, for his memory was semi-reliable only from yesterday, although each hour since was clearer. An indeterminate number of days before yesterday blended together in a fuzzy kaleidoscope of images that could be memory, fabrication, or dream. And before that?

A total blank.

At least he had a first name. It was more than he'd known a quarter hour ago. What a hell of a time to find out he was, possibly, a father-to-be.

Armond shrugged on the shirt, then stood silently

in the doorway, watching the woman named Callie range through his cabin. She seemed more nervous than intent on snooping.

At least she hadn't fled.

From his first sight of her, he'd guessed they'd once been intimate, judging by the way his body remembered hers, even if his mind did not. That was why he'd watched, then approached her the way he had.

They must have slept together recently, for he saw no signs of pregnancy in her. Yet she said they were lovers no longer.

Making love to Callie was a memory he wished he had not lost.

He would have liked to know how she tasted when he kissed her and to remember whether she talked as much or used her mouth in more creative ways when they were in bed.

She was not classically beautiful, nor was she athletic perfection, yet there was a rounded, very feminine appeal to her body. Her wide brown eyes and chin-length hair—brown, shot with gold—roused basic masculine instincts in him, and he'd been hard put to dampen his response to her guileless admiration.

They might be lovers no longer, but he still wanted her.

Even now, he stirred with the remembrance of her womanly body curved into his and the fresh scent of her hair. Her skin was soft and warm, he'd found, and the merest touch—from him to her, or her to him— set his skin tingling as though she'd embraced him with a thousand caresses.

Yet he might have let her return unaccosted except for two things.

Even when she was upset, the corners of her lips tipped in a pleasing smile.

And, in some inexplicable way, he sensed in her a

goodness of soul that touched him like a sparkling, cleansing fountain. Not perfection, for she was not perfect, but no dark deceptions, no cruelty, no . . . evil emanated from her.

Sheer instinct prompted him to reveal himself to her, but instinct alone wasn't something he dared trust; hence the quick frisk. Unfortunately, instinct appeared to be all he had right now.

Instinct, caution, and Callie.

And a child? A man with no memory, he had difficulty accepting the notion. It seemed unreal. Unlike his reaction to Callie, it struck no chord in him, no instinctive response but denial.

Armond stepped into the room. "Callie," he softly called.

Callie, peering into the fireplace, whirled around, her hand to her chest. She let out a breath of air. "You've got to stop startling me like that. Do you cook in the fireplace?"

"When I have to," he answered, having no idea whether he even knew how to start the fire.

She gave him an incredulous look.

Merde! Finding out about himself, about them, while not letting her know about the memory loss, was going to require a delicate touch. Yet, until he found out the who and the why of the loss, he must keep it hidden. "Does that surprise you?"

"For someone who never cooked when we dated and still didn't know his way around a kitchen last August? Yes."

More tidbits. "It's not much of a kitchen."

Callie laughed. "True."

"Would you like something to drink?" He uncorked a bottle of sparkling cherry juice, his only alternative to water or wine. She wouldn't want alcohol and, for him, it was too early for the Pinot Noir that he'd opened last night. His palate could distinguish the nuances of its pleasant fruity taste, he'd found. He might not cook, but apparently he knew something about wine. The wine cellar in this cabin was well-stocked.

"Drink?" Callie answered, glancing around. "Ah, no thanks."

Armond poured himself a glass, then recorked the bottle. He leaned against the cold brick of the fireplace and sipped the juice. "Sit, Callie, and start from the beginning."

Callie perched on the windowsill, her back to the outside. The morning sun had risen high enough that it shone around her, highlighting the gold in her hair. Now that she had lit some place, he found it easier to concentrate. "You know the beginning; you were there."

That answered the question about whether the child was his. And something about her, some instinctual surety, told him Callie wasn't lying.

"I imagine you want to know what happened," she mumbled, suddenly intent on fingering a thread in her shirt. "The desk—My condoms were old. And, remember, I was . . . clumsy, being the first time and all. I, ah, may have accidentally put a hole in the condom. With my nail. So don't worry, it's not your responsibility."

Her desk? The first time? With him or with anyone? Didn't he have more finesse than to take a virgin on a desk? Or any woman the first time? To let her feel clumsy? To let her get pregnant?

Merde, he had a lot to make up to her. It was necessary to set this right. "It's my responsibility, too, Callie," he assured her. "I won't run away from it."

Her response wasn't the one he expected.

"Oh, no," she groaned, making a face. "Mom said you'd be like that. Please, don't offer to marry me, okay? I know it would be only out of obligation, and I really don't need that."

Armond gaped at her. Until he regained his past, he couldn't, wouldn't, make promises or commitments that he might be unable to honor, but she couldn't know that. "You don't *want* me involved?"

"Gabriel women are self-sufficient, strong, and capable. We take care of our daughters just fine."

"You're sure it's a girl?"

"Of course. Gabriels only have daughters. I'll be a good mother to her," she said fiercely.

"I'm sure you will." Armond took another sip of juice, her words pounding at the back of his head. *My child. Without a father.* A sudden ache spread through his chest, as though the shadow of a memory had passed through him. Damn, he hated going by instinct and half-pieced-together clues. It seemed so . . . chaotic. "Why did you come here then, Callie?"

"I thought you deserved to know. My mother said I could tell you later, if I insisted, but I figured you'd hear the news from Mark and Joy sooner. Better it come from me. But I don't expect anything from you."

Armond tried to think if he knew a Joy or a Mark, but the names slammed against the blank wall of his memory. Had he ever met Callie's mother? If he had, he obviously hadn't made a good impression.

"You knew I was here?" From his explorations yesterday, he knew the cabin was isolated.

"I didn't know you were here; I simply didn't have any other place to look. You're not an easy man to locate." She flushed. "I remembered the instructions you gave me."

He was missing too much here. Suddenly the absurdity of the whole situation struck him, and he started to laugh.

"What?" Callie demanded.

46

"You came to this isolated cabin against all advice, and when it obviously makes you uneasy, on remembered instructions, to tell me about my baby, then expect to walk away without me doing a thing with that little newsflash?" *And, to top it off, I don't remember a damn thing about any of it.* "What kind of a man do you think I am?"

Callie looked at him, a curious tilt to her head. "One who doesn't laugh like that. I like the sound, even if I'm not sure I appreciate the cause."

Laughter faded while the words hung between them. This gentleness from her was like a physical touch he felt to his bones, and his muscles tightened in response.

What should he say? How would the Armond she knew respond? So far, Callie had unknowingly fed him the clues he needed, but in this she seemed as reticent as he.

In the end, he said nothing. He picked up his glass and gulped down the drink.

She rose from the windowsill to move closer. The slight air disturbed by her passage brushed his skin like a cat's tail. "Have you caught many fish?"

"What?"

"The FBI office in Atlanta said you were fishing. Hard to believe you took off from your latest assignment for a vacation."

"What do you know about my latest assignment?" The question came out sharper than he intended.

She gave him a questioning look. He must never forget, her mind was quick and agile, as evidenced by the way she switched between multiple topics. She gave clues and answers, but she also knew the man he had been, and she would be quick to spot inconsistencies.

"Nothing," she admitted. "But you always have a

compelling 'latest assignment.' When you were with the New Orleans Police, I used to make guesses about what you were doing. I was usually wrong; the family talent for intuition skipped me." She wrinkled her nose at him. "Your secrets, whatever they are, are still safe."

"You think I have secrets?"

She gave a snort of derision. Apparently that one didn't deserve answering.

Armond started to pace, rubbing one hand along his arm against the prickling of his skin. Wind pushed through the screen, bringing heat and humidity, breaking the ensuing silence. The sun crossing toward noon created new patterns of light and shadows.

Callie glanced around, and her hand drifted toward the CD player hanging at her belt. She cleared her throat. "I'd better get back. You said you'd show me the path."

In this short time with her he'd learned a lot about himself: His name was Armond. He was former police. He worked for the FBI in Atlanta and was supposed to be fishing, although maybe that was code for some assignment. He didn't like to cook. He swore in French.

He wanted Callie more than any woman he'd ever known, and the fact that he couldn't remember any other woman had nothing to do with it.

And she was carrying his child.

Abruptly, Armond made a decision. "Give me a minute to pack."

"You're coming with me?" she squeaked.

He moved closer to her and laid a hand on her shoulder. "It's my child, too. I have a right to be involved."

And in the process he would learn about himself, for he was not letting her go, this woman who held the keys to his past and his present.

* * *

Back in the bedroom, Armond changed into jeans, then shoved the few toiletries and items of clothing stashed at the cabin into a suitcase. Had he prepared this cabin, knowing he might need a place to regroup? Had he left other necessities?

As he quickly went through the drawers, a sense of déjà vu swept over him, and once, before he opened a drawer, he knew it would contain only a deck of cards. Had he gone through these drawers recently, during the hazy days after he'd first arrived? Or was it a memory from before his memory loss?

Too many questions.

A nubbin of a headache pulsed, as it did whenever he tried to remember.

Swearing, Armond shoved the last drawer shut, thrusting away the attempt to remember. Nothing.

Might he have hidden something? Armond tried to remember but ran up against the solid wall of amnesia.

He'd gotten here on instinct; let instinct tell him. He took a tiny step, then another, concentrating not on remembering but on the contraction of muscles and the prickling of skin to guide him toward the bed. He knelt, then lifted the cotton spread, felt along the wide frame, and pressed something. A drawer opened from the frame.

It contained a treasure trove. Money. Credit cards. Some in the name of Armond Marceaux. Some in the name of Adrian Marsten and Marshall Warren. Three IDs, same three names. The hair was shorter and the face clean-shaven, but all were his picture.

Who am I? Callie called him Armond, so he would be Armond Marceaux.

Digging further, he unearthed a gun and an FBI credentials case with a badge. Why had he left his creds here? The immediate answer was that he'd been undercover and wary of being frisked. He thrust the creds case in his pocket, then stared at the gun a moment before picking it up. When he didn't look at it, when he didn't try to remember how to use it, it fell naturally into the palm of his hand. Without thinking, he loaded it with the ammunition also in the drawer, fit it into the holster, and strapped it on beneath his shirt, where its bulk felt familiar.

Obviously he knew his way around weapons.

A color snapshot caught his eye and he pulled it from the drawer. It was a candid shot, unskillfully photographed, but he recognized the two people standing in front of the rearing horse statue. Himself and Callie.

Callie wore a short, vivid red skirt, a tank top, and an armful of bracelets, while he was dressed in linen slacks and an open-necked shirt. Armond rubbed one hand against his bristly chin. Once he had been clean shaven, close cut, and with a damn sight better taste in clothes than those shorts he'd worn earlier. He grabbed at the physical characteristics to hang his identity on.

In the picture, Callie, laughing, leaned against him, while he almost smiled, and his arm rested intimately across her shoulder. It didn't take memory to recognize a male gesture of claim. Armond's palm tingled with deep-imprinted memory.

What had separated them? Was the child her only reason for seeking him out?

Too many questions. Too few answers.

With a frustrated grunt, he shoved the drawer shut and heard something thud against the back.

A jewelry box, he discovered, when he pulled it out. It had been there some months, if the dust on the outside was any indication. Inside was a ring—a single yellow diamond surrounded by smaller stones of golden-yellow topaz.

"Are you ready?" Callie called from the next room.

"Almost." Armond stared at the ring, believing in his gut that it had been for Callie. Yet he'd never given it to her. Why?

His fingers closed around the jewelry box.

Chapter Three

Despite her plan to tell him the news and leave, Callie was secretly relieved to have Armond walk back to the car with her. No way on God's green earth could she have made that return trip alone. He headed straight for the car's driver's side, then halted. She saw his hands and wrists tighten; then, surprisingly, he climbed into the passenger seat without a comment.

"You want me to drive you? Don't you have a car? Or want to drive?"

"No. I came . . . by boat." After that, he said nothing, staring out the window as though to absorb each detail of the route into New Orleans.

Callie gave him a sidelong glance. He'd changed into soft jeans that hugged the right spots without being vulgarly obvious and a long-sleeved, khaki-colored pullover. No logos, nothing so obvious indicated quality, but the cut, shape, and simplicity of whatever he wore bespoke sheer elegance. Armond did not have a huge wardrobe, she remembered, but every piece fit him perfectly, as though chosen for comfort and ease.

She had thought never to see him again, yet here he was, filling the space of her small car and still setting her heart speeding.

The panic she'd had in the woods was gone, but an inner restlessness had her flicking on the radio and punching buttons until she found a song she liked. She tapped out the dance beat, and when the song was over, she repeated the ritual. When she reached for the radio a third time, Armond stopped her with a hand on hers. Smoothly he picked up one of the tapes littering the floor of her car and, without looking at the title, stuck it into the tape player.

She could live with that, as long as she had the music.

The beat from LaBouche's *Be My Lover* filled the car. Not the best choice for a pregnant woman whose hormones made her lust-crazed, but she left the tape in. She liked the song.

Armond leaned against the car door. "How do you keep busy these days, Callie?"

So, no discussion of the past or of the problems behind them. Armond was making it clear they were in "just friends" mode. It was the baby that brought him back, nothing else. Fine by her; she hadn't come to fan old embers or resurrect heart-wrenching hurts.

"Remember 'Spicy Living,' the cooking show I do for Channel Twelve?"

He made a noncommittal sound.

"No, maybe you don't. I started it in March, after you left, and you probably didn't have time to see it when you were here in August. A representative from the American Regional Wine Council saw an episode I did on Louisiana wine, liked it, and hired me to video a series of programs. Did you know there are at least twenty-six U.S. states besides California that produce wine?"

"Some of the wines are very good," he commented. "I had a Pinot Noir last night from a Michigan winery."

"The Council is trying to promote these wines, introduce them to the American public. I'll travel to the areas where the wines are made, visit the vineyards, make some dishes to go with the wines using local ingredients."

"You're leaving the city?"

"Don't you remember how much I always talked about wanting to travel? How you used to say"—she lowered her voice in imitation—" 'Stop talking and make the reservations, Callie.' "

Then again, maybe this wasn't the best memory to dredge up. The one time she'd gotten up the nerve to make plane reservations for the two of them—to New York for dinner and a show, a surprise birthday present for him—he'd canceled their date at the last minute. An organized crime task force multipronged raid, he'd said. Unable to face going alone, she'd given the tickets away.

She gave him another sidelong glance. "In a way, you're responsible for this chance."

"I am?"

"Sure. You introduced me to these lesser-known wineries, I tried some for myself, and that's what gave me the idea for the episode." She fell silent, remembering the last bottle they'd split. Did Armond remember, too? How could he not? The baby she'd told him about today was a direct result.

If he was remembering any of this, they weren't pleasant memories, judging by the tense set of his shoulders. "Wine, though—is that wise? When you're pregnant?"

"I planned to let the winemakers choose the wines to go with the food, and I've tasted enough of them to do a good program. I can pretend to drink it. We'll be on hiatus during part of the pregnancy, while the vines are dormant, and resume after the baby's born. Dion said we'd work around the problems."

"Dion?" His fingers started to drum against the car, then he caught himself and stilled.

"Dion Backus, the ARWC rep who hired me."

"Should you be traveling in your condition?"

"My doctor says it's okay." She glanced over at him. "I'm thrilled about this, Armond. You know I always wanted to travel, but getting Greenwood off the ground kept me too busy. Now, with Joy managing the restaurant for me this year, I finally got the chance and this drops in my lap." She grinned. "A chance to visit some of the places I've always wanted to see, and I get paid to do it." Plus it would give her the financial resources to hire more of the work done at Greenwood, so, after the baby came and Joy left, she wouldn't have to keep such grueling hours. "My life is really together."

Never let it be said that Gabriel women weren't resourceful. And she'd prove that, in this at least, she was a true Gabriel woman.

"We missed them." Hera circled the empty cabin, frustrated.

Zeus leaned against the weathered boards, chewing on a piece of grass he'd plucked. "We wouldn't have been late if you hadn't insisted on changing your clothes. And redoing your makeup."

"The CEO of Peacock Cosmetics does not appear in public with a naked face."

"You could have used your power to appear decked out," he grumbled.

"But inside the visage I still would have been wearing heels, nylons, and a straight skirt. I wasn't going to tromp through the bayou in that!"

Zeus muttered something unintelligible that began with, "Women!"

Hera ignored him, sending a mosquito on its way with a glare. "Where have they gone, do you suppose?"

"Use the far-see smoke. There's no one here to notice."

Hera extracted the crystals from her purse and looked for a suitable stone. "I told you we should have waited. What did you hope to gain by coming here, anyway? We need an excuse to invade their lives, and suddenly appearing in front of them isn't it."

"*You* were supposed to create a fog as cover. I thought we could listen in on them, so next time don't transport us directly to where they're standing. When we find out what they're doing, I'm sure something will occur to us."

Hera gave an exasperated sigh. In all these years, he still hadn't changed in this. Live in the moment, let the future take care of itself. It was that thinking that had gotten them exiled here, which had kept them apart for so many, many years. "Do you see any rocks around here?"

"Southern Louisiana doesn't have rocks. Here, use this." He handed her a large shell.

Not ideal, but it would do. Hera wrote the name of Callie Gabriel on a scrap of paper from her purse, wadded it onto the shell, then sprinkled the far-see crystals over it. She rubbed the ring on her finger.

Nothing happened. The ring stayed cold on her hand.

Hera raised a horrified glance to Zeus.

"Try it again," he suggested in a hoarse voice.

She rubbed again. This time the clouded ring glowed lava red and ignited the crystals. "Just a glitch," Hera sighed as the scented smoke rose.

"Y-Ten-K," joked Zeus.

A vision of Callie and Armond in a car approaching New Orleans formed in the center of the smoke.

"We can't transport there," Hera grumbled.

"We'll just have to wait until they stop moving."

Hera glared at another mosquito. "Then let's go someplace more comfortable to wait."

Zeus took her arm. "I know this charming trattoria— you will adore the squid."

He rubbed his lightning ring and, to their unvoiced relief, the power in it held strong. Both of them knew that these rings were impervious to "glitches," having been designed by a race with eons to perfect them.

Only one thing could make them sputter. The power was dying.

And Zeus's ring was as old as hers.

The city of New Orleans was familiar: Superdome, Crescent City Connection, St. Charles Ave. Signs gave Armond the names of streets and sites he couldn't remember. The labels weren't important; it was the sensations he recognized. The mixed scents in the close air, the burning of the southern sun against his face, these were old friends. For a moment, Armond closed his eyes to take in the city through more primitive senses. This was the place to start looking for himself.

"Where do you want me to drop you?"

At Callie's question, he opened his eyes. Where, indeed? Where to start? *Someplace you think I'd recognize?* "Where are you going?"

Callie pulled the car into the parking lot of a television studio. "Here, first. I'm taping the last episode of 'Spicy Living' today, and I want to make sure everything's ready. Then home to change and back here."

"I'll walk from here."

Outside the car, Callie turned and held out her hand. "Then this is good-bye."

He had no intention of letting her dismiss him so easily.

Armond took her hand, lacing their fingers together as he shifted closer. He liked her hand. It was strong, with fingers scarred and callused from her profession, yet she kept her nails shiny.

"I'd like to see your show," he said, tracing her palm and wrist with his thumb.

"I don't think that would be wise. We agreed—"

"Did we?" He rested his other hand on her belly, knowing the peace that washed over him when he touched her and the faint heartbeat pulsing in his ears were only his imagination. He would at least settle that he would not be shut out of his child's life. "I think this changes things."

She gave a tiny sigh. "Come at four. I'll make sure you have a seat."

"And dinner after?"

"Yes." She sounded breathless.

Good, because his lungs had acquired the same malady.

He had no memory of their lovemaking or previous kisses, so he would make one new, small memory to keep. He leaned forward and brushed his lips against hers. Once, twice. Hers was a taste as complex as a Bordeaux and as sweet and refreshing as iced wine.

No protest from her when he gathered her close. He found himself lost in the pleasure of holding her. A wild urgency beat against his chest, demanding release, but he controlled it with tenderness. Treat her gently, don't frighten her away.

Tenderness. Suddenly the feeling translated to an image, intense and narrow as a laser, that pierced through the black wall of amnesia with precision and ungodly pain. Callie, his first heart-stopping view of her face. No tears or panic, only a tremulous smile and a brave joke that cut straight through his detached reserve to strike the man beneath the cop.

Other impressions followed, pulsing like white-hot strobes through his brain, the images running backward at top speed. Assist the victim. Handcuff the rapist. His hand throbbed. *Justice. This scum would prey on innocence no more.* A knife. An alley with the stink of beer and male sweat. A man pulling her into an alley. Callie, walking alone.

The images cut off, terminated by a searing headache. Armond gasped and fell back from Callie. He pressed his hand against his forehead, trying to squeeze away the pain, and clamped his lips together against the nausea.

"Armond! What's wrong?" Callie laid a hand on his shoulder. "Do you want me to call a doctor?"

He shook his head. Her touch did more than any doctor's remedy ever could, putting the headache and nausea at bay. "I'm fine," he ground out.

"And I'm going to have chicken for supper."

What the hell was that supposed to mean? Armond pulled in a breath. "No, I'm fine now. I've had . . . headaches. They come and go quickly."

"You ought to let my mother take a look at you. She's used feverfew—"

He shook his head dismissively. "No doctors."

"Mom isn't just any doctor. She's the village witch. Of course, she doesn't like me to call her that. She prefers herbalist. Or naturopathic physician."

There was one thing about talking to Callie, he was finding. She soon distracted you from any troubles you might have. The headache and the nausea were fading, but the single memory remained. "Callie, what do you remember about the night we met?"

"Why?"

"Tell me everything you remember."

"Mostly it's not a memory I like revisitin'."

"Please, it's important."

She ran a hand through her hair. "I was walking home from a friend's house. It was night and there'd been warnings about a serial rapist, but I felt safe—familiar neighborhood, people around, only a couple of blocks to go. Instead . . . he attacked me. He was strong and threw me to the ground. All I really remember was feeling so scared when that knife edge touched my throat and so stupid that I hadn't been more cautious. That, and my throat hurt from screaming.

"Then you came. And stopped him. I found out later you'd just started working the area, trying to find the rapist, and somehow you were in the right spot that night."

"You made a joke."

"A silly one. About avenging angels having flaming swords, not flashing fists."

The image was a true one. Lightly he touched her cheek. "That night I thought you were brave."

Her eyes widened. "So why did it take a month for you to ask me out?"

He didn't have an answer for that. Instead, he cupped her chin and gave her a brief kiss. No images, no headache this time. Only two sureties.

That he would want another kiss.

And that Callie was the key to regaining his memory.

Chapter Four

Armond bought a map of the city, oriented himself by street names, then located a barbershop. If he was the man in the snapshot, then he needed to look the part, the better to conceal his memory loss. And perhaps his face would seem familiar then.

Soon he gazed into the mirror held by the barber, rubbed his smooth chin, and studied the features that looked back from beneath the dark, cropped hair. It was the face from the photograph, but this reflection was hard to reconcile with the shaggy face seen in the cabin mirror, the only face in his current memory.

Which person was he? The one who acted only by instincts or the hard-edged, gray-eyed man who now looked back at him?

Which did he want to be?

Why did both exist?

Armond thrust away the disturbing questions. Action was what he needed. Focus. Work on retrieving his memories and life, and trust that the kind of man he was would sort itself out.

Callie said he was a cop, that he'd quit the N.O.P.D. about eight months ago, in February, and that he'd been back in the city two months ago, in August, working on a case. He would start there.

It took him little time to locate the public library and have the librarian show him how to access the newspaper files. Typing in ARMOND MARCEAUX gave him a surprising number of hits. Apparently he'd been a busy cop.

Armond settled in to read.

Half an hour later, he sat back and stretched his shoulders, thinking. Most of the mentions had been a simple statement listing him as arresting officer, with occasional quotes about a case. Twice reporters questioned what had led him to a perp that nobody else suspected, but his answers were remarkable only for their evasiveness.

The case that had brought him back to Louisiana especially interested him. It was ongoing, mired in the legal maneuvering before a trial. Guy Centurion, a local businessman noted for his support of new restaurants, had been arrested for gem smuggling and the attempted murder of Mark Hennessy and Joy Taylor. The reports hinted at other unsavory ventures.

Restaurants. Callie said she owned one. Mark and Joy—Callie had mentioned those names in a context that suggested friendship.

He doubted it was all mere coincidence.

Armond found his name in connection with the arrest. There was also a single picture of him, obviously taken from a distance when he was unaware. Short hair, determined bearing, all-business jaw—he recognized the man in the picture as the one he'd just met in the barbershop, but he felt no kinship to him. The caption identified him as FBI Special Agent Marceaux.

He ran his fingers over the picture, but nothing he read, saw, or felt elicited new memories, only new information and new questions. What terrible things kept him from remembering the past? The bruise in his arm throbbed. Was this connected? He rubbed it to ease the ache, unable to ease the hollow void left by his amnesia.

If he could not have memory, he would substitute whatever knowledge he could find.

In rapid succession he looked up the names of Joy Taylor, Mark Hennessy, and Callie Gabriel. One picture of Joy, hosting a chef's benefit. A description of Mark's tour. Apparently the magician was becoming well known. A couple of positive reviews of Callie's cooking show. Nothing struck a chord of remembrance.

Time to delve further. Opting for a different route, he logged onto the Internet and searched for MEMORY. What he read was not reassuring. Despite research, human memory was still a complex, elusive process subject to physiologic and psychologic tampering. Multiple neurotransmitters, multiple cells and neurons, multiple parts of the brain, all interconnected, all mysterious.

One discussion about types of memory that he found on a Usenet group interested him. Explicit memory was conscious, verbally oriented, and divided into general knowledge about the world and specific knowledge about one's life. It drew on the higher brain centers, like the cerebral cortex. Implicit memory, however, was subconscious and part of the cerebellum, and stored tasks that had become so innate that they required no thought. Like breathing. Or a pro golfer's swing.

Or an agent's ability to handle a gun.

Armond posted a question to the group, asking for further information, then continued his search. Global amnesia like his was rare, often the result of trauma, and could be either fleeting or permanent. Armond fingered the wounds at his forehead. Were these enough to cause his amnesia? Didn't seem likely. So what had? At least the snatch of memory today gave him hope that the loss wasn't permanent. Memory return, if it happened, was often triggered not by sight but by more primitively wired senses, like taste and smell. And by emotion.

For him, that trigger was Callie.

Armond glanced at his watch. Time for a cooking show. He collected the various articles he'd printed out and was about to log off when an idea struck him. He did one final search—Guy Centurion—and found one telling hit.

It was a year-old article, a long interview with Guy Centurion published in a national magazine. The tone was fawning rather than investigative, and near the end the reporter had coyly asked about Centurion's interest in the occult.

"Not occult. ESP. Psychic powers," Centurion had corrected. "It's not a fad. Even the federal government researches potential uses and ways to increase ESP, like with the CIA experiments with LSD or NIH funding for acetylcholine research. And backroom chemists have long cooked up designer drugs to enhance psychic talents. Like DC-909. It wipes out conscious memory but is a potent stimulant of psychic abilities. A highly trained agent given that would make a formidable weapon."

"So what's your involvement?" asked the reporter.

"Only as an interested bystander."

Armond stared at the page and his arms ached, while ice coalesced in the pit of his stomach. *The federal government researches potential uses. Designer drugs that enhance psychic talents and wipe out memory. A highly trained agent would make a formidable weapon.*

Had he been part of some insane experiment?

On her way out of the Gabriel house, which she shared with her mother, sisters, nieces, and the nanny, Callie detoured to her mother's workroom. Always, the first impression here was scent, the aromas of the earth: rosemary, chive, ginger, pepper. Lillian Gabriel had taught them all here—Callie and her two older sisters, Stacia and Tessa; and now Callie's two nieces, Alexis and Kitty. She'd passed on the knowledge of the herbalist: the healing properties of each plant, the risks, the way to achieve balance. Her sisters had soaked up the knowledge.

Not Callie. Her first foray into healing, when she'd given the neighbor's dog an unpleasant case of diarrhea, had convinced her that she had neither talent nor inclination in that arena. Instead, she'd tasted everything, making herself ignobly sick a few times. While her sisters created salves and tinctures, Callie cooked up gumbo, pilaf, and vinaigrette. Her sisters followed their mother into the woods and bayous of Louisiana to harvest plants, all of them overcoming the inborn Gabriel preference for cities. Callie shuddered at the thought and stayed home, chopping peppers and onions.

Yet she'd always loved the scents in the workroom. They were so strong and fresh, she could taste them.

Lillian Gabriel was bent over a small flask of bubbling mud, her pale blond hair caught in a neat French twist.

"Conjuring up a brew, are you, Mom?" Callie called, biting into the apple she held.

Lillian made a face at her. "I do wish you would cease with this persistent reference to me as a witch."

"You're an herbalist and a licensed physician. Neighbors come calling at the workroom for treatment. Some swear you perform miraculous cures." Callie grinned at her. "What would you call it?"

"I'm a holistic healer. I merely point the path to a better way of health." Her mother busied herself with the flask again, adding some liquid in a thin stream.

"Like I said, the village witch. I left corn chowder simmering on the stove, if any of you are home for dinner. And there's cucumber dill salad in the refrigerator."

"Aren't you going to be here?" her mother asked absently, concentrating on the flask.

"No." Best get the confession over with. "I'm going out with Armond after the filming."

Lillian's head came up, and she gave Callie a sharp look. "Armond Marceaux? You found him? You went to see him?"

"He had to know, Mom. Why don't you like him?"

Lillian made an irritated noise. "He's too . . . dominant. From what I've heard of him, he's a good man. Honest, if a bit blunt, loyal, a dedicated agent, and pleasing to look at. But he's a man and not for you. You are a Gabriel, Callie. Don't ever forget that. You know what that means."

Callie knew, all too well. She'd always fought to live up to the Gabriel ideals of independence, strength, and achievement. Sometimes she'd even succeeded.

But finding herself alone and pregnant, wanting this baby so badly and wanting to do right by it, had unleashed weaknesses and differences and needs she'd struggled against all her life. Doubts she didn't have the courage to voice grew so strong that sometimes her bones ached with the confusion.

As if sensing her turmoil, Lillian gave Callie a comforting pat on the shoulder. "Did he propose?" she asked gently.

"No. Armond's not the marrying type either. His work is vital to him, and it doesn't leave a lot of time for romancing. But he wants to be involved with the baby."

"Why?"

"The baby is his," Callie reminded her gently, feeling her heart twist with the memory of what she and Armond had shared before things had gone so wrong.

"Other men aren't this difficult. Why couldn't it be someone else's?" Lillian muttered. "Why couldn't you have slept with someone else?"

"Mom!"

"Sorry. That didn't sound like I intended."

"He and I will work things out."

"That's what I'm afraid of." Lillian gripped her fingers. "Gabriel women have a history of being harmed, badly, by men. Do you remember what happened to Katrina Gabriel?"

How could she forget? Callie's earliest bedtime stories had been the cautionary tales of the two Gabriels who lost their good sense enough to actually marry. "She and her daughter were abused and then killed by her husband, along with two of her cousins."

"And Ellen Gabriel?"

"Her husband ran off with all the money, bankrupting the entire Gabriel household. In the frigid winter that followed almost everyone starved or froze."

Callie knew that Armond would never harm her or the baby, that this time and this place was different, that *she* was different. It was that instinct, and a deep moral sense, that had sent her to Armond's cabin. But her instincts had lied before and, alone, she wasn't strong enough to overcome centuries of Gabriel expectations.

You're not alone. You've got a baby to think of.

"We've gone without male interference and we've done well over the centuries," continued Lillian fiercely. "I don't want to see you break that tradition. I don't want you to get hurt."

"Don't worry." Callie laid her hand over her abdomen. "We'll be fine."

She just hoped, for once, her fallible instincts were right.

Inside the studio door, Armond paused. Blue drapes on three sides of the illuminated set separated it from the snaking cables, cameras, and jumbled equipment and props that filled the dark edges of the room. The poinsettias and evergreen garlands bespoke a Christmas show. Chocolate permeated the air. He'd purposely come early, and the audience chairs remained empty.

Callie wore a festive red shirt, snug white pants, a huge green and gold braid apron, and glitter in her hair. In the woods, the kindest word to describe her was *uncoordinated.* It had been an erroneous impression.

Here she was in her element. With efficiency and skill, she peeled a lemon rind into curling strips. She used them with tiny green sprigs of something to garnish a Santa-decorated dish, while talking to the man beside her.

The man towered above her. Dressed in jeans, he was as tall, thin, and pale as a crane. He sported a multitude of studs in one ear and nostril and a barbed-wire tattoo on his bare arms beneath the rolled-up sleeves of his T-shirt. Armond strolled over to join them.

Callie spared him a quick glance but kept talking to the crane man. "The green beans weren't very good, so I substituted braised celery hearts. Make sure the recipes at the end reflect the change; there's a copy."

"No prob." He pocketed the paper she indicated. "Wait'll you hear the music I've got. Think Santa and blues, with a little country jazz thrown in."

Callie laughed. "Christian, I can't even imagine it, but I'll trust you."

"It's hot, babe." He kissed her cheek, then bustled away.

"Who's that?" asked Armond.

"Christian Perrault, the director. He's also doing the video series." Deftly, she upended a loaf pan onto a decorative plate, then sprinkled paprika and peppercorns around the crunchy-looking dish. She set it, and the Santa dish with a red something inside it, on a warming shelf below the counter.

"What are you making?"

"Chestnut Roast and Red Cabbage Casserole. A Christmas dinner. This show airs in December."

"Chestnuts, cabbage, celery? What happened to turkey and ham?"

She gave him a horrified look. *"Meat?"*

Merde; he'd said the wrong thing. *The vegetarian pacifist. And I'm having chicken for supper.* Her comments finally made sense. Armond would have known that. "Gotcha!" he added quickly. "Your meal sounds delicious."

"Are you teasing me, Armond?" Laughing, she made it sound like a rare event. "I never did convert you. Why did you cut your hair?"

"This is more . . . me."

"I was enjoying the new Armond."

He couldn't tell whether she was teasing him back and decided to change the subject. "Anyone besides Perrault going with you on the video shoots?"

"Dion will be with us sometimes. We'll use local crews, though." She set two bottles of a Rouge Militaire on the counter and poured a small glass of each; the red wine provided a rich complement to the holiday setting. "You know about wine: Give me an opinion. Which would go better with my dessert?"

"What are you making?" He sipped the first. It had a robust taste he enjoyed.

"Chocolate fondue."

He tasted the second wine. "I'd use the first."

"Why?"

Armond tasted the wine again, not sure he knew the words to describe what he tasted. "It's got a faint taste, almost chocolatelike, that complements the dessert. The other is too fruity. I don't think it goes as well with the chocolate."

She nodded. "That's what I'll go with."

"You have a discriminating palate," a voice observed behind Armond. "The first bottle was aged in new oak barrels rather than reused ones."

Armond rotated on his seat to see an enormous figure detach itself from the shadows, looming over them as it closed in, step by slow step. Every muscle tensed. Anticipating what? A threat? Recognition? He shifted on his seat, placing his body between Callie and the figure. Without thought, he reached for the weapon at his waist, but he let the jacket fall back when Callie greeted the figure.

"Dion, I didn't know you were going to be here today."

Dion. Dion Backus, the man who had hired Callie.

"I thought I would treat myself to the pleasure of

watching your final show." Dion Backus stepped into view.

The huge shadow had not been a trick of the light. Dion Backus was enormous, tall and broad, with a beak of a nose and a forest of red hair, although his impeccably tailored suit and lack of flab made his bulk stylish. He kissed the back of Callie's hand, then straightened, smiling, a delighted smile that invited one in return.

Armond didn't smile, and he shifted closer to Callie, studying Backus. Dion Backus didn't set well inside him. Something was off, something rippled across him in warning. The man was entirely too jolly to be real.

And he was looking at Callie with decided male interest.

When Armond gave him no room, Dion studied him back, a long look that assessed, then grew cautious. "Callie, you found . . . a warrior. Introduce us."

"Dion, this is Armond Marceaux. He's with the FBI in Atlanta. Armond, Dion Backus, my boss. Why don't you two sit here for the show. You'll have front-row seats," she said, motioning to the chairs at the counter, then leaving them.

"Are you investigating us, Agent Marceaux?" Dion asked, giving Armond's hand a firm shake before he settled into the chair as commanded.

"No, I'm . . . on vacation. Callie is a friend." And I'm the father of her baby, Armond was tempted to add, but thought better of it. He would leave it to Callie to make her announcements. "Please, call me Armond."

"Where did you learn about wines?"

No clues from Callie for this one. "It's a hobby of mine."

The studio doors opened, letting in the waiting audience. Their conversation stopped as people brushed past them, choosing seats. At last a jazzy riff

sounded over the microphones, then Perrault introduced Callie and "Spicy Living."

Callie, in the kitchen was a sight to feast upon. She
drew the audience in with her perpetual smile and
corny jokes. Her skill was subtle, and she made him
believe even he could make the dishes she demonstrated.

To his surprise, she didn't preach her vegetarian
lifestyle. It was simply a part of her. Instead of warning
against a meat-based diet or extolling the health benefits of her choice, she concentrated on two things:
the food and the taste.

"What do we do now?" she asked the audience
once.

"Add spice!" everyone chorused, in what must be a
recurring theme for the show. Callie had a definite fan
base.

When he tasted the dishes she'd prepared, he understood why. None were the bland beans-and-
sprouts dishes he expected of vegetarian cooking. She
almost convinced him that chestnut roast made a
tasty alternative to turkey. "Spicy Living" was well
named, for Callie's cooking was spicy, savory, and a
delight to the senses.

Just like her.

At the conclusion of the show, some people exited
but most milled around talking, while a few pressed
forward to corner Callie.

Uneasy with the mass of humanity pressing forward, Armond rose and, ignoring Dion's surprised
look at his sudden departure, prowled the edges of
the crowd. He didn't like crowds, he discovered. The
crush of bodies raised the hairs on his arms and tightened the back of his neck. He was too aware of a
brushing touch or a sour breath.

For a moment, his attention caught on an odd couple in their late fifties, early sixties, he guessed. They presented quite a contrast to each other, the woman in trim jeans and silk shirt, while the man sported a baseball cap, flowered shirt, shorts, and sandals. But they seemed more interested in Dion than in Callie.

Armond stepped outside a moment, needing a breath of fresh air, and when he returned to the studio all seemed normal. Even the odd couple had disappeared. Only a young man with a wisp of beard on his chin remained from the audience. The boy ran a hand across his shorn scalp and pleaded earnestly with Callie. "You can't go. I'll miss you too much."

Callie folded up her apron. "The new videos will be on after the new year. There won't be a long hiatus."

"But I've been here for every episode of 'Spicy Living.'" He brightened. "I know; I'll go with you. I've been studying. Remember that salsa you made last month? I improved on it with oregano. Bet you never added that!"

"Oregano? I'd never have thought of that." Callie shook her head. "You can't go with me, Jason, you know that. Your mother; your job."

"Washing pots and pans," he said scornfully. "Chef Bernard doesn't appreciate my talents."

"What about that girl you brought to the last show? Sandy?"

"Mandy." Jason made a dismissive gesture. "She's nice, but it's you I care about."

"You care about my Thai curry."

"Well, yes, but—"

Armond joined them, laying a hand on Callie's shoulder.

The gesture wasn't lost on puppy-eyed Jason. "Who's he?"

"A friend," Armond said mildly.

Jason threw him a suspicious look. "Are you a chef?"

Callie made a choking sound. "Hardly."

That was all it took for Jason to dismiss him. "Your show is an inspiration, Callie. You can't go."

She smiled. "Trust me, you'll like the new format."

"But I can't *be* there." Jason pouted.

"Why don't you let Miss Gabriel finish up here?" Armond interjected smoothly, seeing the slump of fatigue in Callie's shoulders. She didn't need an over-eager fan adding stress. "It's late."

Jason glanced around, as if he'd just realized the studio was empty, and ran a hand across his scalp again. "Sorry, I didn't realize." He leaned over and gave Callie a swift peck on the cheek. "I'll miss you."

Armond's fingers tightened briefly around Callie's shoulder.

When he'd left, Callie turned to Armond. "You didn't need to rescue me. Jason is harmless, and I'm perfectly capable of taking care of myself."

"Humor me. The child is mine, too," he added in a low undertone. The more often he said it, the more real it seemed, the more responsible he felt. He just wished he could remember the conception! Tucking a strand of hair behind her ear, he savored the feel of the silky tress.

Callie scowled at him, apparently experiencing no such tender feelings.

"It's time for dinner," he said. "You did all the cooking, but you didn't eat."

She laid a hand on her stomach. "I could use something, but we have to make a detour first. Christian, is the food packed?"

"Ready and waiting." The director motioned to a pile of boxes on the counter.

"We deliver the food I cook to a women's shelter,"

Callie explained. "Then, let's go to Greenwood. Food's great there." She gave him a grin.

"Only if you promise to sit and eat, not work the kitchen."

"I'll try. Dion," she called out, "you want to help us load?"

A few minutes later, the four of them had the boxes in her car and Callie was pulling away from the curb with a wave toward Dion and Christian.

Armond rested his arm along the back of the seat, the tips of his fingers barely touching her shoulder. At least she didn't shrug him off. One step at a time, Armond reminded himself. Methodical, careful. The tactic worked whether building the evidence for a conviction, searching for clues to your past, or easing yourself back into a woman's life.

Even a woman as reluctant as Callie.

Armond noted with some humor that his mind equated getting to know Callie with a strategic campaign. It would help, though, if the information he had on her was a little more complete.

Hera held the silver orb in her hands, gathering her courage. She and Zeus had gone from the cooking show to get hotel rooms, and she had only a few minutes before he would knock on her door and rejoin her.

Each of the exiles, except Zeus, had been given an orb. Given one chance to contact their home world and request restoration of citizenship and the freedom to return. Some had already done so: Hephaestus, Poseidon, Demeter. If the chance was used, and lost, there would not be another. Only Zeus, their leader, their vision, had been given a sentence that could not be repealed, a warning for those who would foment disruption.

Hera's return would be fraught with conditions; the Oracle would need proof of her regret, her willingness to conform to societal rules and structure, and her redemption. That was why she'd known she had to make reparation to a descendant of Callisto.

If only the son of Ares had not complicated matters.

The silver orb was smooth, cold, featureless except for a single indentation. It was an embodiment of D-alphus, her world.

That was what they had rebelled against, those many years ago when they were young and foolish. The intellectualism, the peace, the bonding of spirit with body. Now, she deeply felt the loss. In some ways she would miss the chaos of this world, miss things like Beethoven's *Ninth* and Numero Duo pizza and magenta. Others, she would have no regret leaving.

Hera took a deep breath, then pressed her ring into the indentation. The cool exterior of the orb vibrated faintly, then settled quietly into her hands. She held it, waiting.

At last a small holographic figure appeared on the surface of the orb. The leader of the Titanic Oracle himself.

"You wish to return, Hera?" The voice was mechanical, halting.

"I do."

It took a few moments for the answer to relay over the vast space. "You've learned the error of your ways?"

"I want to come home. I will no longer disrupt."

Another pause. "How can we believe you?"

"Do you know of Callisto?"

"We do."

"I have chosen her as my proof." Briefly, Hera described what she intended to do. "There is a small matter, a problem that will take some time to settle first. Another man is with her, a son of Ares, but I'll make sure he is sent elsewhere."

"No, he is the one you must mate her with."

"What? Ares does not love. So, too, will it be for his son."

"You question my judgment in this?"

The tone was mild, but the question was a telling one.

Hera subsided. "No, of course not, but you have given me an impossible task."

"Then it should be a worthy demonstration of your sincerity." The image began to waver.

"Wait!"

"Yes?"

Hera bit her lip, hoping she wasn't jeopardizing her only chance. "Zeus. Is there any way you can reverse—?"

"No. The leader cannot return. We cannot allow his energies to unbalance our harmony."

"But he's changed. It was his idea to help these women."

The leader of the Oracle shook his head, his eyes sad. "I'm sorry. It cannot be done. We cannot change the law."

For a moment the flare of rebellion burned again, but Hera quickly doused it. "I understand."

"Does this change your decision to return?"

Hera gripped the orb between sweaty palms, feeling the roaring of her heartbeat in her ears. She sucked in air.

"No, it does not."

Chapter Five

As he exited the taxi for his hotel, Dion Backus replayed his final image of Callie, with Armond walking beside her to the car, a hand resting at her back. Electrifying currents flowed between those two, forces as ageless and as powerful as those that brought his grapes to the perfection of wine. Did Armond know about the baby? That would explain his proprietary air toward her. A son of Ares wasn't keen on love, but protection was definitely his realm.

Frowning, Dion stepped into the hotel. He liked Callie, had contemplated the initial steps to an affair with her, for there was a complexity about her that intrigued him in a way he'd thought himself too jaded to still enjoy. He'd had little doubt of his success in bringing her to his bed, for few women could resist him when he set his mind to seduction.

Then she had told him about the baby.

He had few scruples about sex and pleasure, but seducing pregnant women was one of them.

"Mr. Backus!" the hotel clerk called after him.

Dion detoured past the desk. "Hello, Fernando. How was that Ninety Cabernet Sauvignon I suggested?"

"Delicioso." Fernando leaned forward with a conspiratorial leer. "The woman I was with, she found it most pleasurable."

Dion grinned back. "I've always found that vintage to be quite stimulating. So the evening was a success?"

"I have much to thank you for."

"You're welcome."

"And perhaps you will soon have similar luck. A woman came by asking for you. Of course, I would not tell her your room, but she promised to return."

Must be the charming lady he'd met at the hotel bar last night. Once Callie was off limits, he'd immediately started looking elsewhere. Dionysus, the god of wine, didn't go for long periods without female companionship.

"A woman? Young? Redhead? Hair down to here? Chest out to here?"

"Ah, no." Fernando sounded disappointed for him. "Not so young. A handsome woman, though. Chic."

Definitely not the redhead. Dion shrugged. "If she wants me, she'll come back."

As he headed for the elevators, then up to his room, his thoughts returned to Callie's friend. Armond Marceaux was clearly a son of Ares, and not too many generations removed, judging by the strength of the gods in him.

Ares had always been such a pain. The god of war and justice cared little for fun or pleasures or getting a wee bit tipsy on a summer's eve. He was the dispenser of justice, the warrior for the wronged, the conscience of the gods.

Dionysus hadn't liked being reminded about things such as conscience and the right thing to do and restoring the balances.

Callie and a son of Ares? As lovers? What could she see in a straitlaced man of justice? he wondered as he got out of the elevators and headed toward his room. Hades, the baby couldn't be his, could it? It simply didn't fit.

Still, to his credit, Armond did enjoy a good glass of wine.

No matter, Callie would be leaving soon. "Out of sight, out of mind," he muttered, opening the door to his room. "Problem solved."

"What problem?" asked a feminine voice. The door slammed shut behind him. Dion stared at the couple making themselves at home with his Merlot and biscotti.

"Hera? Zeus!"

Hera lifted a glass in salute. "Long time no see, Dionysus."

Callie loved Greenwood. She loved every dish on the menu and every detail of the offbeat decor, with its slew of eat-low-on-the-food-chain posters, postcards sent to her by traveling customers, and souvenir-shop trinkets.

"I like this decor; it's unique." Armond nibbled a vegetable chip and looked around, as if he'd never seen the place before.

"The grinning cow is new," she said, pointing to a plastic cow with a bobbing head on a spring and a sign around his neck reading EAT MY GRASS. "And Mark's sending back postcards and souvenirs from his tour."

"The Heart of Dixie?" he asked, pointing to a stacked doll with a bright red heart painted on her chest.

"That's been here. Don't you remember your comment when I showed her to you?"

"Ah, no."

"That no female of those measurements could walk upright." She mimicked his no-nonsense, dry tone. To her surprise, his cheeks turned a faint red; she'd never seen a hint of fluster in Armond before. "I thought it was kind of sweet, considering I'd just bemoaned the fact that my attributes didn't exactly stack up."

"Your attributes lack nothing," he said offhand, still glancing around.

Her turn to be flustered, and Callie hastily added, "Mark sent me that flamingo." She pointed to the six-foot, bright pink, floppy stuffed creature with BUSCH GARDENS blazoned on the chest. "And this."

She retrieved a plastic clamshell sporting two sneakered feet from a nearby side table. She wound it up and set it on the open surface between them. The clamshell strutted around on mechanical feet. "Isn't it great?"

Armond burst out laughing. "Callie, that is utterly tacky."

"Yeah, I know. That's what makes it great." His laugh spread like warm caramel inside her. After he'd left, too many times she'd caught herself wanting to hear that rare laugh again.

Charles, their waiter, set plates of eggplant scallopini and spicy vegetable kabobs in front of them with a flourish. "Here you go, dear heart. Armond, can I get you another glass of wine? We have a Ninety-six Bourdeaux you might enjoy."

"Thanks, that sounds good."

"Tell Joy this smells divine," Callie said, inhaling the aroma of coriander, cayenne, and paprika, glad for something to think about beside Armond and all the issues that lay between them.

"Joy has added her own touches, but she keeps the essence of Greenwood." Charles motioned for a busboy to fill her water. "We're all looking forward to seeing your video series. Can you come back at closing? We can have a nice gossip. It's been a week since I saw you last."

Tempting. Charles had been with her since she opened and had almost as intimate, and fervent, a knowledge of Greenwood and its clientele as she did. Callie glanced at Armond, then shook her head. "I have things to do tonight."

Like a conversation she couldn't put off any longer. This was not the place to have it, though, with too many friendly ears to overhear and a good meal to savor. Callie firmly believed excellent food and earnest discussion were not to be mixed, for together neither got the proper attention. For his part, Armond seemed perfectly content to forget the past; for the moment she would, too.

"I'll tell Joy to be sure and come out to see you before you leave." Charles gave her a peck on the cheek, then returned to work.

"Does every man you meet kiss you?" Armond asked.

"I'm a hugger. I told you that when we first started dating. Don't tell me you forgot." Callie dug into the scallopini. "How are your kabobs?"

"Excellent spicing. The mushrooms are a flavorful change from beef or shrimp. What kind are they?"

"Shiitake. They're meatier and don't fall apart with the roasting. My scallopini's good. The only thing it could use is a little"—Callie tasted the dish again, a sudden craving gripping her—"veal." Her fork clattered to the table.

"Veal?" Armond repeated.

Veal? Had she actually said *veal?* Dear Lord, she

wanted veal scallopini. "I'm craving meat. How can I want veal? I've never even tasted veal. I'd rather sleep on an isolated mountaintop than eat meat. *Why do I want veal scallopini?*"

A few diners turned their heads at her rising voice.

"Sorry," Callie muttered to no one in particular and slouched into her seat. She picked up her fork and began shoveling in food. "This is good. I do not want veal in it."

If she said it often enough, her taste buds might believe it.

To her relief, Armond said only, "You're pregnant. You can expect to have strange cravings."

"I expected pickles and ice cream. Not veal and hamburger and pork tenderloin and mounds of crawfish. Right now I'd even eat one of Joy's ostriches."

"Maybe you need the protein."

"I do not need protein. I get plenty of it." She gave him credit for not laughing out loud or suggesting she just eat the meat, but she wouldn't listen to his solutions. "Don't try to fix it, Armond. Just listen to me complain. And never give me meat, even if I beg."

"As you wish." Calmly, he returned to his meal.

Callie scooped up another forkful of eggplant. That was something she'd forgotten about Armond, how easily he accepted her strangest requests. He simply took her as he found her, without judging or trying to change her.

Callie's throat tightened. There had been so much good between them, so much that she'd pushed from her mind, but remembering the good had only made the breakups difficult and painful.

Don't think of the end. Not during dinner. Think of the good, and remember you're a Gabriel. Callie bent back to her veal-less scallopini. The baby would require that she and Armond to interact for many years, and Callie was determined they would deal amicably. She couldn't do that if she dwelt on the past—good or bad.

She eyed Armond from beneath lowered lids. Even for something as simple and basic as eating, he moved with the economic ease of a man very comfortable with his body. Another thing she'd forgotten.

Her heart picked up its pace, filling her with hot, thrumming blood, just as it had when she'd seen him earlier at the TV studio, shaved, hair trimmed, the man she remembered. This Armond was a far cry from the man she'd met at the cabin dressed only in a bare chest and a pair of shorts.

Yet both were Armond.

While she gave him another surreptitious glance, he lingered with each bite of food, each sip of wine, savoring the flavors and textures and aromas.

What would it be like to have him linger over and savor her with that same slowness and attention?

Her fork dropped from her nerveless fingers. Shoot, where had that come from? Wasn't the last time devastating enough?

Yet she couldn't deny that she wished they'd made love a second time, giving them a chance to go slower. Not that she would have wanted to miss the fiery, explosive, frantic first time. Callie let out a small, tremulous breath, facing the stark truth.

Despite everything between them, she still wanted Armond.

Hormones. It had to be the hormones causing temporary insanity. Not guilty by reason of pregnancy.

Armond gave her an intent look. "Are you all right?"

Callie retrieved her fork and stabbed her eggplant. The man missed nothing. "What's happened to you?" she asked around a mouthful of tomato and garlic, desperate for a topic other than her thoughts.

His fork halted halfway to his mouth. "What do you mean?"

How to explain something she barely understood herself? Each moment with him, he shifted further from the uncivilized man of the cabin, who both fascinated and frightened her, and became the urbane, reserved detective she'd dated but could never live with.

He waited, eyeing her with wary interest.

"At the cabin, it was like a veneer had been stripped from you." Callie gave a short laugh at his incredulous look. "You asked. Right now—the haircut, the clothes, your ease with wine, the wariness and control—every moment melds you back to the man I knew. At the cabin, though"—she shrugged—"obviously you've been through something bad—the damage to your face, the scratches on your legs. And with it was a freedom or a ferocity, a wildness, I'd never seen in you. Or rather, you never let me see."

"Christ, Callie, you make me sound like some freaking Jekyll and Hyde." His knuckles were white where he gripped the wineglass.

"Never Hyde," she assured him softly. "And not two people, really, just a part you never let me completely see."

"A part you don't want to see?"

"Maybe. I think sometimes it slips out, though." Like two months ago, when we made a child together, she thought with a sizzle of memory.

Armond hesitated. "Which me do you like better?"

"This one. I'm used to it. The other one scares me."

He swallowed the last of his wine in a quick gulp. "I'm an FBI agent. What you saw just comes with the territory."

The simmering excitement dropped with the dull thud of reality. Callie shivered at his withdrawal, at the echo of isolation in him and in her. His work was always the first priority with Armond.

Focus on the food. At least the veal craving had gone.

Hera sampled the Merlot. A perfect complement to the meal Dionysus ordered delivered to his suite. But then, she expected nothing less from the god of wines and pleasures. It wasn't an expensive bottle, under fifteen, but with Dion price had never been the ultimate criteria for wine. After all, he'd been making it for millennia. For him, it was all a matter of taste.

She told Dion as much.

For a long moment he savored the ruby liquid, lids drooping, a look of pure pleasure over his arresting face; then he let out a tiny, appreciative belch. "We're visiting the Michigan winery that perfected this bottle. Would you like me to fetch you up a bottle or two?"

"Perhaps we will select our own," Hera murmured.

"Ah." His languid look disappeared, though he didn't move. "So, we get to the reason why you seek me out after all these years. Do you wish to heal the rift between us?"

"I sought you before," Zeus said, "but you would not even see me. The rift is not of my making. Yet now you agree. I think we both have questions."

"Perhaps I've mellowed, aged to a finer vintage. I am no longer so angry with you for allowing man to turn from us."

"I could not stop the tide of progress."

"They called you god. You have powers, Zeus, you refuse to explore. You're a fool in that."

Hera saw Zeus's lips tighten and she jumped in before the two started flinging thunderbolts and thorns. "That's the past, Dion. We're here, and you gave us hospitality. Let's start from there."

"Very well. Why have you come?"

Hera saw no reason to dissemble. "Callie Gabriel."

Zeus threw her an irritated look. He always did prefer the roundabout to the direct. "You aren't trying to seduce her, are you?" he asked Dion.

So, maybe he'd learned a few things about direct over the years.

"I thought about it, but in truth I am not."

"Why?" asked Hera bluntly.

Dion smiled. "I draw the line at a pregnant woman."

"She's pregnant?" Zeus exploded. "Who's the father?"

"I don't know."

"Armond Marceaux," said Hera flatly. When Zeus raised one eyebrow in her direction, she flushed and muttered, "I, ah, happened to far-see on her a couple of months ago, and it was obvious they'd, um, just finished. I sent a rainstorm to break them up, but I guess it was a little late."

"What's your interest in a woman from the lineage of Callisto?" Dion asked her.

Zeus answered. "We're trying to unite her with a true love. Break the legacy I left to her line."

The wine choked Dion as he burst out laughing. He coughed, tears streaming, choking out, "You ... two ... matchmakers?"

"Our record is perfect," Zeus said with the booming, haughty grandeur that had stood him well on Olympus.

"Who do you think to match Callie with?"

"A son of Olympus."

"Armond? That son of Ares is the only one around her that I see."

"No," said Zeus. "Not Armond."

"Yes," said Hera. "Armond."

Zeus flashed her another irritated look. "We agreed.

87

Sons of Ares know nothing about love. She'd do better with Apollo's kin, or Hades, or even one of Dion's."

"She'd do more than simply better with an offshoot of mine," protested Dion.

"Do either of you know where one of these paragons is? Does Callie know any?" Hera asked pointedly. The two gods were silent. "I didn't think so. A son of Ares isn't my first choice either, but there aren't a lot of other options."

"No." Zeus shook his head. "Not Armond."

"Definitely not Armond," added Dion with vehemence.

"Our job will be to find her someone else." Zeus.

"Amen." Dionysus.

Hera gave an exasperated huff. The only time these two agreed was on things guaranteed to plague her.

"Our job," she said softly to her husband, "will be to make it work for her."

Zeus swallowed. "How?"

"By teaching a son of Ares to love."

"Impossible," spat Dion.

If there was one thing guaranteed to challenge Zeus, it was the word *impossible*.

He turned from her to eye Dion. "Are you sure about that?"

"You two are going to teach him?" Dion's amusement was clear.

"Who better?" countered Zeus.

"You can't even manage your own love life."

"That's different."

Dion's eyes gleamed. "And I say Armond is too close to Ares to love. Not sex, not altruism, not justice or retribution. Love. The deep, abiding, selfless, *romantic* kind. Would you like to prove me wrong?"

"I always did like a challenge." Zeus snapped his

mouth shut and turned to Hera. "You're awfully silent, my dear."

"You're talking enough for the both of us."

"And I'm taking the opposite position from what I took not three minutes ago. The one you espoused. How do you do it, love?"

"I let nature take its course. What did you have in mind, Dion?" Hera asked.

"I'll get you on the shoot with us—that is why you came to me, is it not?"

Hera nodded. Many unflattering things were said of Dion, but being stupid wasn't one of them.

"You could do the makeup, dear Hera, and Zeus, do you know anything about lighting?"

Zeus brushed an invisible crumb from his shirt. "Well, Apollo always did have more of a talent for it than I, but the god of lightning has learned a few things over the years."

"Will Armond be there?" Hera asked.

"I think I could persuade him," Dion said.

Hera frowned at a sudden thought. "We met both Callie and Armond. Only once and briefly, but they'll know us. We'll need a plausible excuse."

"You could be trying out a new line of cosmetic products aimed for the entertainment industry," Zeus offered. "And I can be looking to expand from fireworks. It's a stretch, but if Dion approves me, who will question us?"

Hera nodded in agreement. The excuses were workable.

"Why are you so eager to agree?" Zeus asked Dion.

"It appeals to my sense of fun?"

"Obviously, or you wouldn't have agreed, but I suspect you want something else. Some additional benefit?"

"We could place a little wager on the outcome," Dion suggested, studying his fingernails.

"What do you think?" Zeus lifted a shoulder toward Hera.

"A wager would add spice to the mix."

Zeus picked up his wine and sipped it. "What is the wager to be? The stakes?"

"The wager? That he bonds with her. But it must be for love, not only because of the baby."

Zeus looked at Hera.

"It's the only way the union will last," she answered.

"Wager accepted. And the stakes?"

"Ah, the stakes." Dion tapped his chin. "I'm prepared to wager the mirror of Aphrodite. She left it with me when she returned home. I suspect it will be useful to you in your future matchmaking."

"What do you want in return?"

"Your rings."

Hera gasped. The other gods had their talismans, that which manifested their abilities—the book of Hermes, the mirror of Aphrodite, the gems of Hades, the shield of Ares—even Dion had his goblet. The rings, however, made them kings and queens, and their power should not be wielded by another.

"Aren't you sure enough of your abilities?" Dion mocked. "And I think we need a time frame."

"The length of the video shoots," suggested Hera.

"Too long. I'll be sporting: the length of the shoots in Louisiana and around the Great Lakes. Two months."

"Two months!" Hera exclaimed.

Zeus motioned her silent. "Will you interfere, Dion?"

"No more than you. I'll leave you the initial moves, but I reserve the right to, ah, protect my interests. What could be fairer?"

Two months? Would that be enough time to teach

a man how to love? If she lost her ring, would she still be allowed home? Regardless, she could not allow Zeus to be punished for her choices; he would need his ring when she left. And he was clearly intrigued by the piquancy added by the wager.

"My ring only," Hera told Dion. "You wager one talisman; we wager one ring."

"My dear—" protested Zeus.

"It was I who insisted on Callisto. Who chose Ares."

"Your ring alone," acknowledged Dion quickly. "Are we agreed?"

A knock sounded on the door.

Dion glanced at his watch. "Make up your minds. If I'm not mistaken, that is our dinner."

Hera glanced at Zeus, then back at Dion.

"Agreed," said Zeus.

"Good." Dion rubbed his hands together. "This will be fun."

"Marceaux's surfaced."

At last. Sweating in the Georgia heat, Special Agent in Charge Conrad Titus gripped the pay phone receiver. "Where?"

"New Orleans," answered the harsh voice of the laboratory guard, one of Centurion's muscle. "He logged onto a Usenet group from the New Orleans Public Library. We don't know where in the city, but we'll find him."

"You'll bring him back to the lab?"

"No." The monosyllable was flat.

Heat made breathing a chore. "Kill him?"

"No. The doctor wants to watch him out in the field."

Those fools. Armond Marceaux, whether he had his memory or not, was a dangerous man. "Let me talk to the psychiatrist."

A moment later the head of the DC-909 project answered in her cool voice. "Yes?"

"Why are you leaving Marceaux free?"

"We need to study how long DC-Nine-oh-nine retains potency without a booster dose or whether the modifications make the memory loss permanent."

"Can't you do that in the lab?"

"Not as effectively. He won't know we're watching, so his responses will be true. And we can see any effects from triggers."

"Triggers?"

"Something in the outer world that stimulates his memory, likely something he has strong emotional ties to—positive or negative."

"I thought you said Marceaux was a perfect specimen because he didn't have any ties."

"I'm just saying, if he gets a surge of serotonin or endorphin release, the drug might lose effectiveness." Titus could almost hear the woman shrug through the phone lines.

"How long?"

"Once we locate him, we'll keep him under surveillance for at least forty-eight hours. His memory won't come back that soon. After that, we'll play it by ear."

"What about his telepathy?"

"He hasn't got any." Her scorn was evident. "The tests were negative."

"Check again," he said softly. "He's got something. It's not a good idea to leave Marceaux out."

"Centurion's already approved it," she said flatly and hung up.

And that decided that.

Titus pulled a handkerchief from his pocket and wiped his face. He didn't have the guts to directly oppose Centurion, not anymore. The man owned him.

It had been so easy to get ensnared by Guy Centurion, one tiny step at a time. Get some intell that resulted in the headline-grabbing bust of a major terrorist plot, then direct your field agents to another site when a small plane lands. One evening with an adventurous, pretty hooker, but we won't tell your wife if you arrest our rival's pimp, not ours. Share in the profit from the sale of gems you don't confiscate and pay for college tuition and surgery bills. It had all been so easy.

He knew the Bureau's assistant director in Washington suspected a rogue—but didn't know who—when Armond Marceaux had been assigned to Atlanta as his first office placement out of training at Quantico, and Titus had gotten a look at the agent's files. Marceaux was a top-notch investigator, a dedicated LE professional, but there was something else. Nobody talked about it, but the knowledge was common: Armond Marceaux had something, some instinct, that let him hone in on a perp.

Titus had managed to avoid meeting the man, since Marceaux had been in Louisiana part of the short weeks he'd been assigned to Atlanta, but the SAC knew his days were numbered.

Then Armond Marceaux had arrested Guy Centurion.

Centurion wanted revenge.

Titus wanted to survive.

Together they'd sent Marceaux undercover to Centurion's pet project.

Together they'd betrayed an FBI agent, a man under Titus's command.

And now Centurion was letting him run free.

Until Marceaux regained his memory, Titus was safe, but he would keep his own tabs on the troublesome agent.

And find out more about possible triggers.

Chapter Six

"I don't need to ask if you enjoyed it," said a woman's voice as Callie scraped the last remnants of tomato sauce from her plate.

Callie pivoted in her seat, then rose. "Joy."

Her friend had come from the kitchen, dressed in her chef's whites, her red hair tightly bound into a neat knot, and her face flushed and sweat-sheened from the heat. The look she split between Armond and Callie was frankly curious; then she smiled at him. "Armond, I didn't know you were in town."

"I'm on vacation."

"It's good to see you; Mark will be sorry he missed you." She gave Callie a hug. "I thought you'd left to do that video."

Callie returned the embrace. "We filmed at the wineries north of the lake. Now we're shooting around the area for the rest of the Louisiana wines segment, plus the cooking segment." She waved a hand, encompassing the humming dining room. "Busy night."

"Mondays have been picking up."

"Where does Mark head next?"

"He's got two more dates in Florida, then he'll have a week off before he starts playing the Midwest. I expect you'll start getting replicas of the Sears Tower or miniature cars." Thankfully, Joy didn't pursue the topic of Armond's presence, although Callie guessed if she and Joy were alone, she'd have been pelted with questions.

"Oh," Joy continued, "do you remember meeting Dani, the dance teacher, at my wedding? She was so impressed with the buffet you did for my reception that she wants Greenwood to cater hers."

"She knows it would all be vegetarian?"

Joy nodded. "She was excited about the idea."

"How's the workload?"

"We can handle this one, but I've gotten other requests. If you want to expand in this area, you'll have to hire a chef de partie. I've done catering before; it might be the time to venture out."

Quickly Callie made a decision. "Let's work up the numbers, but it sounds promising." Once the baby came, this, with the video series, might be a way for her to still work, while delegating the hectic, long hours a restaurant kitchen demanded.

"Good. You ready for dessert? Fresh baklava's on the menu. Armond?"

He shook his head. "No thanks, I'm full."

Callie hesitated. She was full, too, but she had a weakness for baklava.

Joy laughed. "I'll get you a couple of pieces to take home," she offered, bustling away.

Armond tossed his napkin onto the table. "What's the arrangement between you and Joy, Callie?"

Had she told him? "While Mark's completing his North American tour, she's minding Greenwood for me. Next fall I'll come back, and she'll go with Mark on his European tour."

"Can you manage a busy restaurant and a newborn?"

Callie threw back the remains of her sparkling lime juice, then pushed to her feet. "Gabriel women can handle anything."

She just hoped it was the truth.

Joy returned a moment later with the wrapped baklava. "A phone call just came through for you, Callie."

"For me?"

Joy nodded. "He left a message when he found out you hadn't left yet. Do you know a Dion Backus?" At Callie's nod, she continued, "He wants you to meet him in an hour at his suite at the Windsor Court." Her eyes flicked toward Armond. "Both of you."

When Joy left, Callie looked up at Armond. "What do you suppose that's about?"

He gazed thoughtfully after Joy. "I don't know."

Outside, the air had cooled with the sunset, and the humidity had fallen to manageable levels. Callie drew in a breath of city air. It was a nice night for being outside. "We've got some time before the meeting with Dion. Let's go down to the river, by the Aquarium."

They parked at the foot of Canal Street, and in a few minutes they were strolling through Woldenberg Park, a grassy strip along the edge of the Mississippi River. Only the drifting bulk of a barge disturbed the quiet waters beside them. Every fifteen minutes the ferry's horn sounded a lone blast as it prepared to traverse the distance between the banks. Snatches of dance music carried to them with the gusts of wind that ruffled her hair. Callie stuck her fingers in her pockets, close enough to Armond to catch the faint whiff of his soap, but not touching.

They weren't alone. They passed a pair of lovers occupied on a blanket and a street denizen snoring beneath a tree. A huddle of giggling teen girls bounced down the sidewalk. Nobody paid her and Armond any attention.

Families used the park, too. A young couple passed them, pushing a stroller together, while a father gently twirled his daughter in a circle, the girl laughing with delight. Callie stopped a moment to watch, her throat constricting.

"My father was a wanderer, a sailor," she said softly. "He stopped in New Orleans only long enough to deposit his seed."

"Did you ever wonder about him?"

"I used to imagine him coming back and taking me sailing around the world." She resumed their walk along the wooden boards. "Gabriels aren't supposed to miss their fathers, though, so I gave up the dream."

Until she'd gotten pregnant, she'd thought she'd accepted her father's abandonment. Instead, she'd realized she didn't want her daughter growing up like that. Wondering what was wrong with her that he didn't even send a postcard. Pretending she didn't care that she didn't go to the Brownies' father-daughter dance. Angry that she hurt when Gabriels weren't supposed to.

"Do you have anything of his?" Armond's question interrupted her thoughts.

"His genes. And my given name on my birth certificate is California, his home." She gave him a small smile. "But don't you dare tell anyone that."

"Your secret's safe." Armond made a tiny cross over his heart.

"You told me once that your mother raised you. Do you have anything of your father's?"

Such a simple question, yet such a minefield. Armond hesitated, frustrated once more that his amnesia put up barriers. His hands fisted, but he said only, "No." It was the truth, as far as he knew.

There was something else, though, that he needed to know. He swallowed around the tightness in his throat. "Callie, the pregnancy. How did you feel when you found out? Were . . . are you sorry?"

She twisted to look up at him, her face partially shadowed. "My first reaction was disbelief." Her voice was barely perceptible above the night sounds. "I mean, it was only the one time, and we had used protection. How's that for my luck? My second was chagrin. I'd made a whopper of a mistake, and a baby wasn't part of my plans right now."

His fingers flexed. He'd asked and he had to listen, even if it was a stab to his chest. "Did you think about getting an—?" The word *abortion* stuck in his lungs.

"Never." Callie laid a hand on his tense arm. "The disbelief, the chagrin, were fleeting. And always mixed with them was joy. I want this baby, Armond, and I already love her."

Relief embraced him, and he felt the warmth of her smile more than saw it.

"More than anything," she continued, "I want to do what's right for her."

"With you as a mother, she can't help but be beautiful, inside and out." His hand drifted down toward her stomach, pleased she allowed him to touch her there. Was she more rounded? He wished he could remember her before, so he would know. "I can almost imagine I feel the beating of dual hearts."

"She has one by now, a heart, a strong little heart beating away."

"Are you having a lot of symptoms?" he asked after a moment, his hand still resting on her warm abdomen.

"Not a lot. The sight of scrambled eggs nauseates me. I feel hotter, don't need a jacket, but who does down here? And I'll probably have to stop in the bathroom at Jax Brewery before we leave to meet Dion."

"Then why don't we head in that direction?" He dropped his hand, feeling strangely bereft at the loss of contact. Every time he touched her, he felt the goodness in her soul.

They turned in the other direction, and Armond thrust his hands in his pocket. "You found me. What do you want from me, Callie? What do you want my role to be?"

"What do *you* want it to be?"

He didn't really know, Armond realized. He rubbed the back of his neck, looking out toward the water, as if there was some answer in its ageless motion. Only the tinny sounds of a steam calliope on an approaching paddlewheel responded.

He had no knowledge to go on. No knowledge of his work, except to know it was dangerous. No knowledge of himself as a man, what traits he would bring to fatherhood. No assurance that he would be an asset to his daughter's life. All he could do was rummage through his feelings and instincts in a way that felt curiously rusty, as though he tried to avoid them.

"I don't want to disappear from her life," he said at last, sure of that one thing, resuming their walk. "I want her to know her father."

"Then she shall."

"Other than that? I want to be listed as the father on her birth certificate. I want paternity acknowledged by law as well as our agreement."

"All right."

"I'll make sure to support her financially."

"But I don't want you—"

Her protest grated across him. "I'll support her," he repeated, low and implacable.

"We'll reach a figure."

"Joint custody?"

Callie frowned and kicked at a loose pebble. "Remember how many dates you canceled, or shortened, because of some urgent break in a case? You work worse hours than I do, and I'll have my family to help. You can't take care of a baby like that."

"I want regular visits," he amended. Why was he so insistent when he didn't know if he could meet that obligation? But something inside him could not let go. "Can you be flexible with the times?"

"We'll work it out."

What else? He couldn't think right now, not yet really accepting all the ramifications of being a father.

"The rest I guess we can just work out as we go," Callie added.

Armond cast a sidelong glance toward her. He'd been bound up in his own problems—the memory loss, the question of where he'd been, the shock at hearing he was a father-to-be, the attempt to reconcile it all—he hadn't really stopped to consider what this all meant to Callie. He hadn't thought about the changes she was going through and the adjustments she would have to make.

This couldn't be easy for her. She was the one dealing with all the challenges of pregnancy. Something had broken them up, and she still remembered what it was. She could have kept her secret, yet she was here with him, trying to be fair.

"There's one more thing," he said, resting a hand at her collar, craving the feel of her beneath his palm.

"I'd like to try and help her be as smiling, as capable, as loving as her mother."

"Is that how you see me?" Callie turned toward him, her eyes wide.

"Haven't I ever told you?"

He felt her head shake. "Not in those words. You've always closely guarded your feelings."

"Then I've been a jerk." He longed to take her in his arms, not for the chance of retrieving memory but to hold her close, to kiss her thoroughly.

What the hell could have gone so wrong between them?

Somehow he would make it right with her. Some instinct deep inside him insisted on it. He just didn't know how, not until he got his memory back. "Callie," he began hesitantly, "about us . . ."

Idly, his fingers teased a strand of her gold-and-sherry-colored hair. So silky. How many times had he touched her like this? How could he have forgotten it?

Callie pressed a hand against the traitorous fluttering in her stomach. He'd touched her like that, that little gentling at the neck, the night he'd come back to her. The night her daughter had been conceived.

"Don't," she whispered.

"Don't what?"

"Don't do that." She felt his touch clear down to her bones. Wants she'd thought she'd finally conquered burst forth. Armond had a way of slipping past her defenses without even trying, just like he was doing now. It was as though he'd taken them back to the first days of their courtship, when there were no losses and pain.

"Don't touch me like that." The words sounded harsh in the smooth night. She pulled from him and, arms crossed, faced him. "I'm not part of the fatherhood package," she said, her jaw aching. "Being part of the baby's life doesn't mean being part of mine."

"Did you expect that I would be like your father? Ignore my responsibility to you and the baby?"

"I suppose not," she admitted. "You always took your responsibilities seriously." And, when the pregnancy test turned positive, for one brief, insane moment she'd actually thought about marrying the father, if he asked. About forgetting all the reasons why it was impossible. "But I'm not one of them."

Responsible. The word was a heavy lump in her chest. Pregnant, she was simply one of Armond's myriad responsibilities, and that she couldn't accept. She didn't want that, didn't need it. Her fantasies included someone who put her first. Someone who went to work at nine and came home at five, without fail. Someone who wouldn't leave her.

That could never be Armond.

Her chin came up. She needed armor, some defense against herself as much as him. "Gabriel women are independent. Our tradition is clear; we raise our daughters ourselves."

"Tradition? Sounds more like a family curse."

"You don't understand. You never understood my family."

"Then explain it to me. What went so wrong, Callie?"

"Don't pretend you don't know! Eight months ago you left for DC with only a single call telling me you were going—" She shook her head, anger taking the place of regret, pushing back the fact that she bore part of the blame, had been the one to let him down first. She'd been devastated, and only starting to heal when she let her guard down two months ago. When he seemed to need her just as much as she needed him.

What a delusion that had been.

"And the last time! We make love, then you tell me you're staying in Atlanta and going undercover for God knows how long. Twice is enough, Armond. I can't go through that again." Callie's gaze caught the telltale bulge beneath his shirt, the planted-feet stance. "Look, even now you're carrying a gun, standing alert. Whether it's detective or agent, your work always comes first. At heart you're always a cop."

Always a cop. Always a cop. The words rattled inside Armond, setting up a throbbing echo.

She brushed past him, her scent sweet as almond and honey.

Touch, scent, sight, Callie. *Always a cop!* The words exploded in his mind. A thousand stilettos stabbed at the black wall separating him from his past, boring in with unyielding pain. Armond clenched his fists and struggled to stay upright around the pain and nausea. Through the agony, though, he fought to keep the memories.

Light flashed in thin beams from the black wall, a strobe on metal, reflecting a word, a sound, a scent, a picture fragment.

Always a cop.

Loyalty. Bone-deep disappointment, a shadow of the real memory, filled Armond. He set his teeth against the grinding ache in his chest, which augmented the migraine. Vaguely he knew Callie was still talking to him at the water's edge.

"A . . . moment. Please," he gritted out.

She gripped his arm, the brilliant red of her sleeve coming into focus, her voice hesitant. "Armond?"

Armond. Almond. Red. Callie. *Always a cop.* The shards of memory coalesced, assimilated in an instant. The office at Greenwood. A desk with a line of melons on it. Callie beside the desk, nude and blushing pink. Hadn't she said they'd done it on the desk?

Flash. He on a narrow sofa, Callie half beneath him. Clutching him. Holding her. Kissing her gently below the ear. Her red blouse tangled on one arm, and she tasted of almond biscotti. Other clothing strewn around a room.

Explosive sex. Keen release, exhaustion, peace.

What next? The remembered question from Callie burned into his brain in the next flash.

I'm LE. I can't change that.

Won't.

Can't.

Always a cop. You never even called to say you were leaving. How can I trust you, when you leave me alone?

Their words were staccato notes, sharp and short and hurting.

I asked you, but you never came. Never picked up the phone. I need your loyalty.

A flash of a deeper layer. Him. Standing at the cabin. Fists clenched. That bone-deep disappointment filling the hollows of his chest. Alone. Alone. Alone . . .

Alone. A flash of a steel-encased room. Restraints. Lancing pain in his arms. Worse pain behind his eyes. Alone with the poisonous taste of someone's guilt. *Betrayal.* A harsh, sickening knowledge. *Someone betrayed me. Betrayed the Bureau.*

Betrayal.

"Armond, eat this." From the recessed reality, he heard Callie, felt her thrust something sticky in his hand. Real time. The river. Blindly he ate as she commanded, loss and regret and betrayal and anger, both memory and current, throbbing inside him.

Honey dripped on his chin. He was eating honey. And almond. Lights and stilettos vanished, leaving only the residues of pain in his head. And in his heart.

Shaken, Armond sucked in a deep breath. The images were assimilated; the emotions were still raw. He opened his eyes and willed himself to focus on the present, then stared at the sticky sweet in his hands. "You gave me baklava?"

"It was all I could think of. Honey's a curative."

Surprisingly, something in it had helped chase away the remnants of nausea. He took another bite.

Callie watched Armond eat the baklava, her hand resting on his arm. His eyes were open, lucid. A few beads of sweat dotted his forehead, the only remaining clue that something had been quite wrong for a brief moment.

What had just happened? One moment he'd been talking to her, the next he'd stood ramrod stiff, even more military than usual. She called; he barely responded. Eyes shut, lips pursed, with sweat on his brow—he looked ill or in pain.

She'd done the first thing she thought of, given him the baklava. Funny, it seemed to work.

"Sorry," he said, eyeing her warily.

"For what? What happened, Armond? And don't tell me nothing."

"I told you. Headaches. I was under . . . stress at work."

Headaches? Her eyes widened under a shot of fear. "What aren't you telling me about these headaches?"

The muscles beneath her hand turned to iron. "Nothing."

"Omigod, are you sick, Armond? You're not on vacation, are you? You're on leave. Medical leave. What is it? A brain tumor? Is it a brain tumor? Mom knows one of the top researchers at Ochsner. We have to get you—"

"It isn't a brain tumor," he snapped.

"Are you sure?"

"Don't sound so disappointed. Of course I'm sure. It's stress."

His irritation convinced her more than his words that he didn't suffer some deadly malady. "Since when did you give in to stress? You thrive on it."

"No, I don't. I just know what needs to be done and I do it." His mouth clicked shut, as if the words surprised him. "And what happened between us wasn't all my fault, was it, Callie? Why didn't you come to my cabin? Why didn't *you* call? Didn't you think I'd be worried? Disappointed? Hurt?"

Callie gaped at him, startled by his open admission, and a taut silence settled between them. The mask dropped back across Armond's face, as if his outburst embarrassed him.

"Looks like you folks could use a little cheerin'." A street performer dressed in a patchwork suit of red, white, and blue strutted up to them, saving her from having to answer.

"Sorry, we're busy," said Armond, his eyes making a quick assessment.

"Spare a moment for an old man. You won't regret it."

He rubbed his hands together, producing a flash and smoke, catching their attention. With a flourish, the juggler lowered his top hat to the sidewalk, ready to receive whatever donation they might give, and Callie's surprise dissolved into curiosity. Beneath the top hat, the juggler wore another one with a broad brim that shielded his face, so all she could see was a drooping mustache.

"How about a bit of juggling? Time, work, and love?" He patted his pockets and emerged with an old-fashioned alarm clock, a ballpoint pen, and a red plastic heart. He began to juggle.

Callie stared as the odd collection spun between his hands. Despite his appearance, the man was a good juggler.

"Time, work, love. All important, don't you think?" He fixed a gaze on Armond. "Don't you think?"

"Of course," Armond answered, a trifle impatient.

"Especially love. Now you try it." He held the objects, still juggling with lightning speed toward Callie.

She laughed. "I can't juggle."

"You can do what you put your mind to. Catch!"

The plastic heart jumped toward her. Callie caught it just before it dropped.

"See," said the strange juggler. His hands blurred again, and another plastic heart appeared for Armond, who easily caught the white-and-red-striped toy. "You can juggle, too. Just toss me back the hearts, and be prepared."

Callie glanced at Armond, who studied the juggler the way he might study a crime scene; then she shrugged and tossed back the heart. Deftly, the juggler reincorporated it into his act. "Now you, young man."

"Here." Armond flipped it back.

The stranger caught it. He juggled the four objects, then a moment later, Callie found herself holding the striped heart and Armond the red one. They repeated the exchanges, settling into the performer's rhythm with an ease that had her smiling. Then the juggler clapped his hands. So fast he was, she didn't even see the clock and pen disappear. She was left holding the striped heart again, and Armond had the red one.

The juggler bowed to her applause. "You've juggled and exchanged hearts. Pay attention and keep them safe."

Callie held out her heart to return to him. "Here."

He waved it away. "Keep it. A gift. A reminder."

"Thank you." She smiled, then began rummaging in her purse for a donation.

"I've got it." Armond tossed a bill into the hat, then

eyed the man curiously. "You've got a strange act."

"It depends upon what you need," he answered cryptically, claiming the money and settling the top hat back on his head. "Just remember, it takes two hearts to juggle."

He strolled away, whistling, disappearing into the fog that rolled in from the Mississippi.

"What do you suppose that meant?" Armond asked.

"I haven't got the foggiest idea," Callie answered.

They looked at each other, and Callie burst out laughing. "If you could have seen your face when he tossed you that heart."

"And you were staring so hard, I thought you were hypnotized." His low chuckle pleased her.

He lifted a hand, as if to smooth back a tendril of hair dislodged by the river breeze, then dropped it. "Callie, we need to keep things . . . cool between us."

"Yes," she said softly, looking up at the shadows that had fallen over him. "We're adults. We can deal calmly, civilly, with matters at hand."

She wondered if he was lying as thoroughly as she was. Her reactions to this man were never calm and cool. But if he was willing to try, so was she.

"Agreed. The past is past. We'll leave it there."

There he was wrong. The past could not be forgotten.

Hearing the laughter, Zeus smiled. They'd been so tense, so at odds. A little humor was bound to lighten things up, and two people who could laugh together still shared hope.

"They're gone," he said. "You can get rid of the fog."

With a whoosh of wind, the fog disappeared to reveal Hera, watching him. She shook her head. "That suit is really ugly."

"It got their attention." With a rub of his ring, he

removed the overlay to reveal his real clothes. To his relief, the ring's power held true. Must have been a trick of ionization that caused the previous problem. "And maybe the message got through a little, too."

"You had a good idea to seek them out after we left Dion."

"We have a hard task ahead. But, for now, we have some hours free." He leaned over and nuzzled her neck. "I can think of a few more tricks."

To his frustration, Hera pulled away from him. She refused to look at him, gazing instead at the river. "Between us, we need to take things slow."

"Slow? Hera, we are married, and have been for millennia. We've shared about everything a man and a woman can share."

"But we've been apart for a long time. We need to get reacquainted. I've changed, and I think you have, too. I don't want to hurt you," she added a bit desperately.

"The only thing you could do to hurt me is to keep us apart."

Her shoulders stiffened. "Don't say that! We have separate lives now. Different needs."

Zeus's teeth ground. Women. For someone who loved them so much, he really didn't understand the way their minds worked. Well, he had known there was trust to be regained between he and Hera. This time, this matchmaking, he would do as she asked. His hand dropped. "You're calling the moves on this one, my love."

But for the future, he would not be so patient.

Chapter Seven

Conrad Titus jotted down the names of Armond Marceaux's partners when he'd been with the NOPD. They might be worth keeping an eye on. Then he turned back to the files. There didn't seem to be any other close friends, any long-term relationships, except one possibility.

Callie Gabriel.

She was an odd element.

According to the files, Gabriel was an up-and-coming chef in New Orleans. For a city that valued its food traditions, that was an accomplishment. Especially considering Gabriel was a staunch vegetarian in a city where shrimp, tasso, and boudin sausage were prime food groups. Beyond that, her file read like a blueprint for a freakin' bleeding-heart liberal. Besides professional organizations and charities, she maintained membership in the ASPCA, Amnesty International, and Greenpeace. In the past, she'd demonstrated peacefully against animal experimentation, volunteered at a battered women's shelter, and appeared in local theater, while training under a variety of chefs. Lately, though, the report said she concentrated on her restaurant.

Gabriel and Marceaux dated while he was in New Orleans, but sources indicated nothing too serious had developed. They'd broken up when Marceaux left. Not too surprising. A liberal vegetarian and a by-the-book cop? Marceaux was too hard, too focused to find her more than a passing amusement.

Still, she had tenuous ties to Centurion: she'd once approached him about financing her restaurant but backed off, and she'd hired Joy Taylor, the woman Centurion was so stupid as to try and kill.

It might be worthwhile to locate Callie Gabriel.

Files could be wrong.

He closed down the computer, then left to find a pay phone.

"Dion asked you to look at our security? And you agreed?" Callie wove through the late-evening traffic, honking her horn as a taxi cut in front of them. "I can't believe it. For a little note? Probably just an eager fan."

"He's received two notes telling you to stay in New Orleans, to get off the video series," Armond said mildly.

Callie gave a snort of irritation. "I'm a chef. I'm in no danger."

"And I'll make sure you stay that way."

His quiet assertion drew her up short, and Callie shot him a glance. "You're really suspicious about this? You think something's wrong?"

"I'm always suspicious. It's my job."

Dion had gifted him with the opportunity to stay

close, and Armond was willing to take advantage of it, but he *was* suspicious, by both nature and training. Something about the notes rankled. They hadn't seemed a dangerous threat, not that he could put his finger on what prompted that conclusion. It was sheer instinct.

He was learning to trust these instincts, but not when it was Callie's safety on the line.

It wouldn't hurt to do a little investigating into Dion Backus, though. Armond hadn't been surprised to find the man settled into the finest suite at the elegant hotel. Something about Dion bespoke a hedonistic pleasure in luxury.

The wine business must pay very well.

Or he had another source of income.

"Just accept it, Callie," he added. "You're stuck with me for a couple more days."

Callie muttered a profanity. A few more days in close contact with Armond? She wasn't sure if her hormone surges could handle the pressure. Or her heart survive intact.

"What about your job, *Agent* Marceaux?" she protested. Besides, what was all the fuss about a couple of crank notes?

"I'm on vacation. Dion just asked me to keep an eye out for a few days. I won't use Bureau resources, and I'm not taking any compensation." He threw her a glance. "Unless I can talk you into the occasional meal."

Her answer was a noncommittal *hmmph*. "Where do you want me to drop you?"

"For now, I go where you go," he said with the quiet control that characterized the man she knew.

Callie slammed on the brakes, even though the light had just turned yellow. The driver behind her honked, swerved around her, and swung through the intersection as the light turned red.

"Twenty-four/seven?" she asked, trying to ignore the power he still wielded over her heartbeat, dammit.

"If that's what it takes." He gave her a penetrating look. "Callie, trust me, in this at least. It's important."

A single doubt punctured her frustration. She knew enough about Armond's career in NOPD to remember other officers talked about "Marceaux's freaking luck" at untangling cases.

Could she take the chance that there was something to the notes? Could she risk the baby?

In a word, no.

"Fine." The light changed. She spun onto St. Charles Avenue barely missing the clanging streetcar. "I'm going home. You can take the car and start finding out who's behind the notes."

But that was all it would be, strictly business. Civil and calm.

They rode in silence until Armond asked, "Have you told many people about the baby?" He stared out the window, not looking at her, his voice casual.

"A book I read recommended not telling anyone but the father until late into the second trimester."

"So, who have you told?"

"Dion," she admitted. "He had to know why I wasn't drinking the wine. My family." She tried for mutually casual. After all, unwed motherhood was the norm for Gabriel women.

Still, this was a secret she wished to hug a little close for a while longer.

The Gabriel home was a sprawling structure set back within a riot of palmettos, pecan trees, and magnolias in a New Orleans neighborhood aging as gracefully as a Southern lady. Callie pulled into the driveway, then faced Armond.

"We're here. The Gabriel household."

"Is somebody else here?"

"Don't you remember? Mother, sisters, nieces, nanny all living together."

"More tradition?" he muttered.

Callie ignored it. "You don't need to worry; I'll be safe here, and I'm not going out again." She tossed him the keys. "Take the car and pick me up in the morning. Early."

To her surprise, Armond followed her. "I'll see you in," he said, calmly and implacably.

"You want to come inside?"

"Aren't men allowed in the house?"

"Of course. We entertain, and they come to get herbs or do business with my mother and sisters."

"What is your family doing these days?"

"Pretty much the same. Mom runs an active medical practice, badgers the local medical society to adopt holistic healing and alternate therapies, grows her herbs. Stacia just got appointed to the Mayor's Council for Women and Children's Health because of her OB practice's reputation for successfully nurturing high-risk pregnancies. And Tessa? Well, I tell her she's close to inheriting Mom's mantle of village witch. From her trip to China this summer she's added acupuncture."

They reached the side gate, leading to her mother's garden and office. Callie opened it, planning her good-byes, but Armond pushed on into the garden.

"This is . . . unexpected." Armond circled her mother's garden like it was a cage.

Most people who entered the green bower released tension with a sigh and sank onto the grass or one of the wooden seats beside the herb garden. Personally, the sense of isolation made Callie edgy, but, until now, she knew no one else who had that reaction.

"Most people call it serene, but I've always thought serene was overrated," she answered, then tripped over a concrete urn.

With a quick move, Armond caught her before she fell. His strong hands held her steady.

"Thanks." She drew in an unsteady breath, not from the almost fall, but from the spicy scent of his nearness.

"You're welcome." Slowly he released her with an enigmatic look. "Something we have in common? Vitality?"

Callie flushed and smoothed a strand of hair behind her ear, unable to get used to the flashes of this earthier, looser Armond. She nodded toward the building at the end of the garden. "Mom's home; there's a light on in her office. Come any farther and you'll have to say hello," she added, figuring the last person Armond wanted to meet right now was her mother.

"Better now than later," he murmured, following her back.

"Mom?" called Callie, once inside.

"Be right out. I'm tending the mushrooms."

"Mushrooms need dark. And quiet," Callie offered. "We'll wait here."

She watched while Armond took in the details of Lillian Gabriel's medical license, the bells-and-whistles computer, the plump cushions in the seating nooks, touching each as though to commit them to memory. He stopped in front of a portrait of her family, done just last year.

"Are you sure you're not a changeling?"

Her mother, sisters, and nieces all had the characteristic Gabriel white-blond hair and vivid blue eyes, a decided contrast to Callie's golden brown. And there were other differences as well, ones that didn't show up in a family portrait.

Callie laughed. "I asked my mother that once, when I was six and had just finished a particularly vivid Irish fairy tale. Her reaction was vehement, to say the least. I never doubted after that that I was a child of her body."

"And denied you your patrimony," Armond murmured in a low tone.

"Like I said, I got my father's genes. You never met my sisters, did you?" Callie changed the subject. "That's Stacia and her daughter Alexis." She pointed to the woman with the somber child standing next to her. "The other pair is Tessa and Kitty. Kitty is holding Miss Flanders. Kitty and her grandmother had a discussion about whether the doll should be included in the portrait."

"Looks like Kitty won."

"Even at five, she's incredibly strong willed. So is Alexis, although she goes about it a lot more quietly."

Callie gazed at the two little girls, so like their mothers and grandmother. Her throat tightened with longing. Soon she would have a little girl to hold in the family pictures. There would be seven women, all joined by bonds of blood and love.

Would her daughter also be the changeling? Her hand touched her abdomen. Would she have blue eyes? Brown? Or gray? Dark hair or blond? Callie pressed her lips together against the ache of yearning. More than anything, she wanted her daughter to know she was loved and wanted.

Abruptly, she turned from the portrait to see Armond prowling the room again. "Danger does not lurk in these shadows. I think you're taking this security business much too seriously," she complained.

His gray eyes turned stormy as he closed in tight.

"You're my responsibility. I don't take that lightly. No harm will come to you, Callie, while you're under my protection."

"Gabriel women don't need to be kept by a man."

Armond started at the sound of the cool feminine voice. Lillian Gabriel emerged from the door at the back, accompanied by the faint scents of orange and dirt and with an ice blue gaze fixed on him. Her platinum hair was pulled into a chic knot at her nape and her floor-length flowing dress was for comfort, not to hide any figure flaws. "Hello, Agent Marceaux." She gave Callie a peck on the cheek. "Hello, dear. How did today's filming go?"

"Good."

"I'm sorry that emergency kept me too late to see last night's program on TV. And Stacia and Tessa were both out."

"Don't worry about it," Callie assured her. "I know you're all busy."

"I'll watch the tape later." She turned and speared him with that blue gaze again. "Agent Marceaux, why do you think Callie needs a man's keeping?"

"Dr. Gabriel, I said under my protection, not my keeping. There's a difference."

"There's been a couple of kook notes," Callie explained. "Dion asked Armond to look into them."

Lillian Gabriel turned her attention back to Armond. Still decidedly frosty. "I didn't know personal protection was part of the FBI job description."

Okay, so apparently he wasn't on Mom's A list, Armond decided, not surprised. "Only when it comes to Callie. Callie and the baby," he added. He couldn't explain the instinctive irritation that plagued him. It wasn't the restless urge to bring Callie's note-writer to task or the aching need to fill the void of his memories. It was—he shifted his shoulders—a sense that he stood in a totally foreign world, a feminine one that did not welcome him.

"The baby. Are you going to be difficult about that?" She leaned closer.

"Depends upon your definition of difficult." He did not back away.

Callie gave an exasperated huff. "Would you two stop? Please, Mom, let me handle it. Haven't you always insisted Gabriel women are independent?"

"Yes, but you—" Lillian bit off the objection.

"Go about things a little differently and often screw up, I know," Callie finished for her. "But I need to do this my way."

She then rounded on him. "And Armond, stop baiting her."

"I wasn't—"

Callie glared at him.

After a long moment, Armond turned to Callie's mother. "A truce, Dr. Gabriel?"

"Call me Lillian," she grudgingly offered.

"Lillian." A truce did not mean agreement, but for Callie's sake he could be civil. Apparently this was his night for civility.

A smile played at Lillian's lips. "Despite Callie's nonsensical claims about me, I promise not to turn you into a toad."

"I'd wager you wield other powers," he said softly.

"So, is it safe to leave me here?" Callie asked with a touch of sarcasm.

"It seems."

"C'mon, I'll walk you back to the door."

He stopped as they reached the gate. "What time shall I pick you up tomorrow?"

"Six A.M. We're shooting early, before the crowds gather."

"I'll be here." Then, partly because he knew it would

irritate a watching Lillian Gabriel, but mostly because he wanted another taste of Callie, he cupped his one-time lover's cheek with his palm and brushed a quick, gentle kiss over her mouth.

Lush fruit and gentle tannins were Callie's flavor. As soothing to him as the harmonious notes of a delicate wine.

No lancing headache, no flash of memory this time. Just a pleasing kiss.

Armond drove away well satisfied.

He had started this day not even knowing his name. Now he had an identity, Armond Marceaux, FBI Special Agent, at home with the weapon at his waist and reassured by the credentials in his pocket. Yawning and stretching, he tried to categorize what else he'd learned, but his thoughts blurred with fatigue, and perhaps remnants of the source of his amnesia. He parked and found an anonymous hotel for the night.

Despite the fuzzy thinking a few salient facts were clear.

One, he was going to be a father. The mother wanted him involved only peripherally because twice they'd managed to screw things up, but something inside him refused to accept that.

Two, despite that one gut-wrenching memory of what drove them apart, he still wanted Callie Gabriel with a strength he couldn't deny.

Three, someone in the Bureau had betrayed him.

Beside the immediacy of that horror, all the other problems paled, to be handled later. He didn't know who or why or how, only that someone had blown his cover, and the result was this hell of amnesia. Until he found out who, he couldn't risk contacting the Bureau directly. Armond rubbed his sleeve, feeling the soreness of the bruises beneath.

A traitor was going to fall.

And Callie was still the key to it all.

The next morning, Armond watched his memory trigger slip into her car seat and hunch over, her hands clutching an insulated, covered mug. Her hair fell in a gold-brown curtain about her cheeks as she sipped her drink. Her only greeting was an indistinguishable mumble.

"Seat belt," he reminded.

Without looking, she held out the cup to him, then fastened her belt.

He sniffed the drink. "What is this?"

"Try it."

Armond took a sip and made a face. It tasted like honey, ginger, and dried weeds. "What is it?"

"Tessa makes it for me every morning. She says it's to prevent morning sickness." Blindly, she held out her hand.

Armond returned the drink, then closed her door and moved around the car into the driver's seat.

"I hate mornings," Callie grumbled.

"I gathered that."

"Voodoo Museum first."

"Just the thing for six A.M."

He pulled away from the curb, and Callie drank silently while he headed the short distance to the French Quarter. The early hour kept the traffic minimal.

"Does the tea work?" he asked at last.

"No morning sickness. Just cravings." She didn't elaborate further. She took another sip, then made a face. "Yuck."

" "You don't have to drink it."

"Tessa's feelings would be hurt if I refused, and I wouldn't want to deceive her by pretending. Besides"—she tilted her head back and finished the remaining tea—"it does work."

Armond glanced at her pale face, gradually retrieving its color, and her hand resting on her still small stomach. Was she ill or was this always Callie's approach to the morning? Had they slept together through the night so that he would know she wasn't a morning person? These were small details he regretted losing.

She laid her head back against the head rest and sighed.

"Are you feeling all right?"

"I'm fine. I just don't handle the first hour of mornings well." She opened one eye to peer at him from behind the curtain of her hair. "While you look both chipper and coherent. You should wear colors, like that blue, more often."

Armond glanced down at his pullover. He'd chosen it because the sleeves hid the bruises on his arms, and the long, loose design concealed the gun at his waist, not because of any appeal of fashion or color. "I don't own a lot of colors."

Unlike Callie in her short, green skirt and multicolored blouse. She pushed her hair back, revealing double studs—one green, one turquoise—in each lobe, and sat straighter in the seat. "You could always go for an earring."

Despite the early hour, a small crowd had gathered in front of the Voodoo Museum. Armond recognized the video crew, except two additions, an older man and woman. A Lucky Dog cart waited hopefully on the corner, its vendor in the shadows of a doorway. The bright yellow-and-red wiener cart was an odd sight in the early morning. Armond expected business wasn't brisk.

Callie drew in a deep breath. "Lucky Dogs. Do those smell goo—" She broke off abruptly. "No. I did not say that. I am not craving *hot dogs.* Tell me I am not craving hot dogs."

"You don't want a hot dog, Callie."

"You're right. No hot dogs. Hey, Christian."

Christian waved back, the morning sun flashing off his wrist chains.

Callie strode down the sidewalk, without a thought to safety. Armond followed her close, a prickling at the top of his spine, uneasy but not able to put a reason to it. No threats pulsed from the crowds, nothing that felt like danger—

Felt like danger? Where the hell did these feelings come from? What was he? Some kind of empathic freak?

Armond eased Callie's path through the crowd, keeping a watchful eye. The sense that something was off gripped his shoulder blades. In the crowd, a thousand sensations fingered him from the press of bodies or the brush of clothing. A tactile awareness of each touch vibrated across him, just beneath the surface of his skin. It felt like a low-grade hum at the edge of his hearing, unpleasant, irritating, but something continued exposure would blunt. He laid a hand at the small of Callie's back, noting with relief that the hum was abating, then grit his teeth and endured until they emerged from the crowd and the hum faded away.

Had the amnesia heightened his other senses? Like a blind person whose hearing improved, were his instincts working overtime to compensate for lack of knowledge? Or had he lived with this all his life?

God, no wonder he forgot.

Christian grabbed Callie's hands. "You're late!"

"I'm on time. You're always early."

"Well, we've got a problem. The museum is locked

tight. I got the director at home, but he says someone called and changed the shoot to later. He sounded a trifle miffed at being awakened, but he's on his way here."

Armond shifted his shoulders, still edgy. Something was out of place, didn't feel right. The scent of boiled hot dogs lingered in the air, an ugly smell at this hour. Who would buy—?

Armond spun around.

The Lucky Dog cart was gone.

It was a good thing her ring's power had held strong, Hera decided while the crew waited at the Voodoo Museum. No one would have believed her an expert with makeup, not the way she had looked this morning, without a touch of enhancement.

She had not slept well. Fact was, she had missed Zeus at her side. Hades, but she'd wanted his embrace. Yet she could not sleep with him, then abandon him. Despite how idiotic myth chroniclers painted her, she was not a heartless witch.

Armond maintained a protective stance behind Callie, she noticed. He glanced around, taking in details, no doubt. To her mild surprise, he eyed her with curiosity but no recognition. When he saw Zeus, his eyes narrowed, though, as if something familiar had pricked him.

Dion's idea to keep him close by using the warrior's protective instincts was a good one, and she thought her little call to the museum director was a nice added touch to the notes they'd composed.

Christian clapped his hands. "People, we'll start with some exterior shots while we wait. Callie, you haven't met our new makeup and lighting crew."

"Hi, Callie Gabriel." Squinting into the morning sun, Callie stretched out her hand; then her face relaxed as recognition dawned. "You were at the buffet I helped Joy cater. I apologize, your names escape me."

"Zeke Jupiter. Harriet Juneau." Zeus made the introductions, casting a curious glance at a silent Armond. "We also met. At the barn. When you arrested Centurion."

"Yes," Armond answered politely. "It was a . . . hectic moment. You know Backus?"

"Old acquaintance," murmured Hera.

Armond eyed Zeus again. "Have we met somewhere else?"

"I don't think so," Zeus answered innocently.

"Let's go, everyone," called Christian. "Do you have your script, Callie? Feel free to ad lib; I looked at the tapes from the wineries and you did a simply super job. Excellent copy, excellent! We got some great bites to use. This is going to be a spectacular series, and I don't say that to everyone." Christian stopped the running commentary to size up Armond with a hint of something stronger than curiosity. "Looks like you've picked up an admiring fan, Callie love."

"Dion's idea," said Callie.

"My, Dion has been busy. Lighting, makeup, now you." He gave Armond the eye. "What are you doing for him?"

"Security," Callie said.

"Really? We need security? Well, Dion's the boss. And, here I was, hoping he'd finally hired someone to go for coffee." He looked expectantly at Armond.

"No," answered Armond.

"Didn't think so. Now, let's have some action before I get cranky."

They set up the exterior scene, while Hera fluffed powder and highlights onto Callie's face, then began taping. Callie recited her introductory remarks. She flubbed once that Hera heard, but mostly she had it pat, despite repeats using different angles.

Callie had an innate talent at this, Hera realized, then turned her attention to Armond. Reserved, calm, elegant, he maintained a watchful guard near Callie.

Callie was carrying his child. All his protective, possessive instincts were being aroused, and for a son of Ares, those instincts were strong indeed.

Hera fanned herself. And it didn't take the six eyes of Cerberus to see the sexual chemistry between them.

But the love. That she did not see.

Not yet.

Chapter Eight

Armond trailed the crew into the Voodoo Museum, entering beneath the alligator head and broom crossed above the lintel. Inside was stuffy and dark, with herbal dust clinging to the air. While adjustments were made for filming indoors, he glanced around, curious if he'd ever been here before.

The room was crammed with a mix of ceremonial masks, statues carved from dark wood, crosses, drums, bones, and skulls. An altar was fixed in one end, a miniature cemetery in another, and a live python writhed in a glass cage on the far wall.

All very strange to his eye, and nothing that seemed familiar. He probed deeper into his mind, seeking a wisp of memory, only to run futilely against that blank wall and the headache that lurked there.

This place held no triggers; memory stayed firmly locked.

126

He returned his attention to the video crew. Chaos to the uninitiated eye, but no dangers or dirty tricks. Zeke adjusted a light, Harriet dusted the sheen off Callie's, face and then the cameraman lifted the video camera to his eye and began to tape.

To his surprise, Armond found fascinating the director's explanations about the tenets of voodoo and the significance of the various religious tokens, or *jujus*. Callie seemed equally entranced, exploring the displays with ease despite the whirring of the camera and the incomprehensible, to him, body language of Christian directing her to step here or ask this question.

" 'Tective Marceaux. Hey, 'Tective." The whispered greeting startled Armond. He turned to find a wizened woman, her hair and skin more gray than black, sitting behind a display case of leather bags, charms, and amulets for sale. "What, you not even say *bon jour* to Marie?"

"Marie!" *Who was Marie?* Somebody very familiar with him, judging by the twinkle in her black eyes. *"Pardon."* He slipped into snippets of French automatically, and kissed the hand she held out to him. "Lovely as ever, Marie. *Comment ça va?*"

"Bien, bien." She withdrew her hand and tilted her head, studying him. "I did not expect to see you here."

"I'm with the video crew."

She cackled at his answer. "Never with 'Tective Marceaux is it that simple, but always it is for the good." Her eyes narrowed as she continued to fix him with a birdlike stare. Only briefly did it stir—toward Callie—then back to him. "But this is different. You seek a missing piece of your soul."

Armond couldn't stop the astonished look that passed across his face.

"What, you forgot Marie sees the truth?" the little woman wheezed.

"Madame Marie is a priestess of the Spirit Temple," Harriet Juneau said, coming up beside him. "According to the literature I read, you should listen to her. And buy from her."

The two women assessed each other for a long moment, then Marie nodded. "You are wise in such matters. Like a goddess, no? What do you wish to purchase?"

"A *gris-gris.* For myself. And one for my friend, here."

"You don't need—" Armond began.

"Yes, I think it would be wise," Marie said. Without rising from her wheeled stool, she began mixing powders, drawing from bins and bottles beneath the counter. She hummed under her breath as she worked, and it took Armond a few minutes to recognize the old tune.

"Love Potion No. 9."

"Really, I can't accept this," he said under his breath to Harriet. "Regulations."

"Pity." She turned away from him to watch Marie and began to hum the song along with her.

"Then you just pay yourself," interjected Marie, her back still to him. "You not going to let Marie's work go to waste, are you, 'Tective?"

"No." Armond rubbed the bridge of his nose, wondering how he'd gotten entangled with all these women.

Marie handed him a red flannel drawstring bag and wrapped his fingers around it. The ends of the black yarn threaded through the top dangled beside his hand. Marie encased his hand between hers. "I threw in a protection along with opening your heart. It will keep you until you find your true shield. Promise me, 'Tective, until then, that you will wear this. At all times. *Promise me.*" Her whispery voice grew harsh.

"I promise."

"Good." She freed his hand.

Armond loosened the strings to peer inside, but she stopped him. "Do not open. You let the magic out. Just wear it. Ten dollar." She held out her hand.

He gave her the bill, then slipped the black yarn over his neck. The *gris-gris* bag hung below his sternum, so lightweight he barely knew it was there. He tucked it inside his shirt.

"Good," Marie repeated, nodding. "Now yours." She handed Harriet a small vial on a short leather thong. "Burn it and the answers you seek will be yours. When it's done, bury the ashes."

"Why?" asked Harriet, handing her the money.

"It makes good fertilizer," cackled Marie.

Harriet laughed, then stuck the vial in her pocket. "Thank you." She rejoined the crew as they headed into another room.

Armond hung back. Marie wouldn't have any answers about the Bureau, about his betrayal, but she might fill in some other pieces. God knows, he could use something solid. "Marie, what do you hear about Guy Centurion these days?"

"Why you ask me? He don't bother the brothers and sisters. He fleece ladies and gents."

"Like you told me, you know the truth."

"I know he don't like you very much."

Armond wasn't too surprised to hear that.

"But Centurion's off the streets," she added. "You survive, and in time his power will fade. It's the ones on the outside you got to worry about now."

"Like who?"

She shrugged. "I 'spect you got friends, too."

The problem was, how to tell which was which?

* * *

Callie slipped a Zip-loc bag from her backpack purse, a portion of the supply of homemade snacks and dried fruit she kept handy, and pulled out a tomato-and-salsa wheat cracker. Pregnancy didn't give her nausea; it made her hungry. They had finished at the Voodoo Museum and were hoofing it to their next appointment at the Pharmacy Museum, this one confirmed by Christian that no unpleasant surprises preceded them.

"How did you learn to be so comfortable in front of a camera?" Armond asked her, appearing at her side and shaking his head in refusal when she offered him the bag.

Nibbling her cracker, she shrugged. "Nothing to learn. I just pretend there're scads of people listening in and I'm talking to all of them."

"You don't find the thought of all those listeners scary?"

"I like to be with people." With that they reached the Pharmacy Museum, a single old-fashioned room with an herb garden out back. Callie finished her crackers and dusted off her hands. "Time to go back to work."

Armond faded back, allowing her to greet the museum docent, and for a moment her attention split between work and man. She watched as he unobtrusively checked out the room and the herb garden, and her nerves sparked with their familiar sizzle at his fluid movements. Visual poetry in a pair of tight-fitting jeans.

Apparently all was well, for he returned, gave her a short nod, and then leaned one shoulder against the back wall. An edge of tension blunted inside her. Callie considered the notes an annoyance, not a threat, but with Armond close, she had to admit, she always felt safe and unafraid.

She pulled her attention back to her work. "Is it true this was the first licensed pharmacy?" Callie began interviewing the docent. Small, quirky sites like this fascinated her, and she soon found herself sucked into the history of New Orleans medicine, from the use of deadly calomel for yellow fever to the jar of leeches by the door.

The rest of the day followed the same pattern, as they sped from Mardi Gras World, filled with huge, colorful papier-mâché heads used on floats, to the ruminations of Swamp Suzette, who led alligator tours of the bayous. All passed without a repetition of the morning's problems. But the day was long and Callie more than willing to turn the drive home over to Armond late that afternoon.

Tired, she leaned her head against the window, enjoying the smooth ride. Armond drove at the speed limit, used his blinker before changing lanes, and viewed yellow lights as a signal to stop, not to race, yet he always arrived exactly when needed. With him, a drive through city traffic was almost peaceful.

"What's your upcoming schedule?" he asked, his quiet voice joining his solid presence in the confines of the car.

"More location shooting, and I'll film the cooking segment for the first episode. After that we have a few days off before we head up to Michigan and the Great Lakes wineries."

"How do you tie it all together? Cooking, wineries, tourist sights?"

"The shows includes an overall look at the area, a concept called 'agritourism.' You get people to try the wines by getting them interested in the area: attractions they might not know about, local personalities and color, specialty foods. They tour the area; they visit the wineries; they buy the wine. Everybody benefits. The Visitor's Bureaus have been very helpful in getting us set up with what we need."

"It sounds like an interesting concept. Which place are you most looking forward to seeing?"

"All of them. I've never been anywhere."

The conversation came easily and it had often been like that, Callie realized. Armond listened like he cared, and without judgment. Although desire was a constant hum between them, there was also a companionship that she'd never found with anyone else. She'd forgotten how much she enjoyed simply being with Armond.

Callie drew in a breath, savoring the unique mix of flavors and scents that defined him. Then she sniffed again. Something different, a new scent. Something pleasing. Exciting. Her lips tingled with a sudden urge to kiss and taste.

Instead, she leaned forward and sniffed, her nose at a level with his heart. "Hmm, something smells good. *You* smell good." She laid a hand on his chest, his warmth and strength wrapping around her, and felt a small, soft lump. "What's this?"

"A . . . good-luck charm," he said, a faint touch of red at his cheeks, and pulled a bag from beneath his shirt.

Callie's eyes widened. "A *gris-gris* bag? You?"

"Madame Marie—"

"Say no more. I understand." She leaned forward and inhaled deeply of the *gris-gris*. Something about the scent, especially when mixed with Armond's essence, was deeply appealing to her chef's nose. "That really is nice. Sage and rosemary." She tucked the bag back beneath his shirt, giving a small pat when she'd finished. "Wearing herbs is good."

She leaned back in her seat and absently started humming.

"Love Potion No. 9."

The Warrior

*   *   *

The brief rush from the *gris-gris* scent had faded by the time they reached the Gabriel home, though, and Callie discovered she was bone tired. She appreciated Armond's quiet support as he walked with her from the car to the front door.

"Are you sure you don't want dinner?" he asked, unlocking the door, then returning her key.

"Thanks, no, we've got leftovers galore. Would you like to come in for some?"

He hesitated a moment, then shook his head. "I've got some things to do. Are you here alone?"

"See the lights in the workroom? Someone's here." She gave Armond a faint smile. "It's safe to leave. I'm not alone."

Armond hesitated again. Though he said he had things to do, he seemed loathe to leave. Instead his gaze scanned her face, as though she were a mystery to him, and then the gray in his eyes warmed to molten silver. "I know we said calm and civil, Callie. So why do I still want you?"

Callie sucked in a breath at his honesty. The atmosphere of the Gabriel house, usually so serene, took on an electric charge.

"It doesn't go away just because we say it will," she whispered.

He tucked a strand of hair behind her ear, the side of his hand brushing against her cheek.

Such a simple touch, yet it spread through her like a blue-hot alcohol flame. They shouldn't be doing this, she knew. Shouldn't be tempting what could never be. Callie closed her eyes and allowed her cheek to lean against his palm. She had missed these gentle caresses.

Armond shifted closer, the faint scent of his aftershave mingling with the fresh sage and rosemary of the *gris-gris* he wore. His lips met hers in a kiss that brought her every cell clamoring to life.

He cupped her head with his hand, holding her still as he tilted his mouth and renewed the kiss. His lips moved over hers with a firm, commanding pressure. Neither deepened the kiss, each content to linger and relearn tastes and textures.

Slowly, Armond lifted from the kiss. His breathing had acquired the same ragged quality as hers, Callie noted. Yet she was grateful he maintained control. She couldn't have dealt with the flashes of the wilder Armond. Tracing a path of fire, his fingers trailed lightly across the top of her shoulder, then to the crook of her elbow, the pounding pulse of her wrist, the flat of her stomach before he released her.

"We can't ignore this, Callie. If we're going to spend time together, we can't ignore it."

"But we don't need to give into it again. We've made our choices." Her fired-up body didn't seem to agree, but Callie forced herself to step away.

"Why didn't you come to the cabin when I asked you?"

She closed her eyes again, not in passion this time, but in cowardice, then opened them. "I'm not a very brave person, Armond. You're very controlled, but underneath I suspect there's a lot you never let anyone see."

"I was right. Jekyll and Hyde."

"No." Callie shook her head. "I'm not afraid you're going to turn abusive or cruel or anything like that. God, no, you're just the opposite, especially with women and children. When I remember how gentle you were with me the night we met—" She sucked in a deep breath, not knowing how to explain her fears. "Your work comes first."

It was a half answer; she was still skirting the real

issue. There were surface problems, yes, but it went deeper than his job or her family, and that she couldn't understand or explain. It was something within *her*.

He withdrew—his hand, his body, his passion, his brief flash of openness. After a moment he ran a hand across his neck and said flatly, "You're right. I can't do my job, get the answers I need, if I'm distracted. It won't happen again."

He was right to keep things controlled, but Callie didn't like being relegated back to a job description and a responsibility, and she fought to keep the scowl from her face. Damn these emotional swings. From passion to petulance in five minutes. It had to be the hormones.

He never should have kissed Callie, shouldn't have lost control and given in to the impulse. Now, the softness of her lips, the warm press of her round body, and the unique gingery scent of her were imprinted upon him, keeping him aroused and leaving him wanting more. As he strode down Royal Street in the French Quarter, Armond rubbed a hand against the back of his neck. It couldn't happen again, not until he had some answers. He couldn't afford such sweet distractions; he had a job to do, a memory to recover.

The day's heat had given way to a cooler evening, and Armond was grateful for the reprieve. At least it was quieter here than on Bourbon, where the press of the crowd crawled under his skin with an itchy sensation of things unresolved. A block later, he reached his destination, the 8th District police station, and went up the steps into the whitewashed lobby.

This was a long shot, he knew, but some instinct, some familiarity sent him here. Hoping for a spur to recollection, Armond scanned the plain vanilla room.

It was crowded. People moved with purpose, either because they belonged here or because they wanted to be anywhere but here.

None of it disturbed the impenetrable shield of amnesia. He could have stood in a room as foreign to him as an opium den and felt more recognition. Disappointment formed a hard lump in his gut. How could he have worked here and not be able to pull out a single shred of memory?

He prodded the black hole of his memory, but it seemed to suck out the very warmth of thought, leaving him with nothing.

Nothing—until a wild-eyed, handcuffed man stumbled against him, and rancid, positive, instinctual knowledge exploded inside Armond. A foul taste curled the back of his tongue and bile rose in his throat.

The man had murdered tonight, in a drug-fueled frenzy.

Suddenly the very air pressed against Armond. Hot and rank, it clogged his lungs, until each breath was a chore. These rooms were redolent with the guilt of the criminals who passed through them. It crawled across his skin and filled his nostrils, bringing a bitter metallic taste that pressed against the back of his throat. A strange, primal urge welled up: to war, to battle against the evils here, to hunt the wrongdoers.

Armond stumbled backward, away from the scum. His fists clenched in the struggle against this insanity.

"Can I help you?" asked the woman at the desk.

Armond shook his head, trying to make sense of the question. What had he come here for? He couldn't even think of a name to ask for. "No, thank you."

He stumbled out the door, reached the foot of the steps, and gripped the handrail. Slowly, painfully, silently, he mastered the alien sensations, both guilt and the call for retribution, until they lurked quietly behind the questions. What was this? Had he endured this all his life? How?

By never losing control. By knowing he could do something about it.

"Marceaux?" The booming voice pulled him short.

He turned to see a bear of a man staring at him. The officer wore a rumpled tan suit and his tie knot dangled at mid-chest. "Marceaux, it is you. What the hell you doing here?" The voice was both welcoming and cautious.

"Night, Abe," a departing officer called, and the big man waved.

Abe. A name from the newspaper articles he'd read yesterday popped into his mind. Detective Joseph Abramowicz. Armond strode over and held out his hand. "Abe. Good to see you." The handshake was firm, the exchanged slaps on the shoulder familiar, the touch a thankfully cool one of decency and honesty. "I'm in town a couple of days and thought I'd stop by to say hello."

"Working on that Centurion case? Think you Feds can nail him in court?"

"We've got the evidence to make the charges stick."

"I don't care what the charge is or who gets him. Just get him off my streets." Abe shook his head. "You did it, pal."

"Did what?"

"That Hannan woman? 'Guy Centurion will see justice,' when none of the rest of us even suspected the bastard. You got him, and by the book, too."

Hannan. The name clicked into place from his research in the library. Armond remembered reading about the case, now several years old. Sophia Hannan had been set to testify about a small, select, vicious smuggling ring, when she'd disappeared. According to the paper, she'd been found days later, a suspected victim of the men she'd been set to name. What had been done to her was only hinted at in the article. She'd had two small children, who were left orphaned. Armond Marceaux had been the investigating officer.

As he'd read the articles yesterday, he'd been filled with an icy rage at what had happened to her and an equally icy determination that those who had killed her would be brought to justice, emotions he suspected he'd felt at the time.

"Yeah, I got him."

"We're working on a few angles ourselves."

"You got time for a beer?" Armond asked abruptly.

"Sure. So, what you working on that you want to share?"

"Ever hear of a man named Dion Backus?"

In the kitchen, Callie turned the blinds to block out the darkened garden. At night, when she was alone, she avoided the garden. There was a wild quality about it that made her edgy, especially in the darkness.

She turned the small TV on low, needing the hum of conversation, then poured herself a glass of milk. She was used to the hushed serenity of this house, but it never failed to disturb her at first when she was alone late.

Callie drank down the milk, then glanced toward her stomach. "That was for you. I'd have preferred a glass of New York Riesling."

She opened the refrigerator and pored over the contents, suddenly hungry. Opening containers, she dumped leftover black bean burritos and fried vegetable rice on a plate, shook on hot sauce, then stuck it in the microwave to nuke. While it cooked, she finished off a container of cold soba noodles in spicy peanut sauce. The satisfaction from the emergency stash of snacks she nibbled throughout the day had worn off long ago.

"Going to get you used to red pepper and cayenne," she told her belly. "Ginger, horseradish, mustard, chiles are all very good things."

Stacia swore you could tell the state of Callie's mind by the heat and spice of her cooking. Good thing Stacia had been too busy, and gone too often, to taste much of Callie's meals recently, or she'd think her sister was a candidate for a lock-up ward. Most pregnant women avoided spicy or strong foods. Callie craved them.

The microwave dinged. Callie tasted the burritos, added a few green chiles, and warmed the food up a few more seconds. When it was finished, she set it on the counter, added a sliced apple, pulled up a stool, and dug in, the evening news a soft counterpoint.

Pregnancy cravings—spicy food, meat, and Armond.

Hell of a trio.

Callie took a big bite of burrito. If she could only indulge one, she'd do it with a vengeance.

"Maybe it's time you and I had a little talk," she told her stomach again. "You'll probably wonder sometimes, like I did, why your father doesn't live with your mother. Even though it's kind of expected in this family."

She finished up the fried rice, then rubbed her stomach, hoping the baby would feel the love, even if she didn't understand the words. "You see, he's got this job. It's a very important job. He makes a difference to a lot of people."

Callie paused a moment, remembering the night they'd met, the night she'd almost been raped. He'd been so gentle with her, not at all what she'd expected from such a masculine, breath-stealingly attractive policeman. In fact, she'd refused the female officer they'd said could take her statement. She'd felt safer with Armond.

"He's got a passion for it," she told their daughter. "I'm not sure we could compete with that. He puts in a lot of hours, he's gone a lot, to places he can't name and we wouldn't want to visit, doing things he can't tell me about. He's loyal to his friends, he'd be faithful to us, but mentally, emotionally, I'd be afraid his first commitment would always be to the people he helps. I don't want that for you; I can't live with it for me."

She scraped up the fragments of burrito and chiles, knowing even to her baby she didn't tell the whole truth. Something inside her, some fear she couldn't face, kept *her* from the trust, the openness, and the utter loyalty he needed.

Abruptly she stood and snapped off the TV. Enough of Tabasco and soul-searching for tonight.

Callie cleaned up the kitchen, then found the papers describing the wines and sights that would be next on her video itinerary. She poured a glass of sparkling lime juice, then spread out brochures, a map, and her travel books and notes, research for the video series. Their next stop was the wineries near Traverse City, Michigan.

She was particularly anxious to see Michigan's Sleeping Bear Dunes. Why, she couldn't fathom. National Park places generally held no interest for her, but this one did.

There were so many other places she was anxious to see, too. Places between Louisiana and Michigan. She ran a thumb across the glossy surface of a brochure for the Pink Palace Museum in Memphis. Places like this and the Squash Café and the Magic Museum. She and Tessa were going to take the week off, drive up together, two vagabonds on discovery—

As if conjured by Callie's thoughts, Tessa drifted into the kitchen. "Callie, oh . . . you're here."

Callie smiled. Talking to her sister always had an ethereal quality to it. "Want to look at some of the places I thought we'd see?"

Tessa grew sorrowful. "I've been trying to contact you all day."

"Why?" The excitement level plummeted, and Callie's hand tightened on the papers.

"Abbeville."

"Abbeville?"

"I have to go there. On an acupuncture consultation for a child. It's a very exciting case, one I think I can help. They asked me to stay and teach a class in herbals."

Callie tried to respond to the enthusiasm lighting her sister's face. "It sounds perfect for you." Despite her best efforts, the words were flat.

Tessa sandwiched Callie's hands between hers. "I'm sorry, Callie, but I really need to go. Perhaps you can start out alone, and I could join you. Or maybe Mom or Stacia—"

"Hey, don't worry, Tessa. I'll work out something. You just get that child well."

"Are you sure?"

Callie was proud of the breezy smile she managed. " 'Course I'm sure. When do you leave?"

"Day after tomorrow, same as you." Tessa leaned over and gave her an airy kiss on the cheek. "Thanks. I'll see you when you get back. Good luck with your tour." A moment later she was gone, leaving only the light scent of lavender and an ache of disappointment with Callie.

Could she go by herself? Alone? Right. She was as likely to do that as she was to scale Mount Everest.

What if she got a flat tire in some isolated valley? What if she got lost and ended up alone in a dark woods? What if she met a feral hog?

Callie's eye drew back to the colorful brochures and well-thumbed tour books, and a powerful yearning seized her. *She wanted to see them.* The craving was like an empty well that needed fresh water.

Maybe someone else could go with her. Who? Her mother or Stacia? No, they were too busy, had too many important demands to take a week off with her. Her friends? They had trouble coordinating schedules to find time enough for drinks.

Armond.

Armond was on vacation.

Armond could go.

Callie stilled, her only movement the rapid pounding of her heart in her throat. A week alone with Armond?

Impossible.

Not the way her mind knew every move he made, the way her body responded to his touch. Not the way her heart clenched whenever she thought about seeing him again, or about never seeing him again.

She bent her legs and rested her head on her knees.

She'd be a fool to think they could spend days together and not give in to the passion between them.

She'd be a fool to think she could spend days with him, sleep with him, and not be devastated when he left. Didn't she remember the past?

But she'd seen changes in Armond just in these past couple of days. Already they'd spent more time together than they had in a month of dates. His formidable control showed a few chinks.

Was she being given something rare and special—a third chance to get it right?

Callie wasn't in to taking risks and chances, but this one she had to take. For the baby. For herself.

Detective Joseph Abramowicz turned out to be a wealth of information, none of which brought back a single memory.

As far as Abe knew, Backus was clean. He'd heard about the man, even in the short time Backus had been here, for the wine expert wasn't one who kept a low profile. Harrah's casino, a Martin's Wine Cellar tasting, the glittery opening of the symphony season all had seen him in attendance.

Guy Centurion was trying to get out on bail, damn the local bleeding-heart judges, but for the moment he was still sitting on his Armani ass in a cell, compliments of the feds. The man was keeping his nose clean.

Callie Gabriel didn't have any obvious enemies, but he'd look into it, and the notes, for Armond. It was more N.O.P.D. jurisdiction, anyway, but no promises. Other cases had priority. Armond said he understood.

Abe admitted he was a meat-and-potatoes man himself, but the wife liked that veggie stuff and he'd eaten at Greenwood. For a liberal do-gooder, Callie had a knack with the food, and hadn't Armond gone out with her a time or two? The last was asked with a bit of a leer that Armond ignored.

They separated with shoulder slaps and vague promises to stay in touch they both knew they wouldn't keep. Back on Royal Street, Armond walked away, feeling restless. Facts galore, things to investigate, but nothing that stimulated a memory.

Callie, it seemed, was still his key.

The restlessness settled. He would see her tomorrow.

Chapter Nine

With typical New Orleans quirkiness, overnight October turned from a sultry remnant of summer to a wind-tossed portent of winter. As the video crew set up, Callie perched on the stone lip of the goldfish-and-lily pond and shivered in her sweater. Leaves from the massive oaks planted throughout the Audubon Zoo swirled about her feet.

Behind her, monkeys screeched and lions broke the morning with a roar, setting her nerves bouncing faster than water on a hot skillet. First shoot of the day at the zoo, last shoot of the day at the Global Wildlife Center. What insanity compelled her to agree to that?

She buttoned her sweater, watching Armond. He stood with his back to her. His relaxed stance didn't fool her; Agent Marceaux was on duty, surveying the territory. His casual clothes blended with the rest of the crew, but she'd bet no one else's shirt covered a weapon. He circled the perimeter of the shoot, his soft dark hair first lit by sunlight, then shadowed by the oak branches, and Callie's heart did a tiny flip. She loved to watch the way he moved.

"He's a compelling man," Harriet murmured, close to Callie's ear. "And would be intensely loyal."

Startled, Callie spun in her direction. "What?"

Harriet sat down beside her, sponge and sable brush in hand. She spread foundation over Callie's face. "I want to test this long-lasting foundation my research facility developed."

Callie decided she must have imagined Harriet's comment. How could she know so much about Armond? "Why are you doing this? Someone else could test the makeup for you."

Harriet added color to Callie's cheeks. "I won't be here long. I think these new formulas are revolutionary, but I want to be sure. If I'm enthusiastic, I convince my people. If they believe, they can convince others."

"Is that why Zeke's here?"

"Something like that."

"You two been friends for a while?"

"A very long time."

The monkeys chattered again, accompanied by an unearthly screech that lightning bolted down her spine. Callie leaped to her feet, hand to her chest, heart pounding against her ribs. "What was that?"

"Just a peacock," said Harriet. "Come, my pretty pet."

For a moment the comment startled Callie, until she realized Harriet was talking to the peacock strutting toward Harriet's outstretched hand.

Still panting, Callie shifted backward, almost tripping into the goldfish pond. "Careful, he might peck."

"Not me." Harriet crooned to the peacock, and he

spread a magnificent tail and lifted his crowned head. She ran a hand down the feathered neck. "Yes, yours is a beautiful display." She tilted her head toward Callie. "Would you like to pet him?"

Callie thrust her hands behind her back. "No thanks."

Harriet fussed over the peacock a moment more, then urged it on its way. Zeke joined them and held a meter to Callie's face, testing the light, chatting while he munched a pastry.

Callie barely heard him. Eggs. She smelled eggs. Her stomach churned with nausea. "What are you eating?"

"Toaster breakfast. Do you want one, Callie? It's scrambled eggs and cheese. No meat."

"Scrambled eggs?" Callie's stomach turned again. "No thanks."

Armond appeared at her side, an insulated mug in hand. He handed it to her. "Here, drink this."

Tessa's tea. Callie took a gulp, grateful. Without a word, he pulled a cracker from her bag and handed it to her.

"Thanks," she sighed.

His fingers massaged the nape of her neck, not sexual, but soothing and supporting. His touch worked as much magic as the tea, chasing away both nausea and nervousness. "Feeling better?"

"Yeah."

"Callie, sweetie," called Christian, "we're almost ready. This is going to be spec-tac-u-lar. The zookeeper says you can pet the anaconda."

Callie's stomach met her toes. "Oh, swell."

After seeing all running smoothly and noting zoo security at hand, Armond offered a quick word to Dion, then slipped out of the shoot and found the brilliant blue neon sign that caught his eye earlier. INTERNET

CAFE it read, one of the trendy new bars offering connections both personal and cyber. An Internet connection that could not be traced back to him.

At night, the noise level would be raucous, a mix of music, talk, and computer that granted privacy by the sheer fact that nothing could be heard more than two feet away. During the day, however, it took on a subdued, coffeehouse tone. There were some empty terminals, and he snagged the attention of a waitress.

In a few moments he was logged on. Among the items stashed at the cabin had been a printed copy of an e-mail. It was old, nothing useful, except it gave Armond his e-mail server. He logged onto the Web page where he could download his mail and entered his name. Below was the password box.

What would he use as a password? Nowhere had he found a password listing. Armond tried a few words—cabin, nola, agent—and variations of his name and pseudonyms, but each was refused. He closed his eyes, relaxing, focusing not on the password, nor the blanks in his mind. His fingers typed, relying on instinctive memory, then pressed ENTER.

He was in. Mail scrolled onto the screen: a couple from the Usenet group he'd questioned about memory, one from Mark Hennessy, one from someone named Hugh Pendragon, a couple from a "ctitus" with a .gov at the end of the address. He'd grab these pieces of his life in a moment, but first . . . What had he typed to get there?

He played his fingers over the keyboard, remembering the motions. J-U-S-T-I-C-E. He'd typed *justice*.

Armond turned his attention back to his e-mail, scanning swiftly. The one from Mark gave a list of performance dates, offering free passes if he could make any of the shows, as well as a definite curiosity about

Callie. A fleeting smile crossed Armond's face. Joy, apparently, had been talking.

The one from Hugh Pendragon was curious. The tone suggested they were friends, and the message stated simply that he had information regarding the private matter they'd discussed. Who was Pendragon? What private matter? Related to the Centurion case? His amnesia? Why had he asked for Pendragon's help? No answers came from behind the curtain of black, so Armond sent back a noncommittal reply.

The ones from ctitus.gov interested him. Earlier the librarian had been most helpful in identifying names associated with Bureau positions. Conrad Titus was the SAC for the Atlanta office, Armond's boss, and apparently concerned that Armond had not checked in.

Armond's hands hovered over the keys. Titus could be his lifeline. Likely the betrayer was someone whom he'd never met, someone in the higher realms, or he would have known as soon as they shook hands. Surely he'd met his boss.

No, he couldn't afford to trust anyone he wasn't looking straight at. His brief note was a model of ambiguity: assurances that all was well, vague hints at reasons he'd been unable to make contact earlier.

E-mail complete, Armond stretched a moment, feeling the press of fatigue, and his eye caught on a man hunched over a video game. He paid Armond no mind, but something about the man, the tilt of his head or the shape of his shoulders, struck a chord.

This man wasn't Zeke Jupiter, but the feeling was the same sense of familiarity Armond had gotten yesterday when he'd met the lighting expert. Something about Jupiter—and now this stranger—hinted that he'd seen each before, but in a different context. This wasn't a flash of memory; he'd seen them after the amnesia, and given time he'd remember where.

A few questions wouldn't be amiss. Armond headed toward the man, but he slapped a frustrated hand against the video machine, then shoved to his feet, stalked out, and drove away with a roar. Armond stared at the disappearing car.

Cop's suspicion told Armond he'd been followed.

Was it because of his amnesia?

Or was it because of his connection to Callie?

He debated a moment, then headed away from the zoo toward Greenwood. He'd rejoin Callie before they headed north of the lake. In the meantime, Joy Hennessy might have a few answers.

"What are you reading?" Zeke Jupiter perched beside Armond, who was sitting on a bale of hay at the Global Wildlife Center. Armond held the book out to him.

"*FBI Secrets?*"

"I like to know what public perceptions of us are," Armond answered. He'd bought several books last night—about the FBI, about pregnancy and birth—in the hope of filling in some of the gaps of his knowledge or stimulating some memory.

"Are those books accurate?"

"As far as they go."

If only he knew the real answer. Armond closed the book. The clench of his stomach at another reminder of his loss, at another deficiency, was becoming far too familiar.

Concentrate on what you need to get done right now. Take each moment and survive it.

He looked out over the acres of grassland at the Wildlife Center, their final location shoot north of the lake. A tractor-pulled wagon chugged toward them, a pied piper leading a parade of giraffes toward their night quarters, where they'd be protected from the cooler night air. Callie, Christian, the cameraman, and the center's director were on the wagon, taping the late afternoon ritual. Armond had paid more attention to the other visitors than the animals, looking for his tails or suspicious activities, but with the approach of sunset, the thinning jumble of spectators let him relax.

"Are the giraffes always that eager?" Armond asked, seeing the herd gallop after the wagon.

"They're fed when they get here," Zeus answered.

The wagon arrived, the tall beasts milled and stomped, and the center director urged Callie to join the feeding. Her laughing demurral caught Armond's attention. His eyes narrowed and his jaw tightened. She hid it very well, but she was reluctant. The director shouldn't be so insistent. She was pregnant; she might get hurt. Abruptly he strode over and vaulted onto the wagon, heedless of the rolling cameras.

"If she doesn't want to, then accept that," he told the director in a tight voice. "Callie, you don't have to do this."

Callie stared at him. "Armond, we're taping."

"What in blue blazes is going on?" Christian sputtered, then waved his hand at the cameraman. "Cut. Cut. Armond, out of the scene."

"She doesn't want to feed the giraffe," Armond tossed out.

"That was for the show," Callie returned between clenched teeth.

For privacy, Armond turned his back to the others. "You were genuinely scared," he told her in a low voice.

"If so, that's for *me* to deal with," she told him, also too low for the others to hear. "This is my work, Armond."

"And my task is to keep you safe."

"I'm in no danger."

They glared at each other a moment, while the distinct impression he'd just made an utter fool of himself crept across Armond. Without a word he jumped down and strode back to his bale of hay.

"If you're trying to woo her, you're not going about it very well," Zeke murmured as the taping resumed.

Armond gave him a startled look. "I'm not trying to woo her."

Zeke rolled his eyes. "Puh-leez. The way you look at her?"

"I have to watch her to do my job."

"Uh-huh." Zeke rubbed his hands together, and the air took on a sharp charge. The hairs on Armond's arm stood with static. "You have to ignite the air to find out who sent those notes."

"He's right, you know." The melodious voice of Dion Backus came from behind him. "The crew has a pool going. Betting when you and Callie are going to sleep together."

"*What?* That's disgusting." Outrage filled Armond as Backus lowered himself to another bale of hay with a supple motion. The idea of people talking about Callie like that made his skin crawl.

"They do not have a pool," Zeke insisted. "If they did, I'd have been asked to be in it."

Dion gave him an amused smile and then shifted on the bale with a look of annoyance. "Hay itches. No wonder I never had a desire to make love in a barn."

Zeke patted Armond on the arm. "Don't pay him any mind. He likes to stir up trouble. Trust me, any gossip, I'd hear. There is no pool. But I do have just what you need." He reached behind him and pulled out a worn book.

Where had he kept that? Armond hadn't noticed any book in his back pocket.

"That's a perfect blueprint of how to woo a woman."

Armond stared down at the book. Incomprehensible words written in Greek letters graced the front, and when he opened it, more Greek words greeted him. He returned the book to Zeke. "Thanks, but I can't read this."

With a *tsk,* Zeke put the book behind him, then immediately drew it out and handed it to Armond. "Wrong book. This is yours."

It looked like the same book, even to the water stain in the corner, but the title on this one was in English.

"A Guide to Eros?" Armond thumbed through the pages, then read aloud. "For that special evening boil the head of a goat in rosemary and mead."

Dion burst out laughing. "Yes, follow every word."

Zeke waved a hand. "Some of the details are a little archaic, but you get the point. Cook her a meal."

"Callie's a chef. And she says I can't cook."

"Then rub her feet with almond oil. Or bring her flowers. Doesn't matter if they're roses or daisies." Zeke leaned forward confidentially. "Harriet is partial to a willow wreath. I'm especially fond of this advice." He flipped the pages back to a chapter entitled *Eros Unchained,* then started to read. "Picture your love before you go to sleep. Picture her in her perfection and radiance. Recite the ways of your love, the ways she stirs you. This puts her deep into your heart and your actions will draw from there." He gave Armond an expectant look.

"What kind of New-Age babble is that?"

"Zeke, he has the mind of a cop, not a poet," drawled Dion.

"It is not New Age," huffed Zeke. "It is very old age. Ancient wisdom. The wisdom of Eros." He gave Dion a pointed look. "Truer than the frenzy of the maenads."

"Eros was a mere child," returned Dion. "He never understood a man's passions."

"He knew a woman's."

"He has no stamina."

Zeke examined his nails. "Unlike that obvious siren you met last night? She entertained you way too long, Dion. You're losing your sense of style."

"My style is fine. I'm not the one wearing shorts, sandals, and a parrot print shirt."

Armond shook his head at the bickering twosome. "I'm not here to woo Callie. I'm here to make sure she's safe."

Zeke pushed the book back at him. "Keep it anyway; I have others. You may need it one day."

As Armond stuck the book in his pocket, his attention snapped back to Callie, who stood alone on the wagon. The giraffes again! Instead of a docile stroll into their quarters, they crowded her, pushing her, bending their long necks to poke at her sweater or hip. She hid her panic, but it was there in the wide eyes and pale face. His gut tight, he raced over, not caring a hoot if he was acting the fool again, or what any damned pool made of it.

The giraffes smelled like dust as he slipped between them. His nose itched, but he held back the sneeze, afraid it might spook the gigantic beasts. His arm brushed across the *gris-gris* bag, and the odor of rosemary and sage wafted from it. Apparently the giraffes didn't like it, for they parted, allowing him a clear path. Callie was breathing hard when he reached up to boost her off the wagon. "You're getting out of here," he told her implacably.

"Good idea," she gasped, pushing away a wandering nose, and gripped his arm. At once, he saw her breathe evenly.

Shielding her with his body, Armond led her out of

the compound and onto the soft grass. She collapsed onto the ground with a grateful sigh.

"Thanks. I managed the anaconda, but those giraffes—"

Christian raced over to them. "Callie, love, are you okay?"

"I'm fine, just got a little spooked. Won't happen again."

"Great copy, great copy. Armond, you are very photogenic."

Armond fixed him with a look. "Edit it."

"But—"

"Christian, you are not going to use a single inch of me on that footage. Not for an episode. Not for a sound bite. Not even behind a closing credit."

Christian settled with a pout. "It would have made some lovely drama." He turned back to the crew. "We're done filming here. Let's wrap up."

Armond turned back to Callie, glad to see her color had returned. "Do you have something in your pocket that they wanted?"

She shook her head, patting her pockets automatically. "No. I made sure—Wait." She pulled out some food pellets. "I was sure I'd got rid of everything. They must have dropped in my pocket when I was feeding the zebras."

Or had someone put them there?

When Callie raised her eyes to his, for the first time, he saw the shadow of doubt there.

Joy claimed Callie had no enemies.

So, who was pulling the dirty tricks?

"Which one of you had that brilliant idea?" hissed Dion, glaring at Zeus and Hera.

"Pellets in her pocket." Zeus lifted his hand like an errant child in school.

"I added the giraffe pheromone," offered Hera, embarrassed. "It wasn't supposed to be so potent."

"Your schemes almost got my star flattened. Try to think a little next time." He stalked away.

Zeus looked at Hera. "It was the ring, wasn't it?"

She nodded, still remembering the empty pit sensation in her stomach. "I tried to prod the giraffes just a bit, to get them away, but the ring sputtered. By the time it worked again, Armond had rescued her."

"At least my ring is still holding steady."

"Do think we did any good?"

The two gods glanced over at the couple, then exchanged a conspiratorial smile. Protective instincts going strong. They'd just have to be a little more careful next time, not to rouse the warrior, too.

"The lead you gave us about Callie Gabriel panned out. He's with her." The lab doctor was emotionless as ever.

Conrad Titus gripped the pay phone, his hand sweaty. "Has he regained his memory?"

"No sign of it. But he may be suspicious. He keeps spotting our shadows."

"He's an FBI agent without a memory. Of course he's suspicious."

"What can he do without his training?" The scientist was scornful.

"Plenty. He has instinct," said Titus softly, "and if he's with Callie Gabriel, he's found a trigger to his memory."

The doctor's silence disagreed with him.

He didn't have time for these fools. Something had to be done. "Tell your security to bring him in, or I'll go and do it myself." Even at the risk of exposing his ties to Centurion, for if Marceaux was free when he regained his memory, it was all over anyway. That wasn't going to happen.

"Centurion—"

"Centurion is in jail. Bring Marceaux in."

"We need another day to watch him."

Others in the Bureau were starting to question Marceaux's silence, but he could stall the FBI investigation for that long. "Have him back in that lab tomorrow. You're running out of time." He slammed down the receiver and leaned against the phone booth, breathing hard. Neither his heart nor his blood pressure needed this.

It was time to start planting intell against Marceaux. Forging clues that would explain his disappearance and ultimate death. Creating the portrait of a man who would betray the Bureau.

Chapter Ten

"You're going to do what?" Armond asked with pointed quiet.

"Drive," repeated Callie firmly. "Drive to Michigan. Can you dry these off, please?" She handed him a dish towel as she cleaned up the studio kitchen after lensing the cooking portion for this segment.

"Sounds like fun," said Zeke, leaning on the counter.

Dion parked on the stool across from Callie. "Your sister's going with you, right?"

Callie shook her head. "She had to cancel."

"You still have on some stage makeup. Here." Harriet opened her voluminous bag and smeared cream on Callie's forehead, then wiped it off.

Callie, frowned. She hadn't expected an audience for her discussion with Armond, but the trio seemed determined to stay.

"Seven days on the road, seeing the USA." Zeke waved a hand. "Think of it."

"I am thinking of it," grumbled Dion. "I don't think it's wise, and as your employer—"

"Won't Armond be with her?" chimed in Harriet.

Dion threw her a look. "That's what I'm thinking of."

"No interference," warned Harriet.

"Listen to your own advice," Dion muttered.

Callie didn't have the slightest idea what they were talking about, but her concern wasn't with them. It was with Armond, who contemplated them with stormy gray eyes.

"What do you mean 'Armond will be with her'?" he asked Harriet.

"Don't you still have vacation?" she answered. "I just assumed—because of the notes and all."

In the pin-drop silence that followed, four pairs of eyes looked at Armond. His gray eyes narrowed, warning Callie of a later reckoning. Callie gave a tiny shrug. She hadn't intended to broach the subject with an audience, but she'd take all the support she could get.

"When do you leave?" asked Armond in a low voice.

"Tomorrow morning." Callie finished her cleanup. "I need to get home and pack."

Armond held her elbow in a light grip. "I'll see you home. Don't worry, sir," he tossed over his shoulder to Dion. "She'll be safe."

On the ride home, the silence between them was as thick as extra-firm tofu. Even Callie couldn't think of a thing to say. At the Gabriel house, Armond drove up to the curb and parked. He helped her from the car, then leaned one hip against the fender and contemplated her over his crossed arms. "You never mentioned driving."

"I thought Tessa and I were set, but she canceled yesterday."

Armond gazed thoughtfully at her a moment, seeing way more than she wanted him to, Callie guessed. "Do you want me to go with you?" he asked softly.

"I don't want to go alone." That was true as far as it went. She also wanted Armond with her.

After a moment, he nodded. "All right. I'll go."

Something champagne bright and sparkly bubbled inside Callie.

"Using the interstates, we should make it in under twenty-four hours."

The champagne feeling went instantly flat. "I'm not using the interstates. See, I've got it all mapped out." Callie pulled a map from her backpack and laid it on the car hood, where the streetlight shone. She smoothed out the creases. "The route is marked in yellow. Of course, I can be flexible. That's the whole point of this. To see things."

"You start out by going west. We need to go east and north."

"That's because I want to drive the Natchez Trace, and it's here." She traced a finger along the western border of Mississippi. "I can go east in Memphis."

"Why this little jog?"

"The Squash Cafe."

"The Squash Cafe?"

Callie nodded. "It's shaped like a pumpkin and the dishes all feature squash in some form. I've always wanted to eat there." Callie smiled. "Ever since I was a little girl, I read my travel books and dreamed."

The lines around his mouth softened and he lifted a hand, as though to caress her cheek. To Callie's disappointment and relief, he halted before touching her, and his hand fisted.

"Are there any other surprises I should know about?"

Ah, well, he might as well know it all. She hadn't known Armond would be with her, hadn't known about the baby when she'd suggested starting in Michigan and staying at the bed-and-breakfast. Her desire had been to see the fall colors, which were said to be in their peak in mid-October.

"In Traverse City, we're staying at Rochon Estates."

To her surprise, he simply nodded. No reaction.

"You're not upset?"

"Should I be?"

"I guess not. I'd kind of gotten the impression you were estranged from your family." So, the Callie instincts failed again. What else was new?

"My family?"

"Your mother and stepfather. Rochon Estates."

"My *mother*." He raked a hand through his hair. "I didn't realize—I just—" He broke off and swore under his breath in French. Mostly she was glad she didn't understand.

"Do you want to tell them about the baby?" she asked.

"What? *No*. I mean, not yet."

Good! She wasn't ready to face that hurdle either. "Don't worry; when we do I'll make it clear that not getting married is my choice, but I won't shut them out of their granddaughter's life."

"I—" He shook his head.

Callie peered at him, his jaw set and shoulders stiff. Why the shift from indifference to agitation? Damn, this man was confusing. "Does this mean you won't come with me?"

"What? No," he answered distractedly. She wondered if he realized he was gripping the *gris-gris* bag.

"No, I'll go. It's just I need . . . I'll pick you up in the morning. I want an early start."

He left with an abruptness that had her staring after the red taillights.

His mother! An hour later, Armond still could conjure up no image, no sensation of her, but the thought of meeting her both excited and terrified him. He stepped from the shower in his nondescript hotel room and toweled off with brisk, efficient motions. She was a part of his past, could tell him things to fill the inner hollows, but . . . How was he supposed to keep a memory loss from his mother?

And keep it secret he must. The shadows who dogged him, the fool who threatened Callie, the only thing keeping them at bay likely was that they didn't know about the loss and respected his skills. He couldn't risk them finding out how helpless he was.

Armond stared into the mirror. Short hair, gray eyes, no softness. He had known this face all his life, yet it was the face of a stranger, one he'd recognized for only a few days. Angrily, he rubbed his hands across his cropped hair. Not even the texture felt familiar.

He had to get his memory back with no one aware of the loss. He would leave town with Callie, give himself some privacy and some breathing room, prod his memory.

Spend a week alone with Callie? Armond sucked in a breath and glanced ruefully down at his body, already stirring with the mere thought, icy shower be damned. Picture her before you sleep. Recite the ways she stirs you, Zeke had said. It didn't take words or visions to harden him, only a hint of the scent of pepper and ginger, only a grazing touch against her smooth skin, only the sound of her breathy sigh.

How the hell was he supposed to keep control for a week if his unruly body didn't cooperate? By enduring the discomfort or taking care of the matter himself, he supposed. He hated the feeling he was using Callie, but there was no other way. He wouldn't compound the sin, however, by sleeping with her.

Armond caught his reflection again, noticing faint scars amid the fading bruises and scratches. Sometimes he wondered if he wanted to find the answers. Bits of revelation about Armond Marceaux had not been promising. Driven, controlled. A workaholic. Callie said he was estranged from his mother. Why? What kind of man was estranged from his mother and the mother of his child?

He braced his hands on the sink. "Who are you?" he demanded of the reflection.

Gray eyes stared back at him. They were too hard, too knowing. They reflected back the realities of that ugly knowledge that invaded him unbidden, the knowledge of justice demanded. Who wouldn't want to forget?

It was tempting to just chuck it all. Ignore the past, marry Callie, make love to her and raise their child. Twice he'd lost the woman who was barreling back into his soul. Part of him had never forgotten her; all of him still wanted her.

Forget the past, he might, but he couldn't ignore the present. Someone was following him; someone was a danger to Callie.

He had also learned he was a good agent, a respected one, part of the FBI, the premiere crime-fighting unit in the United States. And that surety of guilt—memory or not, wanted or not—he was stuck with the power. He would just have to learn to master it again.

One thing he was sure of: He wouldn't lose Callie

again. Someway they would be together. In this morass of loss, he had found that one irrefutable goal.

After packing, Callie debated between immediate bed and the warm lights of her mother's workroom. She yawned, fatigued beyond mere exhaustion, but she knew she had to let her family know her plans. Sighing, she trudged to the workroom.

Alexis and Stacia were with Lillian. Alexis ground seeds into a fine powder in a mortar, her blond braid bouncing as her small arm worked vigorously. Her focus, however, was intent on Stacia and Lillian, who were discussing the treatment of a threatened miscarriage.

Stacia looked up. "Hi, Callie. I'm sorry I missed your show again this week. I got called to a delivery."

"No problem."

"I'll try next week." She handed Callie a paper. "Here's the list I promised you."

"What list?" Callie scanned the unfamiliar names.

"Sorry, I forgot to tell you. It's the top OB people in the areas you're going to be visiting for the video series. Just in case you have any problems with the pregnancy while on the road. As the rest of your itinerary firms, I'll find out who you should see." She nodded to the paper. "I know most of them and have spoken to them."

"Thanks, but you really didn't need to—"

Stacia patted her on the arm. "I want to make sure you and your daughter have the best."

"We have to take care of you, Aunt Callie," Alexis told her gravely.

Callie perched on a stool next to her niece. "Isn't it late for you to be up?"

"There's no school tomorrow. And we're waiting for Tessa and Kitty to get back."

"Grandma, we got it." Kitty's high voice preceded her into the workroom. A moment later, she careened in, her blond hair streaming behind her, brown bag in hand. Tessa drifted in behind her daughter, centered in a cloud of billowing chiffon.

"Hey, Aunt Callie," said Kitty. "Don't forget you promised to bring me something special from your trip. Mom said she'd bring back a dulcimer."

"I hadn't forgotten. What did you get?"

"Black cohosh," Kitty said proudly, handing Stacia the bag.

Callie blinked. She'd figured it was Kitty's favorite treat—frozen yogurt.

Lillian stuck her nose into the bag. "It smells stronger. We may have to use less."

Tessa, Stacia, and Lillian launched into a discussion about whatever tonic it was they were concocting, while Alexis deftly added a thin stream of lavender oil to her mortar and Kitty hopped up onto a stool to watch.

The five made a striking picture of a close-knit family. Familiar sensations of warmth and longing swept through Callie. Her daughter would have this legacy, the loving and care that went back through centuries of Gabriels. She cleared her throat around the sudden lump. Five pairs of brilliant blue eyes turned to her.

"I just wanted to wish you good-night and tell you 'bye." She backed up . . . and stumbled over a stool. Quickly, she caught herself. "I'm leaving tomorrow. Starting the drive to Michigan."

"Are you going alone?" Tessa asked with concern. "I told Mom and Stacia about canceling, but they couldn't go, either."

"I figured. But, ah, no, I'm not going alone."

"Who with?"

"Armond."

164

The collective recoil was obvious, and Lillian drew in her breath with a hiss.

"A man?" squealed Kitty. "Aunt Callie, you wouldn't do anything so foolish?"

Callie suspected there was a direct quote from Lillian in there. "Sheesh, you'd think I said I was going to dance naked at Mardi Gras."

"Didn't Cousin Nina do that?" Tessa asked absently.

Alexis gave Callie a grave stare. "Are you going to marry him?"

"Of course she's not," exclaimed Kitty. "Aunt Callie knows that bad things happen to Gabriels who marry. Not just to the bride, but to the whole family." She turned bright blue eyes back to Callie. "You wouldn't do that to us, would you, Aunt Callie?"

"It's just a drive," said Callie faintly, feeling cold from her heart all the way to the child developing inside her. "I'm . . . I'm going to bed now." She set her jaw against sudden unshed tears, wondering why she'd hoped for anything else. Had it been anyone but Armond, she'd have felt the same.

A chorus of good-nights followed her as she stumbled out. Lillian, however, joined her in walking to the house. "Are you sure this trip is wise, Callie?"

"Mom, I've never been out of Louisiana. I always wanted to travel, but with training as a chef, opening the restaurant, I never had the chance. Now my job and that urge to travel are coming together. It's an opportunity I can't miss."

"But . . . with Armond?"

"Dion is worried about the notes. Armond is there as protection."

Sadly, Lillian ran a hand over Callie's hair. "Don't lie to me, and especially, don't lie to yourself."

She wanted honesty? "I've tried twice to give him up, and it hurts. I know there are problems, every reason not to want him, but something inside me just won't let go. This is the last time, though."

"Be sure you know what you're doing, Callie. You have a generous heart. Don't let it lead you astray."

Callie walked out of the garden into the more comforting kitchen. She leaned against the counter and faced her mother. "If I were to—Isn't there any way you could accept him?"

Lillian shook her head. "You know our history, Callie. You don't only risk yourself, but all of us. If it was just me—" She shrugged. "But I have Alexis and Kitty to think about."

"It's not right, Mom."

"It's the way it is, Callie. I can't be any plainer. None of us want this, but if you try to bring Armond Marceaux into this family, you are on your own."

Callie braced herself on the counter, her knees suddenly too weak for support. She would be alone.

Alone. The word echoed in her throat and chest, bringing fear and panic, making her dizzy. Her chest hurt, as though an arrow pierced bone and tissue.

Lillian's eyes narrowed with worry. "Are you all right? The baby? I didn't mean to upset you so . . ."

Callie waved a hand, beating back the pain. "We're fine. Just a twinge."

Her mother looked at her with affection, gave her a kiss on the cheek. "I know you'll do what's right. You're a Gabriel." She returned to her workroom and her family.

Callie stood in the kitchen, alone. Tears sprang to her eyes and she rested her hands on her stomach, wondering if the child inside was weeping, too.

Chapter Eleven

Hugh Pendragon sat in his darkened room and watched the dawn settle over the Chicago skyline. His hand rested on the massive dog beside him. Three days ago, the strange mutt had appeared and had insisted on being adopted. His appetite was huge, his bark was window-rattling, but the dog fit him somehow.

When the last lights winked out, he closed the curtains and then turned back to the computer screen to study the e-mail before him.

It was from Armond, a response to the one he'd sent almost a month ago. The answer was terse and unremarkable, simple words to the effect that he was tied up and would be in contact later.

This was late, much later than Hugh'd expected, and showed no interest in what he'd found. Moreover, in the written word—even Armond's normally brief electronic missives—Hugh could hear the soul of a man. This response was lacking. Or different.

Curious.

"Do you know what Armond is up to?" Hugh asked the beast beside him.

The huge dog gave a single bark. Hugh wasn't sure if that meant yes or no, then decided it didn't matter. "We're not going to wait until then anyway. Something is definitely screwing up my old friend's radar. Shall we see where he is?"

Another single bark.

Must mean yes.

Hugh searched through his darkened house—a mausoleum some called it—until he found what he was looking for. The strip of cloth Armond had tied around Hugh's bloody arm the day they'd met.

Four older boys had caught Hugh unaware and surrounded him, threatening him for the crime of attracting the attention of the leader's girl. Hugh hadn't bothered to explain she'd been the one to come on to him. He'd been intent on saving his skin from the four of them.

Then Armond had appeared, somehow sensing the threat. He'd faced down the leader. "This is wrong," was all he'd said, very quietly. The look in his eyes should have been all that was needed, but the four toughs were too stupid to see it.

Four against two. Unfair odds. He and Armond had whipped them soundly. After the toughs stumbled away, Armond had bound the knife wound on Hugh's arm with a torn strip from his shirt, saying, "They won't bother you again."

Hugh had known it for the truth.

Armond hadn't stayed long in town—his mother had moved a lot in those days—but for a few months two boys had found a bond in their strangeness, not that they'd ever talked about it.

Now, Hugh Pendragon picked up the cloth and held it in his hands. He didn't close his eyes. Instead he focused on a small, rusty stain—not his blood; blood from Armond's scraped knuckles.

He never could explain what it was he did, or why it only worked sometimes. The best he'd found was that objects retained an essence of the people who manipulated them, but sometimes that essence was insufficient as tinder.

Armond, however, was very strong.

Hugh quieted the worry for a friend that roiled inside him, seeking to become only a blank slate. The dog, whom he'd named Cerberus on a whim, padded over and leaned against him, his massive head reaching Hugh's thigh. Not demanding, just . . . adding strength.

His hands and eyes burned. He dragged in air, but his lungs felt clogged with smoke. Then the image popped into his mind.

A car, a stretch of winding road, a road sign, a man and woman together. Just as quickly, the image disappeared in the usual wall of fire, leaving the familiar aftermath of fatigue and intense sensitivity to any sensation, touch especially.

It was one of the reasons he kept this room dark and simple and filled with soft fabrics.

Only when his senses quieted did he move.

Armond was with a woman.

Hugh smiled. About time.

Callie and Armond had their first argument forty miles outside of New Orleans.

"Callie, if you persist in stopping every ten miles, we're not going to make Memphis in a week, much less Michigan. And Donaldsonville is straight south."

Callie looked up from her guidebook. Armond drove with expert ease along the narrow road between the sugarcane fields and oil refineries, but his fingers drummed against the steering wheel, a sure sign of irritation.

"The Acadian Village is the last one today, promise. We'll be in Natchez in time for supper."

He made a strangled sound low in his throat. "How can this be any different from Destrehan Plantation, Oak Alley, Laurel Valley Village? They're all old houses."

"You have no sense of history, Armond."

His fingers tightened around the steering wheel. "No, I don't."

"You'll like this. There are demonstrations and audio-visual displays illustrating the customs and cuisine of Acadiana," she read aloud from the guidebook. "Interactive. Don't you want to see that?"

"Fine, we'll stop. But we can't drive these back roads and pull off every time it suits your whim."

"Why not? Turn here."

"Because we'll never—" He broke off abruptly, as the center appeared.

Rather than a regulation tourist building, there were a series of small houses nestled in a clearing. Smoke rose from one, and employees dressed in period costumes ambled through the area or worked their demonstrations.

"Interesting, isn't it?" Callie leaned forward for a better view out the front windshield.

He parked the car and undid his seat belt but didn't get out. "Callie, we do need some sort of plan."

His gentle words scooped a hollow ache inside her. A plan. She knew he was talking about the trip, but she could see future conversations like this one, setting out a plan for their child.

Behind him the afternoon sun lit his hair to a dark sheen, and already a shadow darkened the strength of his jaw. A jaw she longed to line with kisses until she reached his lips. Such a masculine man; every fiber of her wanted him.

And she couldn't imagine him ever part of the Gabriel traditions. She closed her lids tight a moment. Damn those hormones, swinging her from lusty to moody with occasional dollops of fear in the space of a heartbeat. All Armond would have to do was touch her and the lust would be back stronger than ever.

Personal risk wasn't high on her priorities, but she knew why she'd had to take this trip. For her sake, for her daughter's sake. To see if she and Armond could change old patterns, forgive old hurts. Otherwise these memories, and her baby, would be all she kept of him.

"Is there any place you want to see?" she asked, opening her eyes. "Some place you've wanted to see since childhood?"

He hesitated a moment, then shook his head. "None that I remember."

"But there are so many, many places I want to see. While I have this chance."

"You have to be in—"

"I know. You said we need a plan; I have one." She pulled out the map and penciled a slash across Natchez. "We'll be here by tonight and I need to be in Traverse City by next Wednesday. That gives us five more nights."

Quickly she bisected the remaining yellowed route with five slashes. "If I plan the sightseeing so we end up at each of those points by suppertime, then will you agree not to make any complaints about any stops I want to make?"

"You want to be in complete charge?"

She hadn't meant it that way, but—"Yes." Callie held her breath. Armond had never been the laid-back type, willing to let someone else be in control.

"All right."

Callie blinked. "All right? You mean that?"

"Of course I mean it. I wouldn't have said it otherwise. There's just one exception." He tilted her chin up with one finger, drawing her gaze to his gray eyes. There wasn't a hint of joking in them. "If I do give you an order, you obey, instantly, completely, and without question."

"What!" Callie sputtered.

"You're in charge, unless I think there's some danger or risk. Then I am. Trust me enough that I won't tell you to do something unless I think it's necessary. Trust me enough to let me do my job."

His job. She was still just "his job" to him.

Agent Marceaux, that is about to change.

Callie gave him her biggest grin. "All right. I'm in charge unless peril threatens."

And how likely was that?

The first cabin squatted beneath an ancient-looking cypress tree, and Callie and Armond strolled to it. He rested his hand against the small of her back, enjoying the warmth of contact and the motion of her back, and bottom, as she walked.

Visitors were sparse, so they had little competition to watch a man caning a chair, paddle a pirogue, and buy a piece of sugarcane to suck on. The cane was a dry matrix, the juice especially sweet in contrast.

To his surprise, Armond found himself slowly relaxing as he strolled beside Callie. The caress of cool afternoon air, the scents of wood and shrimp, and the pleasure of listening to Callie's enthusiasm all worked a simple magic on him. He had no past, and he didn't want to face the future yet, so he would live each moment of the present.

They'd been tailed coming out of New Orleans, but he'd soon lost their shadows. Callie's unpredictable route would be difficult to pick up again, one of the reasons he'd bitten back his instinctive refusal and let her choose their path, but he'd remained alert.

Until now.

Armond shifted his shoulders. The looseness in the play of his muscles, the absence of familiar, bitter traces of others' guilt, the lack of urgency and purpose, were alien sensations, more unfamiliar than his face. Had he never taken the time to simply relax? Had he never felt peace? Or contentment?

Would this all be lost when he got his memory back?

If so, then he would grab each moment while he could.

"Armond, look at that man whittle." Callie laid her hand on his arm and leaned against him, nodding toward the couple on the porch. "Have you ever seen a knife go so fast?"

A faint, pleasurable stirring rippled through Armond at the press of Callie's body against his side. His attention on her ginger scent, he glanced casually where she pointed.

The sun went behind a cloud, and a shiver slid up his spine. The peace of the afternoon disappeared behind a crawling at the back of his neck.

An older couple sat in rockers—the wrinkled, bald man whittling, his matching partner crocheting. He didn't recognize them, not a feature looked familiar, but some instinctive part of him recognized them.

What was familiar? Where had he seen them? The lab where he'd been held? The FBI? Since he'd come to New Orleans? Had his and Callie's trail been picked up again? He couldn't believe that.

So, where had he seen them? Where had he seen that motion of the hands?

Abruptly he turned and joined the couple on the porch, Callie trailing behind him. "What are you making?" he asked, sitting in one of the rockers.

"A doll." The man held out the toy to him. "Just finished it."

It was a beautiful piece of work. "The facial features are detailed." Armond caressed the smooth wood, his hands enjoying the silky feel even as his brain cataloged the man.

"You discover things with your hands," observed the old man.

It was an insightful observation from a stranger, but true, Armond realized. He did like to touch things; it made them real. "Yes, I believe so."

Callie sat beside the woman, whose crochet hook also moved with lightning speed. "I tried crocheting once but never got the hang of it. My yarn always tangled. What are you making?"

"The doll's dress." The woman's voice was low and melodic, strangely younger-sounding than her wrinkles would indicate.

Callie touched a finger to the tiny frock. "It's so soft."

"I use a special yarn."

"Filaments of spiderweb," interjected her partner.

The woman cast him an irritated look before leaning over and whispering to them, "Don't listen; he has senior moments." She took the dress off the hook and handed it to Armond, gesturing for him to put it on the doll.

Armond complied, still trying to nail down the sense of déjà vu as he awkwardly dressed the doll. Apparently this wasn't in his repertoire of skills. He held up the doll in his larger hands, and for one brief moment a vision stole his breath: his hands, holding a baby, dressing a child. His child. His fingers closed around the doll.

"Is this for sale?"

"Of course." The old man named a ridiculously low price, and Armond paid it.

"You ought to try whittling," said the man, handing him a rough cypress block with a flourish. "They've got knives at the gift shop."

"Maybe I will."

That flourish. Armond's eyes narrowed as he suddenly realized what was so familiar about the man. He had the same movements as the strange juggler who had accosted Callie and him on the levee. "Have you been to New Orleans recently?"

The man shook his head. "I hate cities. Me and the little woman been right here on the bayous all our lives."

"Relatives there?"

"Non."

Maybe it was a doppelganger. Not that the two men looked remotely similar—not even a camouflaging disguise could explain the differences—but characteristic gestures were a hard habit to hide and unique to the individual.

Armond chewed around the puzzle as he and Callie walked away, glancing once or twice at the elderly twosome; then he shook his head. The pinch in his chest reminded him that it wasn't possible to banish the cop in him.

He glanced at Callie. "Do you want to go to the souvenir shop?"

"Do I mind stopping in a souvenir shop? Think about it. At Oak Alley, who bought the stuffed pirate with the massive sword?"

Armond smiled, allowing his doubts to slip back a little, desperate to recapture a fraction of that strange peace he'd felt earlier. "And the Great American Dances limited-edition souvenir plate of the Cajun two-step."

"Who bought the Dr. John tape?"

"Only because I was tired of listening to Chumbawamba and Rednex."

"The book, *Magic in the Swamp*—that's yours, too."

"In case your mother rethinks her decision not to turn me into a toad." Armond touched her arm, setting off the shower of desire inside him again, and determined to ignore it as well. "C'mon, let's see what damage we can do to our wallets here."

One knife, one book on great crimes in Louisiana, five miniature bottles of hot sauce, and two pralines later, they were back in the car. Callie, munching the ice from her soft drink, gave him a smug smile. "Aren't you glad we stopped?"

"Don't gloat."

"Gabriel women don't gloat. We ooze assurance."

"Don't ooze."

She smiled again. "And thank you for buying the doll for our baby."

"You're sure it's a girl?"

"Well, it's too early for an ultrasound to confirm it, but Gabriels always have girls. Besides, even if it were a boy, he could still play with the doll."

One look told her what he thought of that idea.

Callie broke out in a peal of laughter, and, impulsively, she leaned over. "Thanks for stopping. And for the doll." She kissed his cheek.

All thoughts of peace shattered in a single burst of

desire. It wasn't enough. A kiss on the cheek wasn't what he wanted. Armond swore under his breath. He'd been counting on her to remember they were wrong for each other, since he couldn't remember any such thing.

She was making this damned difficult.

Callie drew back, surprised at her boldness. But today—things had been so different with Armond. *He'd* been so different. For the first time, a sliver of hope cut through her wariness. This trip was a time for chances.

Hoping she wasn't making a major mistake, she slid across the shadow of his beard, then kissed him again. On the lips.

He tasted of sugar and pecan, of cola and ice.

He tasted like the man she wanted.

Above the fizzing and sizzling, Callie heard her own sigh of pleasure as she leaned into him and deepened the kiss.

For one heart-lurching moment she feared she was the only one participating. Then Armond's hand cupped the back of her head and his fingers tangled in the strands of her hair. He held her still, right where she wanted to be, and took charge of the kiss.

The fizzing spread, from lips to chest to the tips of her sensitive breasts to toes and all parts in between. Callie pressed closer, seeking release for the ache building inside her. Her fingers kneaded the muscles of his shoulders.

His arms came around her, holding her in a fierce, protective hug, though he pulled away from the kiss. "Callie, we can't do this." Armond's voice was a frayed thread.

"What, you never went necking in a car?"

"If I did, I sure as hell didn't do it in a public parking lot. Besides, I can't do my job—"

"Armond, do you see any mad note-writers here?"

Armond drew a deep breath, trying to quell the fire in his veins, trying to think of one good reason they shouldn't find the closest motel and say to hell with making Natchez. A flash, a movement seen from the corner of his eye, grabbed his attention, and he jerked his gaze to the Acadian Village, loosing Callie from his embrace. What had he seen? All looked normal, except—

The old couple had vanished.

Armond frowned as another connection formed, dousing the fire that had licked his veins. The juggler, the whittler; he'd seen that flourish in someone else.

Zeke Jupiter.

Yet, they looked nothing alike, and he got none of that instinctive wary knowledge from them. Armond rubbed the back of his neck. Maybe the memory loss was only a symptom of insanity. Next he'd be seeing sinister clowns and knitters.

He turned back to Callie. She was facing forward, her seat belt on, her sunglasses shielding her face. "Let's get going," she said tightly.

The last residue of the afternoon's contentment faded.

"The little woman?"

"Senior moment?"

Zeus and Hera finally materialized in Zeus's hotel room, glaring at each other, sparks and fog swirling about the room.

"Did you have to tell her about the spider filaments?"

"Senior moment!"

Her mate's unbridled fury broke through Hera's annoyance. He was so magnificent when he was angry. Her lips twitched. "Maybe 'senior moment' was uncalled for. You have all your faculties. And talents."

"Thank you." Zeus's anger visibly receded, and he rubbed his chin. "We'll have to use the far-see smoke next time. I think Armond recognized something of us."

Hera fingered the ring. "I think we should leave them alone these days."

"How can we be sure they will proceed to love without us?"

"Zeus, my husband, did you not see that kiss?"

He thought a moment, then smoothed her hair. "It was as enticing and teasing as one of yours. We can trust them for this week."

Hera fought the lurch of her heart.

Zeus's fingers tightened around her hair. "There is another reason we should not use our powers again."

"The rings," Hera said flatly. The power, this time in both rings, had again failed when they first tried to transport away.

"Aye, the rings. Unless we find a way to recharge or replace the crystal, our powers are in their twilight. In the meantime, we had best conserve their use."

Hera gave a rueful smile. "Even if he wins the bet, Dion might not be getting such a prize."

Zeus picked up her hands with his. "So, we have this week. What about us, Hera? How can we use this time?" His thumb ran across her knuckles with enticing slowness.

"You know," he said softly, "I want you back at my side. I want to not wonder when you're going to disappear again for years too numerous to count. I want your love. I want your trust."

Hera tried to memorize the gentle insistence of his touch. Memorize it for the remainder of her years, when it would be lost to her forever.

She should not give him any hope, but when he was

with her, she was weak. Resolve seemed a lonely companion, and homesickness a mere phantom.

At the least, she should tell him of her plans to return home. But that one niggling doubt, that vestigial lack of trust, remained. When they had first come to this world, when she had needed him most, he had turned from her. Had shamed her and fought her. Yet, because she understood the pain that fueled his actions, because she, too, had done unworthy deeds, she had, at last, forgiven.

But trust?

If he found out she sought to make amends with Callie to return home, would he refuse to help? Would he side with Dion? If he did, could she prevail against the two of them?

She withdrew her hands. "Don't fall in love with me again. We have no future, only moments in time."

Zeus's lips tightened, and the golden aura of his powers surrounded him. Even with the weakening crystal, he was still magnificent. "Just this moment? I am not willing to accept that. Tell me one thing: Do I fight only the demons of my past, or is it a demon of the present, too?"

She hesitated, then said, "There are barriers of today."

"The rings? Does the loss of power frighten you?"

"Some. But I have learned other things in these years, and have other resources."

"As have I. So, what is it? Another man?"

Hera shook her head. She hated that black knot inside, the ugly seed of doubt that kept her silent, but she could not ignore it. "Let's not think of this now. We have a week."

"Passion and amusement?" Zeus asked.

"And, perhaps, we begin to look for a way to restore our full power."

The Warrior

Dion stared into the goblet of Amontillado, alternately popping an olive or an almond into his mouth between sips. What he would do for the far-see smoke or transporting talent of Zeus and Hera; he would like to see the progress of Armond and Callie. Alas, those were powers the leaders reserved to themselves.

Unless I get Hera's ring.

Life had grown boring of late, at least until Zeus and Hera had arrived. He should be grateful to them for livening things up, but groveling really wasn't part of his nature. He smiled around a taste of the sherry. The bet added an extra charge to the situation; he wanted to be sure he won.

Gods never played to lose.

He swirled the wine in the goblet. A very special goblet it was, the goblet of Dionysus. Dion lifted it to his lips and drank deep.

"In vino veritas."

In wine is truth. Callie would not drink of it while she was pregnant, but perhaps he would give Armond a taste. Who knew what he might learn from that son of Ares?

For a moment the thought of Ares distracted him. Had Ares ever returned to their home of D-alphus? Likely.

Dion laughed aloud, remembering how Ares's formidable temper would ignite whenever he heard the developing myths. It infuriated the god of war that humans could not tolerate his rational side, his justice, and so they had taken from him all the qualities of good and given them to a fictional goddess, Athena.

Of course, Dionysus had taken every opportunity to remind the war god of that fact.

He took another sip of his wine, feeling the haze of alcohol settle over him. Perhaps he would find a companion for the night; he did not tolerate a lack of sexual release for very long. The god of wine and mirth reveled in unrestrained fun and hedonistic pleasures.

Few remembered that Dionysus was also the god of the cruelties of drunkenness, the truths found in wine, the death and regeneration of the vines. All could be found in a taste of his goblet.

With his goblet and Hera's ring, he could amuse himself for a good many years.

Chapter Twelve

Armond disliked coming back into a city. Even if Natchez was smaller than New Orleans, crime was a universal blight. The undercurrents vibrated across his nerves in a way he didn't like but was learning to ignore by trusting his instincts to tell him when it was important.

Alone with Callie today he'd relaxed. She was too energetic to be deemed calm and peaceful, his reactions to her too primitive to be deemed civilized, but when he was with her something inside him stilled and loosened.

The only problem was avoiding the minefields planted by his amnesia. He'd thought about telling her, asking her help in retrieving memories, but innate caution kept him silent. If Callie knew, others might also, and he couldn't take that risk.

Armond pulled into a hotel on the outskirts of town,

eschewing the plain motels for a touch of luxury.

Callie gave a low whistle. "Not the Motel Six, is it?"

"I want a suite." Adjoining beds with Callie would be too tempting; separate rooms wouldn't let him keep an eye on her.

"I'll check out the restaurants," she said. "See if there's one I like and make reservations. But I want a swim first."

He waited, watching the sway of her hips as she strolled off, before he turned and handed the clerk his credit card. It wouldn't do for her to hear the clerk call him Mr. Marsten. Mostly he'd pay by cash, but when necessary, he planned to rotate the pseudonymous credit cards he'd found at the cabin. If someone was looking for him, maybe they wouldn't know the Adrian Marsten or Marshall Warren identities.

They swam, then ate dinner and talked—a pleasant evening between a man and a woman. For some reason Armond had given himself permission to relax, to be off duty. Callie'd seen his rapid switch from lover to LE at the Acadian Village, so she doubted it would last, but, for the moment, she enjoyed it.

Afterward, though, tempting as it was, Callie turned down his invitation to dance in favor of a return to the room and a warm shower, feeling pregnancy's undeniable fatigue claim her. After she'd finished her shower, Armond took his, while she curled up in a chair with a book.

"I thought you'd be asleep," Armond said.

"I was reading." Callie looked up, and the book she'd been staring at fell to her lap.

He was coming from the shower, towel drying his hair and wearing only a pair of khaki shorts that rode low on his hips.

She bit her lip as she watched him walk closer. Picturing Armond in the shower had chased away sleep, despite her tiredness, and, now, seeing him nearly nude started her unruly hormones dancing. He was all sleek muscles and powerful grace. Her heart did that little flip it did whenever she caught sight of him anew, and the seltzer water in her blood got a new dose of bubbles. A dusting of dark hair spread across his chest, but he was clean-shaven, despite it being bedtime.

He tossed aside the towel to pull on a long-sleeved T-shirt. Beneath it lay his gun, which he deftly hid almost before she had time to see it.

Part of him was the man who held her chair, opened doors, and ordered with the competence of someone who knew exactly what he wanted. Part of him was the man who tenaciously sought criminals, who handled a gun as easily as he used a corkscrew, and who had given her a baby in one very untamed night. Today, for the first time, she'd seen a new side, a man content to be with her. Sometimes he seemed a complete stranger.

"What? Did I forget a spot?" He rubbed a hand across his chin as he crouched beside her.

Callie smiled, realizing she'd been staring. "Sorry. No, you're clean." She trailed the back of her hand down his smooth cheek.

He pulled away. "What are you reading?"

As a siren, apparently she had a lot to learn. She held up a thin book. "Just studying about the places I'll be visiting for Dion. Look, here's a picture of your stepfather's vineyard."

He stared at it for a long moment, one finger tracing the steep-roofed house set among acres of vines. "What do you plan on videoing while you're there?"

"Do you have any suggestions?"

He shook his head, silent, still looking at the picture.

"One place I'd like to see is Sleeping Bear Dunes. It's a National Lakeshore. The legend about it—I don't know, it somehow really got to me."

"Tell me the legend."

"Don't you know?" She couldn't believe he didn't remember the local myth.

"I'd like to hear you tell it."

"It's a Chippewa legend. Long ago, in the land that is today Wisconsin, a mother bear and her two cubs were driven into the vast waters of Lake Michigan by a raging forest fire. The water was cold, the waves powerful, but they swam and swam, fleeing the monstrous fire. All grew tired, and the cubs lagged behind. At last the mother bear reached the opposite shore and climbed a bluff to search for her offspring in the lake. She never found them, yet still she waits, a dune reaching to the sky. The cubs drowned and became the Manitou Islands just offshore."

Callie sniffed and wiped a tear from her eye. Her other hand rested protectively on her stomach. True, it was only a legend, but she'd felt the mother bear's pain when she'd read it, sympathized with a maternal instinct that would wait through eternity to protect a child. As she would do anything to protect this baby. "It's stupid, I know, but it always catches my throat."

He leaned forward and kissed her damp cheek. "It's not stupid, Callie. Not when it's part of you." Too quickly he pushed to his feet. "Will you also be visiting the Manitou Islands?"

"No. Only the South Island has regular boat service, and it's limited in the fall. North Manitou is a wilderness." She shuddered. "I can't imagine going there. Ever."

* * *

Armond heard Callie tossing restlessly in the bed. Lying on the sofa in the living area of the suite, he stacked his hands behind his head and waited. Sure enough, as she had done twice tonight, moments later she got up and padded to the bathroom. The room was hushed and dark, so he followed her progress as much by sound as by sight. When she shut the door, he got up and leaned against the wall beside the bathroom, waiting for her.

"Are you okay?" he asked when she returned.

"Fine. Pregnancy is not kind to the bladder." She settled back into bed, propping the pillows at the small of her back. "I think I'll read a little if you don't mind." She reached toward the light.

Armond stopped her hand before she could snap it on, then sank at the edge of the bed. "You can't sleep?"

"My back aches a bit," she admitted.

"Maybe you sat too long."

"Are you suggesting we make more stops tomorrow?" she teased.

"If it keeps you comfortable," he answered seriously. "Now, roll over."

Dutifully, Callie complied. She must be uncomfortable if she wanted no discussion on the matter.

Armond pushed up the T-shirt she wore as pajamas over her hips, revealing silky pink panties and the elegant curves of her bottom and spine. Callie stirred and gave an unintelligible murmur, which he quieted by a gentle croon. "I'm just going to rub your back."

"Darn," she whispered.

He stroked her back and neck and arms, easy and slow, until her sigh of pleasure reached all the way to his heart. His thumbs kneaded gently along her spine and lower muscles, wherever he felt tension. Her skin became soft and pliant beneath his hands. It gratified him to feel her relax.

There were no lamps on in the room and the heavy hotel drapes kept out all light, except for the small crack at the center, where they weren't drawn together. The yellow sliver of streetlight was enough for him to see the outline of her sherry brown hair against her back and pillow. Mostly, though, he felt: the satin of her panties, the silk of her skin, the tiny ridges of her spine, the smooth bones of her shoulders.

All his senses seemed keener tonight, not just the odd one that kept him alert and ready for danger, that knew of guilt or wrongdoing. The only danger here tonight came from his reaction to Callie: the powdery scent of her, the dry taste of the cooled air surrounding her, the play of muscles—hers and his—as he massaged.

In the quiet night, the intimacy between them seemed a deep river—not sexual this time; he wouldn't let it be—but placid on top, endless and dangerous below.

"Callie?"

"Hmmm?" She sounded relaxed and sleepy.

"How's your back?"

"Better." She was silent a moment, then rolled over to face him. "Can I ask you something?"

"You can ask. I can't promise to answer." His hands atop the T-shirt rested on her warm abdomen.

Her smile was a little sad. "Why did you stay with me?"

"The notes—"

She shook her head. "Do you realize this is the longest stretch we've ever spent together? And you weren't thinking about anything else—a case, a victim, a criminal—you were thinking about what we were doing. I didn't feel . . . alone. Was it only the job,

Armond? Do you care for me?" A ghost of a smile crossed her face. "Beyond desire, I mean."

Words seemed glued in his throat, yet he had to say something. "Yes. I—" He floundered, unsure how to describe what he didn't understand himself. "—care."

She gave a tiny laugh. "I think that's the most you've ever admitted. Why now? What's changed?"

Because the feelings seem stronger? Because I have nothing else to guide me? "I don't know," he answered honestly, resting his hand on her body. "The baby? Because I'm on vacation?"

"When is your vacation over? When will you leave?"

He took the question at face value, although he suspected there was more there than he understood. When would he leave?

With all the insanity—the amnesia, the notes, the shadows, the baby—he'd not really thought beyond the immediate future. If being with Callie these days did not trigger his memory, then he had to take other steps. He would have to return to the Atlanta Field Office where he was assigned, Armond decided, and hope he unmasked the traitor before being taken out.

"After you finish in Michigan," he answered at last, feeling the clutch of loss in the decision.

She didn't say anything, only nodded as though she expected the answer, and then she sat, drawing her legs up. Only her green-painted toes rested against him. "Have you always wanted to be a cop, Armond?" she asked softly, wrapping her arms around her legs. "Did you ever want anything else?"

He thought a moment, about the fingers of knowledge that touched him, about the impossibility of ignoring them. "I can't imagine doing anything else."

"Why? Why is it so vital to you? Why must you do it?"

He knew in his gut that it was the right thing for him, but he didn't know why. For explanation he drew on primitive emotions and instincts, not facts. Hunting—for his identity, for the person out to sabotage Callie—felt as natural as putting his pants on. His hand curved, as though around the butt of a gun or the handle of a knife. Protecting Callie and their child was as vital as his next breath. Satisfaction at balancing the scales was matched only by the peace and satisfaction he found when Callie held him or cared for him.

"It's important. It's important to stop people like—" Pain lanced through his head, swift and sharp, as he came up against the blank wall of names. "—like Guy Centurion. And I'm good at it." At least, he believed he was. "It's part of me," he added honestly. "My soul. My genes."

It must have been the wrong thing to say. He felt a shudder ripple through her, and she laid her head against her knees.

"Your face changed when you said that. You left me. You became the warrior." Her voice was so low, he barely heard her, but her response could not have been clearer. She couldn't accept that part of him. She shifted again, her feet moving so that last small contact between them was lost.

A sudden chilling shot of solitude coursed through him. It wasn't words, so much as a gut-level understanding. *You're alone. You always will be.*

Alone. The cabin. The ring abandoned there. Callie's office. Cold, hollow, alone.

The fading bruises on his arms throbbed, and his forehead joined in. *Alone.* The pain grew, a pulsing headache against the black wall at the back of his mind.

"I think I'll read," Callie said, reaching over to snap on the light.

Armond flinched against the sudden slash of brilliance. It stabbed at him, ripping through the black wall encasing his memories.

Bright lights. Eyes hurt. I'm alone. Figures blotted out behind the searing wall. The burning of a needle in his arm. The overwhelming metallic taste of something so very wrong. I have to get out. No help.

Through the rent of amnesia, out poured sensation. His wrists burning as he struggled against bonds. Hands touching him, and the sure knowledge of their wrongdoing curling his tongue. Incoherent voices until one command stood out.

Tell us what your mind knows, Special Agent Marceaux.

His answer. *This is wrong.* A string of French curses.

Their reply. *No telepathy. Disappointing.*

On the hotel room bed, Armond pressed his forehead against the palm of his hand, trying to blot out the raw feelings sweeping through him. Keep the memories. Handle the pain.

Memories, yes, but so new they felt as real as the first time. *Guilt. Touches of evil and the madness of dispassion magnified a thousand times.*

The drugs. Identity leached out, one drop at a time. One thought retained—escape.

What is your name?

I . . . don't . . . know!

Betrayal.

Armond's stomach roiled and his muscles readied with the need to stop it, to combat the evil of that room. Lash out. Stop them. He was alone. They thought him powerless.

But not for long.

He had escaped.

"Armond!" Callie's voice cut through the maelstrom like a splash from a cool spring.

"Touch me, Callie. Hold me," he ground out.

She knelt and gathered him close.

A measure of coherence returned. The headache still demanded its due, but he could look at the memories, could follow them to pull out others. He felt again each stab in his veins and fought against the burning of the drug. Recoiled from the evil that had swept through him with the repeated injections. Experienced the madness as they stripped away his learned defenses and control, stripped away his identity, his soul, leaving only the raw powers and alien sensations.

Callie was his anchor, her arms around him formed his shelter. The tripping beat of her heart became his peace. He didn't want to need her, but right now he had no other choice.

How long they sat together—his breath finally slowing, his heart returning to its beat, while Callie silently held him—he couldn't say, but at last the pain receded.

Armond sat upright, removing himself from Callie's murmuring support. He ran a hand through his hair, grateful that his fingers, at least, were steadier than his insides. This was getting damn embarrassing.

These memories he had understood. A drug had been given to him, like the one he'd read about in his research. It enhanced this insane "talent" of his, while stripping him of explicit memories, leaving only the implicit, the instinctual, the primitive, the basic. Because they had not understood what he did—Hell, how could they? Even he didn't—they'd deemed the enhancement a failure.

But the memory loss had fascinated them.

He rubbed his arms, feeling the knots of the injections, and a shiver of cold rippled through him. The laboratories had been very cold, near freezing.

How he got there, he didn't yet know, except for one simple fact: He'd been hunting someone, someone in the Bureau, someone working with Guy Centurion, and had been caught instead.

Chapter Thirteen

"Armond." Callie's hands rubbed against his arms, bringing blood to his cold flesh. "Are you all right?"

"That question's becoming a habit with you." Circulation returned with a roar, and he maintained an even tone with effort.

"Only because you keep spacing out on me. Another headache?"

"Yeah." Despite the fading pain, he felt almost exhilarated. This one had brought him real clues, and he could feel the edges of the wall crumbling. At last he had a real hope that the loss wasn't permanent.

"Are you sure you don't need to see a doctor?" Callie asked.

"Trust me. I'm sure."

"Let me get you some Tylenol. I've got some in my bag." She stretched one foot out.

Armond stopped her with a hand to her shoulder,

and it was as though he'd grabbed a lightning bolt. Blood coursed through him. "The pain's gone. Thank you, Callie."

"For what?" She was a golden siren with eyes wide and soft brown, hair tangled about her shoulders, and shirt hiked up to her hips. The pink panties peeked out above her smooth, strong legs.

"For being here." Her feminine scent, ginger and shampoo, teased him. The pulsing of the headache was replaced by a more primitive beating, low and deep. The aftermath of survival? The release of endorphins? He didn't care.

More basic instincts took over.

Protective instincts. To shield Callie and the baby and be the man they needed.

Sexual instincts. He wanted Callie. Armond leaned over and kissed her.

Despite the storm inside him, he forced himself to keep the kiss restrained. A pressure on the lips, the touch of his tongue. She tasted like a Southern summer rain. His hand slipped from her shoulder to her hip to the curve of her thigh and nestled her flush against him.

When she clutched his shoulders, he tunneled his hands through her hair, soft as a kitten's fur, holding her close. But when she opened her mouth for him, restraint fled.

He'd been crazy to think he could kiss Callie and not want more.

It was the witching hour; they were alone; crisp sheets beckoned. Over the soft fabric of her nightshirt, his hand cupped her breast, his thumb rubbing lightly against her tight nipple. The caress was subdued from what he truly wanted.

Wanting more, Callie moaned and leaned against his palm. So easily his touch banished fears and doubts. Her sensitive breasts tingled with the need. When Armond brushed against her other breast with the back of his hand, she sighed. "Yes. That feels so good."

She tugged up the hem of Armond's shirt, then pulled it off him and tossed it aside. Immediately, her hands came back to the crisp hairs on his chest.

The bruises and scrapes there were healing, like the one on his forehead. She ran butterfly strokes the length of his arms, admiring with sight and touch. Perfect. Perfectly shaped muscles, the perfect masculine strength of his wrists. There were bruises and brush burns there, too, and knots in the crook of his arm, but before she could do any more than notice, Armond bunched her shirtfront and pulled her close.

"That tickles," he growled.

She grinned at him. "I like a man with a great pair of arms."

"See anything else you like?"

"A few things." She lifted her chin. "Going to give me a ravishing kiss?"

"Nope. This." He gathered her in his arms and held her tight against his ribs.

Callie leaned her head against his chest. Ah, this was what they'd missed the first time. Time to play, time to savor. His arms holding her close and safe. They were a man's arms—exciting, strong. The pounding of his heart echoed the rhythm of hers. It was good to know that he wanted this as much as she did. Her fingers teased playfully down the front of his shorts. Yes, he definitely wanted her.

Armond grabbed her hand. "Not so fast."

Callie pushed on his shoulders, urging him down to the bed. He resisted, and she was powerless to move him. "Next time we can be slow," she offered.

"It's a deal."

Then he caressed her again, kissed her, and her warrior claimed her with a frantic, rising need that spiraled between them. He was intense, untamed, and he roused primitive instincts in Callie, wild feelings that both thrilled and frightened her.

Her hands wrapped around his waist.

She felt the hard gun at his back.

Callie drew back, ice lodging in the pit of her stomach. "Get rid of that. I hate it. There are no enemies here."

Her words died out, leaving only their harsh breath against the silent room. Both sat utterly still for uncounted heartbeats. Callie stared at Armond, his eyes dark and unfathomable, his face pulled taut with need. The healing bruise stood out in stark relief against the shadow across his cheeks.

When Armond broke the tableau, though, it was not to kiss her. Or to remove the gun. Instead, he stroked a hand across her hair. "Callie, we can't do this."

Callie's hormones screamed in frustration. She was losing him, being left behind to whatever drove him. "I want it. Get your job out of this bed." Her hands ran frantically across his chest, down his arms. "Damn you, Armond, don't stop now."

He looked down, where her hands gripped his elbows, and she felt him withdrawing.

"Don't you want me?" she asked.

He gave a hollow laugh and flexed his hips against her. "Does that feel like I don't want you?"

"Then why not finish?" She reached for his zipper.

He grabbed both wrists and held her arms apart. Callie squirmed and twisted, but Armond's grip was unbreakable. His voice was tight. "Don't make this harder."

"I'm not the one with the hard problem."

"You don't know how close to the edge I am." The

raw edge of control slipped, his hips jerked toward her, and she saw the tight nipples of his chest.

"Good. Why stop?"

Control slipped, but it didn't give. He drew in a long breath. "There are too many . . . complications."

And this wouldn't solve any of them, she knew. Callie writhed, still unable to break free. Deep down, her sense of fair play admitted this wasn't easy for him, either, that only Armond's restraint and formidable self-control kept them apart. Tonight, however, Callie wasn't into fair play.

"Dammit, Armond, I don't like to argue with people, but trust me, you are making a major mistake here."

He gave her a swift, hard kiss that broke off quickly enough to convince her that he wouldn't be changing his mind. "I'm being a gentleman, here. That's what you really want."

"I hate it when people tell me what I want." She stopped struggling and glared at him, blinking back tears with anger. Talk about being a failure in the femme fatale department. Then she saw the way his gaze lingered on her chest, despite the T-shirt still covering it. She saw the glitter of desire in his eyes and the flush of his cheeks. If she pushed him further—

No. Sex would solve nothing.

"All right." She gave in.

He loosened his grip, and a strange expression, almost like pain, crossed his face. She snapped off the light, then folded her arms over her chest. "I'm going to bed. Go back to your sofa. I got the message; this won't happen again."

It was a bald-faced lie. She'd go back in his arms in an instant.

Curling onto her side, she turned her back to him

and pretended to sleep. A woman had to save face somehow.

Armond stared at her back, mentally stringing curses at his ineptitude. He'd made a complete hash of that, but, when she'd held his bruised arms, mentioned their enemies, his responsibilities to her had come crashing down, slicing through the desire.

How could he protect her if he was sleeping with her? How could he break the rules like that?

That doubt paled behind one crashing, freezing fear. He might have put her in danger. By coming back to her, had he drawn his enemies' attention to her?

He'd rather carve out his own heart than bring harm to her and the baby.

So, what should he do about it? He allowed one final curse against the memory loss that had forced him into this, then settled down to solve the problem. Automatically, he picked up the piece of wood and knife he'd gotten in Louisiana, opened the curtains a bit to let in the moonlight, and began to carve, watching and thinking.

Common sense said he should leave, but two very instinctual reactions kept him in place. One, if he had drawn attention to her, she'd be helpless if he left her. Who else could he trust to guard her? If she were in danger, from the note writer or the lab Nazis, then he was her best protection.

Two, despite all rationale, he could not bring himself to leave her again.

His brain said leave. His instincts said stay.

He was learning to trust the instincts.

"Here's your tea."

Callie opened one bleary eye to see Armond crouched beside her bed. Mutely, he held a paper cup toward her. She slid her hand as far as the edge of the bed, then waited. He put the cup against her palm, then wrapped her fingers around it.

The cup was hot. Felt good. Callie's eyes drifted shut.

"Careful, you'll spill." Gently Armond braced her drooping hand. "Time to get up."

"No."

"Next time I'll arrange late checkout, but if you want a shower before we leave, you'll have to get up. Besides, morning is a pretty time to see the Natchez Trace."

Callie groaned, tried to push upward, and failed. After last night's humiliation, sleep had proved as slippery as an unpeeled grape. Mornings never ranked high with her, but as mornings went, this one qualified as the dregs.

The mattress tipped as Armond settled onto it. His arm scooped beneath her shoulders and without further word he had her upright. He guided the cup to her mouth.

Hot, steamed weeds. Tessa's nausea tea. This morning, Callie was grateful for the familiar brew. She sipped in silence until her eyes began to focus.

"Where'd you get this?" she asked, lifting the cup.

"I bullied the kitchen staff."

"I'll bet." She sipped again, then added a grudging, "Thank you."

"You're welcome."

"How long you been up?"

"A while."

Probably hours. And he looked good in the morning. Callie hunched over her tea.

Armond must have sensed further conversation wasn't on the morning's agenda because he sat beside her in silence while she shed the zombie. When she finished the tea—it did help—she stumbled to her feet toward the bathroom.

"Will you be okay?" Armond asked.

"I've been showering by myself for a long time."

"Pity," he muttered, so low Callie thought she must have misunderstood. At least he had the good sense not to follow her into the bathroom.

The hot water felt heavenly. Callie turned her face toward the shower spray, letting it cascade across her as she woke up. Her hands rested on her belly and she looked down.

"Forget about your mommy's actions last night. Gabriel women are poised and confident. They're sultry and alluring if they choose. You remember that, little one. Poised and confident. You'll be like that."

Poised and confident? Callie was coming to the sorry conclusion that she was never going to manage that aspect of being a Gabriel woman. At least around Armond Marceaux. She just hoped she could muddle through the rest of the morning.

As they angled north through Mississippi, Callie watched the foliage surrounding the Natchez Trace Parkway pass by her car window. The air outside took on a fall chill, and she was glad she'd opted for baggy jeans instead of shorts.

"Do you want to stop at the overlook?" Armond's question broke through her reverie.

At least he'd again showed uncommon good sense by not mentioning last night. "Of course."

He pulled the car onto the narrow lane and wound up the hill to the small parking lot at the top. When he stopped, Callie got out and walked over to the overlook. Below her was the main road, but, as it had been so far, it was empty of other cars. Before her stretched green, only faint touches of red foretelling the fall colors still ahead. Hills, meadows, and forests rolled out before her. Beautiful. Nature in its raw bounty.

The initial fluttering of panic started in her chest, only to calm to a manageable queasiness as Armond joined her.

"Pretty, isn't it?" he commented.

Callie nodded, then sucked in a breath as he laid a hand on her shoulder.

"It seems isolated, but look, there's a herd of cows." He pointed out the distant farm.

She moved from his touch. She'd turned down his offer of sex last February when she failed to come to his cabin; he'd turned down her offer last night. Except for one blazing miscalculation two months ago, they were clear and even on that point.

Somebody should let her libido in on the agreement.

She could be cool and poised, she could handle easy companionship, as long as he didn't touch her in that gentle way.

Armond's fist clenched and his hand lowered. "I'm sorry, Callie, about last night."

"Yeah, me, too." Great, *this* he wanted to talk about.

"I shouldn't have started something I wasn't going to finish."

"I never would have pegged you for a tease."

"Do you still respect me?"

Callie turned to stare at him. The corner of his lips twitched.

She fought the bubbling humor that diluted her embarrassment. "Isn't that usually the woman's line? Or should I turn into the tease?"

"God forbid. I was only strong once."

His answer was so filled with heartfelt horror, Callie burst out laughing, and in a moment Armond joined her. It felt good to laugh with him; Callie didn't like being at odds with anyone, but especially not Armond. She held out her hand. "Truce?"

He picked up her hand and kissed the back of it. "Truce. Today we are simply tourists."

Play tourist they did, and Callie reveled in every moment. The Natchez Trace Parkway was idyllic. The Mississippi Petrified Forest was intriguing. The world's largest magnolia was a waxy beauty. And the flower garden made of discarded gum wrappers and strings was, well, unique.

As they pulled into Memphis, she had to admit that the day had gone more smoothly than expected. Armond was solicitous, polite, and charming. All hints of passion were ruthlessly squelched. In its place remained the perfect companion she'd dated for so many months. She'd had a good time with him.

She was also annoyed as hell.

Too bad she didn't have the guts to confront him about it, truce or not. What could she say? Stop being so nice? Not when that was exactly what she'd thought she wanted from him.

It was a pregnant woman's prerogative to be contrary, but this was ridiculous.

In defense, Callie reverted to her favorite motto: When in doubt, cook.

"Let's find a motel with a kitchenette," she suggested. "I want to cook supper."

"You're not too tired?"

"Not for the meal I'm craving."

"What," he asked, wary, "are you craving?"

"Pasta. Olive oil. Onions, peppers, garlic, some mustard greens, ginger."

"I'm sorry I asked."

"Humor the pregnant woman."

Armond gave her the resigned look that men have been giving their pregnant women for an eternity. Not to her surprise, he did find a motel with a kitchenette. Her next stop was the nearby grocery store, which, she was pleased to discover, carried a good variety of chiles as well as fresh vegetables and whole-wheat pasta. Callie roamed happily through the store.

As he followed her, Armond found his natural inclination was to gravitate toward the deli, bakery, and take-out. Apparently he didn't spend a lot of time in grocery stores, except maybe for coffee and dry cereal. Going with Callie was a decidedly more sensual experience, he decided. He paid no attention to the food, only to Callie.

She smelled peppers and held them for him to judge, not that he could tell any difference beyond green or yellow. She tasted a tiny leaf from a bunch of greens she then added to their cart. She weighed oranges in her hand. She hunted for miso, charmed a salesclerk into going into the back and bringing out two bunches of fresh broccoli, and helped a fellow shopper decide between serrano or jalapeño chiles. She skipped aisles, then backtracked when she remembered something else she needed.

Once he caught her lingering over a package of fresh chicken. "No meat," he reminded her. Hastily, she shoved the package back.

It was the same in the motel kitchen. Armond loved watching the way she moved when she cooked, when she lost all awkwardness and doubts. He liked the play of muscles in her arms and shoulders, the way she bit her lip in concentration. He liked a woman who knew how to handle a knife. He elected, though, to keep those thoughts quiet, when waiting for him tonight was a single room with two beds and very little room between them.

Callie handed him a knife and brought him into the center of her whirlwind of activity by pointing to the celery and peppers and commanding, "Chop." And she had the decency not to laugh at his mangled attempts.

The knife did not feel awkward in his hand, but using it on vegetables did. Armond wondered briefly what that said about him, then watched, fascinated, as Callie combined raw ingredients, a minimal kitchen, and skill to create a meal whose color and aroma set his mouth watering.

She wouldn't let him taste it until they were seated at the small table on their patio overlooking the hotel garden. Armond uncorked a nonalcoholic bottle of sparkling cider and poured two glasses while Callie dug into her plate.

"I hope you don't mind if I start," she said around a mouthful. "I'm starved."

"Go ahead. What do you call this dish?"

"It doesn't have a name. It's just things I threw together. Anyone could make it."

Didn't Callie realize how special a talent she had? It wasn't the healing skills of her family. It was something unique: She had the ability to bring comfort. Armond set the bottle down with a thunk. "Why do you say that?"

She shrugged. "Everyone cooks."

"I don't. With no recipe, a strange kitchen, ingredients you just chose, not everyone can make a meal that smells and looks as good as this. It's like you have this"—he shook his head, looking for the word—"intuition about food."

"I never believed my intuition and instincts were too reliable."

"They can be." If he had learned anything recently it was not to ignore those gut-level feelings.

Except the one about taking Callie to bed, of course.

"But cooking seems like such an ordinary skill."

He gave a snort of irritation. "You own a restaurant, a good one, and have you ever watched yourself on TV?"

"Not if I can help it. I always see the flaws."

"You make it look easy, when I know it isn't." He sat down and speared a mangled pepper in illustration. "Those are gifts."

She stopped eating to tilt her head and look at him. "You really mean that."

"Of course I do."

"You think I'm talented?"

"Don't you?"

She sat back, looking pensive. "I never really thought of it like that." After a moment she nodded toward his plate. "How do you like it?"

Armond laughed. "I haven't tasted it yet."

"It's a little spicy."

"I like spicy." He grabbed up a forkful and ate.

A little spicy! "Callie," he gasped, grabbing for his glass. "That's hot!"

"The extra chiles too much? By the way, milk works better than water at combating the fire." She scooped up another mouthful and ate.

She didn't seem to be having any problems. No sweat broke out on her brow. She could breathe without gasping. Armond took another taste. A very tiny taste. It was still hot, but this time other flavors, intense flavors, good flavors, broke through. "You like it this hot?"

She nodded. "Still think I've got talent?"

"That, and a cast-iron throat."

Chapter Fourteen

They lingered over coffee Armond bought from the motel restaurant. It wasn't gourmet, but it was hot and strong. By mutual accord they left off the lights and sat in darkness. Moonlight tinted the garden leaves silver, but otherwise the night was dark and still. So still Armond could hear the soft inhale-exhale of Callie's breath and catch the faint scents of spices and pepper.

A scene both romantic and dangerous to his peace of mind, yet Armond sat quiet. The faint tension of desire hummed through him like the tiny buzz from a bottle of wine, pleasurable but under his control.

"What color do you suppose the baby's hair will be?" Callie's pensive question hung in the quiet night.

"Brunette. Golden-brown hair like her mother, I hope."

"No blue-eyed blondes for us," Callie added with a

laugh. "Maybe she'll have your gray eyes. Do they run in your family?"

"They're rare." It was a safe guess. He didn't have the slightest idea, and tonight the evasions sat heavy on his conscience. He preferred to be straightforward about things, Armond realized with a start, yet he had held secrets all his life. He rubbed his forehead, chasing back the first throb of headache that accompanied the sudden knowledge. "Have you thought of any names for the baby?"

"Some. Do you have any suggestions?"

"Don't name her, or him, after someone in the family," he said after a moment. "At least not the first name. A child should have her own identity."

"Not big on family ties? How about Louisa? Callie, California. Louisa, Louisiana."

"Louisa's pretty."

If it was a boy, he could be Louis. Despite Callie's claim, Armond couldn't stop thinking of his child as a son. Male egotism, he supposed, although he felt no strong urges that the family name had to be continued at all costs.

Because you know no family lineage. The thought slid inside him, accompanied by another throb. When he was relaxed and open like this, these tidbits of self-knowledge seemed to return more easily, sidling in like unannounced guests. Armond set the coffee down just in case the memories also returned. He would not frighten Callie by letting her witness another bout of pain.

"I want her to like spicy food," Callie said after a moment. "And I talk to her when I cook, telling her what I'm doing."

"That's why you mumble in the kitchen," he teased.

She flashed him the grin he loved. "Are you telling me I talk to myself?"

"Only part of the time. The rest you're talking to someone else."

That pretty grin again, then her gaze returned to the garden. "My grandmother brought me into the kitchen when I was a baby; that's where I first learned to cook. I'd forgotten that until now; it was so long ago."

"So cooking's as much a Gabriel trait as healing."

"Maybe Louisa will have both." Callie tilted her head and looked at him. "What family talents might she get from you?"

"Perhaps a talent for winemaking," he said easily, hiding an uncomfortable thought.

Would his child have this strange gift that plagued him? It wasn't something he'd considered before. It wasn't a legacy he would wish on his child. But if it was a legacy, he would be there to help.

Unlike my father. A stab of an ancient betrayal sucked away his breath.

When a gust of breeze blew across the garden, it startled him with its burst of cooler air and the unpleasant aroma of old grease from a nearby restaurant. That quick pain pierced the black wall of amnesia. Images of betrayal tumbled through in a jumbled mass, mingling with the grief of repeated losses.

Nausea roiled in his throat as he saw and experienced. Waiting in a greasy restaurant. A boy and a woman. In the garden, Armond gripped the chair arms, knowing the image was an early one. That made it no less powerful. He guessed the woman beside him was his mother, and they waited for a father he'd never seen, a father who never came. His first taste of betrayal. His first taste of the crush of panic when he realized a man at the cash register had done something bad, but not knowing what and not knowing what to do about it.

Never again. His was, ultimately, a solitary path.

Another image crashed through with a jabbing pain. Waiting at a cold and sterile police station. Knowing friends were killed in a vicious, bloody fight. Vigilante justice gone bad, all because *he* had known who started the turf war.

Never again. The law would be his route.

Waiting for Callie at the cabin.

Never again. He would not be vulnerable.

But Callie had refused to give up her hold on him.

Each image flashed like a strobe, bright and piercing and tormenting. Armond sat rigid and silent in his chair, his eyes squeezed shut as the assault of emotional pains long forgotten competed with the physical pains of headache and nausea. At last all faded, and the tension left his shoulders, leaving him sore from head to gut.

He drew in a careful breath and glanced over at Callie. She gazed dreamily out at the garden, unaware of his turmoil. A faint gleam came from her gold-brown hair, and her lips held that perpetual half-smile. Her hands rested in an unconsciously protective gesture against her belly.

Desire mixed with the fierce need to keep her like this, keep her safe. He didn't want Callie to be touched by the visions he saw, didn't want her to guess the indescribable hells that came to him without his will.

He could answer, now, her question about why law enforcement was so important to him. Without the law, knowing who was guilty wasn't enough. Without the law, the only way of bringing them to justice was through vigilantism, and that he could not tolerate. That was not the way.

LE was all he could depend on.

If his job was LE, it was time to do his job. Abruptly, Armond pushed to his feet. "I need to go out for a while. Lock the door behind me. I'll take a key."

"Is this one of those command times? When I need only obey?"

"Consider it a strong suggestion."

"All right." Callie watched, in silence, as he left.

Armond had had another one of his headaches. Callie sipped her coffee. This one was over more quickly but had left him more shaken than he'd been before. Stress? Not bloody likely. Something was going on.

Although she couldn't believe he was sick, and he firmly believed he wasn't, it wouldn't hurt to get another opinion. Frowning, she dialed home, planning to leave a message on the machine.

To her surprise, Lillian was home, and Callie briefly explained the problem.

"You should stop this crazy 'tour,' Callie," was her mother's advice. "Fly straight up to Michigan. The Munson Medical Facility there is excellent."

"Armond says he doesn't need a hospital. I thought you might have some alternative suggestions to help him."

"Aspirin. He needs tests."

"Mom," she said softly, "I'm worried. Can't you help?"

There was a moment's pause, then her mother sighed. "Pressure points. The soft spot between his thumb and forefinger—pinch it. Apply deep pressure for one minute on each side. Keep repeating, and the headache should ease. And put ice on his temples. Very briefly, as the ice can be painful. That's all I can suggest without seeing him myself. Do you want me to meet you at your next stop?"

"No!"

Lillian was silent; then she gave a mild curse. "I knew this would happen. You're falling for him again."

"Damn it, Mom, how did you get that out of one word?"

"I'm the village witch, remember? Didn't you two learn anything last winter?"

Callie gripped the phone. "What do you know about last winter?" She hadn't told anyone about the aborted trip to the cabin.

"Armond called here, looking for you."

Armond had called. "What did you tell him?"

"The truth. You were out with that nice Frederick Frasier."

"Mother! That wasn't a date. Frederick is a chef, a friend, and we were doing our monthly demonstration at the New Orleans School of Cooking."

"Frederick isn't just a chef, he's chef at Voisin. And you always went out for drinks afterward. Your Armond just didn't wait to hear all that."

"And I bet you weren't real quick to squeeze it in, either."

"Remember, you are a Gabriel, Callie. Gabriel women raise their daughters alone. I'll be blunt; men contribute sperm. We do not welcome their interference, especially a strong man such as Armond Marceaux. He can only break your heart when he leaves. And he will leave."

"I know that," she whispered.

"Don't disappoint me," her mother continued firmly. "Your choices affect us all."

Callie bit her lip. Instinct told her there was a flaw there, but she wasn't strong enough, didn't trust herself enough, to argue. "Trust me, I won't forget."

There was silence on the other end, then her mother's voice gentled. "Tell me, what have you seen on this grand tour?"

Callie related all the stops they'd made and the ones she was planning to visit as they headed up to

Kentucky, and soon they fell into the easy conversation that had so characterized her life growing up. At last Callie yawned and looked at her watch. "I'd better get to bed, Mom."

"Take care," Lillian said softly.

"I will."

"I'll come up to Traverse City when you get there. We'll find out what's wrong with Armond." Her mother hung up before Callie could protest.

Armond found another Internet Cafe and was soon logged onto his e-mail. Conrad Titus was still worried about him, urged him to come in from undercover. Just a few days, he assured his boss, without explaining the delay.

For the first time Armond felt his confidence had some basis. He felt the block giving. Each day, new pieces of himself returned, slipping him back into his old, comfortable skin. He just needed a little time.

A short missive from Abramowicz proclaimed the notes a dead end. As the odd feeling of being watched had abated since they left Louisiana, Armond began to wonder if Callie wasn't right in her assessment that the notes were no threat.

One e-mail puzzled him. From Hugh Pendragon, it read simply: *Wrong answer.* Apparently Pendragon hadn't liked the last contact. Who was the man? What part was he playing? Armond considered asking Conrad Titus, then decided against it, opting still for caution.

Just a few more days to keep the balls juggling.

The last message made him smile. From Mark Hennessy again. It was clear Mark had found out about Callie's pregnancy, for the note was filled with a good-natured ribbing about sexual prowess and sperm strength, but the underlying message was clear: make an honest woman of her.

No bigger prig than a reformed rake, thought Armond with amusement, suddenly realizing he instinctively knew a lot about Mark Hennessy. *Don't you know I would if I could?*

Armond leaned back in his chair, stunned. He would marry Callie if she'd agree. Give their child his name. *His* child would not be raised a bastard. Like him. He sucked in a breath, knowing it was the right thing to do, but that didn't make it any less frightening. Ever after was a long time, and if he took vows he would keep them.

If he hadn't lost his memory, would he have come to the same decision? From the last snatches of memory, he knew he thought that he was destined to be alone, that he'd never marry and must follow a solitary path. Not knowing yourself forced you to abandon a lot of misconceptions and preconceived notions, though, like that one that had sat with him for so many years. Being with Callie before he remembered he shouldn't be had let her work her magic on him.

Of course, he'd have to be careful not to scare Callie off with those odd talents of his, but he could do it. She didn't want to know about his LE work, and he recognized now that he was adept at keeping the compartments of his life separate. Callie would be the woman he came home to, the haven away. His peace.

He flipped off the computer and left to find an open gun shop with a shooting range. He needed to keep in practice.

Callie drove through the Kentucky hills, enjoying the feel of the car swooping down inclines and around curves. Her fingers tapped to sounds of Faith Hill on the radio. Country seemed the basic radio choice in these parts. Armond sat beside her, studying the map and a guidebook, not seeming the least bit concerned that Louisiana was flat and this was the first time she'd ever driven hills like this, if you discounted the High Rise bridge over the Intracoastal Canal in New Orleans.

For the past two days they'd continued the light, friendly relationship that Armond had adopted since their morning at the overlook. He was the charming companion from their dates, and if secretly she missed the wild man from the cabin, she didn't admit it aloud. They maintained the facade by virtue of never touching each other.

With one exception: At night, when her back hurt, Armond would gently roll her over and massage away the aches, leaving her muscles and tendons loose and her insides aching instead with the need to hold him and have him moving inside her.

Yet she did nothing, made no move of invitation. Not until she knew he wouldn't draw away again.

This morning, however, she'd come perilously close to the conclusion that she wanted him enough to take that risk. She'd awoken when he'd gotten up from the sofa. She'd glanced at the clock and given a mental groan at the hour, but she hadn't fallen back asleep. Instead she'd watched as he'd stretched and rubbed his hands through his hair and across his chest, the play of muscles as elegant as a ballet. She watched him perform a rigorous routine of exercises that looked like some cross between yoga and a martial arts regimen, and her heart tripped on the power and beauty of it. She watched as he checked his gun and holster, checked a knife he had hidden somewhere. This was the man at the cabin, the hidden warrior.

And at last it didn't frighten her. It was part of him as much as the genial companion of the past and the caring man of the present.

It was stupid to have these days together and waste them sleeping in separate beds. There would be plenty of time for that later.

Then he'd left to run, quietly locking the door behind him, and she'd taken a cold shower instead.

Callie pressed the gas pedal to maintain speed up a hill. "The fall colors are getting more intense," she observed, seeing the southern green giving way to reds, oranges, yellows, and browns.

Armond glanced out the window. "They look like the sunny side of a rainbow. And they're not even at full peak."

"The sunny side of a rainbow. I like that image, but I can't imagine a whole forest of such brilliant colors. What's it like?"

"Wait and see for yourself. The colors should be at their peak when we get to Michigan."

"I don't want to wait. I want to see it all. Now."

He laughed, the laugh that seemed to come much more easily to him the farther they got from New Orleans. "Greedy. Why didn't you ever travel before, Callie, if you were so eager?"

"Too busy, I guess. And I didn't want to go alone. It's not fun if you can't share it with someone."

"You're close to your family. Couldn't one of them go with you?"

"Tessa and Stacia are nine and ten years older than I am. By the time I was old enough to go, they were firmly entrenched in their careers. They're all so busy. Hey, look, is that a hawk?" She pointed to the swirling bird.

"A bird of prey of some kind."

Callie averted her eyes back to the road when the

bird swooped down for a kill, and Armond returned to his map.

When she and Armond were dating, they'd never had this much time to spend together. The demands of running Greenwood on top of all her other activities had kept her busy, and Armond's job entailed long, odd hours as well, so that they had snatched evenings when they could.

These past seventy-two hours they'd laughed a lot and talked a lot. Mostly their talk centered on the present. Armond avoided talk about the future, although he seemed willing, anxious even, to listen to her talk about the past. Not about the issues dividing them, but about the small matters, like listening to Harry Connick, Jr., at Jazzfest.

"There is someplace I'd like to see." Armond looked up from his map, breaking into her thoughts. "If we head south at the next interstate, we should reach there by suppertime."

"South? Armond, we're almost to Lexington."

Armond just raised a brow. "Your point?"

"We're going north. I thought you expected to spend the night in Lexington."

"We'll still be close enough to make our next stop. Besides, I'm not the one who insisted on an extra day's jog across the length of Tennessee to see the House of Johnny Cash, Davy Crockett's birthplace, and the Museum of Ancient Bricks."

"You were impressed with the brick from the Tower of Babel. Admit it."

"Once we found the museum."

"I couldn't help it that there were no signs on the building. So, where do you want to go?"

"Mammoth Cave. You can't drive through Kentucky without seeing Mammoth Cave."

"I can. Why do you want to see a damp cave?"

"Asks the woman who spent an hour and a half in the Ventriloquism Museum."

"At least I didn't make you tour Graceland."

"*Merde,* no. There are limits to a man's patience."

Callie burst out laughing. Armond had stayed true to his promise, letting her choose where they would go, but, yes, she supposed there were limits even to his good nature. Mostly she avoided National and State parks—pristine nature—but if Armond wanted to go to Mammoth Cave . . . Callie turned south. "Mammoth Cave it is."

She just hoped he didn't plan on her going on one of those cave tours. Nothing more uncivilized than being underground with no natural light, dripping water, and rocks.

He unfolded a brochure. "I've got a list of the cave tours we can take. How about this? It's got . . . oh, wait, no, it won't do."

She took her eyes from the winding road to glance at him. "Why not?"

"Three hours. No bathrooms. And I suppose the lantern tours are out. We'll find another, *ma chérie.*"

Swell. The tiny thrill at hearing him call her *chérie* almost made up for the prospect of facing all that great outdoors.

"Marceaux has some kind of psychic talent." The doctor's voice sounded almost eager over the phone.

Titus refrained from an I-told-you-so. "What is it?"

"Not telepathy; I'm not sure what it is. It's nothing I've ever seen. That's why we missed it at first; he didn't respond to the usual tests. But the brain waves . . . something is definitely there. I want to study him some more."

Titus shivered at the cold excitement. If it had not meant his own survival, he could not send another member of the Bureau to that hellish cave of stainless steel.

A desperate man could not afford scruples.

"And now you've lost him," Titus said softly.

The doctor was silent a moment. "Marceaux surfaced in Memphis, then disappeared. Use your Bureau to find him."

"No." Bringing in other agents increased the risk of his exposure. He'd continue to use Centurion's men.

So, think. Where was Marceaux? Titus pulled out a map. Callie Gabriel was scheduled to be in Traverse City, but they hadn't followed any of the logical routes there. In fact, no one seemed to know where they were, no one who could be discreetly questioned, that is. And he didn't want a confrontation in Traverse City, when Marceaux would be waiting, when there might be interested witnesses.

Titus looked at the map again. Where might they surface? If Marceaux was giving the woman a little vacation in exchange for sleeping privileges, where might they go? Only one spot stuck out.

Mammoth Cave.

Chapter Fifteen

If a grandmother could do it, so could she. While Armond talked to the ranger, Callie sidled over to the white-haired woman who was bent over, tying a tennis shoe. This tour was small, since it left from a remote part of the park rather than the main entrance.

"Hi," said Callie. "You ever go on one of these tours before?"

The grandmother straightened. "Dozens. I love caves." She directed an irritated sniff toward the ranger. "And they say I'm too old for the spelunker's expedition."

"Spelunker's—?"

"Cave crawling." The woman gave Callie a friendly smile. "I hope we see some bats this time."

Bats? Oh, sh—Callie hadn't realized there were bats. "Are there other animals? I, uh, thought we were going to see, you know, cave stuff."

"Animals are 'cave stuff.' " The woman leaned forward. "I hear the crickets are really big. And this tour goes by the underground river."

"What's in the underground river?"

"Eyeless, albino fish, shrimp, and crayfish."

That did it. Callie eased over to Armond and the ranger.

"There are about two hundred steps at the beginning of the tour," Armond told her, then he turned to the ranger. "My wife is pregnant. Is it dangerous for her?"

His wife? Then again, she couldn't see Armond announcing to a strangers "My traveling companion is pregnant." His wife. Callie was so bemused by hearing Armond call her that, she almost missed the ranger's answer.

"We consider it moderately strenuous, sir." The ranger gave her an assessing look, probably noticing that she wasn't ungainly yet. "If she was fit before the pregnancy and her doctor hasn't given her restrictions, she should be able to do it, but if you have any doubts, we'd prefer you stay topside."

Armond touched her shoulder. "The tour is about to leave. Do you think you can handle it?"

He was giving her an out. She had three choices.

One, she could stay up here alone, in the remote woods, with the ticks and the bears. Yeah, right; that possibility ranked with such likely events as her eating a whole goose and leaping tall buildings with a single bound.

Two, she could ask Armond to skip the tour and stay with her. He'd do it in a heartbeat, she knew. Skip the one thing he'd asked to do this trip—if you didn't count the kissing parts.

Three, she could go with him. It couldn't be that bad, could it? Not with Armond at her side.

Armond's gray eyes searched her face. Callie guessed that her complexion had turned pasty, because he abruptly turned to the ranger. "No, we'll—"

"I can go," she interrupted.

Armond shook his head. "No, Callie, we'll stay—"

Callie looked over at the gray-haired woman doing toe touches. "If Cave Granny can manage, so can I. I'm physically fit." She flexed one arm. "I lift heavy pots, stand on my feet for hours. Being a chef is tough work."

His mouth lifted in that smile, the one that melted her insides softer than chocolate in the sun. "A regular Jack Lalane. Are you sure about this?"

"Sure, I'm sure," she lied. "What Louisiana girl wouldn't be looking forward to seeing blind crawfish?"

"A vegetarian one?"

"Where's your sense of adventure?" She tapped him playfully on the arm, wondering how she'd gotten herself into the position of persuading *him* to go.

"We gonna sit here jawing all afternoon or are we going to see some caves?" demanded Cave Granny.

Armond and the ranger both looked at Callie.

Ah, hell, she'd come on this trip to see new things. "Let's go," she said brightly.

The cave wasn't so bad. It was cool inside—a perpetual 54 degrees, said the ranger—and Callie was glad she'd brought her jacket. As they descended the steps into the earth, the ranger explained the forces that had created this, the longest recorded cave system in the world. Callie paid more attention to the rocks glistening with dampness and the lights clinging to the slippery walls.

Armond walked in front of her, yet he repeatedly

looked back, missing nothing of her careful descent. Once, her foot shifted on the steps, a slight hitch in her traction, and he was there, almost before she realized the slip herself, steadying her. His palm, warm and strong, supported her until she took the next step.

At the bottom, Callie found herself in a vault so large she could barely see the top. All around her was stone, the foundation of the earth. The solid walls shimmered and danced before her eyes in dizzying vibrations. Her chest hurt, as though the full weight of rock and dirt pressed on top of her head. She looked at the ranger, at Cave Granny, at Armond, assuring herself she wasn't alone, and her breath came a little easier.

Armond laid a hand on her shoulder. "Are you okay?"

"Fine." The man didn't miss a thing.

"I must caution you not to touch any of the formations we see today," intoned the ranger. "The oil on your hands will seal off the delicate balance of dissolution and precipitation, and destroy a process that has continued for a thousand years. And removing anything is a federal offense."

A thousand years of nature at work. Callie grabbed Armond's hand and, to her gratitude, he wrapped his fingers around hers and held her tight.

With his solid nearness and silent support, the panic faded, and Callie began to enjoy the tour. The formations were beautiful. Lacy fans and webs of gypsum, columns and falls of limestone, and jagged crystals of selenite formed an eerie landscape of solid-on-solid. Callie stared, entranced by rocks so unique they had their own name: Soda Straw, Snowball, Bridal Veil. She forgot she was descending a mile into what the Greeks would have deemed the gates of

Tartarus in her fascination with things she'd never thought to see, in her pleasure at touching Armond and feeling the brush of his body against hers. His masculine scent was a welcome comfort in the oddly unscented air of the cave.

She had everything under control.

The ranger stopped their small group. "Most of us never get a chance to see what true darkness is, but the brave first spelunkers had to face it, knowing that if their candles blew out, they would be lost forever. Just to give you a taste of what they faced, please be absolutely silent and don't move."

Then he turned out the lights.

Black. Black, black, black. Not a speck of light, not a shadow. Faint gasps from the tourists, then utter silence. Except . . . water dripped and tiny claws scratched on the rock. Nature at its most primitive.

Alone. She could see, feel, sense, hear no one around her. The dark was so complete, even the existence of her own body was in doubt.

Instant panic.

Callie's lungs heaved, seeking air in the smothering blackness. Her free hand jerked, or she thought it did, but there was only a sensation of movement, and she wasn't sure where her hand ended up.

Her breath rasped against her teeth, but the blackness, the raw nature, squeezed her chest, keeping her screams in her throat. Her nails dug into Armond's palm. Somehow he knew, somehow he found her in that stygian hell, for he wrapped his arms around her. Callie knew she was trembling against him, but she couldn't pretend to be strong and pretend she didn't care. She leaned on the haven of his solid, strong body, buried her head against his chest, clutched him close.

"Turn on the lights." Armond's voice rang out,

though Callie knew the reality must have only been seconds of darkness.

The blessed light returned.

It didn't take long for the ranger to assess the situation. He was over at once, talking to Armond in undertones. Totally humiliated by her weakness, Callie still couldn't leave the safety of Armond's embrace. In the primitive part of her brain, the blackness still pressed against her. She couldn't move, not a step forward, not a step backward.

My wife. Can't go on.

Not safe. Wait.

I'll manage. FBI.

She heard snatches of the conversation between the ranger and Armond. Both knew she couldn't go farther. Rather than abort the tour for the rest, the ranger wanted them to wait here for him to radio for help in getting out, while Armond insisted she needed to get out now, and he could get them both to the surface.

The ranger looked to Callie, then gave Armond a thorough assessment. What he saw there must have reassured him, for he nodded. "The route is marked by the low lights."

"I've been watching."

Callie guessed he'd noticed every detail of their route in. There was very little that escaped Armond's quiet observation.

"We're going back, Callie," he said in a low voice, his hand stroking her hair, gentling her.

It didn't stop her trembling, but it did help her breathe.

"Just take a step with me. That's it. One more step; it will get better, I promise. Ah, *ma petite,* you're doing it."

With his soothing voice, he led her back the way

they'd come. His body supported her, never let her feel the cool air against her side. Each foot back to the entrance, Callie focused on resonant voice, warm skin, careful touch, and felt her panic receding, her heartbeat slowing, her breath easing.

In its place came complete and utter humiliation.

At the top, she sank down onto a picnic bench and buried her head in her hands. Armond sat beside her, one arm wrapped around her shoulders. He tugged down her hands, then tilted her chin up with one finger. "Keep your head up. You'll feel better."

She wasn't sure if he meant physically or emotionally, but she was sure nothing could let her feel better about being such a fool. When she looked into Armond's gray eyes, though, she found no laughter, no annoyance, only sympathy. A brown leaf twirled between them, caught in an autumn breeze. His thumb traced beneath her eyes, and Callie feared she'd been crying and didn't even know it.

She didn't want his pity.

Callie stiffened her jaw, ignoring the ache as her muscles relaxed. "I'm sorry for that. I'm all right now."

His expression said he didn't believe her, but he wisely didn't voice the thought. "You want to talk about what happened down there?"

"Not really."

His thumb stroked gently against her cheek and his fingers burrowed beneath her hair. "But you're going to tell me anyway."

Armond was better at patience than she was. Callie sighed. "I have this little thing about being alone."

He frowned. "You must have been alone sometime."

"It doesn't bother me in the city so much, but in places like this, the great outdoors, I get a little crazy." She waved a hand around. The hardwood forest surrounded them. Callie didn't know any tree names, ex-

226

cept for the white-barked birch; she only knew the trees were sturdy and surrounded by a litter of brown and autumn leaves. Denuded vines and brush filled the spaces between. She and Armond were isolated in a silent world of nature. Callie shuddered and turned away. "Out here, my brain says, 'How pretty,' but my gut says, 'Something really, really bad is going to happen.' "

"Ah, *chérie,* this place is tame compared to most places in the world."

"Maybe places you've been, but I've never been out of New Orleans." She rolled her eyes but still couldn't move from the slow stroke of his hand. The panic inside her was rapidly turning to something else. "God, I am such a wimp, but in that darkness, I was so utterly alone."

"It's not being a wimp to face your fears."

"I didn't face them. I turned into a quivering, gasping mass of gelatin."

"You faced them by going into the cave. You just didn't conquer them. Yet."

She sat with him, letting the cold inside her transform to something smooth and warm. If her breath caught again, it wasn't because of fear, but because of the need he aroused so easily.

"Have you ever been afraid of something, Armond?" she asked at last.

"All the time," he answered promptly. "It goes with the territory of what I do."

"No, I don't mean the very real dangers you face." She didn't even want to think about the men with weapons, the crazed evils he must have faced. Even though she knew how capable he was, she didn't want to think of him vulnerable like that. "I mean something irrational. Did you conquer it?"

He was silent, and she felt the tension in his back

where her arms surrounded him. She laid her cheek against his shoulder, knowing he wasn't going to let her see that secret piece of him. "That's okay; you don't have to answer."

She lifted her head, and as the panic receded, Callie realized she was hungry. Starving, even. She rummaged in her pockets, only to discover she'd eaten her last batch of snacks.

"You got anything to eat?"

Armond shook his head.

They'd left their car at the main parking lot and taken a shuttle bus to the tour start. Callie checked her watch. "The tour won't be back for another two hours, and the shuttle is even longer. How far is it to the visitor's center?"

"Two miles."

"Let's walk back."

"I don't think that's a good idea. It'll be through the woods, and there won't be a ranger around if we run into trouble. Besides, you're pregnant."

"Pregnant, not incapacitated. I walk a lot more than two miles one night in my kitchen. Please, let's walk back." She didn't want to just wait here, starving. And maybe walking back with Armond would give her the courage to confront, and overcome, that stupid fear. She was so tired of being afraid.

Callie drew a deep breath. "As for no ranger, what do I need a ranger for when I've got you?"

He stared at her a moment. She wondered why gray was always described as cool and misty. Armond's eyes were like molten silver, and the metal etched straight into her heart and lower. She swayed forward, her lips parting.

He stood. "Let's go."

Armond left a note for the ranger, then stayed close to her as they started down the narrow deer path. It didn't look like a well-traveled route, but Callie had no doubt Armond had studied the maps and knew exactly where he was going.

They walked in silence, the only two people in this remote corner of the park. She wished she had her CD player. Callie's nerves started caterwauling, the fluttering panic touched her stomach, but she trudged on, drawn by the pressure of Armond's hand grasping hers.

Soon he started talking to her, pointing out first a colorful leaf, a patch of red berries that he claimed would make her very sick if she ate them, a mushroom, the sound of the wind through the trees. Then he stopped and wrapped his arms around her, pointing her toward the forest.

"Look," he whispered.

She forced herself to look at the details of the land before her, not thinking of it as nature, but rather as a pattern of shadows or a shading of colors or a source of the green foods she loved to eat. "What?"

"There."

Her gaze followed where he pointed; then a giant tremble spread through her as she saw what he'd noticed. A huge spiderweb, with the spider in the center. The spider was orange and black, like some gruesome Halloween creature, and Callie shook harder. She really, really disliked spiders.

"Look at the waterdrops on the web," Armond said. "There're only a few left, but they glisten like liquid diamonds. See the web sway in the wind, delicate as a strand of hair, yet strong."

"Like the thread on the doll's dress."

"Exactly." His breath was warm against her ear. Did she imagine the brush of his lips against her neck? As he continued to murmur sweet facts, gradually, she saw a bit of what he saw, not with the eyes of fear, but with the eyes of wonder. And as panic receded a second time, the desire came back all that stronger. Not that it had ever truly left. With this man, she seemed to go around in a constant slow simmer.

His voice trailed off, leaving only the rustle of leaves. Armond's arms were a powerful band around her, his body flush against her back, and now she noticed the semiarousal pressed against her, though he made no move. His scent teased her, and when she shifted, her breasts brushed against the curve of his arm.

That he noticed. She felt his intake of breath.

"Going insane," he said, breaking the silence.

Callie turned in his arms. "Excuse me?"

"You asked about irrational fears." His jaw worked a moment, then he continued, "There were times in my life, I feared I was going crazy. It is the worst thing I can imagine. To lose control of your very being."

Callie stilled, holding her breath, afraid the slightest movement would shut him down again.

His face was raw, harsh. "Don't take this wrong, but sometimes, when I touch you, when we . . . kiss, it scares me. Like right now. I feel uncontrolled." He bit off the words, as if he couldn't give voice to any more.

"You feel this?" Callie took one of the biggest risks of her life. She stood on tiptoe and kissed him.

With her emotions so close to the surface, with her body and skin primed by his touch, it was instant forest fire. Smokey Bear wouldn't have a chance against this one.

She felt Armond's deep inhalation, and the fire whooshed into a raging inferno, consuming them both in its wildness. He pulled her flat against him and his fingers tunneled into her hair, holding the back of her head, holding her in place for the tilt of his head as he deepened the kiss. She opened for him, mouth and heart and soul, and his tongue swept in, claiming her mouth. Her heart and soul he'd long ago owned.

At his waist, her fists bunched the fabric of his shirt. She wanted to pull it off, wanted skin to skin, heedless of the fact that they were smack out in the open. He crushed her to him, but his hands could no more stop their mad exploration than hers could. Chest, neck, wrists, pelvis, hair, thighs, her hands fluttered to any part of him she could reach, while he found a sensitive spot behind her ear that made her shiver. He tunneled beneath her shirt and she rediscovered the exquisite texture of his palm on her breasts.

When she touched him low, began an erotic massage atop the straining fabric of his jeans, though, he broke away.

"Callie. We can't do this. Not here."

He wasn't going to stop the burning. Not this time. Callie gave an unladylike curse and grabbed his belt, pulling his hips against hers. "Do you hear anyone coming? Didn't think so."

His hands cupped her cheeks. "You should have a bed."

She fumbled with his belt, couldn't figure out the buckle. "If I'd wanted a bed, I wouldn't have started this."

"It's the aftermath of fear."

"I'm not on fire because of *fear.*"

"The baby—"

"Should meet her father."

Armond gave a strangled laugh. "Callie—"

"Shut up, Armond." She looked at him and knew her heart was in her eyes, but she didn't care. "The only reason you should stop this is if you don't want me. Otherwise, give me one good memory of being outdoors."

Those gray eyes burned. "Last chance. It won't be delicate."

"I don't care."

With a muttered curse, he bent to her again. He kissed her with an expert kiss that stripped her of any semblance of reason.

Only feel. Only burn.

He backed her up to the edge of the path, then stopped, looking.

"What now?" she gasped.

"Poison ivy."

"None?"

"None." He braced her against a smooth-barked tree, then his hands jerked down the zipper of her jacket. He tugged open the buttons of her blouse, shoved her knit shirt upward with an impatient gesture, and then he leaned forward and took her breast in his mouth. For all his urgency, he suckled easily on it while his hand treated the other side.

Her breasts were so sensitive, though, and Callie gave a tiny scream of pleasure. It echoed clear and deep.

He immediately halted, his breath warm against the moisture left on her skin. "Did I hurt you?"

"No. Don't you dare stop now." She kissed his neck, stroked his hair, touched him low, undid his zipper. To hell with the buckle.

"I won't." He undid the buckle for her.

She slipped her hands inside, ran them across the silky length of him, the taut skin and damp tip. "Come inside me, Armond," she begged, past pride or coherence.

"Callie," he groaned.

She made short work of her jeans' fastening, slipped out of one leg, and then leaned back against the tree in invitation.

Armond accepted. He surged inside her, seating himself to the hilt.

It felt so good. He felt so good.

"Ah, Callie, I wanted to remember this," he breathed.

Callie wrapped her legs around his waist, trusting in his strength to hold her. His hands supported her shoulder blades, keeping her from rubbing against the tree as he filled her with long strokes, nearly pulling out, then plunging back deep. Their clothing was barely disturbed, just her breasts and two vital areas exposed, but her skin burned with the pressure of him, the friction as they rubbed against each other.

Too fast, too high, so soon she reached the flash point. She wanted to draw it out. She couldn't wait. Her body jerked with the pleasure, tightening on him, a drawn-out sigh escaping her.

Armond gave a guttural shout and spilled deep inside her, his hips pulsing against her.

Fire flashed to blue-hot, a single explosion that folded down upon them in a red afterglow as Callie sagged against the tree, savoring the weight of Armond against her.

Neither spoke.

At last Armond nuzzled her neck, giving her a tender, intimate kiss that left her with a silly grin and a pleased heart. His hand moved down her back, then came to the front to caress her abdomen, and his little finger curled around her belly button. "You've got a navel ring."

He said that as though he'd never seen it, yet he'd talked about it before. The glow cooled a tiny bit.

"Are you okay?" he asked.

Still out of breath, she could only nod.

He smiled a little against her neck, and his fingers rubbed against the slight curve of her belly. "Too fast, but at least this time you weren't a virgin."

Callie froze, her breath caught in her throat.

Armond's hand stilled, almost as if he realized he'd said something really stupid.

Callie unwrapped her legs, hoping they would support her weight, and pushed against his shoulder, willing him to look at her. He met her gaze, but she couldn't read the expression in his guarded eyes.

"What are you talking about? Don't you remember our discussion—?" The words died as a whole lot of odd facts clicked into place.

Ah, Callie, I wanted to remember this.

The glow died to ash, and she knew the other side of gray.

"You don't remember, do you?" Frantically, she searched his face for some denial, while she clutched her shirt together.

She got back a blank.

"You don't remember any of it."

Chapter Sixteen

Armond cursed. The incredible pleasure; he'd wanted to hold on to it with both hands, reconnect in some minor way. This was why men never talked after sex. Their brains weren't engaged.

He hated the wounded look in her eyes. Hated that he had put it there.

He'd begun to believe he would get his memory back without her, or anyone, ever knowing. How wrong he was.

She was fumbling with her shirt, her pants. He tried to help, but she brushed him away. Instead, he righted himself.

"How much have you forgotten?" she asked flatly.

"Everything about my identity and my life."

"At the cabin, you didn't recognize me, so coming back to New Orleans had nothing to do with me or the baby. Why did you come back?"

Best to give her the remaining truth. "Because you recognized me. And you seemed to trigger my memory."

"Those headaches?"

"Memory flashes."

"And I didn't guess a thing." She gave a shaky laugh and pushed away from the tree. "All along, you've been using me for a walk down memory lane."

It was the truth, at least in part, although what happened today, the wild feelings she aroused in him, had nothing to do with his memory. Armond didn't think she wanted to hear that; it would be up to him to show her.

"Callie—"

"Don't." She held up a hand, then started down the path. "Don't try to convince me you care about me, or our child, when you didn't even remember its *conception*. I'm surprised you believed me."

"I never doubted you."

Her snort of disbelief said it all.

"I do care about the baby. I swear, Callie, she's not going to grow up without a father. Not like we did."

She ignored that. "You are one hell of an actor, Armond Marceaux."

One thing they had to get clear. He grabbed her elbow, then dropped it at her glare. "Callie, you can't tell anyone about the memory loss."

"What?"

"Do you think I would have kept it from you if it wasn't important?" He shoved up his sleeves and pointed to the crook of his arm and the veins on his wrists. "What does that look like?"

She stared at the fading bruises, her jaw set. "That you've been shooting up. Except you'd never touch that poison."

"Somebody gave it to me."

"They addicted you?" She raised stricken eyes to him, and from the concern he drew a faint hope that he hadn't destroyed everything between them.

"No. The drug was something designed to enhance psychic powers. It's not addictive, but it did have the effect of wiping out my memory."

"You don't have psychic powers," she scoffed. "Do you? Oh, God, Armond don't tell me you're a mind reader or have telekinesis or can start fires."

"Of course not." Something told him now was not the time to expose the odder aspects of his psyche.

"Why would they give it to you, then?"

"I was hunting someone, a traitor in the Bureau, and I ended up in some Frankenstein experiment as a result. That's all I know for sure, and until I get my memory back, I don't know who."

"You don't know who to trust?"

"I know I can trust you. *That's* why I came back with you."

That seemed to give her pause. "How did you know you could trust me?"

"Because there is something about you, Callie, that is radiantly honest."

She frowned. "I don't know that I like being transparent."

"Not transparent. Honest. But you see why I couldn't tell you. Why we can't tell anyone else."

She took off back down the path. "No."

"Because somebody's looking for me, and only if they think I can do them some harm will they come cautiously. I'm buying time; and I need you to help me use it. I need you to help me get my memory back."

"Is that why you made love to me?" she asked, not looking at him.

"I made love to you because I wanted you so badly I was cross-eyed with the need."

He heard her breath catch, and her pace picked up. It was a start.

"And, Callie, remember, if I say duck or run, you do exactly that. That part hasn't changed."

Her sucked in breath was sheer irritation this time. At least there was one positive result from all this. Callie didn't have a single panic attack all the way back to the Visitor's Center.

Armond caught a faint herbal waft from the *gris-gris* he, for some God-only-knows reason, still wore about his neck, and the brief unpleasant odor drew him short. *For protection,* Marie had said.

He halted at the trail head and put out a hand to stop Callie. The hairs on the back of his neck stood up, while the odor from the *gris-qris* strengthened, urging him to look. Something about the Visitor's Center parking lot was off. Armond searched, wondering what had alerted him.

"What is it?" Callie asked.

"Shhh. Keep in the shadows. Don't let anyone see you."

"What—?"

He waved her quiet. There; standing by the bulletin board, studying the park map. Two men, casually dressed, but with the beefy physique of a couple of toughs. Not a gay couple; that much was obvious by their body language. And no wife, kids, girlfriends joined them. He supposed they could be two men out seeing the sights together, but he doubted it.

Armond scanned the parking lot. That was their car, the one that looked ordinary but sat low on heavy-duty tires, indicating it contained more equipment than it appeared to have. The one parked next to Callie's car.

So, they knew about her.

He looked over at her. "I am so sorry I got you into this, but I will get you out."

She leaned closer, looking over his shoulder. Armond ignored the faint scent of wood and leaf from her.

"What do you see?" Callie asked.

He pointed out the two men and the car.

"Are you sure? They look so ordinary."

"I'm sure," he said flatly. He drew in, turning himself over to the instincts and intensive training that would have to serve them here.

"What are we going to do?"

"*I'm* going to get us out of here, then we're going to drive straight up to Traverse City, where you can be safe and I can finish this. After that, we are going to get married so my daughter will know that her father cared enough to give her his name. No child of mine is going to be illegitimate."

"And then?"

"Then if you tell me to leave and go straight to hell, I will do just that." Especially the part about going straight to hell.

"Not much on the details of planning are you, Agent Marceaux?"

"Field agents have to be flexible. Now stay here until I signal it's safe for you to come out."

They were going to have to have a little more discussion on some of the finer points of that plan, Callie decided, but that could come later. The matter of him leaving her to go after the two men alone took precedence.

"What about the amnesia? Can you do this alone?"

He flashed her a look that was pure male hunter. "This isn't knowledge, this is instinct."

Not that she was much of an asset in this situation, but there must be something she could do. "Let me—"

"Stay here, Callie. Don't move, not even your little finger." There was no argument allowed in the steel command. He gave her a quick kiss. "I don't want to be distracted worrying about you."

"Men always say that."

"Because it's true. Your job is to make sure they don't see you."

"Not much of a job."

"But a vital one."

She caught a glimpse of his face as he left—impassive, determined, cool, emotionless except for the eyes. The eyes gave away how instinctual this game of hunter-and-prey was to him.

Then the warrior disappeared into the underbrush.

Mindful of her single job, Callie stayed in the cover where Armond had left her, careful not to move and draw the two men's attention. Instead she waited and watched, trying to see some sign of Armond, yet hoping she wouldn't. Because if she could see him, certainly their two stalkers could, too.

He remained invisible as a phantom.

A bus pulled into the parking lot, the one they would have been on if they hadn't left early and come through the woods. If they hadn't stopped, hadn't made love, the two men might have caught them at the center.

The two men waited by the bus, hidden from the doorway, alert. If she and Armond had been on it, they would have walked right into the men's trap. When the bus was unloaded, the men stopped the ranger and spoke with him. He pointed toward the trail head. Right where Callie was hidden. The men hurried toward her, hands going for what she guessed were weapons.

Damn, damn, damn. Where was Armond?

She tensed, ready to run. Where? Those two men

looked mean and strong. Where could she run that they couldn't catch her? She'd seen how silently Armond could move and knew she didn't have a prayer of evading them by stealth.

Armond said not to move. She'd put her trust in him, trust that he knew what he was doing. She kept frozen in place, the only things moving her stomach acid and her eyes. Even her lungs seemed to have stopped as she watched the men close in on her.

Staying was a stupid decision.

Too late to change now. They'd reached the brush at the edge of the parking lot and plunged into the woods, not fifty yards from her.

They came into the woods and then . . .

The one at the rear went down. Armond slid out from the brush. She didn't see what he'd done—karate chop, Vulcan nerve pinch, knife, God she hoped it wasn't a knife—but only one remained.

The fight between them was swift, silent, and primal. In the end, Armond was left standing, drawing in slow breaths and gazing at the man at his feet. Then he raised his head and stared at her, his face hard and masculine, his gray eyes blank.

This was the warrior underneath the polite companion.

This was the part of him that would take him away from her.

The stiffness deserted Callie and she leaned against a tree for support. Armond swiftly searched the men, took the ammunition out of their weapons, then a moment later was at her side.

"They aren't—You didn't—" She couldn't bear to complete the questions.

He shook his head. "They're just out cold."

"Who are they?"

"No ID on them."

"Were they going to kill you?"

"I think they want me back."

"But you don't want to go back."

"Not on their terms."

She looked at the downed men, saw the weapons at their sides, remembered the steel of their faces, and understood just a little why Armond had kept it all secret. "Do you want to wait until they wake up? Question them?"

He shook his head again. "Too risky. We need to get out of here. Head straight up to Traverse." He laid a hand on her cheek, and she saw the blaze of desire rise in the aftermath of danger. But he made no further move. Instead his hand dropped and the mask slid into place. "I'm sorry. You'll get your trip sometime."

Callie shrugged. "In the meantime we need to get your memory back. You said I trigger it? How?"

That taut desire flashed again. "When you kiss me."

"Fishing is boring." Zeus crossed his legs and braced them on the rail beside his pole.

"Maybe if you used bait . . ." Dion sipped his wine, making no pretense at fishing. He came out here because he liked being on the water, not because he wanted to handle slimy things.

Zeus lifted a haughty chin. "The king of gods does not resort to worms."

"Then use your ring."

"My ring? Ah, well, yes, my ring. All right." He pointed toward the water and rubbed his lightning ring. A tiny electrical bolt sizzled against the Gulf waters. "Hades, missed."

Zeus studied the dark waters, aimed again, and this time crowed in delight when a large, stunned fish rose to the surface. "It just takes patience."

"Patience? You?"

"I'm learning." Zeus nabbed the fish and put it in a cooler of water. Dion knew as soon as the fish had recovered enough to avoid predators Zeus would toss it back. The fun was in the hunt, not the kill.

"Hera," guessed Dion, "is being difficult."

"Hera is being impossible." Zeus sat back in his recliner and put his feet up. Apparently the fishing was over.

"You must want more than she's willing to give." At Zeus's sharp look, Dion lifted one shoulder. "Hera has always been your weak spot. Would you like some wine?" He lifted a goblet.

"From your goblets? *In vino veritas?* I don't think so." Zeus pulled a can of beer from a cooler and popped the top. "Although maybe you could let Hera drink of it."

"I can arrange that." Dion grimaced as his former leader tilted his head back and took a long swallow of the beer. Beer was a drink he never could stomach.

Zeus shook his head. "Tempting, but I'm trying to prove I've changed. I don't think that would further my cause."

"You've changed?" Dion laughed. Except for not seducing any beauteous female within reach, Dion didn't see many changes in his mercurial companion. Zeus had never been mellow, a trait that had caused him endless problems on D-alphus, a trait that had drawn the restless Dion to him. "Impetuous, easily bored, know-it-all genius, arrogant; which one have you given up?"

"You know me too well, Dion." Zeus chuckled, then turned pensive. "It is good not to have to wear masks."

"Which we must with all others," murmured Dion.

Zeus acknowledged the truth with another drink of

beer. "Do you ever regret, Dion? Do you regret following me?"

Dion rubbed a finger along his goblet. The wine in his goblets did not affect him as it did others, but truth in this would not be amiss. "Regret? No. I have enjoyed Earth. Had I stayed on D-alphus, I likely would have scandalized the Oracle by becoming their first suicide. Too many traditions, too many rules. I was suffocating there, Zeus, and suffocation is a very slow death." He sipped the wine, enjoying the buzz and the bite of it. "In truth, I think we all felt that."

The wind picked up with the lowering sun. "Still frustrated Hera says no far-see on Armond and Callie?" Dion asked.

In answer, Zeus crushed his empty can. "I admit a certain curiosity. Humans can get themselves into so much trouble."

"Let's look now. Hera would keep you on too short a leash."

Zeus gave him a knowing grin. "You are trying to foment trouble. I know she'll be here any moment."

Dion shrugged. It was worth a try. "So, before she gets here, tell me, what is it you want of Hera?"

"She's up to something; I want to know what."

"And?"

"For her to admit her place is at my side."

The wind died.

"How about you admit your place is at *my* side?" An irritated Hera strode across the deck to join them.

Dion gave her an appreciative appraisal. Hair still midnight black, figure still stacked, she was quite the queen, and that nipped-in red suit of hers was anything but starchy.

"I thought that might get a rise from you, my dear," answered Zeus mildly, delving for another beer. "You look in fine temper."

"I'd say magnificent," Dion agreed.

"Keep your pants zipped," Zeus warned.

The king of gods understood him so well. If Hera had not been soul-bonded, or been soul-bonded to anyone but Zeus, he would have welcomed her into his bed. As it was, the forbidden remained a piquant constant.

"Sit down, Hera love," Dion invited. "Would you like some wine?"

"Thanks, as long as it's not in the goblet of Dionysus."

Dion laughed. "Would I try that on you?"

"If you thought you could get away with it." Hera accepted the crystal glass filled with amber Chardonnay, then looked around. "I thought you were fishing."

Zeus retrieved their single fish, then tossed it back into the Gulf. He stretched back out on his lounger. "We have shown too much restraint these past four days, my dear. Now that we've all caught up on the demands of our businesses, it's time to return to our matchmaking project."

Hera drummed her fingers against the chair arm. "I agree."

Zeus burst out in laughter. "You are just as curious as we are!"

"I—" A faint pink tinted Hera's cheeks under her flawless makeup. "Yes, I admit it. I am curious. I brought the far-see crystals."

"Then let's get started." Dion finished his wine, while Zeus and Hera prepared.

The cedar-scented far-see smoke wafted into the briny air of the Gulf, bringing with it the image of a car speeding down the Interstate.

"Where are they?" asked Zeus.

As if in answer to his question, a road sign flashed past. Toledo. Ohio, just near the border to Michigan.

Hera frowned. "I thought they were taking back roads."

"And I didn't expect them to be this far north," added Zeus. "Not with two days still to go."

Had something gone wrong? Dion rubbed a thumb against his buffed nails, keeping back the smile. "Focus closer."

Callie and Armond sat in the car, Armond driving, Callie talking. Even through the haze of the far-see smoke, Dion could see the set of Callie's shoulders, the grip Armond had on the steering wheel.

Not the posture of reunited lovers.

"Something's wrong." Hera had come to the same conclusion. "It looks like they're heading straight to Traverse City."

"Then we'd better get there quick," said Zeus.

Things were going well. Dion cast a covetous glance toward Hera's ring. Soon it would be his.

Chapter Seventeen

The spit of land known as Old Mission Peninsula bisected Grand Traverse Bay, once home to Ottawa canoes and sawmill schooners headed to the vast waters of the Great Lakes, just beyond the bay's mouth. From the car window, Callie watched the slate-blue water of the bay lap against the rocky shore. Today, only a few hearty souls in a sailboat braved the brisk winds and choppy waves. She'd read Lake Michigan's water was cold even in summer, and although the sun shone with a clear brilliance, she'd bet that water was icy.

To her left, fall colors formed a vivid carpet. Jewel-decked trees garnished the houses on the peninsula, and bushes of flaming yellow and red formed the accents. Leaves danced across the narrow road in a spirited gavotte.

Soon, however, the houses gave way to tracts of

orchards, vineyards, and patches of withering sun-
flowers as the road rose to the spine of the peninsula.
The land was narrow enough that she could see the
surrounding bay below on both sides. A high, narrow
land encircled by water—the trick of nature gave this
tiny, twenty-mile strip a unique microclimate, more
temperate than expected in a northern climate. Here
farmers could grow apples, peaches, and the region's
noted black cherry. More recently, grapes for wine
had diversified the crops.

She and Armond had taken four days to go the first
half of the distance here. They made the second half
in twelve hours.

Twelve hours in which Armond consistently drove
one mile an hour under the speed limit and the stops
were exactly timed for her bladder capacity. It should
be hard to stay angry in the face of such perfection
for a whole half day, but Callie managed. Mostly by
spouting out every single tiny fact she could remember about Armond.

She claimed it was to help him with his memory.
The reality was that it effectively avoided other topics, and by returning the memories to him, she hoped
she could wipe them out for her.

It wasn't working.

For one thing, it only emphasized how little she really knew about Armond. As they finished the last
miles, she voiced her thoughts. "You know, for dating
you almost a year, I really don't know much about
you."

"You know what's important."

"I know you worked for N.O.P.D. for five years; that
you've been with the FBI for eight months. I know your
mother was French, but you were born in this country. I don't know where, though."

He hesitated, then his lips twisted in a brief, rueful

motion. "Neither do I. I do know she came here looking for my father, and we moved around a lot."

"Did she ever find him?"

"I don't think so."

No wonder Armond was adamant that their child would know her father.

The wind, unhampered at this height, gusted across the top of the peninsula and rocked the car. Armond was silent a moment, while he kept to a steady line, then said, "Those facts aren't what I meant by important, though. History doesn't matter. What matters is how you're living your life now; the kind of person you are. I know a lot about you."

"You have no memory," she scoffed. "What do you know about me after so few days?"

"You're someone who genuinely likes people. Who smiles a lot, at least until I put that frown on your face. You don't do frowns well, Callie. They're not natural."

Callie pressed her lips together, trying at least for enigmatic.

"I know a lot of other things about you. That you're not the preaching type, because you never go on, trying to convert someone to your vegetarian lifestyle. That your hands are your window to the world as much as your eyes; you like to touch things, same as me. That you like your food spicy. Really spicy. That you'll be a good mother. Sexually . . . well, we've proven that compatibility. I know that you moan and get sexy soft when I kiss you here." He took his eyes off the road a moment to touch her neck, then he gave her a slow, wicked smile. "And I know that you snore when you sleep, *ma chérie.*"

"Snore! I do not."

"Well, a little heavy breathing. Maybe it's the pregnancy."

Kathleen Nance

Callie crossed her arms. She did not snore. "Why do you say I'll be a good mother?"

"You care about people. You cared enough to come looking for me when everyone was telling you not to."

"Big mistake," she muttered.

"Maybe for some things, but not for the baby."

"Don't tell me you remember all this about me."

He shook his head, fingering the small *gris-gris* bag he wore. "I've just been watching."

"Cops are good at details, aren't they? And you needed every one."

"I did what I had to do." That implacable note was back. He really didn't regret using her as he had. Or at least the cop part of him didn't.

She might be able to forgive the deception, understanding a little why. What she couldn't forget were the hopes he'd raised, then dashed, when she'd found out any changes were an illusion, a smokescreen to cover the amnesia.

It was lowering, however, to think he'd observed so much about her, while she'd been too caught up in herself to even realize he had amnesia. She crossed her arms. "All right, I'll play the game. Let's see, what have I learned about you these past days?"

Not facts; those she hadn't learned. But what things were so instinctual to him that they defied even the loss of memory?

"The SA abbreviation for Special Agent could mean Straight Arrow in your case. You're quiet; of course that could partly be because I mostly talk enough for two. Cautious. Courteous. Protective. You know wines. I never saw you carve before, but you do like to use your hands in creative ways." Quickly she squelched the crazy yearning to find out just how creative his hands could be in bed.

"It's not a bad list," Armond observed quietly.

"No."

Some of the knowledge was not reassuring, however. He could be deadly, untamed. He carried weapons, probably more than she was aware of. Those two men at Mammoth would have been dead if Armond had wished it.

It was the part of him that held her back. The job would always be first for Armond. He would leave without warning, be gone for an unknown span of time. Never settling, always restless.

It was also the part of him that called to instincts in *her* that frightened her. Wild, rebellious ones that had no place in her life.

Callie leaned against the chilled glass of her window to glance over at him and her heart did its familiar flip-flop. Armond looked so good sitting there, dressed in a fisherman's knit sweater and jeans. The clothes were loose, comfortable, but he wore them with an instinctive flair that she loved. His aftershave was a green, woodsy scent, his innate masculine scent a clean one her chef's nose appreciated. He drove with ease, despite the wind, and the late afternoon shadow of a beard did nothing to soften the line of his jaw. When he glanced over at her, his gray eyes were somber.

"Reach any conclusions?" he asked.

She loved to look at him; she loved to listen to his voice. She loved—

Stunned, Callie pressed back against the cold, hard window. "Conclusions?"

"About how much you know about me? Is it enough?"

Not nearly enough. Except for one really big, hit-me-between-the-eyes-because-I-didn't-see-it-coming conclusion. The pleasures of being with him again, making love to him, bearing his child . . . one fact marbled through it all.

She was in love with Armond Marceaux. Had been for months, since before he'd left New Orleans. Gabriel women didn't fall in love. Gabriel women didn't marry. Leave it to her to be the odd one out and then make a complete stew of it. She loved him, it scared the wits out of her, and she didn't know what to do about it.

"Enough for what?" she managed.

"To marry me. To give our baby two parents."

How could she marry him when his feelings for her were gratitude and comfort and lust, not love? Armond wanted to marry her, but not because he loved her. Because she was his responsibility. Because she gave him memory.

Callie shook her head. "It wouldn't work. Gabriels who try to form lasting relationships only end up with heartbreak and disasters for everyone."

"That's bull, Callie. An excuse."

She loved him, but she would not marry him. Not unless he loved her enough to make her and their baby the most important things in his life.

Callie gazed out at the passing vines and cherry trees and water. She couldn't deal with this now. Not in the close confines of the car, where her every breath brought his clean masculine scent and his every motion drew her eyes to the play of muscle and strength.

"Can we talk about this later?" Like much later. "You just missed the winery entrance." Callie pointed to a small, discreet gold-and-green sign that said only RO-CHON ESTATES.

After a quick glance in the rearview mirror, Armond braked, did a U-turn, and then turned down the lane to the winery.

The Warrior

The final yards of their trip were completed in silence.

Vines, green and heavy with plump grapes, were tied to rows of wire and posts, allowing the vines to grow both up and parallel to the ground. The acres of vineyards spread on either side of the car, funneling toward a small blacktop parking lot beside the winery tasting room and guest house. The building, done in the style of a European chateau, looked perfectly natural set among the vines. Add clear skies overhead and the bay in the background and it became a postcard photo op.

As he parked, Armond wondered if he'd ever been here before. Logic dictated he had. From the brochure, he knew Bernadette and Norman Rochon, his mother and stepfather, had opened it fifteen years ago. Since, according to Callie, he'd been thirty on his last birthday, that was when he was of an age to be in his last years of high school. Likely this was where he had learned about wine.

He recognized none of it.

Callie's intell on this part of his life was skimpy; apparently he'd not been forthcoming about his past or his family. Why? Natural reticence? Need-to-know caution? Or some fatal rift?

Outside the car, he drew in a deep breath of fresh air, sweet fruits, wine, and turned earth. The faint screech-screech of wire rubbing against wood accompanied the drone of the wind, and his hand automatically brushed away the irritating, ubiquitous fruit flies. This, now this was familiar.

None of it evoked his memories, however. None of it returned his past.

He saw three people out in the fields, looking at the grapes. A man and a woman he didn't recognize. His mother and stepfather? The third figure he did recognize: Dion Backus.

What was he doing here already? And if Backus was here, could Zeke Jupiter and Harriet Juneau be far behind? As if on cue, the couple appeared around the back of the guest house.

But Armond's attention was snagged by the dark-haired woman returning from the fields. Was she Bernadette Rochon? His mother? Armond expected he should have some reaction to give him the answer, but from this distance she was simply a stranger, an attractive older woman who had aged well walking beside a man casually dressed in hip boots and corduroys, but with an erect bearing and distinguished steel-tinged hair.

Armond tugged the hems of his sleeves, neatening his sweater, the ingrained habit of a man more used to wearing a suit, he realized. He smoothed his hair, then stopped, annoyed with himself.

Yet he couldn't quell the odd feelings inside. Expectant. Waiting. For what?

The other shoe to fall?

All hell to break loose?

Any number of cliches could fit.

"Dion!" Callie called and waved.

Dion waved back.

"Callie, Armond, you made it," boomed Zeke. "You're early."

"We thought we'd do the tourist thing in this area before we start filming," replied Callie.

"Liar," accused Armond under his breath.

"Do you want to tell them why?" she muttered back.

"Not a chance."

As they converged, Armond noticed Zeke Jupiter, Harriet Juneau, and Dion Backus eyed Callie, while the other couple stared at him. The woman had her hand to her throat. It wasn't hard to read the shock on her face.

"Dion, Zeke, Harriet, I didn't expect to see you here." Callie, bless her, jumped into the gap.

"We also wanted to sightsee." Harriet gave her a welcoming hug. "How was your trip?"

"Interesting."

"Did you see the Squash Cafe?"

"Yup, and I've got a ton of pictures to prove it." She turned to the last couple and stuck out her hand. "Hi, I'm Callie Gabriel."

"Norman Rochon." The man returned her hearty handshake. "And this is my wife, Bernadette."

The woman pulled her gaze from Armond to greet Callie.

"Bernadette, Norman, delighted to meet you." Callie waved a hand, encompassing the vines and guest house. "This is so beautiful; we're excited you let us film here."

"Dion has been telling me about the video series," said Norman. "We're looking forward to the publicity."

The conversation buzzed around Armond, but he could not tear his eyes away from his mother.

"Armond?" she said hesitantly, moving closer. Her hands closed to fists, as if to keep her from reaching out.

Norman Rochon wrapped an arm protectively around his wife's shoulder and stuck out his right hand. "Armond, good to see you, son."

And that, Armond decided, pretty much told him about his relationship with his mother. He swallowed. She was a stranger; he shouldn't feel this hollow ache. "It's good to see you, Norman. *Maman.*" The cordial words were stilted, an unnatural response when buried instincts told him it was touch he needed. On im-

255

pulse, he stepped forward and kissed her cheek. She smelled of powder and Chanel No. 5. "You look well."

She gripped his arms. "Oh, Armond."

Oh, Armond. The headache beat against him, threatening to scrape away the edges of the block. No, not now! He needed the memories, but not now. Not when they'd all see his vulnerability. Why couldn't this come when he was alone?

Quickly he stepped back, hoping the loss of contact would cut it short. Another jab of pain hit the bridge of his nose from the inside. A gust of wind, thick with moisture and carrying the nip of fall, attacked his thick-woven sweater.

Shivering in a cold, dingy apartment. Oh, Armond, there's nothing for us here. Another move.

His lips pressed together against the nausea. Sweat, from the struggle against the onslaught of images and pain, beaded his forehead.

"Armond!" Callie's voice echoed. "Another headache?"

Other voices joined Callie's.

"Is something wrong?"

"Is he all right?"

Damn, damn, *damn!* "I'm fine," he ground out.

Bernadette touched the healing bruise on his temple. "You've been hurt."

At her touch, with dizzying rapidity, the images shifted, exploded. Nova brilliant, nova agonizing.

His mother telling him she had a new man. His mother crying because of him. Betrayal.

His mother, older. Fixing his battered face. Boys were killed tonight, she said. Oh, Armond, why do you fight so? Why do you never talk about the devil inside you?

No devils, Maman. He had lied then, for he would never admit what drove him. But he'd learned well how to hide it. *This won't happen again.*

It never had. One violent night taught him fighting was no answer. Justice was.

At last the images retreated behind a fading black curtain.

Again, though, the knowledge remained.

Armond sucked in air against the receding nausea. He'd taken responsibility for his mother all his life, and that night he added new responsibilities. For his actions. For those who could not defend themselves.

He opened his eyes to find everyone staring at him, and he gave a mental curse. What excuse for spacing out? He brushed off a fruit fly that landed on his cheek, stalling a moment.

Callie touched his shoulder. "What did you remember?"

Another time her wide-eyed concern would have been welcome, but her soft-spoken question wasn't soft enough. Ominous silence followed.

"Remember? Is something wrong, Armond?" Bernadette asked. Callie's cheeks reddened as she realized what she'd inadvertently revealed. *I'm sorry,* she mouthed, before she turned and gave Bernadette a bright, false smile. "He was so lost in thought that I thought maybe he'd remembered, the, um, the words to the song we were talking about on the way up."

His mother's incredulous look suggested that "lost in thought" wasn't exactly his modus operandi, and he'd heard his voice in the shower enough to know he didn't give a damn about song lyrics.

Besides, Callie couldn't lie worth a damn.

"But you said 'headaches,' " argued Bernadette.

Armond could almost see the diagnoses running through his mother's mind: migraines, seizures, tumors, blood clots.

Apparently Callie did too, for she stepped in before he could salvage the moment. "Armond says it's nothing to worry about, and I believe him. It's just—" Her mouth clamped shut, as though she knew she was about to reveal too much.

"A wound to the head? Headaches? 'What do you remember?' " drawled Dion. "Armond, is there a story here?"

Harriet stared at him, too wisely. "You've got amnesia," she breathed.

Armond didn't have to answer; the look on Callie's expressive face said it all.

Chapter Eighteen

"Electricity. That's what you need, Armond." Zeke Jupiter leaned against the polished wood of the tasting bar, rubbing the odd ring on his finger. "One good zap to the temples. I've been experimenting—"

"No." Armond splashed a Chardonnay Reserve into his wineglass and took a large swallow.

"But—"

"No." Electricity? As if dinner hadn't been enough of a nightmare.

After the flood of questions about what had happened—which he'd turned aside with a tale of a blow during a case, a temporary leave, and assurances that he was mostly recovered—Callie and his mother decided to fill in the gaps—ostensibly for him, but mostly, he suspected, for each other. Why else would they include such annoying revelations as that they considered him to have an utter lack of skill in communication?

If any of it had brought back his memory, he would have tolerated it better, but he absorbed the facts as though hearing someone else's biography. They had no meaning to him. He learned the details, but he didn't "own" them.

Afterward, in defense, he retired to the genteel tasting room for a glass of wine and Mozart on the CD, hoping for a reprieve, hoping Callie would join him. He'd gotten used to the quiet evenings with her.

She had, but the tag team of Zeke, Harriet, and Dion also followed and surrounded him in the chairs, leaving Callie half a room from his reach and Bernadette puttering in the kitchen. At least Norman had the good sense to stay out of the onslaught as he held a quiet conversation with Miguel, the field manager.

Now, it seemed, they'd moved to cures.

Harriet perched beside the enormous grand piano. "The herbs in your *gris-gris*. We could burn them."

"Burnt leaves aren't going to help."

"How do you know until you try?"

"C'mon, Armond, go for the burn," Callie teased.

"Memory?" Miguel, the field manager looked up from his discussion with Norman. "My grandmother, she had trouble with her memory. We give her vinegar and honey every night. Six months. It works. Now she remembers all the bad things we did. Too much memory not a good thing."

"Perhaps stimuli," suggested Dion. "Tastes and smells."

"No, he needs a little jolt," insisted Zeke.

"Give me the herbs," Harriet said with an irritated huff, holding out her hand.

Armond handed her the bag from around his neck. At least Harriet's was a better option than being zapped or drinking noxious brews or stimuli. The *gris-gris had* alerted him at Mammoth, although Marie's love-potion claims seemed farfetched.

Harriet looked around "Norman, do you have an ashtray?"

"We don't allow smoking in here. Destroys the ability to taste the wine."

"Then we'll have to go outside."

Shortly, Armond found himself sitting on a stiff, wrought-iron chair with an ashtray of herbs in front of him. Clouds scudded across a sliver of moon, and the freshening night breeze carried the sound of a cow lowing on a neighboring farm.

Harriet stared at the heaped leaves, as if not sure what to do next, while Zeke cleared his throat and glanced around the circle of watchers.

"You need to light them, Harriet," Dion said, an odd current of amusement lacing his voice. He tossed over a book of matches. "Forget your matches? Or forget how to use them?"

Zeke caught them one-handed. "We'll manage," he answered, irritated. He lit one, cupped his hand around it, and then set it to the herbs. They ignited at once, sending up thin tendrils of smoke.

"Breathe the smoke," said Harriet. Her hand on the back of Armond's head urged him to bend over, like with some primitive vaporizer.

Armond leaned, breathed in, and immediately started coughing. He wrenched his face out of the smoke. "Those stink!"

The penetrating stench spread.

"Yeeeuwww." Callie grimaced. "That's worse than a Port-o-let."

"Smells like the pit of despair in Hades," complained Dion. "Do something."

Armond poured his Chardonnay on the smoldering

261

mass, putting out the embers, but the odorous smoke thickened.

Harriet batted at the smoke with both hands. The breeze picked up, gusting and swirling around them, drawing the smoke upward and dissipating it. At last they were left with only the scents of grapes and damp earth and cool autumn.

"Any memories?" asked Harriet eagerly.

"Only of unmentionable bodily functions," retorted Armond.

Wrong answer. A headache ripped through senses numbed by the foul odor. *The lab; one room reeked with the smell of vomit, a storm sewer, rotting fish, and dredged mud.* As quickly as it came, the image vanished.

So rapid was the episode, Armond thought no one noticed. Except Callie, who looked at him with doe-eyed sympathy. At least she had the sense to keep quiet this time.

He'd escaped through a storm sewer. Hokey, but sometimes simplicity was best.

"Would you like some more wine?" murmured Dion, fingering his goblet.

"No thanks." After the stinks of the *gris-gris* and the images, the mere thought of food or drink made his stomach roil.

Harriet rubbed her chin. "There's got to be some other herbs that would work."

Zeke rubbed his hands together. Static electricity formed in the dry air, little pricks of light dancing from his palms. "I still say he needs electricity."

Armond pushed to his feet. "No. No more less-than-miraculous cures. My memory will come back in its own time." *He hoped.* He left the *gris-gris* bag—empty of herbs and finished with its purpose—on the table and escaped to the vineyards.

There, he joined Norman as the older man walked through the rows of grapes, the moon's power barely strong enough to penetrate the clouds and illuminate their path. As they walked in silence the breeze lessened, and the sweet-vinegar scent of wine settled around them. Behind him, the estate readied for sleep. Even the ubiquitous fruit flies had retired with the night and the cold. Vineyards and deep waters spread out before him. On the far left, at the foot of the bay, were the lights of Traverse City, but to the front was only a moon sliver on water and vines.

The scene tugged him with a faded sense of déjà vu. He guessed he had seen this before, many years ago. "It's peaceful here."

Norman only nodded.

"Will you be harvesting soon?"

"Probably end of the week. The migrant workers are finishing another vineyard tomorrow. We keep an eye on possible rain or snow and test the Brix. It's close to perfect. Fall was good this year, long and warm. I expect a bumper harvest, like Ninety-eight."

Norman pulled a few grapes from the middle of a bunch and offered them to Armond. "Taste. You were always good at predicting when the Brix was high enough."

"Brix?"

"The sugar level. We're hoping for a Brix of twenty-two."

"I remember things that are ingrained and instinctive," Armond answered the unasked question. "Facts like Brix and alcohol level are buried somewhere." The purple grapes were sticky, sweet, and bursting with juice. "What kind are these?"

"Pinot Noir. Mean anything to you?"

Armond shook his head.

"Your mother hoped you would take over the vineyards one day, but I always knew you wouldn't be settling here."

There it was again, the assurance that he wasn't a settling kind of man. Instinctively, Armond knew they were right, but whenever he looked at Callie he couldn't shake the feeling that there was a woman worth settling with.

The question was, could she accept and settle with him?

"How long did I live here?" Somehow, in the dark and peace, with Norman's easy conversation, it seemed easier to listen to these sterile facts.

"Three years. I married your mother when you were fifteen. You hightailed it out of here before the ink was dry on your diploma. And you never looked back."

"College?"

"Marines first, then the University of Alabama." He laughed. "You were always a Southern boy; you never said much, but I could tell you hated our winters."

Southern boy. All these days, he'd never thought of himself as that. Somehow, he believed he never called anywhere "home" long enough to figure it shaped him.

"Where in the south did I grow up?"

"All over, I guess. Neither you nor your mother talk much about those days." He stopped to peer at the vines, then pulled a pair of clippers from his pocket and snipped off a bunch of purple grapes. "There's a dusting here. Gotta check for noble rot. Although the sweetness wouldn't hurt these." Grapes clipped, he returned to his walk, and Armond followed.

"I gather Bernadette wasn't much of a mother to you while you were growing up," Norman continued. "She was pretty wrapped up in her own single-mom troubles. By the time I met her, she'd worked out a lot of issues, but it was too late to mend the rifts between you. Bern said you were a hell-raiser when you were younger, but I never met a boy so self-contained and focused as you were. No trouble, but I never had the slightest idea what you were thinking."

Armond rubbed the back of his neck. He could guess what had happened. A neglectful mother, a son who learned independence early, the secret he carried within him setting him apart. Sometimes, perhaps, it was better not to know so many truths about yourself.

"I haven't come back much, have I?"

Norman shook his head. "You remember her birthday, send Christmas packages, call every now and again. But I doubt you'd be here now if you hadn't forgotten whatever it was wedged between you two."

Almond pulled a grape from a plump bunch and slowly ate it. "Likely not." Same as with Callie. The remembered sense of betrayal and loss was so strong that he wouldn't have risked feeling that again if the amnesia hadn't forced them all from the ruts in which they were trapped. Fresh start, no baggage—they'd come together as they were now, not with remembered barriers blocking their way.

Armond had never thought to be grateful to the amnesia, to the men who had done this to him for whatever perverse reason, but in a convoluted sense he was.

Didn't mean they weren't going to see justice, however.

Norman stopped and brandished the thick metal clippers at him. "Don't start something you won't follow up, hear. Don't go giving your mother hope there's going to be more, then go back to the quarterly phone calls. I won't have her hurt like that."

"I won't."

"Good." Norman turned toward the cluster of buildings, apparently having finished his night inspection.

Armond saw Callie sitting on the patio of her guest room. The overstuffed rocker creaked as she set it rocking with her feet. She shouldn't be out this late. She got so tired these days, she should be in bed.

"Your Callie is excited about filming a harvest," Norman observed.

"She's not my Callie."

Norman gave a snort of amusement. "Then you're slower than I thought. You two heat up the room just by walking in. She forgets to look at anything but you, and you hover like a wild stallion caring for a single mare."

"I'm just on vacation."

"You're never on vacation, son. You've got some agenda, but I wonder if even you know the whole of it." Norman stopped him with a hand to the arm. "About this amnesia: You might look up a man called Hugh Pendragon. Lives in Chicago."

Armond gaped at Norman. The unknown correspondent of his e-mails? "What do you know about him?"

"Just that you mentioned him once, said if I ever needed a PI, he was my man. He sounded like a man you trusted."

So, maybe it was time to meet this Hugh Pendragon. "Do you have a computer I could use? One connected to the Web?"

"In the office."

Armond hesitated a moment, then voiced a nagging question that had cropped up since his first retrieved memories. "Did my mother ever tell you my father's name? Anything about him?"

Norman shook his head. "Not a word." He cleared his throat. "I looked at your birth certificate once. She listed your father as 'Artus Marceaux.' I tried to find out about him, thinking you might need the information one day, but met a blank wall and quit. Truth is, I didn't want to find him, so I didn't try too hard."

"I understand." A name, and he had a lot more resources at his command. Using Bureau sources for personal needs was strictly forbidden—he knew that much from his reading and his common sense—but there were, perhaps, other routes.

Norman clapped him on the shoulder. "Good night, son. See you in the morning." He returned to their living quarters.

Norman's revelations still whirling inside him, Armond headed toward the office, then detoured into his room to get some of his notes.

"Armond"—Callie stood in his doorway—"can we talk a moment?" Through the open doorway, the winter-edged wind whistled through his room, and despite being dressing in sweats, fuzzy socks, and a blanket, Callie shivered.

"It's getting cold," he observed.

"That's why I'm wrapped up in so many layers. Do you think it will snow while we're here?"

"No idea. Come on in. Close the door."

The door shut behind her, but moonlight through the window reflected off her sherry-brown hair. Armond's throat tightened. She looked so beautiful, both mysterious and achingly familiar. He'd been given another chance, and he wasn't going to let it slip by him.

"I wanted to apologize," she said at once. "You told me not to tell, and the first thing I do is go and blab. I swear, it was an accident. I was concerned, and it . . . just slipped out. I tried to make it better, but"—she gave a self-deprecating laugh—"Callie screws things up again. I am so, so sorry. I just wanted you to know."

She turned to leave.

"Wait." In a moment Armond was at her side. He clasped her hands, and her blanket dropped to the floor. Small hands, strong hands. "It's okay, Callie. I probably would have had a hard time fooling my mother, anyway."

"You fooled me."

There was nothing he could say to that. "I had to keep the amnesia secret as long as I could; I would do it again, given the circumstances. But I am sorry that it meant deceiving you. The other things, though, about you and the baby—those were the truth."

After a moment's silence she nodded toward the vineyards. "Learning a few more truths?"

"More than I want to know."

"Anything you want to talk about?"

He shook his head, then moved behind her and began to rub her shoulders and neck, protectiveness and desire mixing in equal, undeniable measure. "Have you been drinking your milk? You need to get plenty of calcium."

"You've been reading the pregnancy books again, haven't you? Hovering does not become you." Despite her teasing, Callie found it strangely endearing that such a big man, such a masculine man, such a hard man in some ways, was fussing over her.

Armond chuckled, low and deep. "Sorry. Lean forward."

Callie complied, and he rubbed her lower back, finding with unerring accuracy the muscles that ached late at night. "That feels *soooo* good," she purred, sinking slowly to the edge of his bed as her knees lost starch.

The mattress dipped as he sat behind her. "Getting warm? You need to take off a few layers." The warm caramel of his voice spread across her with smooth heat.

Callie gave him a startled glance over her shoulder.

His smile was innocent. "This back rub will be more effective that way. I want to give you some relief."

Didn't he know that his touch had other parts of her body demanding relief, too? In a growing haze of need, Callie pulled off her sweats.

Armond chuckled again when he saw the flannel shirt and jeans beneath. Efficiently he stripped off those and her thick socks, leaving her in T-shirt and panties. "Now, lay down," he commanded, turning down one side of the bed.

"Bossy, aren't you?" Following Armond's gesture, Callie laid facedown on the bed.

He was right; this was much better. His hands were strong and sure on her back. She supposed somewhere in his training he'd learned about pressure points, about muscles and nerves. Used one way, the knowledge could be incapacitating. Used this way, it was heavenly.

When he included her arms and shoulders and legs in the bargain, Callie gave a sigh of pure satisfaction and settled down to enjoy. Her muscles relaxed, becoming pliant and soft. She was a limp noodle.

A limp noodle surrounding strips of jalapeño. Inside she was feeling the burn, only her rebellious muscles refused to do a thing about it.

"When shall I tell them?" he murmured.

"Who? What?"

"My mother and stepfather. When shall I tell them you're carrying their grandchild?"

Callie groaned. "Please, let's wait. Just a little bit." Like after she'd left. When she didn't have to face them.

"All right," he said at last. "On one condition. You tell them with me. And explain why you won't marry me."

269

"You don't play fair."

"Yes, I do, but I play to win."

"And winning is?"

"A child with two parents."

Nothing about love. He said nothing about love. Only responsibility.

His hands strayed from their ministering path, sliding across her hip to cup her belly. "I'm going to love watching you grow round and start to lumber."

"Don't sound so pleased about it. I'm the one who has to try and get my pants zipped." Obviously he wasn't feeling the burn she was. No man could be lusty while thinking of a woman shaped like a bear.

"You're getting tense," he observed.

"How surprising, with you comparing me to a clumsy bear."

"I happen to like bears."

"I happen to be afraid of them, and I certainly don't want to look like one." She took a deep breath. "Are you going to be around to watch this transformation?"

He paused. "As much as I can. As much as you'll let me. I want us to marry."

"Gabriel women don't marry," she muttered. She buried her head in the soft mattress, resisting the siren of her heart. *For how long would he stay?* whispered the insistent voice of reason. Until he was transferred? Until she woke up beside the untamed, restless man she'd glimpsed? Until his memory returned and the changes she'd seen evaporated?

It always turns out bad, for the bride, for the family. You wouldn't do that to us, Aunt Callie?

If she knew he loved her, enough that he'd be willing to put her first, that he wouldn't allow the job to take him away, then maybe, just maybe, she could take that risk.

Did he love her? She was too much of a coward to

ask, afraid of the not-right answer, and in that moment Callie despised her fears. But despising wasn't strong enough to overcome them.

" 'Gabriel women don't marry,' " Armond repeated impatiently, rolling her over. "Stop hiding behind Gabriel tradition. What do *you* want?"

Callie drew in a ragged breath. "To stop being afraid. That's why I didn't come to your cabin. I was afraid. Am afraid. Of this wildness, this urge to go against every tradition I've been taught, and what it would do to my life."

I want to know if you love me. Her gaze drew inexorably downward and hormones zipped into all the necessary places. "I want you to love me," she whispered.

Hot silver filled his eyes, and he gave a guttural sound of approval. Or agreement. With one impatient gesture, he pulled off her shirt and undershirt. Relaxation vanished with doubt in a heat as sudden as it was powerful. All she could think was that this was the man she loved, this was the father of her child.

With a boldness that surprised her, she lifted her breasts to his perusal. His eyes went right where she expected. She saw his breath quicken, saw the fabric of his jeans strain.

Armond swallowed. "I'm not strong around you, Callie. Don't do this unless you want me inside you quicker than you can say, 'Yes, please.' "

"Yes, please," Callie whispered.

A savage air, triumphant and compelling, settled on him as he hastily shed his clothes until he stood before her, gloriously male, ferociously aroused. For one moment Callie wondered if she was certifiable, risking her heart like this; then Armond was beside her on the bed, drawing her into his arms, kissing her until she forgot everything but him and his strong body.

The press of his shadow-roughened cheeks against her breasts. The grape-and-wine taste of his tongue sweeping against hers. The masculine scent of outdoors that clung to him. Sensations overloaded her.

Despite his claim, though, he didn't slip inside her quick as yes-please. Instead he stroked her—high and low—until her skin felt so scalding hot that butter could melt and dance on it.

Callie gripped his shoulders, rising to kiss him on the lips, earlobe, neck, shoulder, anything within reach. "Come inside," she invited.

He shook his head, the short cut of his hair a silky caress against her cheek. "I want to savor you and enjoy you, like a fine meal or a fine wine. It's a pleasure we've denied ourselves." Then he touched her, low, on one very sensitive, throbbing pressure point.

"That's not savoring," Callie gasped, "that's devouring."

"Wonder how it tastes," he murmured, and before she could think, he had replaced his hand with his tongue and lips.

Slow and lazy, he savored while Callie sizzled. A small scream rose in her throat as pleasure engulfed her. He moved up, capturing the sound with his mouth, and held her close as the orgasm shuddered through her.

"Let me show you how a chef savors," she said when her voice returned, and she pushed at his shoulders. He rolled over, taking her on top. The delight of having him beneath her hands, beneath her body, beneath her mouth, brought the simmering back to a roiling boil.

When she tasted him, on his masculine pressure pointer, his growl of surprise and surrender, her power over him, was a finer satisfaction than any dish she'd ever prepared.

And when he entered her, a long, sure stroke that seated him fully, when slow-and-lazy turned hot-and-frantic, when the pleasure drew to a hard, tight knot that exploded, when his guttural release echoed in her ear, she knew.

Her instincts were right, claimed her heart in joyous abandon.

He had to love her.

Chapter Nineteen

Callie was sound asleep when Armond slipped from the bed. The hour wasn't late, and he wanted very much to stay in this peaceful comfort, but he had work to do. Besides, she had to be exhausted, and she would sleep better without him hogging the mattress.

When the cautious plan to wait until his memory returned had been replaced by the urgent need to bind her to him, he didn't know, but somewhere it had. None of his reactions to her were things he understood or knew how to manage. A good agent shouldn't ignore something just because he didn't understand it, but on this he had no references, no resources.

So he retreated to the solace and necessity of work.

Quickly he donned his clothes, then pulled the covers to her chin. He added an extra blanket, not wanting her to be cold without her nightgown. He

straightened her heap of clothes, then gave a depre-
cating laugh at his obvious delay tactics. He leaned
down and kissed her gold-brown hair, spread out on
his pillow just like he had fantasized.

"Sleep well, Callie."

Then he left. Could be snow coming, he decided on
the short walk outside from his room to the main
building. The air held a frosty bite. All was quiet as he
passed through the corridor where Callie's room was
located, then to the tasting room and winery office.
He turned on the computer.

It was past three A.M. when Armond finished, but he
was pleased with the results. Passing through the
tasting room on his way to his room, he was surprised
to see Dion at the bar, a bottle of wine and two unusual goblets set in front of him. He wore black satin,
an outfit Armond didn't think he'd ever seen on a man
in public. At least not in the conservative Midwest. It
could be either pajamas or sophisticated attire for a
swanky party.

Seeing him, Dion waved a desultory hand. "Come,
join me in a glass. I weary of drinking alone."

Armond detoured. He was tired, but there were
some things he needed to tell Dion.

"What are you drinking?" Armond settled onto a
stool beside Dion.

"Ice wine. Very sweet, very smooth, very complex,
very expensive. Sort of like a woman should be, no?"
He filled the other goblet.

Armond didn't answer, his attention caught by the
gold goblet Dion handed him. Its glitter and sheen at-
tested to the fact that this wasn't a fake metal. "I didn't
know Norman had glassware like this."

"He doesn't. I travel with my own. They are spe-
cially designed to bring out the flavors of the wine, to

Kathleen Nance

enhance its special gifts. Taste my wine. See if you don't agree."

Armond sipped the wine. The first taste was the sweetness of grapes left on the vine until the last moment, until the snows blanketed the vineyard. But complex flavors soon evolved: a hint of oak and cherry, the faint tang of tannins. All perfectly blended, all perfectly tasted.

"I don't think I've ever had a wine this good."

"Likely not," murmured Dion. "A special wine in a special gold."

"What kind of man travels with his own set of wine-glasses? Especially ones like these."

"A man who appreciates fine things." Dion smiled. "Drink more."

Unable to resist the beckoning bouquet, Armond complied; then he held up the goblet, studying the detailed etching. The craftsman's skill was superb. *Vinifera* vines, thick with grapes ready for harvest, curled around the lip and the stem. On one side of the bowl was a young man, surrounded by frenzied dancers, all female, mostly naked. The beautiful, curly-haired young man watched the dancers with an amused smile and weary eyes that had seen too many vices. The figure resembled a younger version of Dion, even down to the matching smile. As though he enjoyed a joke that few could appreciate.

A word was etched on either side of the erotic scene, but Armond couldn't read the Greek. "Do you know what this says?"

"Evoe," answered Dion. "It means joy in the worship of Dionysus. And the three vines are the madness, the relief, and the truth of wine." He pointed to the other side of the goblet, where the beautiful god, chains at his feet, the telltale smile on his lips, watched pirates leap into the sea. "Dionysus."

Dionysus. The Romans called him Bacchus. Dionysus. Bacchus. Dion Backus.

Armond blinked, gave a short mental curse. He must be tired if he was making insane connections like that. He took a large swallow of the wine, still amazed at the taste of it.

Likely Dion, seeing the connections of his name and his profession, had commissioned the glasses, and the artist had used his patron's features in gratitude.

"So, what do you think of the wine?" asked Dion.

"Excellent," answered Armond truthfully, continuing to enjoy the nectar of the gods.

"What are you doing up so late?"

That reminded Armond of one reason he'd accepted Dion's invitation. "I need to be gone for a few days. Callie will be safe here, and there are a few things I need to follow up." He hesitated, then added, "Despite the amnesia, I've been investigating the notes, but I'm beginning to think whoever wrote them poses no threat."

"You're right." Dion fingered one earlobe. "After you left, Jason, Callie's energetic young fan, confessed to writing them. Puppy love, but he soon realized that was not the way to win his lady's admiration. He was contrite and embarrassed, so I forgave him. I'm sure Callie will, too."

"You're likely right. Callie doesn't hold a grudge." And the other incidents could have been sheer coincidence.

Armond took another sip of wine. Something about Dion hummed inside him, like an irritating gadfly, but it remained too minor to set off his alarms, and the faint alcohol haze blunted the annoying sensation.

"Callie has a bright future ahead of her." Dion's lids half-lowered in indolent grace, but the spark gleaming deep in the moss-green depths was sharp. "With this video series, with a successful restaurant in New Orleans, she's going to be the darling of the food community. Given the right mentoring and assistance, I see her as the unique feminine version of Emeril, with his books and television programs and restaurants."

"Mentoring? By you?" Callie had that potential, it was true, if she wanted it. But the idea of Dion as her champion sparked a primitive instinct of denial.

Dion gave a negligent shrug. "Her family has a lot of power, too." Abruptly, he changed topics. "You said you were leaving. Where are you going?

"Chicago." He hadn't intended to tell anyone but guessed it wouldn't matter that Dion knew.

"Why Chicago?"

"There is a man there who might have some answers," Armond surprised himself by replying.

"Then you'll want to get an early start. I'll tell the others for you, and we'll keep busy with the production."

"I should be back before the weekend." He wanted to tell Callie himself, but she needed her sleep, and he would be gone before she awoke. A vague voice warned Armond that if he was starting early, he should be going to bed, not sitting here drinking.

Dion topped off the goblet, and once more the wine was an irresistible temptation.

Armond settled back on his seat. "Maybe one more glass."

"*In vino veritus,*" murmured Dion, lifting his goblet.

She was naked, Callie realized when her bladder woke her with its routine middle-of-the-night demand. And alone.

Three times she'd made love to Armond.

Three times she'd ended up alone.

This did not bode well.

The room was cold when Callie scrambled out of bed. Fall was giving way to winter, and she donned the sweats on her way to the bathroom.

Mission accomplished, Callie decided to return to her own room, unwilling to face the questions and looks if she was seen coming from Armond's in the morning. She put on her socks, then gathered her remaining clothes and blanket and went outside.

The patio bricks were cold and rough, even through her fuzzy socks, and she shrugged on the blanket as a shield against the frigid air. The moon no longer beckoned; thick clouds covered it. No lights shone in any of the rooms except the tasting room, and the only other illumination was the occasional safety light. Wind shoved her hair into her eyes and Callie impatiently shoved it away.

And stood, entranced. A snowflake!

A single flake made a lazy circle downward, drifting with the whims of the wind. Callie stuck out her hand and caught winter in her palm. For a single moment it was white and lacy against her pale skin, then it melted into a pinprick of cold water.

A snowflake. She'd held a snowflake. Callie had never seen snow, and now, in a little miracle, she had actually held a flake. More flakes came down; not enough that she thought they were likely to turn into an actual storm, but enough that she wanted to share it.

When she entered the dark, quiet corridor leading to her room, she heard low voices, probably male, coming from the tasting room at the end. Maybe Armond had gone there. Wanting to share the beauty of the snowflake, Callie slipped noiselessly down the corridor.

Maybe it was a business meeting she shouldn't interrupt. Callie's steps slowed; she'd look first before interrupting. If it was none of her business, if it wasn't someone to share a first snow with, then she'd leave as quietly as she'd come.

Her socks slid across the cool terra-cotta flooring, and the slickness ran a faint shiver up her spine.

"What are you doing up so late, drinking by yourself?"

Armond. She would always recognize Armond's voice, the slow and distinct pronunciation. Why had he come out here instead of staying with her? She paused in the shadowed edge of the doorway. Dion was with him, Dion facing her, Armond with his back to her. Something about Dion's face, the almost cruel amusement, kept her in place.

"I do not require much sleep," Dion answered. His lazy, hooded glance swept across the room.

Callie melted farther into the shadows. She didn't think he'd seen her.

"I find wine a steadfast companion when others are engaged in their own pursuits. Like you and Callie." Dion swirled the wine in his glass, his dark gaze fastened on Armond. "You slept with her, didn't you?"

Callie's breath caught in her throat.

"No." Armond's answer was blunt.

Dion frowned and glanced at the goblet.

"I didn't sleep," her lover added.

Callie's mouth dropped open. Somehow she'd never envisioned Armond as the type to boast with the boys.

Dion's frown, cleared, replaced by the amused smile. "Ah, yes, so literal. I must remember that. You had sex?"

Don't answer. Her lips pressed tight together, willing him to match her silence.

"Yes." Armond shook his head, as though to clear it, and set the wine down on the bar with a thunk. Yet his voice, his movements were not those of inebriation. He sounded cold sober. "What's your concern about what we do?"

"I think of myself as sort of a father figure to her."

Armond gave a snort of derision. "Your feelings aren't fatherly. Trust me, I'm learning how a father feels."

Dion tilted his head, eyeing Armond with hooded eyes. "The child she carries: Is it yours?"

"Yes."

Callie flinched at the bald answer. Not four hours ago he had promised to keep their secret, promised to give her time. Was this how men talked when they were alone together? No wonder her family wanted little to do with this half of the species.

"What are you going to do about it?" asked Dion.

"Marry her."

"Callie agreed?"

"She will."

"Why do you want to marry her? Do you love her?"

Dion's question, and Armond's pause, filled Callie's throat. She couldn't breathe. Her hand fluttered down to cup her stomach protectively. She didn't want to hear this.

Her feet remained frozen to the tiles. Not even for her heart's sake could she move.

"She and the baby are my responsibility," Armond said at last.

Responsibility. Inside she spasmed with the pain of the word. Outside, she could not move an eyelash.

"But do you love her?" persisted Dion.

Armond threw back the last of his wine. "I'll take care of them, be a faithful husband."

"Then you don't love her," Dion said softly, not questioning this time.

"I don't know what love is."

Callie pressed a fist to her mouth and found the strength to back up. She would not cry, she insisted, even as a tear slipped down her cheek. Gabriel women were strong. Inside, she was shredded. Outside, no one would know.

Just before she passed from sight of the doorway, she found Dion's dark gaze trained in her direction, though he made no acknowledgment of her presence. Lost in thought?

Or had he been aware of her all the time?

No matter. Whether Dion had led the conversation or not, Armond had answered freely.

As she retreated, she drew a shuddering breath that forced back the tears. Gabriel women were independent. She would take this job and make it shine, for her future and her baby's future.

Armond could have his name on the birth certificate, his visitation rights, his time with the child.

She just wasn't going to be part of the mix. This baby was hers to raise, hers alone.

Alone. It hurt so much to think about it.

Shivering, cold to her bones, Callie made it back to her room. She burrowed beneath the covers and buried her head under the pillows.

But she didn't cry.

Armond came into the room, moving as silently as a shadow, but she knew he was there. He didn't say a thing, and she knew he thought she was asleep. Instead he left something at her bedside. Then he leaned down and kissed her, tenderly, sweetly, as though he was a man saying good-bye to a lover.

Callie fought to keep her breathing shallow, fought to keep herself from jumping up and snarling at him, attacking with nails and teeth. That was animal instinct, the response of a beast caught in a trap, and her instincts were lousy. She would be strong, independent, rational.

He wore a mask, the mask of the lover, and she'd believed it. Just as she'd believed the mask of the sophisticated, urbane companion. And the mask of the devoted family man.

But underneath was the warrior. The core that knew no love.

For a moment his hand stroked her hair.

A mask. A mask, she reminded herself.

He left, as silently as he had come.

Then the tears came. They clogged her ears and riveleted down her throat until she had cried herself dry.

Dionysus carefully washed his goblets and put them away. A good night's work. Getting Armond to drink from his goblet had been a fortuitous chance. He, however, had always taken full advantage of the chances given him.

Tomorrow Armond would not feel a hangover, for such was the gift of Dionysus, nor would he have a clear memory of the conversation, just bits and pieces. Likely he would attribute it to the lingering amnesia or a little too much of the grape.

Dion had known Callie was there, of course, and it had been no difficult feat to direct the conversation. Despite the wine, Armond had been astonishingly unforthcoming, but he had said enough.

The goblets gleamed, and he polished a remaining speck from their surface.

It had been a gamble to ask Armond about love, but then, Dion had always loved to gamble, to take exquisite chances. He had gambled that Callie expected love. And that the son of Ares was incapable of it.

Or, at least, incapable of recognizing it.

The gamble had worked.

In vino veritas. Yes, but truth was a fluid concept, shaped by perception and knowledge. Armond might be in love, or he might not be. But if he didn't recognize it as such . . . his answer was the truth of the moment.

Dionysus stored his goblets in their lambswool-lined box, then examined his manicured hands. Hera's ring would look very good on his finger.

In the morning Callie found a note at her bedside, with her name scrawled across it in Armond's bold handwriting. She tore it up without reading it.

At breakfast she discovered one more fact.

Armond had gone.

Chapter Twenty

Do you love her?

As he drove the winding miles along the Lake Michigan shore, that question haunted Armond. He didn't remember a lot about his conversation last night, just disordered fragments and the uncomfortable sense that it felt oddly easy to talk to Dion.

Only that single question, and his answer, stood in stark relief.

His answer had been true last night; he didn't know what love was. Love wasn't mawkish hearts or boxes of chocolates or passionate ballads, that much he did know, but what it was, what it felt like . . . That was a mystery. His only relationship that he could reliably predict would be loving, that with his mother, was strained, to say the least.

How could he say he loved Callie?

He knew he genuinely liked her. He liked being with

her, liked her smile, liked how her offbeat ways challenged his habits. She was honest and loyal, two traits that drew him to her like tides to the moon. In her arms was respite from the bombardment of others' guilt, from the taint it left inside him. And he didn't need a memory to know that what happened between them in bed was very special. The thought of marrying her, of raising their child together, was not a difficult one.

But were those things love?

That he didn't know, and something in him resisted exploring further. Love meant vulnerability. It meant letting Callie see parts of his soul that he was afraid to expose.

Why did he and Callie need love to make a marriage work? Weren't mutual respect and caring and liking and passion enough?

Callie needs it. Given her family history, it was the only thing that could give her the courage to take the risk.

The traffic around him slowed as streams of fall-color gawkers clogged the scenic roads to *ooh* and *aah* over nature's brilliant display, and his thoughts pulled back to his surroundings. *Merde,* he was getting maudlin. The answers weren't to be found by sappy philosophizing. Someway he'd figure this out. Impatiently, Armond left the back roads and headed toward the interstate. He'd need to get on the Skyway soon to make his way through Chicago.

Yet, at the back of his mind, the question still churned.

Do you love her?

Zeus sidled over to Hera. "Dion did something," he hissed, pretending to busy himself with the lights.

"I know." Hera snapped her makeup case shut, then

cast an irritated glance at Dion, who lounged on a tree stump, a cup of coffee in his hand. "Look at that smile. We go to bed with Callie and Armond disappearing into his room. We wake up with him MIA, her needing an extra layer of makeup—"

"—and Dion looking like the Minotaur that swallowed the sacrifice," Zeus finished. He rubbed his ring, and a single clap of thunder sounded.

"Places!" called Christian—the director had arrived early this morning with his crew—and clapped his hands. "Callie, sweetie, Norman, just a little more to the right. That's it."

The cameraman started filming Callie and Norman's passage between the vines. Christian's elaborate body language directed them down the lighted row to a vine trimmed of any dried leaves or skinny grapes. Callie's colorful embroidered vest waved in the breeze, and Hera could see the fruit flies around her, but Callie was poised enough not to wave them away on camera, focusing instead on her host.

"Mr. Rochon, with forty acres of grapes, how do you know when to harvest?"

"Part science, part art, part luck." Norman, not a talkative man, warmed under Callie's interest.

She really was good at this, thought Hera; then, taking advantage of the lull in their responsibilities, she followed Zeus to Dion's side, flanking the troublesome god.

Dion looked between them and sighed.

"Dion, where's Armond?" Hera began.

"Chicago. He went to visit a friend."

"What did you do?" demanded Zeus.

"Do?" Dion raised one brow. Anyone who didn't know him would swear he was innocent of any wrongdoing, but feigning innocence was a talent of Dionysus.

"Armond gone. Callie weepy-eyed. You're behind it."

"Oh, that. Nothing really." Dion buffed his nails on his shirt. "A son of Ares cannot love; we all know that. I just got him to admit it."

"The goblet of Dionysus." Zeus's teeth ground together.

"The wine speaks only the truth."

"And Callie heard?"

Dion gave Zeus a pitying glance. "It wouldn't have been very useful if she hadn't."

"But we all know how the truth twists when you tell it."

"Tsk. And you never practiced deceptions, Zeus?"

"That was a long time ago," Zeus muttered.

"Oh, come on. You were a master of the subtle." Dion ignored Hera's sniff of disbelief. "Remember the time you gave yourself the shape of a swan and came to Leda at the pool? She petted your feathers. She crooned over you. When she was nice and ready you turned back to the man and—"

Zeus smiled fondly. "Nine months later—twins."

By Hades, these two were a trial. Hera cleared her throat.

At least Zeus had the grace to look embarrassed. He rubbed the back of his neck. "Sorry, my dear. Temporary lapse."

Hera rolled her eyes. *Just let me finish this match successfully, just let me get back home.*

Every time her resolve to go home faltered, every time she thought she was united with Zeus beyond the bonds of their vows, something like this happened to remind her of the past. She knew exactly how Callie felt, what put the shadow around her eyes, for she, too, doubted Zeus's love. In the past that doubt led to centuries of hurt and chilling mistakes. Now it propelled her home, and she would not be deterred.

"Zeke! Zeke!" called Christian. "Could we get a small spot trained on this bunch of grapes? I want a close shot of it. I want our viewers to see the dew, to taste these gorgeous fruits. Callie, Norman, that was fabulous, really fabulous. Dion, we have got a hit on our hands."

"I hope so," Dion called; then he turned to Hera, while Zeus adjusted the lights. "You might as well give me your ring right now, love."

"Not bloody likely. I've got until the end of this shoot." She left Dion sitting alone on his stump and came to Zeus's side. For a moment they watched the resumed filming.

"We're ready to harvest." Norman glanced up at the iron skies. "And from the looks of it, we should start tomorrow. Before it snows or rains."

Callie's eyes widened. "Snow."

Norman smiled. "Not too likely this time of year, but always a possibility. Harvest time is a family affair. Would you like to help?"

A smile broke across her face. "I'd love to."

Again Hera felt the tug of kinship. Callie was a strong woman. Despite her private misery, she got on with her life.

"I have an idea," Zeus said, drawing her attention from the production. "To teach Armond about love we'll buy him a dog. Or a bird. A pet. He loves that, shows he can love Callie."

"A pet?"

"All right. Bad solution. I know! He needs a good example. Like us! Me!" At Hera's incredulous look, Zeus lifted his hands. "Okay, I'm not exactly the poster child for eternal fidelity. But I'm working on it. A masterpiece in progress. At least I can teach him how to woo a woman. That book doesn't seem to be helping."

"Might help if he could turn himself into a swan."

"I have other techniques."

Just then Hera saw Callie, hurrying after Norman and not watching her step, catch a toe on one of the snaking cables. Her arms pinwheeled, seeking balance, and she might have succeeded if her other foot hadn't landed on the side of the mound of grass between the vines. The angle sent her crashing sideways onto the vines and wires, and her temple smashed against the top of the post. She collapsed in a heap.

Hera's heart pounded against her ribs as she joined the crew in racing to Callie's side.

Blood trickled down her face from a gash in her forehead.

"Callie!" shouted Christian.

Callie didn't answer.

Hugh Pendragon's residence was huge, as was the beast barking through the barrier of wrought iron. The house had none of the welcoming traits the word *home* implied—cheerful curtains, bright flowers, toys or bicycles strewn about the lawn. Instead, it looked like it belonged on a misty moor or in the depths of the Black Forest instead of amid the city limits of Chicago.

Armond opened the gate, a shiver spreading through him at the touch of cold metal, and stepped inside. At once he knew why Pendragon lived here. Pure isolation. Even the air was hushed. The bustling sounds, the acrid aroma of exhaust, and other urban tensions vanished as he walked into the grounds.

Except for one—the reverberating bark of the dog bounding toward him. The animal's head was so massive, it looked like there were three of them, and his eyes were red lasers.

"Friend," said Armond, standing his ground before the dog. "I'm a friend."

The dog skidded to a halt and his massive head, his *one* massive head, tilted, as though the beast was studying him. Suddenly it seemed as if he recognized Armond, for he gave an excited bark and leaped forward. His paws landed on Armond's shoulders, and Armond staggered back under the onslaught of slobbering tongue and doggy breath.

"He seems taken with you," a man's cool voice observed.

"That thrills me no end." Scratching the animal behind the ears—at least it stopped the slobbering—Armond looked past the dog for the voice's owner. The man appeared to be nearing thirty and no stranger to physical fitness. The unrelieved black of his jeans, shirt, boots, and hair were a startling contrast to his pale skin. The only colors about him were the brilliant green of his eyes—glittering emeralds filled with intelligence—and a blue jewel, a rare diamond, in his ear.

Hugh Pendragon, Armond guessed. Likely women would find the face intriguing, handsome even, and the man a challenge.

The man gave a low whistle. "Down, Cerberus," he commanded.

Immediately the dog dropped to his four feet. He whined, looking back, but the man simply shook his head. Cerberus's low whoof acknowledged both his acceptance and his disappointment.

"Cerberus?" queried Armond.

The man shrugged. "The mythological guardian of the gates of Hades. It seemed to fit. He's a stray who adopted me and has taken it upon himself to guard my gates. As you have seen."

"Hugh, good to see you." Armond held out his hand. Pendragon shook it. "You, too. What's up?"

Armond hesitated a moment. He'd asked only to meet with Pendragon, giving no specifics. But the fact of his amnesia was no longer a secret, and in the touch of the handshake he'd detected nothing that would characterize the men he sought. "Amnesia. My memory starts from a week and a half ago. Before that—mere snippets."

Pendragon didn't seem surprised. "I'd wondered. Let's go into the house and talk. Did you eat?"

"Not yet."

The inside of the house was as unique as the outside. As they traversed to the rear, Armond caught glimpses of other rooms. It looked as though Pendragon had hired a handful of mad decorators and given each free rein in a single room.

One was obviously an office, judging from the huge desk, comfortable-looking desk chair, file cabinets, computer, and fax machine. One room was stuffed with objects that had no discernible connection or order: dilapidated toys; rocks and branches; weapons, both modern and ancient; odd bits of clothing. The glimpse was too brief to take in more. Another room could have been found in a Japanese home with straw mats, a single black lacquer table, a sand garden, incense burners, and bare walls except for two delicate watercolors. One was sheer, sensual comfort: walls covered with fabric, the thickest pile carpet he'd ever seen, a water fountain in one corner, and a divan covered with pillows.

The kitchen Pendragon led him to was definitely in the high-tech category. Callie would love it.

"Would you like something to drink?" Pendragon offered.

"Just water."

Pendragon got them both a glass of water, then opened the freezer. "You get your choice of Stouffer's, Lean Cuisine, or Mrs. Paul's."

Armond laughed. "All this equipment and you only use the microwave?"

"As if you're one to talk. Ronald cooks for me, but he's on vacation." He pulled out two cartons and soon had them nuking. "It's good to hear you laugh."

"Callie tells me I don't laugh much."

"Callie?"

"Somebody—" Armond broke off and shook his head. How could he explain Callie? "Never mind."

As if sensing Armond's need for him to begin explanations, Pendragon perched on a stool and began to talk. "We've known each other almost sixteen years; we met when you saved me from a nasty beating compliments of a quartet of thugs. Do you remember this cloth?"

Armond picked up the strip of cloth sitting on the counter and rubbed his thumbs across its soft surface. There were rusty stains on it. He wrapped it around his hand, testing the weight of it. "No—"

The image blindsided him with its pain, cutting off his denial. *Warning the four thugs. Binding a bloody gash.* He saw it all, smelled the garbage left for pick-up, tasted the astringent guilt of the gang at the back of his tongue, felt his cool anger and determination to set this right.

As abruptly as it came, the image left.

It was the second time something other than Callie had triggered the memory. The block was breaking.

Armond laid down the cloth. "I remember. Four

against one wasn't fair odds, especially since they were bigger than you."

"Did the memory just come back?"

"Triggered by the feel of the fabric. Sight doesn't do it, but other cues—a taste or a smell or, in this case, a touch—bring back moments that are laden with emotion."

"Well, you seemed cool enough that day, but I guess I had enough fear for both of us."

"I was angry at the injustice."

"We became friends that day." Pendragon fingered the rim of his glass. "Two outsiders united in a common battle against the world. At least until you moved a few months later. But we ran into each other occasionally in our work, and the friendship remained."

"What do you do?"

"I find people. I'm a licensed PI and my specialty is finding missing people."

Armond sensed there were some deeper issues in that simple answer, but now was not the time to pursue them. "Did I hire you?"

Pendragon nodded, but the microwave dinged, forestalling further explanations. He held out two steaming trays. "Fettuccine Alfredo or Sausage Lasagna?"

"Fettuccine." After a week on Callie's vegetarian fare, avoiding meat for her sake, the thought of sausage was vaguely nauseating.

Pendragon pulled out a loaf of French bread and a tub of butter, refilled water and ice, and then they both began eating.

"Before we go into why you hired me," Pendragon began, "you might find something else interesting. Two months ago we were both working cases that overlapped in a man named Guy Centurion."

"I read about him. I arrested him for attempted murder and smuggling. What was your tie?"

"A man hired me to find his missing daughter. Turned out she was in to the drug and prostitution scene in Atlanta, but the funny thing was, she didn't remember any of her past. Blow on the head was the consensus, making her easy prey for the boyfriend's lies. I took her back, and eventually her memory returned. Father was happy, girl was recovering, boyfriend was behind bars. End of story."

"You didn't buy it?"

"I bought it as far as it went. It just seemed there had to be more. So, out of sheer curiosity, I went digging on my own. Turns out the boyfriend worked for Guy Centurion in the Atlanta branch of his organization." He paused, looking expectantly at Armond.

Atlanta. "I was assigned to the Atlanta office."

"Fresh out of Quantico. You'd been after Guy Centurion while in the NOPD, and I figured you hadn't quit because you were a fed, you'd just expanded your ability to nail him. The girl's memory loss was just too convenient. I wanted to find out if you knew something about Centurion that might connect, so I went to see you."

"What did I tell you?" The back of his neck tightened. Had he talked to Pendragon as candidly as he'd talked to Dion last night?

Pendragon gave a bark of laughter. "You must have lost your common sense along with your memory. You're a fed, and the most closemouthed bastard I ever met. I'd reached a dead end, though, figured what the hell, but I was still at a dead end when I walked out of your office. Since then I've gotten busy with other things, and I dropped it. You done?" Pendragon gestured toward the trays.

"Ah, yeah, sure. Thanks, it was good."

"It was edible," Pendragon corrected. "All I've got for dessert is fruit. Strawberries or pears?"

"Strawberries."

Pendragon dished out two bowls of hulled berries.

Pleasant as it was to realize he had at least one friend—two if he considered the Mark from the e-mails—Armond still didn't know who the traitor was. But he had learned two things; It was a good bet Guy Centurion was involved, and Atlanta was a place to start looking for answers.

He hated the thought of not going straight back to Callie, but this needed to get resolved first, before he could deal with the thornier emotional issues.

"There's something else." Pendragon handed him a piece of paper. "I got this fax from you right before you disappeared."

Armond looked at the paper. It was a list of names, some crossed out, and on the top was "Keep this" in his recognizable scrawl. A frisson of excitement slid up his spine.

"Do the names mean anything?" asked Pendragon.

"Yes and no." No headache, no flashes of knowledge, no instinctive reaction. "From my research I recognize some. They hold different positions in the Bureau." Several were in Washington, the rest from the Atlanta office.

Pendragon nodded. "I looked a few up and discovered the same thing. I guessed the crossed off names were ones you met."

Armond gave him a sharp look. How much did he know?

Pendragon's fingers tapped lightly against his glass and a slight smile played across his face. "That's just a guess on my part, you understand. You and I, we don't talk much about speculations."

So Pendragon knew the strange abilities Armond

harbored, and the man had his own secrets to hide. He was telling Armond that they shared a mutual pact of no questions, no confessions.

"You want to talk about any of it?" Pendragon asked.

He did, Armond discovered. Wanted to lay out what he knew, and Pendragon was not only someone whom he trusted, but someone who would understand and maybe have some insights.

The facts, however, seemed so meager. "I was assigned to the Atlanta office right after I finished my training at Quantico, but I spent time in New Orleans nailing Guy Centurion's ass, then went straight to an undercover assignment. I don't know for sure what it was, but I think it involved a lab Guy Centurion sponsored."

"Do you know what they studied?"

"Psychic powers, I think."

Pendragon raised a brow. "That fits what I know about Centurion. Sounds like you didn't get a chance to meet a lot of the Atlanta Bureau staff."

"Or all the people at HQ."

"What happened?"

"My cover was blown on the assignment and the lab people included me in their experiments. Amnesia is a side effect," Armond said flatly; then he gave a hollow laugh. "All that, and they didn't find any talents they recognized."

"How long does the memory loss last?"

Armond shrugged. "I don't know, but I think they were watching me before I came north."

There was silence for a moment, then Pendragon asked, "Who blew your cover?"

"That's the question, isn't it? Logic says it's one of those men on the paper. My guess is, something in my tracking of Guy Centurion made me suspicious of a rogue agent."

"So you went hunting to find out who, and someone got scared."

"That's the way I play it."

Pendragon shook his head. "Betrayal's a bitch."

"It sure is."

A cop's survival depended upon his partners, upon the trust they shared. They couldn't go into the situations they did if they were also having to watch their backs. Loyalty was a paramount virtue. Cops resisted any idea of one of their own turning, but, given enough proof . . . The response to betrayal ran cold and deep.

Armond looked at the list. One of these people had betrayed the public trust, had betrayed a fellow agent. He had a narrowed-down list of where to start. And he had a place: the Georgian copy shop where this was faxed from.

"Don't go to Atlanta," Pendragon said.

"Are you telepathic?" Armond carefully folded the paper.

"I'm a PI. It's what I'd do in your place. But you need your memory back; you need to know what you found out, why they erased it. Otherwise you've got no ammunition, no proof."

"I'll think about it." Pendragon's advice was sound. He should go back to Traverse, concentrate on Callie's ability to return his memory. But the itch to know, to *do* something, was strong.

Pendragon cleared his throat. "Different subject."

Armond raised his brows.

"Last winter you asked me to find someone named Artus Marceaux. Most damned difficult search I ever tried." Pendragon rubbed a hand against the back of his neck. "I guessed, from the name, he was, um, a relative."

Last winter. Right about the time he'd bought an engagement ring. "For a man who doesn't deal in speculation, you certainly make a lot of guesses."

Pendragon smiled. "But I rarely share those guesses, so consider yourself lucky today."

"What did you find out?"

"That he was dead. He died twenty-five years ago, trying to keep a village in Africa from being slaughtered by a rival tribe. This is my report." Pendragon reached into a drawer and handed Armond a thin manila envelope. "There are more details inside."

Armond stared at the envelope, not opening it. What could it tell him that would erase this sudden emptiness? He had no memories of his father, suspected he'd never had any. But hearing about his death . . . his chest ached for a loss that could never be reversed.

"I'd asked you for something personal of his," Pendragon continued. "This was the only thing you had." He handed him a steel-linked belt.

A circle of brass with a single blood-red ruby in the center connected the links. Carved into the brass was the figure of a man. He held a sword upraised, and on his arm hung a shield that resembled the buckle. Beams of some type came from the shield. In the background were slaughtered soldiers and rejoicing peasants. Greek words circled the scene.

"I had those translated," Pendragon said, pointing to the words. "They mean 'War. Wisdom. Justice.' "

Armond's fingers clutched the belt, the link to the father he'd never known. Abruptly he wrapped the steel links around his waist. The metal should have been an unaccustomed weight, but he found it comfortable. As if it had been designed for him.

"Thank you," he told Pendragon as he made a decision. Enough with waiting. He'd go to Atlanta. But he couldn't go without telling Callie. "Can I use your telephone? It's long distance."

"No problem." Pendragon gestured toward the kitchen phone.

Armond was surprised when Harriet Juneau answered the phone. "Hi, Harriet. You doing phone duty?"

"Everyone's busy, and I was sitting nearby."

"Is Callie free? I need to talk to her."

Harriet paused, then said gently, "She's not here, Armond. She's at the hospital."

"What?" Armond gripped the phone, his hand suddenly trembling. The hollow ache became a sharp pain. "Is she okay? What happened?"

Was it the baby? Did she miscarry? Dear God, don't let her lose the baby.

"She tripped in the vineyard and hit her head; she was unconscious for a few minutes."

"Is she in danger?"

"I haven't heard."

"I'll be there as fast as I can. Tell her—" He bit off the words and swallowed hard against the knot in his throat. "Tell her I'm coming."

It took him mere moments to give a hasty explanation to Pendragon and be on his way. Ignoring all speed limits on the way back, Armond discovered the gnawing fear kept with him, pressing his foot to the accelerator.

Was this what it meant to love?

Chapter Twenty-one

It wasn't her bladder that woke Callie; it was someone slipping into her room. She held her breath, feigning sleep, her heart pounding in her ears. Ohmigod, what did he want? There wasn't much crime out here. Why her room? She had no valuables. Thoughts tumbled in concert to her somersaulting stomach. *Now* she had to go to the bathroom. She didn't want to pee in the bed.

Slowly she slitted her eyes, afraid he'd hear her eyelashes.

The intruder was a big dark shadow. He moved stealthily. No sound of footsteps. No sound of breathing. Only the whisper of air at his approach. He stopped at the side of her bed. She heard a click, and a laser-width beam of light swung across the carpet onto the bed.

Only one man she knew moved that quietly. Only one louse always smelled like the outdoors. Only one cad could bring her from a sound sleep with tingles circling the back of her neck.

Armond.

The beam swung across her face, faltered at the bandage on her cheek and temple, crossed over her eyes. She scowled in the brightness. The light swung back toward her glare.

"Would you get that light out of my eyes?" she growled.

"Callie? You're awake?"

"I am now." She could see him, now, in the moonlight, and her heart squeezed tight in her chest. "And you're leaving."

Armond ignored her, sitting beside her on the mattress. "I didn't mean to wake you. I wanted to see how you were." He touched her bandage. "What happened? Are you all right? Dizziness? Headaches?"

"I'm fine." She shifted, her butt aching. "Except the tetanus shot hurts."

"Tetanus?" He swore softly under his breath, then asked again, "What happened?"

"I tripped on a light cord. You know, clumsy Callie in the outdoors. It wouldn't have been a problem except my face scraped a rusty nail. No permanent damage, but it was bloody and needed a couple of stitches. Filming tomorrow's going to take some creative makeup and camerawork to hide it."

"Shouldn't you be in the hospital? Weren't you unconscious?"

"I had the breath knocked out of me. They thought I was out, but I wasn't."

"And the baby?" His hand rested lightly on her belly.

"Snug as a bug." Dammit, he was doing it again, fooling her traitorous instincts with the mask of civilization. She moved from his touch. "I had everybody tiptoeing in here to check on me until I finally convinced them what I needed most was solitude and sleep."

"All right." He tossed off his jacket, then stood and began pulling off his shirt.

He obviously expected to come to bed with her!

"Stop!" Callie bolted upright, her hand up in the classic gesture.

Armond looked at her in confusion; then his face cleared. "I know you're tired. I only want to hold you, assure myself you're all right."

There it was again, that caring and tenderness, the same caring and tenderness he'd shown her the night they met. It was part of what made him such a good cop.

Then he pulled his shirt off the rest of the way.

Dang, the man had a fine pair of arms. Chest wasn't too bad either. And those sleepy gray eyes. Rampant hormones urged her to hold out her arms, welcome him back to her bed. Callie grit her teeth. Being pregnant was a bitch in some ways: meat cravings, learning every bathroom between here and New Orleans, backaches, horny hormones.

Armond saw the way her eyes devoured him and he smiled, very sexy, very knowing.

No, she couldn't do it. Not and survive when he realized a baby wasn't enough to keep them together. Armond was honorable. Once he said his vows, he'd be faithful to them, but she couldn't live watching him take more assignments, work later hours, disappear undercover. She pressed back against the pillows.

She couldn't live with him knowing he didn't love her.

"I want you to leave, Armond. For good."

He went utterly still. "What?"

"Leave. Now. It's not going to work."

"What's not going to work?" He spaced the words as though he were dealing with some street drunk who needed placating in words of one syllable.

"Us."

The gray eyes narrowed. The mask slipped, just a tiny bit. "Are you mad because I left? I left a note."

"I tore up your note and, no, that's not it. That's your job, I know that. It will always be your job."

"This is a pregnancy thing, isn't it? Your emotions are all—" He waved a hand around, a male floundering to explain something inherently foreign.

"No, Armond, finally I'm *not* listening to my emotions." *Liar.* Callie wrapped her arms around herself, shivering despite the heat of the room. Must be the wind from the temperature dropping outside. Absently, Armond handed her her robe to wrap up in. Damn him! He could make this easier. Do something nasty.

"I'll list you as father on the birth certificate, you can have open visitation with the baby, but anything else . . . It's over." There, she'd said it. Got it out. It was done.

Why did she feel like she'd just swallowed a chicken whole?

"Have you been talking to your mother?"

"No! This is my decision. A rational, logical decision."

"You?" Armond fisted his hands at his waist. "What did I miss? Because I remember the last few days pretty clearly, and the last time we were together, you were on top of me and using your mouth a lot more satisfactorily than this insane conversation."

Callie flinched and her cheeks turned red with memory. Oh, yes, the warrior was definitely coming out. She rose to her knees, clutching her robe, her armor, tight about her.

"You didn't miss a thing. Neither did I. I wanted to

show you a snowflake. Instead, I heard your conversation with Dion." She steeled herself to say the words. "You don't love me, Armond."

She waited for a denial; not that she would believe it, but it might make her feel that at least he was trying to salvage something.

Instead he swiped a hand across his neck. "*Merde,* that Dion is a troublemaker."

Now Callie was getting angry. "This isn't about Dion. It's about you. And I won't marry a man who doesn't love me."

"Callie, until I get my memory back—"

"Don't use your memory as an excuse. If you loved me, you'd know it."

"Would I? I can say the words, if that's what you want."

Fury, hot as steam, burst inside her. "I wouldn't believe you," she spat.

"I know that I care about you, Callie. On the way back up here, I broke a lot of speed laws because I thought you were hurt. I know that when I'm gone from you—" He broke off when all she could do was shake her head.

"Doesn't it count for something, Callie, that whatever I do feel for you, it's happened twice?"

Startled, she looked up at him, but he was fishing in his discarded jacket. He handed her a jewelry box. "I would have given this to you if you'd come to my cabin. There was no baby bringing us together then."

Holding her breath, Callie opened the box. It was a diamond, a stunning yellow diamond surrounded by smaller stones, topaz maybe. Armond had always had such an eye for the beautiful. Her finger itched to wear it.

He'll break your heart, Callie. Gabriel women don't marry. The Gabriel legacy is very, very clear. We raise

305

our daughters alone, for to do otherwise brings only pain and destruction. To all of us. The warnings drummed into her from birth sounded their beat.

The village witch was the village wise woman.

Do you love her?

I don't know what love is.

Very slowly and softly, she closed the box. She put it against Armond's palm, then wrapped his fingers around it. She looked up at him. Please, let her say what she must, let him be convinced because she knew she would not be strong enough to say it a second time.

"No, Armond. I will not marry you. Not only because you don't love me, but because I don't—" Her voice faltered. She couldn't do it.

Her hand went to her stomach, linking her to the most recent addition to the Gabriel line, linking the present back to centuries of tradition. For her daughter's sake. "—because I don't love you."

The last word was so soft, so broken, yet Callie knew he had heard. A muscle twitched in his cheek and his hand splayed across his abdomen, as though she'd speared him with a dagger. His eyes closed, shielding their misty gray from her.

Another headache, she realized.

Yet she didn't raise a hand or speak a word in consolation.

His hand spasmed around the unusual belt he wore. He clutched tight the buckle, fighting a silent battle; then, as quickly, it passed. His eyes opened.

They were still gray, but not a soft mist or an exhilarating storm. This was the hard steel of a blade.

"This isn't over between us, Callie." His voice was low, determined. Then he snatched up his shirt, pivoted, and left as silently as he had come.

The warrior was preparing for battle.

* * *

Despite being on the road all day, despite physical and mental exhaustion, Armond knew sleep wasn't his lot tonight. He'd gone other nights without sleep; he'd survive. And he had an aversion to lying in bed tossing and turning. At the least he could do something productive. Or get stinking drunk.

He detoured into the tasting room, poured himself a glass of Merlot, downed half of it in one gulp, and then filled the glass again. Glass and bottle in hand, he headed back to his room. Once there, he stripped off shoes and socks, found his notes, and then sprawled in the rose-fabric chair. Morosely sipping the wine, he couldn't bring himself to open the file and start working.

"Merde," he complained in an undertone. His insides were scoured and raw. How could Callie deny what sizzled between them? How could she ignore it? He didn't believe, or didn't want to believe, that she didn't want him.

I don't love you. Her words echoed inside him, reverberating against his hollow chest like a pinball.

In her room those words had triggered another headache—a blinding, near debilitating montage of images. Ones no one should have to face a first time, much less revisit with original clarity and pain. Callie leaving him abandoned at the cabin those months ago. The child Armond scrubbing and showering but unable to wash out the taint of knowing and realizing it forever set him apart. *His mother telling him she didn't love him.*

They had repeated in an endless circle, the headache nearly unendurable.

Only when he'd grasped the shield of his father had he been able to break off the nauseating cycle with the remembered satisfaction he got whenever he brought a vile criminal to justice. He was cool. Strong. Sure of his purpose. It was the feeling he'd sought all his life.

Then . . . he'd opened his eyes and seen Callie kneeling on her bed. Wide-eyed, hand on her belly, lip caught between her teeth, bundled to her chin against the cold. Mad as hell at him, yet still concerned.

For the first time in his life, justice wasn't enough.

Because Callie had burst into his soul.

Callie. Spicy, offbeat Callie with her kitschy decorating habits, her ability to talk to anyone, and her smile that made any day seem sunny.

Was he in love with her?

His gaze lit on the pile of books at his bedside: LE and FBI books, pregnancy and child-care books, and, at the bottom, the quirky little volume Zeke had given him. Following a strange compulsion, he retrieved the book, and when he set it in his lap, it fell open to a page labeled "The Arrow of Eros."

"Eros aims and the arrow pierces," he read aloud, sipping his wine, "unmindful of class or convenience. Eros sees only the needs of the heart. To truly know love, look where the heart resides first."

Where the heart resides first. The needs of the heart.

He had been given a choice today: Traverse City or Atlanta. Callie or the job.

He had no past. He had only the present and the future. And when he looked into the future and saw no Callie in it, it was a future without spice and zest.

Armond set his wineglass down with a thunk, his fingers shaking. He finally had the answer to Dion's question.

He loved Callie Gabriel.

A smile broke out, outside and in. He *loved* her. Chocolate hearts, mushy ballads, till-death-do-us-part, I'll-learn-to-eat-raw-jalapeños love. And, he thought—hoped, really—that deep down, some-where, she loved him. Or could love him.

And if he told her that right now, she not only wouldn't believe him, she'd probably put Cajun Fire Sauce in his next glass of wine.

There had to be something he could do, something that would make things right. Make Callie realize how good they were together. Somehow he'd have to show her that he meant what he said.

That was okay. He was better with actions than words.

Armond picked up the book and started to read.

"You failed," Titus accused the doctor, savoring the feeling of having the upper hand again.

"I'm sending men up to Michigan—"

"No," he interrupted, soft and deadly. "You've al-ready made too many mistakes. I'll bring him in my-self." He hung up the phone and stared at it a moment. "Or perhaps I will do him a favor and simply kill him."

Marceaux was a superb hunter, relentless when tracking his quarry. Even without a memory, he would eventually follow the trail back to Titus. The matter had to be handled now, and personally.

Titus stood and shrugged on his jacket. He strapped on his gun, enjoying the familiar weight of it. There was a reason he'd kept training despite being out of the field. He was still the best marksman of anyone in Atlanta. Once out of the building, he'd call Centurion for the backup. Centurion wanted Marceaux gone al-most as much as Titus did, but this time he was calling the shots.

Time to finish this.

Chapter Twenty-two

Callie scooted her plastic bin—Norman had called it a lug—between the rows of vines. Snip with the clippers, a bunch of grapes went into the lug. Go to the next bunch, move to the next vine shoot, get a new bin when this one was full. The tractor chugged between the rows, picking up the filled lugs and taking them back to the winery. Grape harvest was repetitious work. And tiring.

The *chick chick chick* of her clippers was the slowest in the field. Her hands were sticky with fruit juice, sweat dripped down her back despite the cold of the day, and the fruit flies were an irritating plague. Yet Callie loved it.

Though she worked alone, her slower pace leaving her lagging behind the experienced harvesters, she found she didn't really mind. She could hear their voices and the wheeze of the tractor. Her fear of being alone in the outdoors had kept her from a lot of gardening, except for a city-style herb garden at Greenwood. This silence and simple pleasure in the scents of earth and sun was a new experience.

The crew had filmed the harvest, a nonstop operation that processed the grapes from vine to vat in the minimum time possible. According to Norman, since these grapes were to make a red wine, they would go from the picking to the crusher/stemmer, then directly to the Roto-vat with the skins, where the yeast would be added for primary fermentation. Later the juice would be pressed out for secondary fermentation. Brix, pH, tannic acid, external temperatures—all were changeable factors that made winemaking an art, not a science.

Callie found the whole process frenetic and fascinating, but she'd been glad when Christian switched the crew into close-up shots without her, so she could come out here and pick.

Reaching the end of a row, Callie stopped and stretched her shoulders. Fatigue gripped her with cat's claws. Though most of the afternoon was left, she'd better call it a day. Tomorrow they'd be shooting the final shots at the winery and the cooking portion of this episode. She already knew what she would make—yeasty herb bread, sunflower-seed-crusted root vegetables, and cherry-apple torte. Norman had chosen a Riesling accompaniment. The following days they'd film the tourist shots: Gwen Frostic's studio and printing press, the Old Mission Peninsula lighthouse, a fudge factory, and Bower's Harbor Inn, with its resident ghost. The only place they hadn't gotten permission to film was at Sleeping Bear Dunes. The dune grasses were too fragile and the sands too unstable for the equipment and crew. Callie felt the pang of disappointment, but the Dunes weren't a place she would go by herself.

Then they would be gone, heading to the next winery.

And Armond wouldn't be coming with them. Dion had told her that Jason had admitted to writing the notes, and although Callie found it hard to imagine the youth being so foolish, she accepted that the incident was over. Armond was an FBI Special Agent down to his bones, and with his memory returning he would soon be back on the job. Callie's stomach clenched, anticipating the loss. For this would be the last break. There would be no more chances for them.

Immediately, as it had, oh, every few minutes, whenever she'd thought of Armond, her gaze found him. He was the lodestone, surrounded by a vibrant energy that pulled her heart with unerring accuracy. He was talking to Zeke and Harriet, one hand rubbing the back of his neck in a characteristic gesture.

Now that she knew about the loss, she could see the signs of his memory's return. Just as she feared, the old Armond was settling back into his skin. She saw it in the way his focus turned from live-in-the-moment to careful plans. In his silent watchfulness. In his abrupt departure yesterday. In the air of resolute purpose that became his shield against personal involvement. In the somber way he practiced the karate-like motions with body and knife when he thought no one watched.

Callie had watched, unable to tear her gaze from the play of muscle, the sheen of sweat, and the low-slung jeans. It might be the last time she would see him like this, and the knowledge had scalded worse than hot grease.

Now, as he shared a joke with Zeke and Harriet, his low, caramelized laugh spread sweetly through her.

Callie stopped short in her trudge back to the guest quarters, her heart palpitating, her knees weak. The clear, cold air drew Armond into sharp focus.

With her attention on all the returning problems, she'd never noticed, until now, that there *were* changes. For one, he laughed more. For another, he'd eaten her vegetarian fare all week, even at restaurants that offered a choice, just so she wouldn't be tempted by her abnormal meat cravings. When they were dating he'd always chosen restaurants with a vegetarian entree, but he'd never hidden his preference for a well-cooked steak or a dish of Shrimp Remoulade.

Then he turned, as he had done every time she'd stared at him with her heart zipped into her eyes, and his gray eyes both devoured and cherished her.

There was the biggest change of all. His eyes held a softness she'd never seen in him before, a softness that appeared only when he shared an intimate touch or look with her.

The special agent took in each detail, she knew, as instinctive to him as breathing. But it was the lover who had brought her water as soon as her squeeze bottle emptied and had scrounged up a tomato-and-sprouts pita, then told her to sit and eat when she'd first started to feel woozy from hunger.

To her disappointment, this time he turned away and resumed his conversation with Zeke and Harriet.

What did you expect, Callie? You told him to get out of your life. You told him you didn't love him. You know you can't live with a man whose first priority is the victims he helps, while you get the crumbs.

A man who, by his own admission, doesn't love you.

Each time Callie had battled her wilder instincts and pesky hormones, forcing herself to respond with a cool thank-you instead of jump-his-bones ardor. She couldn't face waking up alone one more time.

Yet, she admitted now, this week Armond had given her so much more than mere crumbs.

How long could it last, questioned the cruel voice of reason, the voice of centuries of Gabriel experience? How long after his full memory returned before the charming veneer covered the dedicated warrior, leaving only scraps of time in his life, and no heart in his soul, for a wife and a child? Better that the break be now and be clean, not a series of fraying good-byes.

Without him, at least she would have her family.

With Armond, she would be alone. Isolated.

Irrational or not, Callie couldn't stop the nausea that rose in her throat or the sharp pain that pierced her chest like an arrow. Her hand pressed against her belly. She just couldn't take the risk.

"So, you'll help me?"

"Help you?" Zeus beamed and clapped Armond on the shoulder. "Of course we will. You know, from the first moment I saw you two together, something said to me, 'Zeke, they'd make a good couple.' "

"I told you that," Hera said, irritated that he'd forgotten.

Zeus waved a hand, dismissing the comment. "Who gave him the book that suggested this picnic? Now, I've got just a few other little suggestions, Armond. To start with, take nectar with you."

"Apricot nectar?"

"That piffle? No, this is a . . . family recipe. Honey and dew and a pinch of ginger and—Never mind, I'll make some for you."

"Honey and Mountain Dew?" Armond's voice gave a clear opinion that he thought Zeus was nuts.

There were times when Hera agreed.

"Not Mountain Dew, dewdrops," corrected Zeus. He

leaned forward and whispered conspiratorially, "Drives women wild."

'Course, he did have a point about the nectar, Hera conceded. That, some far-see smoke, a few bites of ambrosia . . . she and Zeus had made some potent memories with those.

But nectar and ambrosia? The combination was much too stimulating for humans. Hera nudged her husband silent.

"What time do you want Callie at the park?" she asked Armond.

"Tomorrow morning. Before sunrise."

Zeus gaped at him. "Does it have to be that early?"

Armond nodded. "She's got filming the rest of the day, and I have a flight to Atlanta. I'd take her myself, but I doubt Callie will voluntarily set foot in my car."

Hera eyed Callie, who'd turned away. That seemed a sure bet. "In other words, you want us to kidnap her."

"Persuade her."

"She'll be there," Zeus promised.

"Thank you. Now, I've got some more arrangements to make."

He headed away and was almost out of earshot when Zeus called out, "One other suggestion: Never drink with Dion Backus."

Armond drew up short and stared at him. "How did you know—? What do you—"

"Let's just say I'm very well acquainted with Dion."

Hera recognized Zeus's accompanying innocent smile, the one that promised there would be no further explanations, only evasions. She'd seen it many times herself.

Apparently Armond recognized it, too. "Remember, sunrise." He pivoted and left.

"And how do you propose we get Callie out before

sunrise?" Hera asked when she was alone with Zeus.

"We'll think of something."

"You mean, *I'll* think of something." Zeus had always been the one for the grand schemes and grander dreams, while she worried over the tiny details.

"No, I mean *we'll* think of something," Zeus retorted. "We're a team in this, Hera."

A team. Two working in concert. For a time, before the exile, they'd been a perfect match. These past weeks they'd recaptured some of that, and she was so grateful that the last memories she would have of him were these, not the bitterness that drove them apart for so many centuries. Yet, despite the fun, she still longed for peace and for home.

She had to tell him soon. Now. That she would be going. She couldn't keep him hoping for more. Even if he stopped helping her, she had to tell him. She owed Zeus at least that small honesty.

Absently, she rubbed her ring, and a tendril of fog formed over the deep waters of the bay. "Zeus, there's something I need to tell you. About the future, my future."

"Not now, Hera." His thunder clapped faintly in the background, cutting her off. "Let's finish with Armond and Callie, then we can talk about us."

"But—"

"No!" Thunder moved to his voice. "Please, Hera, my love, later."

As if afraid to hear what she had to say, he strode away, leaving her watching, hungry for every view of him. Did he suspect? Although Zeus could be self-centered, he was also very smart, and their soul bonds made their emotions and reactions to each other especially acute. He must have picked up her reluctance, her refusal to discuss any lasting intimacy.

She was weak and could not persist in the face of his refusal to listen. She would wait to tell him. It would be only a few more days before Callie and Armond admitted they loved each other.

Or before they broke irrevocably apart.

Armond sat in the darkened tasting room, a glass of Cabernet Reserve at hand, Pendragon's notes about his father in front of him. The hour was late. Everyone else was in bed, Pachelbel's *Canon* played softly in the background, and he was alone, finally, with the few bald facts known about his father's life.

He fingered the belt. So much about his father was mysterious. Artus Marceaux had been a very private man who spent his life bringing justice to the weak.

"I thought I heard music." Bernadette Rochon came into the room, wrapped in her robe.

"I'm sorry, I didn't mean to wake you. Norman—"

"Is still snoring." A sad smile flitted across her face. "I guess a mother never stops listening for the sound of her child, settled safe in bed."

Without her makeup she looked older, softer, definitely more tired, but with her bone structure she would always be beautiful, Armond decided. She must have been very young when she'd had him, not more than eighteen.

"You missed supper. Would you like me to cook you a steak? You know, I heard eating raw beef and oysters increases the blood flow to your brain. Maybe you should try it. For your memory."

Armond's stomach roiled at the thought; steak had lost its appeal. It had to be love when a man gave up a good steak. "No thanks, *Maman*. I already ate, and I think my memory's coming back all on its own."

Bernadette's gaze caught on his waist, and her hand

gripped her robe lapels tight. "Where did you get that?"

Armond laid a hand on the buckle. "It was my father's, wasn't it?"

"Yes. He said it was a family heirloom. I threw it away; you must have fished it out of the trash. You never told me."

"I don't remember any of it. Why'd you throw it away?"

"Other than you, it was the only reminder I had of him. And it was a day I didn't want any reminders."

But me, you couldn't get rid of. "Did you hate him that much?"

Bernadette sighed and sat down. Without asking, Armond poured her a glass of wine, and she slowly sipped it, as if gathering her courage. "Hate. Love. Two sides of the same coin. Once I loved him. Then I hated him." Her fingers tightened briefly around the stem of the glass. "I never could talk to you about your father. That was wrong of me."

"I wouldn't remember now, even if you had. I do have one memory. You and I were sitting in a café, waiting."

"I'm surprised you remember. You were only four."

So young. When his memories returned, they didn't care how deeply they'd been buried.

She continued. "Your father was a mercenary—a hired gun, I guess you could say—though he claimed to work for those who needed justice."

A shiver skittered down Armond's spine. *Like father, like son?*

"Tell me how you fell in love with my father. What happened between you that turned love to hate?"

Bernadette was silent a moment, gazing into space. "We met in Marseilles when he was between jobs. He was mysterious, masterful. Magic. He swept me off my

318

feet and, despite his profession, he was always careful with me."

"Not too careful," said Armond. "You got pregnant."

Like father, like son?

She blushed and hurried on. "He had to leave for another job; where, I didn't know. His work was a thing separate from us, but he did warn me that often he would be absent and could not write. He left only a post office box number in Atlanta where I could write. When I found out I was pregnant, I wrote. Many times. He did not answer, so I saved my money until I earned enough to come to the U.S., where you were born."

"Did you ever see him again?"

She shook her head. "I wrote, weekly, but I only had one answer, a letter asking me to meet him at the café in Atlanta."

"And he didn't show up." It was not a question.

"No. I had talked so much about your father, you felt the disappointment as keenly as I." She gave a small smile. "You did not handle it well. I remember at the cash register, you starting kicking some stranger and shouting 'You did it!' It was *tres* embarrassing."

The stranger at the cash register. His mother didn't know it, but he hadn't attacked the man because of his father's desertion, but because of the strange knowledge of the man's guilt.

"I knew then," Bernadette continued, "I couldn't keep waiting for him; I couldn't do that to you. I had spent almost five years looking for him; I wouldn't spend another minute. We had to get on with our lives." She sighed. "It might not have been the best decision, my son, but it was the only one I could make at the time."

Armond fingered his glass. "Did you hate me, too?"

"Never!" Her shoulders gave a tiny twist. "Sometimes I was afraid I might," she admitted. "You were, are, so much like him. Your looks, the way you move and talk, this air of—" She waved a hand, looking for the word. "Noble purpose, I guess. Every second I looked at you, I was reminded of him."

"I had another flash of memory," Armond said hesitantly. If he didn't bring it up tonight, in this night of truths, he never would. Too much silence had festered between them already. "You said you didn't love me."

Her face turned white, and her eyes widened with stricken shock. "What? *Non,* never."

He nodded. "You were sitting at your dressing table, crying. I don't remember why you cried, only that I was the cause. You looked at my picture on the table and said, 'I hate you. I don't love you. I never loved you.' Then you swept your hand across the table, knocking everything to the floor." Even in the telling, the words had the power to hurt, to leave him cold and empty. Each soft-spoken syllable rang in his ears and his heart.

Bernadette stared at him, then her head fell back and her eyes squeezed shut. Two tears fell to her cheeks. "I didn't know you had seen that, heard that. Is that why it all changed between us?"

Armond gulped the last of his wine, then stared out the windows. "It's all right. It was a long time ago."

"It is not all right," she said fiercely. She gripped his chin and turned his face toward hers. "It is not right that my son has thought for many years that I do not love him. I was not talking about you. I was talking to the picture beside yours. *I was talking to your father's picture.*"

Dumbstruck, Armond could only stare as his world tilted.

She shook her head. "I was crazy in those days; I'm not proud of it, but—" She gave a shrug of resignation. "My life was a shambles: another town, another flea-bag apartment, another lousy job. Exotic dancer, a new low, even for me. But I thought I had a chance to break out; I had this new man, you see. Except that day he found out I had a little boy and he told me *adieu*. You must have overheard."

Armond waited while she drew in a shuddering breath.

"Perhaps you were just an excuse for him. Perhaps he knew I still loved Artus. The day he left was an anniversary, eight years to the day when I met Artus. Too long to ache for a man who was never coming back. I wanted him out of my heart, out of my life. That was what you saw."

It was the day she'd thrown out the belt, Armond guessed, his chest constricting with their shared pain.

"I cried for twenty-four hours straight, but when I stopped wallowing, it was to find you had closed down. I tried to find out what was wrong, but you would simply give me a quiet stare and say, 'Nothing.' I never got back my little boy, and I never knew why." She swallowed hard, and Armond saw the sheen of tears in her eyes. They matched the ones clogging his throat.

"Sometimes it is those small, pivotal moments that really shake you up. I saw what a pitiful creature I was becoming, and it disgusted me. I went back to school, got a more respectable job, and eventually met Norman. I was doing it for you, but I'd already lost you. I don't ask your forgiveness, only perhaps a little understanding."

Could he expect Callie to forgive him for some of his mistakes if he couldn't forgive his mother? Armond laid a hand on hers. She gripped him tight, an

321

embrace that went straight to his heart in a warming flood. "I do understand."

Bernadette leaned over and kissed Armond's cheek. "Thank you."

"I love you, *Maman.*"

The tears welled up in her eyes, spilled over her cheeks. Her fingers were tight around his, so tight, as though she would never let go. "And I have always loved you, my son."

"He didn't abandon you," Armond said after a moment. "He was killed. I have a report from a private investigator I hired." He slid the envelope over to her.

After a hesitation she picked it up and clutched it to her chest. "Thank you."

"Are you happy now? Happy with Norman?"

"Very much so. I think that's what gave me the courage to talk to you. The past is gone."

In that she was wrong, but he didn't tell her so. The past was never gone. Even when he didn't remember it, it shaped him. It still lived on in him.

Callie hunched her shoulders and stuck her hands into her jacket, trying to keep warm. Wind raced across the bay, piercing her clothing layers and freezing her neck. She wished she had a cup of Tessa's hot weeds tea—not to drink, but to warm her hands. Zeke Jupiter's enthusiasm over this early excursion to see the sunrise over the bay and collect Petoskey stones had sounded more appealing and been more persuasive last night.

Of course, it might have helped with the sunrise part if the beach he picked faced east instead of west.

"Why are we looking for these Petoskey stones?" Harriet grumbled.

"Because they can be found nowhere else in the world," Zeke answered. "And this beach is supposed

to be the best place to find them. They look like this."
He held out a key chain. On the end was a brown stone
in the mitten shape of Michigan.

Even in the murky light of pre-dawn, Callie could
see the stone's smooth surface, patterned with hexagonal starbursts, had been polished until it gleamed.
"It's pretty. Unique, too. I read about these. Something
about this area being undersea at one time, and the
single-celled creatures fused and became rock. Zeke,
can you see the pattern in an unpolished stone?"

"I was told if you put a raw stone in the water the
pattern is clear. Callie, you take that part of the shore,
Harriet will look here, and I'll go over there."

Rocks, not sand, littered the shoreline. Callie me-
andered in the direction in which Zeke had pointed,
her head bent, not so much watching for Petoskey
stones as making sure her sneakers didn't slip on the
damp, uneven ground. Every so often she danced
back from an energetic wave lapping across the rocks.
Wet feet accompanying a cold nose and neck she
didn't want.

The brisk air was damp, but since it came from
fresh water, it carried none of the scent of brine and
seaweed she associated with the beaches of the Gulf.
Instead it was almost odorless, so cold and pollution-
free that it made her think of a pristine snow field.

Or at least what a Southerner imagined a pristine
snow field could smell like.

As brushes of sunrise pink and gold painted the sky
above, though, the rocks became clearer. Callie began
to ignore the cold and Zeke and Harriet talking softly
behind her, intrigued by her hunt. Several times she
thought she'd found one of the prized stones, only to
be fooled by a bit of dirt or shell.

Suddenly Callie stopped. Was that stone patterned?
It looked different from the ones she'd already tested

and found lacking. She bent down and picked it up. Maybe. When the next wave came ashore, she stuck the rock into it, wetting it. Damn, that water was frigid.

Callie held up the dripping rock, peering at it in the coloring morn. It was! It had the distinctive pattern!

"Look! I found one." Jubilantly, she turned around to share her find with Zeke and Harriet.

They had disappeared.

Callie bit her lip, rapidly scanning the rocky shore lined with pine trees. No one. Only the wind played its tune through the creak of the tree boughs. They must have gone into the trees or were around that small bend in the shore. Panic fluttered against her ribs.

"Zeke? Harriet?"

No answer. They wouldn't play a childish prank on her, would they? Of course, they didn't know about her phobia.

Callie sprinted toward the half moon of beach where they'd first come out. She hadn't gone far; they couldn't have gone far either. Her feet slipped on the wet, wobbly rocks, almost causing her to lose her balance. She forced herself to slow down, afraid of adding a sprained ankle to the scrape on her head. But the beating panic and the whistling wind set her trembling.

If only she had her CD player, like she had that day at Armond's cabin.

"Zeke? Harriet?" Her voice was a high-pitched whisper.

"Callie." Armond stepped out from the line of pines. He took one look at her and closed the gap between them in three beats of a racing heart. His arms folded around her and his body shielded her from the wind. "Ah, Callie."

She rested her cheek against his chest, reassured

by the slow beat of his heart. Tension receded.

His fingers softly caressed her hair. "You're trembling. You're cold. I'm sorry."

It took a few more moments for the words to register. Callie reared back, her eyes narrowing. "Why? What are you doing here?"

To her surprise, his neck reddened, and not from the cold. "I know you wanted to see Sleeping Bear Dunes. I wanted to take you there, but I knew you wouldn't come with me, so I got Zeke and Harriet to help." He rubbed the back of his neck. "I didn't know what else to do. Unfortunately, our timing was off."

Sleeping Bear Dunes. The one thing she'd really wanted to see up here, and the one thing she was going to miss. How did he do it? Know just the right thing to tempt her?

"I'm supposed to be filming today."

"I've cleared it with Dion. He, ah, let's say he owes me one. We have this morning. I promise I will be the gentleman."

She and Armond alone? Callie shook her head. "This isn't a good idea, Armond."

"There are some things we need to talk about, Callie. Someplace where Zeke isn't threatening to zap me with electricity, and Bernadette isn't hovering and Dion isn't"—he gave an irritated shrug—"being Dion."

"What more can we say to each other?"

"Please, come with me, Callie."

She'd never heard him ask anything like that, with his emotions raw in his throat. God help her, she was ten times the fool for even thinking of it. Each time she swore this moment was the last with him; then she gave in to the lure of his voice and his touch.

She shouldn't do this, Callie knew. She shouldn't give in to the vulnerability lingering from her bout of panic. She shouldn't open herself to Armond's special brand of seduction and hurt.

Each time she got her heart shattered a little more.

"Callie, one last chance. If not for me, then for our baby."

Had her mother ever given her father any kind of a chance? Callie wondered suddenly. Had Lillian ever tried to make things work, or had she just accepted the Gabriel traditions as Callie had been doing?

"Please." His voice was a mere whisper in the wind.

She wasn't a typical Gabriel. She never had been and never would be, Callie admitted sadly. Perhaps, then, she was to be the one to take a chance with a man.

Slowly, Callie nodded. "All right, Armond. One last chance."

Chapter Twenty-three

To Callie's surprise, Armond avoided the main entrance to the National Lakeshore, going north, instead, to Pyramid Point.

"Why up here?" she asked.

"Because no one will be up here."

Armond wasn't joking when he said no one would be up here; there was hardly even a road. Callie stared in dismay at the parking blip—lot being too fancy a word for this blotch in the gravel, rutted road. Around them loomed the pine forest, its sap scenting the air with a faint aroma. A scraggling of hardy wildflowers lingered at the forest edge.

"I'm surprised you could find this place," she said.

"I scouted it out yesterday. The road felt familiar as I was driving up, and I think I used to come up here with my date and, we, um . . ." The back of his neck turned red as his voice trailed off.

This must be a first; she'd flustered him twice in a morning. "Are you telling me this is where you went parking in high school? And you told me you didn't like necking in a parking lot." She gave a tiny tsk-tsk. "Shall we see the dunes? There are dunes here, aren't there?"

"Down that trail. Wait, your coat. It'll be cold."

While Callie donned her coat, Armond fished a blanket and a basket out of the car trunk. He gave her a critical once-over, then reached back into the car. "You need a hat. Or at least a scarf. Most body heat is lost through the scalp. Do you have gloves?"

"In my pocket, along with an emergency supply of snacks."

Gently he wrapped the scarf over her head and snugged the ends to cover her exposed neck. Definitely warmer, though the heat in Callie had nothing to do with the scarf and everything to do with Armond. When he was finished, however, he stepped away, refusing to touch her further. Apparently he was going to keep good his promise to be the gentleman.

The forest soon ended, except for a rare scrubby tree, and the pine needle–littered path gave way to grass, reeds, and, mostly, sand. The dunes surrounded them, cutting off both wind and sound. If anyone else were here, they would never know it, except for a Yeti-sized trail of footprints left in the sand.

Callie's breath quickened and the muscles in her calves tugged with the exertion as they made their way up a small hill of sand. No need to worry about cold on this trek; she was working up a sweat. She let the scarf dangle about her neck, preferring her hair to be free, even at the expense of a cold head. Occasionally she glanced behind her, making sure Armond still followed, that she wasn't alone out here.

She recalled the one time she'd tried to go herbing

with her mother and sisters. What a nightmare. She'd never felt safe, even though she'd been sitting within view, while they concentrated on gathering the herbs. Her mother had said all Gabriels preferred the city, but they mastered it when they had to, and she'd believed Callie had conquered her phobia of the great outdoors. Callie hadn't—hers seemed so much stronger—but she hadn't said anything. Instead she'd been so tense, so scared, that she'd spent the night throwing up and missed her first-grade play the next day, a play in which she had had the lead as the chief daffodil.

Yet, at the cabin, at the beach, and now here, all places guaranteed to send her into a blithering panic, with Armond—she glanced back again.

Good, he still followed, and he gave her an encouraging smile. "Are you doing okay? We're almost there, I think."

"I'm fine." She was fine. All those places, with Armond there, she did feel safe. Because he was *with* her, not bringing her, then leaving—in spirit if not in body—to do his own thing.

Between the mounds of sand, it was quiet, so, when Callie crested the last one and the wind ran free again, the cold and the noise were shocking. The wind seemed a choir, the soprano notes coming from the shaky-leafed trees and the alto notes from the other trees. The tenor was a low, continuous drone across sand and grass, while the punctuating bass came in with the waves that washed up across the expanse of lake.

And such an expanse it was. In many ways it reminded her of Lake Pontchartrain at home, but this water seemed wilder, less civilized.

Blue came in so many shades: pale, almost green near the rocky shores; deep sapphire over deep water; smoky, darker than the pure gray of Armond's eyes, at the horizon. White clouds danced in the blue skies overhead, but in the distance she could see they had swollen dark underbellies.

Armond came up beside her. He pointed to a smudge of land. "That's North Manitou Island. One of the little bears of legend."

"The one that's a wilderness."

He nodded. "Those clouds look like snow. We may not have long." To her surprise, he sat down on the sand and started to remove his shoes.

"What are you doing?" she asked with a laugh.

"Preparing to run down the sand dune. You have to take your shoes off for that. Wanna join me?"

Armond, proposing something silly and playful? "Sure."

"Just be careful not to tip too far forward. Face first in the sand hurts."

Callie smiled, bemused by this playful side of him, then took off her shoes and socks. Her toes dug into the sand. It was cool on top, damp beneath.

"Is it safe?" She pointed to the red sign, warning them to keep on marked trails because of collapsing sand on the dunes.

"I wouldn't bring you if it wasn't. Just follow me."

"All right." Callie started down, a little awkward at first, but each step brought more confidence, more technique. She followed Armond's easy stride, almost flying between bounds, digging her heels in the sand with each landing to keep her balance, exhilarated at the sensation of freedom.

They reached the bottom together, Callie breathless and laughing, Armond not even breathing hard but also laughing.

"That *was* fun." Impulsively Callie wrapped her arms around his neck and kissed him. And knew her mistake when she felt him still. Quickly she backed away.

"No regrets, Callie," he said softly. "Whatever happens, one thing I don't want you to have is regrets." Then he smiled and gripped her shoulders to face her toward the dune they'd just run down. "There is one bad thing, though, about running down a dune."

Callie groaned as she eyed the expanse of sand towering above her. "Climbing back up."

"Climbing back up. So, we'll rest, eat, talk, then we'll climb up."

"Much more slowly than we came down."

"And return to our lives." His hands dropped from her shoulders, and he turned to spread out the blanket.

Would there be anything changed between them? Or would they be going back to say good-bye?

Dion yawned. The video crew scurried around for their shots, Zeus and Christian were heads deep in a lighting discussion, and Hera lent a hand to the cameraman. Maybe he should do something. Pull a switch or something.

He gave himself a mental shake. Video was a slow process of retakes and edits; he'd never have the patience. His role was what he did best—set things up, smooth the glitches and hitches, let others tread the grind. He needed a hitch or a glitch to fix. Nothing exciting was stirring.

Even his Callie-Armond project seemed doomed, along with the prospect of acquiring Hera's ring. The lovebirds had taken off to Sleeping Bear Dune early this morning; not a good development for one wanting them apart. Especially since those two were worse than Zeus at his most randy. Looking at them melted snow beneath your feet.

Norman Rochon clomped up from the vineyards, heading toward the vatting area, but he detoured to

Dion and handed him a bunch of grapes. "Thought you might like a taste."

Dion popped a handful of grapes into his mouth, the juice bursting across his tongue. "Those are perfection."

"Only way to eat 'em, fresh off the vine."

"With none of the tiny mites and webs washed off," Dion agreed. "Your vineyards are a charm," he told Norman honestly, for no one appreciated the beauty of a pampered vineyard and grape more than Dionysus. "Thank you for letting us film here."

"Our pleasure. We're hoping for some increased sales."

"Just don't grow so big you lose touch with the vines, the earth, and the grapes. Nothing is more important."

Norman gave him a steady look. "Except family."

Dion's gaze strayed to Zeus and Hera, heads bent as they plotted together. "I wouldn't know," he said softly. "I lost my family a very long time ago."

"Sorry to hear that."

"Hello?" The arrival of a stranger cut off any further conversation.

Just as well, thought Dion. Maudlin wasn't his style.

The newcomer was spiffed from his short hair to his suit coat to his shined shoes. Dion frowned. Had to be one of Armond's co-workers. Everything about the man screamed fed.

"Can I help you?" asked Norman.

"I'm looking for Special Agent Armond Marceaux."

"And who might you be?"

The man flashed a badge in a blue leather case, then flipped it back into his pocket. "Conrad Titus. FBI. Mr.—?"

"Norman Rochon." He shook the agent's hand, then angled his head toward Dion. "Dion Backus."

Dion did not extend a hand. Conrad Titus had an irritating karma.

"What do you need Armond for?" asked Norman.

"I'm afraid that's confidential. If you'll tell me where he is, I won't bother you again."

Norman hesitated, then said, "Sleeping Bear Dunes. Pyramid Point, I think. I expect they'll be back after lunch."

"They?"

"He went with a friend."

Titus nodded, not seeming surprised. Or maybe it was just fed inscrutability. He pivoted with precision and took his leave.

There was a power to the FBI, Dion realized, if one look at that badge had Norman talking. Curiosity stirring away his ennui, he trailed into the tasting room, then perched on a stool and watched out the window as Titus left. The agent had two other men with him in the car. These two sported the haircut, the suit coat, likely the shoes, but something about them sneered "faux-FBI." The cruel set of the mouth, perhaps.

Dion frowned again. Perhaps he should talk to Zeus and Hera? A little far-see smoke might not be amiss—

His thoughts broke off as a sporty car whisked into the parking lot and parked with efficient precision. A vision emerged from the car: ice blonde, supple, old enough to have experience. She walked with a determined step into the tasting area and glanced around with the assurance of a woman who knew what she wanted.

Dion liked that in a woman.

Nice breasts, too. And blue-blue eyes.

The dregs of boredom vanished under a blooming haze of interest. "Can I help you?" he asked, content to perform the host's duties.

"I'm Lillian Gabriel. I'm looking for my daughter, Callie."

"Do Petoskey stones wash up on this beach?"

"I don't know. We can look." Armond secured the remains of breakfast in the basket. Bernadette had packed enough for a dozen. He wrapped the blanket around it, forming a neat bundle.

Conversation between them during the short meal was surface only, frustrating Armond. He'd tried to draw them into more intimate areas, but Callie neatly ignored his cues. Weren't women supposed to be the ones who initiated all the relationship talks? It certainly would have made things easier.

Except that Callie thought their relationship was settled. She thought it was over, Armond reminded himself glumly as he joined her at the water's edge.

Callie bent down and examined a pebble, then dropped it. "Not a Petoskey."

Armond kicked at a small rock, looking for something to say. This was ridiculous. He'd never had trouble talking to Callie before.

Because she usually carried the conversation.

He was on his own here, and he couldn't even open his mouth. Wasn't even sure anymore what he wanted to say.

When he'd first had the idea of bringing her here, he'd thought it would give him a chance to convince her that he loved her, persuade her that they were good together. Then he'd found out about his father, about the pain his mother had endured.

Like father like son? The phrase had lingered at the back of his thoughts the rest of the night.

Armond grabbed at something, anything, to say. "Look, a rowboat. Do you suppose it's seaworthy?" He turned it upright. The boat looked timeworn, its weathered board graced with a few flecks of faded paint. "There aren't any big holes."

"There's also only one oar."

He skidded the boat nearer the water. "It floats. Maybe—"

"Don't even suggest it. I like terra firma under my feet."

"Bobbing seas not the best thing for a pregnant woman?"

"I don't do well in nature, but at least here I have solid ground under my feet. Out there—" She waved a hand toward the water and shuddered.

Armond abandoned the boat idea. It hadn't been a very good one to begin with; just a stalling technique.

"My sister Tessa would like this," Callie mused, her hands in her jacket pocket. "She keeps a sailboat out on Lake Pontchartrain and is teaching Kitty how to sail. Tessa always was a regular fish in the water, and now Kitty is, too."

"Like you're feeding your daughter jalapeños so she'll like spicy food?"

She laughed. "And like how Mom taught Stacia all she knew about herbal medicine. Like mother, like daughter runs in the Gabriel family, I guess."

Like mother, like daughter. Like father, like son. What traits ran in the Marceaux family? Armond chose a flat rock and absently skipped it along the surface of the water, once, twice, three times, unable to ignore any longer that nagging question. Did he really expect Callie to wait, like his mother had, for a man who might disappear for good every time he went to work? Was that what he wanted for the woman he loved?

He looked over at Callie. She walked with head bent, studying the rocks at her feet. A beam of sunlight turned her hair to gold, and the wind touched her cheeks with red. Just looking at her filled his chest with an ache of longing so intense, it stole his breath. She brought color to his life, the vibrant colors of autumn and spice and sunset.

Armond picked up another rock and skipped it, four times. Callie needed someone she could rely on twenty-four/seven, not just when the job permitted. As the pieces of his life returned, as the memories of who he was, and how he was, returned, he began to understand what she meant.

Her family gave that to her. He did not.

She had a world of success waiting for her.

The wind swirled, and an eddy of sand prickled against his face. His eyes stung and watered.

He couldn't ask that sacrifice of her. Ask? *Merde,* he'd been demanding it. *We're going to get married, Callie.* What an arrogant SOB.

A lump clogged his lungs. He had to let her go. Callie had accepted what must be; now he would, too. But not while she still thought that he considered their few times together merely a good time.

He cleared his throat, and she looked at him expectantly.

The words would not come. He could face a drugged-out pimp, could maneuver safely through a high-speed chase, could thrill to the snap of cuffs on some guilty scum, but he couldn't find the courage to say "I love you," then let her go.

Instead, he picked up another stone and skipped it.

"Will you show me how you do that?" Callie asked. "Skip stones?"

"Yeah, sure. You have to find one that's thin and flat."

"Like this?" She picked one up.

"That looks good." While he showed her the wrist flick, touched her hand to keep it flat, and explained the angles, her scent, fresher than the surrounding nature, teased at him. She had strong hands, a chef's hands, but her hair was soft where it touched his cheek. He watched her face light in excitement, then cloud in disappointment as her first try at skipping dropped immediately into the water. At once, she sought another stone.

Armond rubbed his aching chest. Marriage meant she needed him to be there for her. Could he quit the Bureau, quit LE? Be what she wanted him to be? Once, the thought would never have crossed his mind, but knowing this was his final hour with Callie forced him to ask the unthinkable. Could he?

Even without his talent, or curse, he was a damned good cop. He knew it without false modesty, and the world needed good cops. Could he read the paper each day, see the stories of murder or fraud and know that if he were there, at least one victim might have been saved or at least one perp would be behind bars and couldn't rape or savage again?

An icy shiver ran through him, and his thoughts tumbled against each other. Could he endure that foul taste of guilt and not be able to do anything about it? He felt the weight of the gun he carried, and his fingers brushed against the leather case holding his badge.

Despite the cold, sweat broke out on his brow and his stomach roiled. The nauseating prelude to memory. White pain flashed in his head, carrying an image of him holding that badge the first time, pride and satisfaction surging through him. Flash to a deafening boom, the echo of the first time he'd fired his gun to stop a maniac bent on killing a hostage. A teenaged Armond in the shower, his arms raw, trying to scrub out the taint he had no recourse against, lying in bed and fighting the nausea of knowledge, of trying to ignore what he knew he should do.

The onslaught vanished, leaving him shaken.

He'd tried to forget what he was, what he could do, and found he couldn't. Even amnesia hadn't erased it. At the end of that path lay the insanity he'd feared all his life. If he quit, he would end up destroying himself and destroying anything good that lay between him and Callie.

He drew in a deep breath, knowing now what he must do.

Plop. Another of Callie's stones dropped like dead weight. Lips pressed together, she picked up another. "Can you show me that wrist flick again? This time I've got the perfect stone. I know I can do this."

"Sure." He stood behind her and wrapped his arms around her, knowing it would be the last time. She stilled for a moment, then relaxed against him. She was made for his arms, insisted his rebellious libido. He put a small distance between their bodies and took her hand in his.

"Like this," he said, wrapping his hand over hers and positioning it. Just from this small touch, his belly tightened with acute need. "Like this." He moved her hand in the skipping motion, repeating it until she nodded.

"I can feel it."

"Now you do it, Callie." He let go of her and clenched his fists against the loss.

She bit her lip, concentrating, flicked her wrist, let go of the stone . . . and it skipped. Three skips before sinking to the bottom.

"I did it!" Callie jumped around to face him, clapping her hands. "I did it."

"You did." He smiled, sharing her joy.

She cupped his cold cheeks with her palms, spreading instant heat through him, and stood on tiptoe to kiss his lips. "Thank you."

At once, he was lost in the kiss. Lost to all reason

and common sense and knowledge of the right thing to do. Instead of pushing her away, his arms came around her, pulling her pliant body against his. Curves to planes, soft to hard. She didn't hesitate or pull back. Rather, her arms gathered him close.

It was a devouring kiss he gave her, for it was a kiss that would have to sustain him with its memory. No matter what happened in his life, he could not forget this last kiss.

And it was a frantic, forgiving kiss she returned. Callie did not resist his hunger. She met every stab of his tongue, tangled him up with hers. Her fingers slipped through his hair and held him where she wanted him. His heart pounded in his ears, mixing with the beat of hers against his chest and the throb of blood in his groin. He lifted, she gave a soft mewl of protest, he angled his head to deepen the kiss.

Gradually the fierceness ebbed, giving way to tenderness. He rained kisses on her damp eyelids, her cheeks, her temple, her neck, then back to her soft, soft lips for one final taste of coffee and cinnamon and Callie. Then, slowly, he ended the kiss.

His forehead rested against hers, their shaking breaths mingling. "I love you, Callie."

Why had the words been so hard to say, when they were so utterly right?

He loved her? Callie pressed her lips together against the joy blossoming in her chest. He loved her.

"I know what you heard me say to Dion," Armond continued, "and it was the truth then, as I knew it. Truths change. I was in love with you; I just didn't recognize it. I know you may find that hard to believe, but I do love you."

After that kiss, after everything that'd happened, how could she not believe him? His soul had been in that kiss. She knew because hers was there with it. "I believe you. And I love you, too, Armond."

In answer, his arms tightened around her, holding her so very close and cherished for a moment; then he loosened her. Callie looked up at him. His gray eyes held that tenderness, that softness.

And that cop determination.

"So why do I feel a huge 'but' being added?" she asked.

"I can't quit the Bureau. I can't quit being a cop, and we both know you can't live with me like that."

Callie closed her eyes as the truth gripped her chest. She had been asking, demanding really, that he change to suit her notion of a husband and father. How could she ask that of him?

Because the rest of what he said was true, too. She couldn't live like that. Alone. A tear slid down her cheek, as she opened her eyes to look at him.

He wasn't angry. He wasn't demanding.

He understood exactly what she wanted and he accepted it. Armond had always accepted her without conditions, without trying to change her, without fitting her into the mold of tradition.

He loved her enough to give her up.

Did she love him enough, was she strong enough, to fight for him?

She opened her mouth, although what she would say she didn't know, but he put a finger over her lips, silencing her. "Don't say anything until you hear the rest of what I have to say."

Callie nodded, and he lowered his hand. She waited for him to begin.

"I think what I do is important, necessary, but there's more." He let out a sharp breath. "I'm different. I have been for almost as long as I can remember."

"Two weeks?"

He smiled at her gentle tease. "From the snippets I've retrieved, most of my life."

"Different? How?"

"I know when someone's guilty."

Callie shook her head. "I don't understand."

"One of the things that makes me such a good cop is, I have this instinctive knowledge when someone's guilty of something. I don't have to waste time figuring out 'whodunit.' I *know* who."

"You read their minds or something?"

"No. I can . . . feel it. Taste it. When I'm hunting a criminal, it becomes part of me until the person is brought to justice. So you see, when I feel this, *know* this, I have to do something about it. That's why I can't quit, why I can't be the man you want. I'd go mad."

This was too much for her to grasp so quickly. "You live with this all the time?"

"Mostly I learned to ignore it when I didn't need it in my work." Briefly he touched the belt at his waist. "I think my father may have had it."

"Will our baby?" Callie's hand fluttered to her belly.

"I don't know that either."

Her baby might be . . . different. As different from her as she had been from Lillian. She stepped away from him, unsure, confused, buffeted by too many conflicting emotions and fears.

Armond accepted her withdrawal with his usual aplomb. Except it was a mask, she realized, and with it he covered tight the passions, and the strangeness, beneath.

No, not a mask. A necessary part of him, all the pieces making up the whole man she loved.

"What do you feel with me?" she asked. "I'm not perfect."

"This is a guilt drawn not from imperfection and regret but from evil. One of the things that drew me

341

to you, Callie, from the very beginning, is the basic purity in your soul. With you, I was at peace. I never expected to find that in another person. I expected to spend my life alone."

"Is that why you fell in love with me? Because I was the only woman you could tolerate being close to?" She could barely get the words out around the vice squeezing her chest. She had thought there would be nothing worse than hearing him say he didn't love her, but this was coming damn close.

He pondered her question a moment, then shook his head. "That allowed me to get close enough to you to fall in love. I fell in love because . . . Who knows why? Because you smiled a lot? Because you color my life with brilliant hues? Because you make me feel as if I could move mountains for you? Because you spice up everything with peppers and ginger?"

"I don't use peppers and ginger in everything."

"I was speaking metaphorically."

"Oh."

They stared at each other a long moment, Callie too scared and confused to think of how she could answer.

"We'd better be getting back," he said at last. "Those snow clouds are moving in. And you have a shoot to finish."

"You're leaving, aren't you?"

He nodded. "Someone in the Bureau is working with Guy Centurion and knows I'll follow the trail back to him. I need to find out who betrayed me, betrayed the Bureau."

That clipped note was back in his voice. The hunter, the warrior, the man who needed justice was back. He would always be back. "You're going back even without all your memory?"

"I have enough."

342

"You don't have a name yet." Callie laid a hand on his chest, faint with a sudden fear for him. A sudden fear of losing him that was worse than any pain of being alone. Beneath her palm lay the warm strength of his heart. "You could be walking right back into betrayal. Armond, stay here, stay with me until you have it all back. It's too dangerous."

"I can't. I may never get back my memory, and I've wasted enough time."

A sudden fluttering in her womb startled Callie; then she wrinkled her nose at the tingling that seemed to come from the metallic belt he wore. An unpleasant taste, like overripe Gorgonzola cheese, puckered her tongue.

Gray eyes darkening, Armond stared at her a fraction of a breath, then spun around to face the dunes, placing her behind him. She felt the muscles of his back tense and knew, from the way his head shifted, that the warrior was analyzing something.

"What—?"

He motioned her silent with a hand. "We're going to head to the edge of the beach, behind that spit of a dune." He spoke from the corner of his mouth, his voice low as the wind, not looking at her. "Slow, as though nothing's wrong."

Until he'd said that, until he'd gone into warrior mode, she hadn't realized anything *was* wrong, but she didn't argue. As they'd agreed, he was a cop, and a damn good one.

"Special Agent Marceaux." A lone figure appeared at the top of the dune. FBI, Callie guessed. Only an on-duty fed would wear wingtips and a suit coat on a sand dune.

Armond's hand settled near the gun he carried. "Yes?"

He'd brought a gun to their picnic? For once, Callie

ignored her pacifistic views long enough to be grateful. Something about the man above them set her teeth on edge and her insides shriveling. She'd bet he wasn't here to skip stones and slide down dunes, and on an open beach like this she and Armond were the proverbial sitting ducks.

"Conrad Titus. FBI," the man called. "You haven't reported in as ordered."

"When I'm undercover, I can't always follow your schedule," Armond answered.

Titus shook his head sadly. "You're not undercover, Marceaux. You never were. It's the drugs."

"Drugs?"

"You've used them a long time. Longer than we realized. Hallucinogens, others. They fueled your paranoia."

Armond halted his imperceptible shift toward the concealing dune and tilted his head, as if studying the truth of Titus's words. Callie followed his lead, her calf scraping against the beached boat.

Surely Armond didn't believe the accusation? He didn't even take aspirin, and the only thing he drank was wine, which, to a French-raised boy, was as commonplace as mother's milk.

"You're not a junkie," she whispered fiercely. "This guy is full of crap."

"I know that!" Armond hissed back. "He may be full of crap, but he's not alone. I caught a movement to our right."

"How many?"

"At least two. Maybe more."

"What do we do now?"

"I'm working on it."

Chapter Twenty-four

"We'll get you help." Titus took a step down the dune.

"Stop right there." Armond whipped out his gun and held it steady on Titus.

Swearing under his breath, Titus skidded to a halt, his slick-soled shoes losing their grip in the sand. He forced himself to play the role of concerned superior. "Don't make this worse than it is. Put down the gun, come quietly with me, and we'll allow you to resign. Minimum of fuss, and you get the help you need. You fire on a SAC"—he spread his hands wide in a gesture of trust designed to bring him closer to his own gun—"and you won't have a hope in hell of surviving forty-eight hours. You know that, Marceaux."

Marceaux's gun didn't falter.

This time, the calculated risk wasn't going to work, Titus realized. The first had succeeded when he'd revealed himself at the winery, after watching for a time and concluding that Marceaux wasn't there. When he'd heard Marceaux had come to an isolated beach it had seemed the perfect time to bring him in without all the hostile witnesses. It would have been so much easier if Marceaux and the woman had simply believed his tale. Marceaux would have been brought in, then disappeared, leaving the woman to be relieved at her escape from a drugged-out agent.

From their looks, neither one believed him.

Covering up the deaths of an agent and a civilian would be harder, but it could be done.

"Shouldn't my daughter be back?" Lillian Gabriel raised one blond brow.

Dion glanced at the clock, startled that so much time had passed, then frowned. He'd started debating wines and New Orleans restaurants with Lillian and completely lost sight of the fact that he'd assured her that Armond had said they'd be back by lunch.

Armond was the type to be punctual to a fault.

"Was it your intention to distract me, Mr. Backus?"

"Of course not," Dion said impatiently, his finger rubbing distractedly along his chin. That FBI man should be getting to the dunes about now. Hadn't he been intending to ask Zeus and Hera about the far-see . . .

He shoved to his feet. "Excuse me, my dear," he offered absently, then hurried out, leaving Lillian scowling after him.

Hera was with Zeus, putting away the lighting equipment in preparation for moving into the kitchen, where Callie was supposed to be getting ready for her cooking segment. "We may have a problem," he said tersely, explaining about Conrad Titus. "We need to do a far-see."

"Why didn't you come right away?" spat Zeus, thunder echoing in his voice.

Hera nudged him, pointing toward the tasting room as Lillian emerged onto the patio, where she was waylaid by Bernadette Rochon.

"A woman? Hades, Dion!"

Dion glowered at Zeus for his hypocrisy. As if he'd never gotten distracted by a woman before! "She's Callie's mother. At least I kept her away from them." No sense in telling Zeus and Hera that had not been his original purpose. He had a feeling they guessed it anyway.

"Come to my room," commanded Hera.

In a moment they'd gathered in her room. After carefully locking the door and pulling the shades, Hera retrieved her geode and the far-see crystals. Zeus rubbed his ring to light the crystals, but only a fizzle came from it.

"What's wrong?" Dion scowled. Was this some kind of a trick?

"Nothing." Angrily, Zeus swiped a hand over his ring and a sharp bite of electricity came from it, igniting the crystals.

Hera, however, wasn't pretending. "It's our rings, Dion. They're losing power. Even if you win mine, you won't be getting much of a prize."

Dion stared at her, unable to do anything but believe the utter sadness in her voice. A god without power? It was unthinkable.

"Look!" Zeus's exclamation brought their attention back to the smoke.

Armond and Callie stood on a rocky beach, looking up a dune at Conrad Titus. And, hidden from view, the two faux-FBI fanned out, treading carefully over the sand until they could surround the couple.

* * *

There was always a possibility Titus wasn't his man, that he was working under false information planted by the true traitor, Armond realized. Still, he held the gun steady. He wouldn't know for certain until he touched Titus.

Of course, that possibility was about as likely as him taking up a career in ballet.

Which meant Callie and their baby were in danger.

A wisp of fog, fronting the swollen clouds, rolled in from the water and seeped beneath the knit of his sweater, chilling him. He'd been in worse situations, but the blossoming fear in his gut was new. It both tore at his focus and sharpened his senses, and Callie was the reason.

Behind him, he felt her shiver, from cold or fear or both. She touched his shoulder, as if needing reassurance, and even through the sweater's thickness her fingers were icy.

She might have had a chance to escape from here if she convinced Titus she believed his drug story, but Callie was too honest and loyal to lie so thoroughly. Besides, odds were Titus wouldn't wait for her to start asking questions later.

That left it up to him.

He wanted to give her a comforting touch but didn't dare the distraction. He forced himself to concentrate on the men circling him, drawing on instinct honed by hours of training to do what had to be done.

Where were the others? Sneaking around the dunes was difficult with the unstable sand, but he figured he had at max two minutes before Titus's backup reached their position and he was outgunned.

"What's your answer, Marceaux?" called Titus. "I'm getting impatient. And we wouldn't want the lady to get hurt."

The threat to Callie settled the issue. As he'd

guessed, Titus not being the traitor was about as likely as him strapping on toe shoes.

Armond's heart pounded against his ribs. Just let Callie be safe. If he'd needed proof that his lifestyle wasn't for her, today provided that in spades. *Don't make her pay for my mistakes.*

"You'll let Callie go?" he asked, stalling.

"Of course. I'm not the one putting her in danger."

Callie's fingers dug into his shoulder.

"You promise she'll be safe?"

"No!" hissed Callie. "I won't go."

"Of course," answered Titus.

Armond recognized the lies, but at least they bought him seconds while he searched for a way out. The dunes before them were too steep. They hadn't gotten close enough to the side of the beach to take refuge in the sand there. The boat? In clear sight of land they'd be dead before they reached the lake currents.

A faint whistle, like the wind through a reed, sounded to his right. One man in place. The man on the left, not there yet.

Protection. Justice. The twin drives sparked through him, amplified through the linked belt at his waist. They sharpened his instincts and clawed at the black curtain of amnesia.

Something about the dunes to the left. . . . Behind the protective wall of sand to their left, something there to help them. Armond forced breath through his lungs, rolling back the nausea. He couldn't afford to remember more right now.

Go. Before the third man whistled. Even if he didn't make it, Callie might.

"The dune to the left," he told her, so low his words barely had voice. "Stay between me and the shore;

I've got the gun. Hide in the dunes." *If I don't make it.* "On two."

Her fingers tightened again, telling him that she understood; then she dropped her hand.

Callie. He would not let her or the baby die. The tidal wave of protectiveness, of fear, of determination rushed through him. Wind whistled down his back. Pale fog swirled around his feet, a cold tether.

Fog. A different day. A death.

His lips formed around the words to set them running.

His voice was drowned by the nausea of pain. Lightning shot from the belt to his skull. Red, then white, exploded behind his eyes, and a flood of memories surged into him.

Warning. Sands unstable. The crimson words on the warning signs ripped through the black barrier of his mind. *A young boy suffocated on the sands piling into the sinkhole. The searchers. Armond, found him.*

Dimly, beneath the pain, Armond understood why he'd said left. A sinkhole. Just to the left, a huge hole separated the shore from the dunes. Titus would lose time going around, giving them a chance to escape.

"Go," he croaked, trying to keep in front of Callie, but his legs were made of sand. This time the memories didn't stop with the images. Past fear for the boy blended with present fear for Callie. Memories of the painstaking search drew out memories of pushing himself in boot camp and the academy. The wall of amnesia ripped under the onslaught, and its shredded remnants stabbed at him like excruciating white-hot daggers.

He heard the whistle of the third man.

Too late. They were surrounded.

"The boat," he rasped. It was their closest escape, their only hope now. Her only hope, actually.

Callie clambered into the boat, and Armond shoved it out into Lake Michigan. The frigid water numbed his legs and he stumbled forward, freeing the boat from the rocks.

Armond glanced over his shoulder. Titus shouted something and raised a gun. Armond let go of the boat and turned. Fighting to focus eyes blurred by the pounding pain, he aimed.

Two retorts, one his. But Titus was still standing. One—

Armond reeled back from the impact, and blood blossomed on his shoulder. There was no pain. At least, none sufficient to compete with the blinding pain behind his eyes and the suffocating pain in his chest that Callie might be next.

Had to get her out of here.

"Get in the boat!" Callie shouted, grabbing the oar and propelling the boat.

Armond shook his head, fighting to clear it. Fighting the onslaught of a lifetime of returning memories. The relentless images competed with the lumps of ice that were once his feet. *Hold on. Hold on. Get her where they can't see her.*

The boat was still in clear range. If he turned, took the time to get in, Titus would have a clear shot at Callie. He backed up against the boat, shoving it out with his butt, still facing the shore, his body a shield.

"Hades!" shouted Zeus. "They're shooting."

And Armond was placing himself between Callie and the bullets. "We have to do something," Hera gasped. "If only the fog—The fog!"

She cupped her hand around the far-see smoke and rubbed her ring. It wheezed, only thickening the fog a small amount. She tried again. Not enough. She didn't have enough power. "Help me," she pleaded with Zeus.

He saw at once what she was trying to do. He laced his fingers with hers, palm to palm. Both of them rubbed the rings. Not enough. Her fear for Callie and Armond coalesced to a stormy knot.

"Again." She pressed her thumb against the ring, pouring every ounce of panic into it. Zeus matched her.

The rings glowed, a flash bright as sun. Lightning bolts shot out from the metal with a thunderous roar and hurricane power into the far-see smoke.

The image disappeared behind thick waves of rolling fog.

Slowly Zeus loosened their hands. He stared down at his fingers. Hera dropped her hand, her body heavy, her arm too weak to bear the weight of the lifeless ring.

"You did it," crowed Dion. "How long will you let the fog stay? Let's transport over there, see if we can do something."

Hera raised her eyes to his. Suddenly the room seemed devoid of color and of life. "We can't," she said softly.

Dion's brows knit. "Can't what?"

"We can't transport over there. We can't dispel the fog."

"Why?"

She lifted her hand to show him the ring. It was dull and lifeless.

"We used up the last of our power," said Zeus softly.

Hera turned from the deadened ring to gaze at him, refusing to give in to the tears that threatened. "I'm sorry."

"It was my choice, too." He picked up her hand, the one without the ring of the gods, and softly rubbed a thumb against her knuckles. "At least our last act as gods was one of good, not one of greed or gain."

They were silent a moment, the thick smoke still lingering in the chintz-filled room. Its damp cedar scent wrapped around her nose and throat, leaving one final memory.

Dion cleared his throat. "About that fog . . ."

Hera tilted her head. "Yes?"

"The power of the gods created it. Without your power to dissipate it, how long is it going to last?"

Hera sat back in her chair. She looked at Zeus.

He shrugged.

"I don't know," she told Dion.

Chapter Twenty-five

By the time Callie got Armond into the boat, she had totally lost her sense of direction in the disorienting fog. Not a sound or a shadow gave substance to the featureless landscape. The only direction she could be sure of was down, because her feet were planted there, and even that was iffy. It was like being in Mammoth Cave again, only surrounded by gray light instead of black darkness.

The gray closed on her, plucking at her breath, and Callie fought the rise of bile in her throat. She couldn't afford to give in to panic. Armond's life depended on her. He'd been ready to stand between her and Titus. Only the sudden fog, so impenetrable it hid them from view as effectively as a wall, had persuaded him to struggle into the boat, where he promptly collapsed. So now she had to help him.

Only the panic wasn't listening to reason.

Barely able to see Armond for the thick fog, Callie knelt beside him, where he sprawled in the bottom of the boat. She touched his cheek.

His face was wet. From the lake or fog? Sweat from the exertion? Was he sick? As she had at his cabin, Callie wished that she could heal him. Or at least know which way to head for help.

"Armond. Armond, what's wrong?"

His answer was a groan. His mouth pulled into a brief, silent grimace; then he slitted open his eyes. They were pain-glazed, tuned to some inner torment. A headache, she realized, wiping the sweat from his face. The signal of the return of his memory, and the worst she'd ever seen.

"Sorry, Callie," he moaned, his voice like sand.

"It's the memory, isn't it? How can I help?"

"No honey this time?" His lashes fluttered, then squeezed shut. The light must hurt his eyes; hers ached from the diffuse glare that reflected off every suspended droplet of water.

"Sorry. Fresh out of baklava."

"Touch me. Need . . . to know . . . here."

"Sure." Callie laced her fingers with his. "And you keep talking to me." The fog absorbed her breathless voice. "Please, just . . . talk to me." She wrapped her arm around his shoulder, braced the other on his damp sweater. "C'mon, let's get you upright."

When she tried to pull him upright, though, he flinched from her. What? She lifted her hand, then stared in horror at her wet and sticky palm. In the diffuse light, now, she saw the darkness coating her fingers. In the cool air she smelled the copper of blood.

He'd been shot. Her panic yielded to the greater fear for Armond. His sweater was soaked with his blood. Hastily she felt beneath the clothes and found the oozing hole in his shoulder. At least the cold water seemed to have stanched the flow of blood, but the wound needed to be bandaged.

No medical kits on this heap. Callie frantically tore the scarf from her neck. She might not have earned the village witch title, but living with three healers and working around hot grease and sharp knives had taught her a modicum of first aid. She pulled her gloves from her pocket, pressed them against the wound, and tied them in place with the scarf. Not the most sterile, but at least he wouldn't lose any more blood, hopefully, until they got out of this.

If they got out of this.

Callie looked around, then quickly averted her eyes downward when the wings of panic beat against her chest. They would get out. It was only fog. How long could it last?

And, for the moment, they were safe from the men on shore.

Careful to approach from his uninjured side this time, she wrapped her arm around Armond's waist and pulled him upright. "C'mon, Armond, sit up. Sit on the bench with me. This floor is damp and hard, and your clothes are wet. You don't need any more dampness." *And we both need to know we're not alone.*

Silently he struggled with her onto the single bench. She pulled him close and he collapsed against her side. Just feeling the weight and heat of him helped.

She wasn't alone. She had two people to save—Armond and her baby.

"What now?" she said aloud, needing the sound of a voice, even if it was just her ragged tones.

"Follow the shore," Armond answered unexpectedly, his voice a thread, his eyes closed.

"There is no shore." She eyed the boat. "And only one oar."

"Away from . . . them." He faded away, and his weight was heavy against her.

At least the fog would prevent the men from coming after them, but when it lifted she and Armond better be someplace else. "So, which way's shore?" Callie muttered.

Shouldn't the waves be washing toward shore? She peered over the side of the boat. Waves lapped against the weathered wood. No help there.

"It's too cold to swim. These waves don't seem to be washing anywhere but against the boat. I can't see where to steer. With my luck, I'd steer us out to the middle of a gazillion-acre lake. Does Lake Michigan have currents? Maybe we should just drift? What do you think?"

No answer.

Callie knew she was babbling, but the sound of her voice helped her hold back the fear sitting on her chest, creeping outward, threatening to engulf her.

"The suggestion box is open for what I should do next. Row? Talk? Sing? Whistle 'Dixie'?"

"Sing." Armond moaned, startling her.

Sing. Of course, every song she'd ever learned immediately left her head except for one: "The Wreck of the Edmund Fitzgerald," Gordon Lightfoot's ode to one of the Great Lakes' legendary sunken ships. "Is this fog the Lake Michigan equivalent of the gales of November come early?" she asked a silent Armond.

He didn't answer, slumped heavily against her, and Callie guessed that he'd lost consciousness. Between the gunshot, the loss of blood, and the debilitating headache, she was surprised he'd kept conscious as long as he had.

He just had to hang on until she could get them some help.

He wanted her to sing, so she would sing, and hope

357

to keep the terror at bay. She held Armond close, then started singing about the shipwreck, trying to be strong and brave.

Callie didn't know how long they drifted; long enough to become hoarse and heartily sick of shipwreck ballads. She'd forgotten to look at her watch at the beginning, and when she'd remembered they'd been aboat for some time. She glanced at her watch. Two hours at least.

Armond had slipped in and out of consciousness, and now he was leaning on her so still and so heavy that she was sure he was out. It couldn't be good for him to sit in his wet clothes. She felt his forehead. Was it cooler? Hypothermia setting in? Hotter? Feverish? Whichever, she had to get him to help soon.

Callie risked looking up. She'd only survived this long by concentrating on Armond, the weight of his body against hers, the sound of his thick, uneven breath. The fog drained away all sensation, until the deprivation had her doubting eyes, ears, and even the touch of her fingers. Instead she watched the play of pain across Armond's face, studied the fringe of his lashes. She'd traced the line of his lips, tested the rapid but steady beat of his heart beneath her palm, even tried her mother's suggestion for getting rid of migraines using pressure points.

The fog still surrounded them. Gray, gray, gray all around. No one here.

Her stomach churned, and it seemed the boat spun in a frightening whirlpool. Dear God, she'd added hallucinating to her list of symptoms. She could almost imagine there was a smear of darkness against the unrelenting light.

Callie blinked and rubbed her eyes. There *was* something there. She gave Armond a gentle shake.

"Armond, land." She grabbed the oar and put her back to steering the boat to shore.

Land. Doctors. Heat. Food. People.

Callie could hardly breathe, so anxious was she to be with people, but her heart sank as she neared the land. She could see little, and the little she did see wasn't promising. There were no roads, no houses, no people, no lights. She stood, ignoring the teetering of the boat, while she peered through the fog. The shore was dense with trees, their yellow leaves gleaming against the gray. They must have ended up at one of the Manitou Islands instead of the mainland.

The wilderness islands. There were bears here, and deer, and poison ivy, but no people.

The panic she'd fought through the endless bobbing in the mind-sapping fog burst out. Callie dropped to the boat bench, shaking, her breath coming in rapid gasps. She couldn't do this. Not one more moment. Tears spilled from her eyes. No more. She grasped her hair in her fists and rocked while a scream bubbled up her throat. No, no, no.

Beside her, Armond stirred, a soft groan escaping his lips. "Callie? *Ma chérie?*"

The endearment, so soft, but the only sound in the endless silence, broke through her panic. Callie froze, her breath and muscles like ice. Even her heart thumped slow in her ears. A final tear rolled down her cheek.

Armond needed her. Her baby needed her. For them, she would do what must be done. Callie dragged in two deep breaths, willing herself to move. She couldn't afford the self-indulgence of panic. Her hands dropped to her sides. Her limbs still shook, leaving her aching, but her mind began to function again.

They had to land, but the shore was rocky and inhospitable. Then Callie blinked, unable to believe her eyes. Looming out of the fog, only a foot away, a landing stuck out into the water. A boat landing for backpackers and hunters.

Paddling as hard as she could, Callie maneuvered the boat near the dock, but she couldn't let go of the paddle long enough to grab the dock. "Armond," she called, "wake up. Please wake up. I need your help. We're landing. Grab the dock. Wake up, Armond!"

That finally penetrated. His gaze was still laced with pain and confusion, but as he looked around, Callie saw comprehension dawn. He grabbed the post of the dock, wincing but not complaining, and held on, helping Callie maneuver the boat to the shore. They stumbled onto land and collapsed on the leaf-littered shore. Callie grabbed the dirt with both hands, overjoyed. The fog still hung over them like a blanket, they could be stranded here for days, but at least the land wasn't covered in bobbing waves.

Armond rose unsteadily to his feet. Callie hurried to his side, bracing him against her. He draped an arm across her shoulders and looked around. "Where are we?"

"One of the Manitous, I think."

"Probably North," he said, his voice weak. "There should be a Coast Guard station near."

"The Coast Guard?"

"The historic Coast Guard station."

"Oh." She laid a hand on his cheek. "How are you feeling?"

"My memory's back. All at once it's come back."

"That must have hurt."

He started to shrug, then stopped, as though the motion hurt. "It's fading, but I'm still having trouble focusing my eyes." He rubbed a hand across his chest. "Did a semi drive over me?"

"Titus shot you."

"Is he—?" His eyes darted around, and she felt him tense. His hand automatically reached for his gun.

"I don't think he can come out after us with this fog, and there weren't any other boats around. Besides, how would he know we're here? For a while we're safe."

His tense muscles relaxed just a little. "You're right."

"We need to get some rest. You've lost a lot of blood. You look terrible," she added. His skin was white, his lips pinched, and his eyes were heavy shadows.

"You're doing wonders for my ego."

"Your ego is just fine, but your body's a bit mangled. Here, lean on me. Let's see if we can find one of the buildings."

It was a measure of how bad off he was that he didn't protest her assistance. Callie bit her lip, knowing she had to find him shelter. She could feel the faint tremors of utter exhaustion rippling through him, but at least he stayed upright. They traced the edge of a path until they reached a clutch of buildings nearly obliterated by the fog. Unfortunately they were all locked . . . until Armond calmly picked the lock on one labeled MARRIED CREW HOUSING.

Callie lifted one brow. "Another rule broken?"

"Just get inside."

There was no furniture inside, but it was marginally warmer. Callie rubbed her arms, feeling the cold now.

Armond fished in his pockets, his slow movements attesting to his weakness. "I've got matches. I'll get kindling and we can use the fireplace—"

Callie stopped him with a hand to his shoulder. "You can barely stand. I'll get it. What do I need?"

"Sticks. A couple of bigger logs."

"Isn't it illegal to burn stuff from a National Seashore?"

"I think we can be forgiven for this." He sat down heavily and took off his shoes.

Callie left the small haven and faced the outside. Leaning against the closed door for strength, she stared into the fog. If she went out in it, she could get lost. She'd seen how easy it was to lose your bearings in fog, how quickly you were alone. The panic that had been with her all her life raised a hurrah, curling in her stomach. Callie set her jaw against it.

She'd just have to mark her way back.

Taking a deep breath to put steel in her spine, she stepped forward. A second step, three more, then she looked back. The building was a fuzzy white. She found a package of crackers in her pocket, part of her perpetual supply of nausea food, and laid it on the ground as a marker.

Forward into the fog. Her steps grew more confident until she glanced back and saw nothing but a tiny dot of orange cracker. She halted, unsure as the fog swirled around her, enveloping her in silence. It stole her confidence as surely as it stole every sensation. She could see nothing except white light, could feel nothing except the cool clouds.

She was utterly alone.

Callie stood stock still, breathing deeply, facing the panic burning inside, refusing to give in. She had to do this; Armond was depending on her. And she was so damn tired of being afraid. Her fears protested, feebler this time, knotting her stomach.

She was much stronger than she had ever believed, Callie realized. She'd faced a madman with a gun and survived a trip in a rowboat on Lake Michigan. Her vegetarian restaurant was a success in a town that glorified andouille sausage and mounds of boiled crawfish. This video series was a good one, and she was partly responsible. Those weren't the accomplishments of a slouch.

Her skin prickled with the cold and with the nerves, but Callie waited, rubbing her arms. She was alone; she'd come this far, she wasn't going to let this beat her.

Outside was hushed and mysterious. Fog swirled in graceful eddies, an op-art pattern of gray on gray. Slowly, gradually, the last remnants of her panic receded, and Callie drew in a long breath. Replacing the panic were feelings she'd never experienced. Quiet peace. Acceptance.

Armond had always accepted their differences; it was time she did, too. She loved him—a strong, honorable man—and she wanted to raise their child together. She wanted her daughter to know her father, to see him sitting at school plays and softball games. She wanted marriage, ring, license, all the ties, and Gabriel tradition be damned. Her family would have to accept it or they'd miss out on sharing her joy.

Callie swallowed hard. She had no illusions about Armond's job and the fact that she would often be afraid for him. What she no longer feared was herself, she realized, her heart giving a tiny flip. Yes, she would sometimes be alone, but she would never be abandoned. Their life together wouldn't be a placid one, but it would be a rich one.

Now she just had to convince Armond of that.

She laid a hand on her stomach. "Trouble is, little one, I've done too good a job of convincing him that we're wrong for each other. Your daddy's kind of stubborn, and when he thinks he's doing the right thing . . ." She shook her head, caressing her belly. "We'll just have to convince him of a different right thing. After all, I'm kind of stubborn, too."

The fluttering in her stomach had nothing to do with panic. It was too early in her pregnancy for a quickening, but Callie was certain what she felt was her daughter's approval.

She stepped out into the fog to gather kindling, dropping her packages of dried apricots, granola bars, and crackers in a Hansel-and-Gretel trail back to Armond.

When Callie returned with the sticks, Armond was stretched out on the floor, his shoes, socks, sweater, and jacket off. Sweater beneath his head, jacket on top. His hand curled above his head, resting on his gun. Her makeshift bandage graced his otherwise naked chest. He was sound asleep. There wouldn't be many moments when he was so vulnerable to her.

Her knees went weak with love and desire. Callie knelt beside him, knowing she could do nothing about the sweet need. Yet. One hand grazed his arm. Beneath her palm was smooth skin, hard muscle, masculine power. She'd always liked a nice pair of arms on a man, and Armond's were mighty fine ones. She didn't intend to lose the pleasure of feeling them around her, of feeling them hold her while he plunged inside her. A mischievous smile broke over her. "Armond thinks he's going to be strong and give me up for my own good. Well, I've got a few tricks he's going to have a hard time resisting," she whispered to her belly.

First, however, other basic needs required attention.

Callie started a fire in the fireplace. One advantage of being a chef was that she was quite adept with fires. A paper rattled in her pocket, and she pulled out one of the packages she'd collected on her way back to Armond. Next thing, though, was water. She went to the door and stared out at the fog a moment, then stepped out. The silence was beautiful and peaceful, not a thing to be feared.

Munching her cracker, she searched around the building, then the nearby grounds, for a container. At last she found a forgotten plastic bottle. She rinsed it in the lake, filled it and drank her fill, and then filled it up again and carried it back to their shelter.

Armond snored softly. Callie took off her shoes and damp sweatshirt and jeans. She laid down beside him, her front to his back, and snuggled beneath his jacket, pulling hers on over the top of them. His skin felt reassuringly cool, his heartbeat steady beneath her palm.

Callie laid down her head and slept.

His shoulder hurt like hell. His head was tolerable. His hip, pressed against a hard surface, ached. But his back, ah, his back was in ecstasy. Armond let out a small breath of pleasure.

Callie pressed against his back. Her breasts were soft against him, and the curve of her belly fit in the small of his back. Her even breaths were warm and moist against his skin. Her gingery scent teased him, stirring his blood through his heart and groin. His chest wasn't doing so badly, either, he realized, because her hand rested protectively against his sternum.

Odd to think of Callie protecting him.

Because he'd done such a poor-assed job of protecting her, Armond thought with disgust, effectively dousing desire. He opened his eyes, confirming memory. Titus. Guns. The boat. North Manitou wilderness.

Sometimes amnesia could be a blessing.

With a soft sound almost like a purr, Callie burrowed against him. He could get used to waking up beside her. They'd never shared that pleasure, but already he found himself longing to make it permanent, longing to turn around and take her in his arms and slip inside her with a smooth stroke. Be her husband and not simply the father of her child.

Yeah, he made real good husband material. He had his memories back, and nothing in them reassured him that he could be what Callie needed. When they'd first returned it had felt like looking at a vivid movie of someone else's life, with all the flaws and faults detailed. Yet already he could feel the memories settling back inside, becoming part of him.

You're different, whispered a rebellious voice. *Callie says you laugh more. You told her about the guilt, and you never trusted anyone enough to do that.*

Because he knew she would never betray him.

Because with her, his soul was at utter peace.

Because her leg had just draped over his, settling her sex firmly against his butt. Warning flares ignited inside, bringing desire and stirring him to arousal.

He couldn't drag her into his world, Armond thought desperately. *Merde,* he'd almost gotten her killed. He'd go through an eternity of hells in this life not to experience that one again.

And he had to get out of here before he forgot all his good intentions and turned and claimed her. Armond slid his hips to extract himself from her velvet grip. In her sleep Callie murmured a protest, and her hand splayed on his abdomen, holding him tight, then slipped beneath his jeans. Her little finger shifted, a tiny movement that caressed the tip of him. Armond held his breath, holding himself still as a rock. When she did it again all of him became rock-hard. Her finger moved again, this time to circle him.

The little tease wasn't asleep. Armond sprang from their makeshift bed, ignoring the protest from his shoulder, and turned, hand on hip, to glare at her. Brilliant sunbeams glinted through the windows, lighting the room with their glow. They must have slept through the day and night, and the fog must have lifted.

They had to get . . . out . . . of . . . The thought vanished as Callie gave him a sleepy, unrepentant smile and shoved her tangled hair from her eyes. His chest ached at the sight. She was so beautiful in the morning.

"You're going to have to stop doing that," she said with a yawn.

That's what he'd planned to tell her. "Doing what?"

"Leaving my bed so quickly. We've never had a nice, leisurely wakeup."

Armond refused to admit he'd been thinking the same thing. "We agreed, Callie, that our lifestyles don't mesh. Don't make this harder."

"Harder?" Her eyes flickered to his readying sex, then back to his face as she rose and stretched. Her thin undershirt rose, revealing the tiny ring in her navel. Her pointed nipples told him that she'd been aroused by their morning snuggle as well. Her tongue slowly traced her lips. "I intend to make it as hard as possible, Agent Marceaux. You see, I've changed my mind."

"What?" His brain was definitely losing out on the blood supply. When had Callie turned into a such a confident, sensual tease?

"I've changed my mind. I want to marry you."

"You can't—You don't—" His higher functions were definitely deteriorating.

She looked straight at him, not hiding her need and her vulnerability. "I love you, Armond, and you told me you love me. Was it a lie?"

Armond shook his head. "But Callie, my work—"

"You will do the work you need to do. I wouldn't ask you to stop, any more than you will ask me to stop the video series or start eating meat. Because I've realized something. Even if you aren't physically with me all the time, we're together here"—she touched his chest, right above his heart—"twenty-four/seven. Whenever I really need you, you're always there for me."

It was so tempting to believe her. "I almost got you killed."

"Not you. Titus. And you stood between him and that boat. You were willing to give your life for me."

"Any good agent would," he said gruffly.

She didn't dignify the lie with an answer. Instead she took a step closer. Armond backed up. Callie followed until he bumped against the end of the warm fireplace. "We belong together, Special Agent Marceaux, and I'm going to keep telling you that until you believe it. You loved me enough to give me up. I love you enough to fight for you."

Armond swallowed tight.

Callie leaned against him, seating the thin fabric of her panties against his tight loins. She wrapped her arms around his neck and her hips swished against him. "And I'm not above fighting dirty. Didn't I tell you, Gabriel women are very determined." She kissed him.

Lost in the haze of desire, Armond barely heard the door open.

"Hey," called a man's gruff voice. "You jumping the gun on the deer hunt?"

Armond whirled around, putting Callie behind him. *Merde,* he'd left his gun on the floor. He was about to lunge for it when the reality registered and held him.

The man who stared from the doorway was dressed in a flannel shirt and work pants, bright orange vest and orange hat with ear flaps. A hunting rifle hung from his back.

The hunters, selected for the annual October hunt to cull the overpopulated deer herd on the island, had arrived.

Chapter Twenty-six

As they drove the final yards down the blacktop road, Callie was relieved to finally get back to the winery.

The hunters were nice men, she supposed, but she always felt uneasy around hunters, Armond being the lone exception. Knowing that several of them, crowding behind their astonished comrade, had seen her nearly naked didn't help with the comfort factor.

She'd almost won the battle for Armond, too, until their untimely interruption. She'd almost gotten him to admit that they were too right for each other to let the differences stand between them. Then a bunch of orange-flapped men in fatigues and flannel had ruined it.

No hunter was going to win against her.

Yet from the time he'd offered an undertone explanation to the ranger and arranged their transport back to the winery, she'd seen Armond withdrawing and the warrior taking over. She'd lost the nerve for seduction, and her attempts at conversation were met with monosyllables. With his memory back, she knew exactly where Armond's focus had shifted: to Conrad Titus and to bringing a traitor to justice.

She'd better get used to it, but he could have at least waited until she got her engagement ring back.

The harvest had continued during their twenty-four-hour absence, and the pickers were at the far reaches of the vineyard. Despite her fatigue and uncertainty, everyday concerns began to intrude. She hoped Dion and Christian weren't too upset with the delay in the shooting schedule. Please God, just let her slip in unnoticed, change into something clean, comb her hair, and brush her teeth before she had to deal with the inquiries.

Nope, she'd used up all her store of good luck, Callie realized when a crowd of eyes fixed on her and Armond as soon as they entered the tasting room. Bernadette, Norman, Zeke, Harriet, Dion, and—Callie swore under her breath.

"Mother," she muttered.

Lillian Gabriel rushed over and enveloped her in a hug. "Darling, we were so worried. Where have you been? What happened? Were you caught in that ungodly fog?" Lillian's concern washed over her, bathed her in its familiar warmth. She settled back and brushed Callie's hair off her face. "Are you all right?"

"I'm fine. It's a long story."

"Your face is scratched. You'll need some aloe."

"Thanks. A branch caught me when I was collecting kindling."

"Kindling?"

"Although, I must admit, after the bullets, the forest seemed almost pleasant."

"Bullets!" Lillian's shocked gasp was echoed by the collective.

Questions bombarded them, but Callie ignored them, focused on the drama of Lillian and Armond. One arm wrapped protectively around her daughter, her mother glared at Armond over Callie's shoulder.

"Bullets?" she spat. "What are you thinking of, putting her in danger like that? I want you to stay away from my daughter. If I have to get a restraining order, I'll do it."

"Don't you think that's Callie's decision, Dr. Gabriel?" Armond said, his voice a mere growl.

"I think Callie knows what's expected of a Gabriel woman."

Callie plucked her mother's arm from her shoulder. "Stow it, Mom," she said gently. "I've never been a typical Gabriel, and I'm starting some new traditions. Like marriage."

"Marriage?" From Lillian's shocked reaction, you'd have thought Callie announced she was auditioning for lead stripper at the Velvet Kitten Club.

"Marriage?" breathed Bernadette Rochon, looking expectantly between Callie and Armond.

"What about our history?" protested Lillian. "You risk—"

"No, I don't. All those other Gabriel unions were missing something, you see."

"What?"

"Love," Callie said softly. "I love him. And he loves me. That's what's bringing us together, nothing else. And after all, as the man said, it's my decision. Armond is going to be my husband, and the Gabriels will have to get used to that."

"Marriage?" asked Bernadette again. "Armond, you're getting married?"

"Well—"

Callie didn't give him time to offer an objection. "He'd better. After all, he's the one who got me pregnant."

"Pregnant?" Bernadette's eyes widened.

"The least he can do is offer to marry me, don't you think?"

"Armond—" started Norman sternly.

Callie cast a sidelong glance at a silent Armond, wondering how he'd taken her little announcement.

"You little witch," he said, his undertone laced with humor.

"I told you I fought dirty."

To her surprise and delight, he burst out laughing, cutting short Norman's lecture. "She failed to mention I asked—"

"—demanded," Callie corrected.

"—demanded that she marry me, and she refused."

Now everyone looked confused. Armond gripped her elbow lightly. "If you'll excuse us," he said to the crowd, "I think Callie and I have some things to discuss." He propelled her toward his room.

To her disappointment, it wasn't a declaration of love he began with. "I have to leave, Callie. Now."

"You're going after Conrad Titus, aren't you?"

"Yes. He's got a twenty-four-hour start on me, and he'll be disappearing. I can't let him go. This has to be settled before I can do anything about us."

"All right." At least he was talking in terms of *us.*

Armond blinked. "Just 'all right'?"

"I told you, I've grown up. I won't come between you and your work. I'll only demand one thing of you—that you come back to me. While you're with me, love me with everything you've got, not because it's the right thing to do but because it's the only thing you can do. While you're not with me, do your job the best you can, and know that you will be coming back to me."

He looked at her, stunned; then he traced the line of her jaw with the edge of his hand. "I never saw you stand up to your mother like that."

"She'll come around." At least Callie hoped she would, but she couldn't live her life around her mother's expectations. Not any more. "Now, go."

"You're sending me away?"

"The sooner to get you back. There's just one thing you need to do first."

"What?"

She held out her left hand. "The ring."

He laughed and a moment later slipped the diamond on her finger. He leaned over and gave her a quick, scorching kiss, and then, as silently as the fog, he was gone.

Conrad Titus had disappeared by the time Armond began the hunt, but thanks to FBI resources and a little unacknowledged help from Hugh Pendragon, he located the man just as Titus was about to slip out of the country through an isolated airport. "Going somewhere?" Armond dropped into the airport seat beside Titus and laid a hand on his shoulder. The metallic taste of the man's perfidy spread from his tongue to his stomach, curling around like a serpent.

Titus turned, startled, then sagged in his seat as he saw Armond and the phalanx of agents with him.

This was one who would not escape justice, Armond thought with satisfaction, who would do no more harm. They had him dead to rights, and soon they'd have the lab and one more piece of Guy Centurion's empire. Titus was the type who would yield whatever he knew in a plea bargain for leniency.

"The smears against me that you planted weren't

quite thorough enough," Armond said conversationally. "They might have worked if I hadn't come back memory intact. Or if the director hadn't already figured out someone was supplying Guy Centurion with intel. He just didn't know who."

"What triggered your memory?" Titus asked.

"Your threat to Callie."

A spasm of irritation crossed Titus's face. "So if I hadn't come after you—"

"I'd have still hunted you down, you son-of-a-bitch traitor," Armond replied softly, then jerked his head toward the waiting agents. Stone-faced, they snapped on the handcuffs as they read Titus his rights, then led him away.

The taste of guilt evaporated, leaving only satisfaction. Armond stood and brushed his hands clean on his trousers.

There was something else this time, something more than satisfaction.

Love. This time he had someone to get home to.

"You won." Aphrodite's mirror clattered on the table before Hera.

She looked up from her game of bows and bolts with Zeus to raise a quizzical brow toward Dion. "Armond isn't back yet."

Dion shrugged. "He will be. I was wrong. Those two are a match, both disgustingly proper."

"You can keep the mirror," Hera told him. "My ring wasn't much of a prize to bargain with."

Dion hesitated, then thrust the petite mirror back in his pocket. "Never let it be said Dionysus did not take advantage of a generous gesture." Uninvited, he sprawled into the empty chair by the polished wooden table. They were alone in the corner of the tasting room; the others had gone to bed. He pointed to their nearly equal piles of colorful cubes. "Who's winning?"

"I am," Zeus crowed. "Hera already owes me a foot rub."

Hera understood his glee; nine out of ten games of bows and bolts, she beat him. Tonight, though, was different.

Zeus leaned forward, his dinner-mint breath caressing her across the table. "I want it with almond oil," he murmured, both commanding and inviting.

Almond oil and the hot springs of D-alphus—their special time after the ceremony of bonding. Why tonight did he have to be so much the man she'd wed? Did he have to raise the specter of those special evenings? Tonight she was going home.

"Almond oil," she agreed, her heart heavy in her chest. If only he could come with her, this man who held too much of her soul. But the Oracle had denied her request again, and with utter finality. Ask another time and her permission would be revoked. That thought made her bones ache as though she'd been struck with influenza.

So did the thought of leaving Zeus.

Dion fingered an unclaimed cube. "What will you be doing next? You're welcome to stay with the video series."

Hera shook her head. "We always knew this was only for this short time. We both have other responsibilities."

"My secretary, Mrs. Hunsacker, is breathing fire to get me back in the office," Zeus added. "The woman is a stricter guardian than Cerberus." He looked at Hera. "What do you suppose happened to the beast? Cerberus, not Mrs. Hunsacker."

"Cerberus can take care of himself."

"True. What are your plans, Dion?" Zeus shook the three hexagonal dice.

"We'll finish the video series." He tossed the cube up and caught it. "I thought I might console the mother."

Zeus gave a crack of laughter. "Dionysus, always the god of pleasure."

"You know me." Dion shrugged. "She's an interesting woman."

The answer was typical Dionysus, but there was something new in his eyes, Hera thought. A loneliness. An admiration. She wished she would be here to see what developed.

Zeus threw the three hexagonal dice, then gave an exuberant shout as it came up three yellows. He separated out the cubes from Hera's pile, then gave her an expectant leer. "That makes a full bow and a storm for me. You'll soon have to add the legs to that rub."

Abruptly Hera rose, her throat clogged with tears. She couldn't continue, couldn't pretend that everything was fine and casual. "It's late and I'm tired. I concede the game."

These past days with Zeus, she'd seen how much he'd changed, and she'd fallen in love with him all over again. Leaving was flaying her heart into tiny pieces.

But missing home after millennia of loss was crushing her by slow, excruciating centimeters.

She gripped the edge of the table. The vineyard was quiet; everyone but the three gods had gone to sleep. But what she had to say was private, for Zeus alone. "Zeus, I . . . Will you come with me? I need to tell you something."

"Of course." His grin was expectant, knowing, then it faded as his gaze locked with hers. "Dion, will you excuse us?"

"Of course," murmured the god of wine and pleasure. "Don't I always?"

Zeus followed Hera out. His nearness, his scent teased at her. Despite the years his body was still firm and trim, and she'd come to like the salt and pepper of his hair. Mostly, however, she had come to like the man he was today. And that she could not regret, though it made the leaving so very much harder.

"Where are we going?" Zeus asked when they passed her room.

"Over there." Hera pointed to an open grassy spot, a pinnacle on the spine of the peninsula, and a few moments of silence later they reached it.

Zeus's lips darkened to a scowl when he noticed the bag she had packed. "Are you leaving?" he demanded.

"Yes. I'm going home."

"To Chicago?"

Slowly Hera shook her head. "I'm going home to D-alphus. They said if the matchmaking went well with Callie and Armond, I would have paid my debt to Callisto, the woman I harmed. I could come home. I tried to get them to agree to take you—"

"I don't want to go back," roared Zeus. "I like it here."

"Even without your powers?"

"Even—" He broke off, then nodded. "Yes, even without my powers. Don't go, Hera." He gripped her shoulders, then bent and took her lips in a kiss that seized her heart. "Don't leave. Don't you remember how it was? How we chafed at the restrictions and the blandness?"

"You chafed," she said softly. "I liked the order."

Zeus reeled back, as if stunned. "I thought you felt as I did."

"You assumed. You never asked."

"But you came with me."

377

"I was your wife," she said simply.

"Wasn't there ever love? Was it only duty?" His eyes were dark shadows in the smooth face.

"It was love and duty. And we've recaptured that."

"Then stay with me." Zeus gripped her hands tightly. "Stay with me. We're doing good things here. We're good together."

"But you can't give me what I want. Home. I miss it, Zeus." Tears welled in her eyes. "I miss the hot spas and the clipped greens and the yellow sky and the hours of meditation."

Zeus dropped her hands. "You really want this?"

"I want you, but I need D-alphus."

Zeus swallowed hard and stepped farther away from her. His hands shook, but his voice was steady. "Then I'll let you go. But do it now, before I lose my courage."

She wanted to give him one final kiss, hold him one final time, but it would not be fair to either of them. With her heart in her stomach, with her vision blurred from unshed tears, Hera retrieved the orb she'd carried since her exile. She looped the handle of her satchel over her shoulder, then put her fingers to the indentations of the orb. It hummed and glowed, until the image of the leader of the Titanic Oracle appeared. He glanced once at Zeus, then kept his gaze firmly on Hera.

"You are ready?" asked his tinny voice.

"I am."

"Then rejoin us, my daughter." The orb resumed its humming and glowing, stretching out the light to envelope her. Through the haze of gold, Hera saw Zeus watching her, without movement; not even his eyes strayed. The gold intensified, so rich she could barely keep her eyes open against the glitter, but she did, her gaze locked with Zeus.

The *gris-gris* charm she'd placed around her neck shattered in a glistening flash, sprinkling her with the fragrant residue.

This was wrong.

"No!" she shouted, soundless behind the hum. "I can't go."

With a flash the glow enveloped her, and she disappeared.

Hera, once queen of the gods, lately queen of cleansers, vanished from Earth with a sharp crack of ethereal thunder.

Zeus stared at the spot where she'd vanished until his eyes were so dry they burned. She was gone. She was really gone. Hera, the other half of his soul, was gone.

And nothing could bring her back.

She was gone because of him. He had been foolish and cruel in the past, self-centered and heedless and hurting. But he had just atoned for those misdeeds, because he had just paid the ultimate price.

Hera was gone forever.

A sharp noise woke Callie, a distinct contrast to her usual wake-up call of overactive bladder. When the noise wasn't repeated, though, Callie snuggled back down in bed, grateful for the pile of covers atop her. She had about drifted off when another noise disturbed her—the soft sound of her door being opened.

Someone came into the room, recognizable by no sounds, only by the familiar curling lick of heat in her belly. "Armond?"

"It had better not be anyone else," he whispered in mock sternness. He sat beside her on the bed.

"Did you get Titus?"

"I did. He won't bother you again." He kissed her on the nose. "And I did miss you while I was gone."

"I missed you, too." She wrapped her arms about his shoulders and pulled him down for a more complete, satisfying kiss. They were both breathless when it finished.

"Are you sure about this, Callie? About us?" His strong fingers caressed her hair and cheek with gentleness. "God knows, I'm no matrimonial prize."

"You are to me. Knowing you has made me stronger."

"And knowing you has given me a joy I never expected."

"Does this mean you're accepting my proposal?"

"Yes, it does. I've given you up too many times—after the cabin, after this"—his hand cupped her belly—"at the beach. I'm not going to do it again." He picked up her left hand and kissed the glittering diamond. "Callie, will you marry me?"

"Yes," she answered simply.

His arms tightened around her, drawing her close to his heat, and he shared with her a kiss of promises and forevers.

Callie tried to draw him onto the bed, but he resisted, rising instead. She scowled at him. "Aren't you going to join me? Ah, dang it, Armond, don't tell me you're getting one of those let's-do-this-right urges that will insist on celibacy until the big day."

"No!" His heartfelt horror reassured her, as did the efficient manner in which he stripped off his shirt. And when he assessed her with those knowing gray eyes the heat in them was a definite plus.

Callie fingered the bow on her flannel nightgown. She hadn't expected Armond back so soon, and the night had turned colder, but now she was heartily sorry for the flannel and the thick, fuzzy socks. "Not the most seductive, am I?"

"I am about to burst my jeans with wanting you."

She gave him a delighted smile. "I turn you on?"

"Callie, you could have on a full-body chastity belt and you would still turn me on. You will turn me on when you're lumbering around with a nine-month belly, although I won't do anything too vigorous about it, and you will turn me on when we celebrate our fiftieth wedding anniversary. First, though, I want to show you something."

He held out his hand; she took it and rose, not shivering at all with the loss of the pile of covers as another heat filled her. He led her to the door that opened onto her isolated patio.

"Close your eyes," he told her, and Callie complied.

The whoosh of cold told her that Armond had opened the door; then he led her a couple more steps forward. Crisp, fresh wind whistled against her flannel gown, until Armond stood behind her, his body flush with hers, his arms snug around her.

"Open your eyes, Callie," he whispered.

Outside was a whirl of white and cold, but pressed against Armond, wrapped in his arms, Callie felt the cold nowhere but the tip of her nose. "It's snowing," she exclaimed softly.

The promised snow had finally arrived. Soft, white, cold flakes drifted to the ground, surrounding them with nature's bridal veil. The night was hushed, reverent, filled with the silent eddies of snowflakes.

"It's beautiful," she breathed.

Armond kissed the side of her neck and nipped her earlobe, just above her earrings. "You told me, that night you overheard me with Dion, that you wanted to show me a snowflake. Now I want to show you one, to replace that memory."

With only snow and silence as company, he extended her hand, his cradling it from beneath. Snowflakes fell to her palm, which he then pressed against his cheek. She felt the roughness of his chin, the cool of the snow, the strength of his jaw. He kissed her palm, warming it with his breath, warming her body with the light strokes of his other hand.

"I love you, Callie."

It was a beautiful memory. "I love you, too."

He turned her in his arms and kissed her—solid, strong, exciting. Only a long time afterward did she lead him back to the bed. This time he got in bed with her, pulling her close against his snow-cooled chest. This time he wouldn't be leaving before morning, she was sure.

Forever she would be in his heart.

As he would be in hers.

Callie still remembered the way to Armond's cabin.

" 'Park below the levee, walk back one mile,' " she quoted to herself, trudging through the narrow path. The leaves had mostly disappeared since the last time, as had the squirrel, but the blue heron soared above. Smiling, Callie stopped a moment to admire its graceful glide. She still preferred the city, but the debilitating fear was gone. When she started back up, though, she carefully avoided the spider silk spanning the walk. She would never like spiders.

" 'Twenty minutes, that's all it will take. The path will narrow, then disappear, but you can make it, Callie,' " she recited the instructions. "And will you be waiting this time, Armond?" He was flying in from Atlanta today, and she'd sent him an e-mail asking him to meet her here.

Three months ago he had given her a beautiful memory of snow. Likewise, she now wanted to banish any lingering unpleasant memories of the cabin.

And she had something to tell him.

In the intervening weeks, they'd both been busy—

she with the video series and Armond with work and the Guy Centurion–Conrad Titus case. They'd snatched together whatever weekends, days, and moments they could, spent a fortune on telephone charges and flights. And gotten married, thanks to some efficient assistance from Lillian Gabriel. Joy was throwing them a belated reception tonight.

Callie was looking to the future together, though. The video series was on hiatus until spring, and Armond had been granted a transfer to the New Orleans Field Office.

The path in front of her closed, and she plunged through the final barrier of trees.

The clearing was still, the cabin shuttered.

"Armond?" she called, receiving only silence. Dang! Had she gotten here first? She peered into the windows but didn't see any evidence of Armond, so she went around to the back.

The green-black waters of the bayou were placid. No alligators and no feral hogs. No Armond.

There was no shadow, no sound that gave her warning, but in one second she sensed someone behind her and in the next she found herself surrounded by a pair of strong, warm, masculine arms.

"Looking for someone?" asked a low voice close to her ear.

Recognition was instantaneous. Callie sagged in the embrace. "Armond, Mother of Mary, you scared me." For one endless, grateful moment she reveled in the missed pleasure of his arms around her.

"Not my intention." His hands swiftly patted her down. Not frisking her this time. Callie grinned. Her straight-arrow husband was copping a quick feel.

Swiftly she turned and wrapped her arms around him. She stood on tiptoe to kiss him. "Dear Lord, but I missed you."

His kiss was everything that she'd missed. "I missed you, too," he growled, swinging her up into his arms.

"Your shoulder—"

"Healed." He shouldered open the back door, headed toward the bedroom.

"I have something to tell—"

"Later," he commanded.

"Gonna take me to bed first?"

"Yes."

She grinned at him. "Good."

Armond reveled in the feel of having Callie back in his arms. She fit him so well, her skin to his, her soul filling all the hollows inside him. Ah, but he had missed her. He lowered her to the bed, followed her, rapidly dispensed with clothing.

Their lovemaking was hot, swift, potent, uninhibited. Here in the wilderness there was no one but him to share her cry of climax, no one but her to moan at the guttural sound of his release.

Afterward, filled with the glow of satiation, he rested his hand on her belly, lightly stroking. She was definitely rounding and he loved to feel it, loved to know she protected their child deep inside.

"There's something I need to tell you," Callie said, looking up, her face dappled with sunshine.

Armond stilled his gentle stroking, uneasy at the note in her voice. Nothing showed in her eyes. "What?"

Callie swallowed hard, shooting his worry up higher. "I had an ultrasound yesterday."

Everything inside Armond tensed, stealing his breath. Was she having some symptoms? Bleeding? Had they found some problem? With her? With the baby? His fingers closed. "Why? Is something—?"

She rested a reassuring hand on his arm. "I'm fine.

The baby's fine. The ultrasound was just a routine precaution."

Relief washed through him. Armond buried his face in her neck, pulling her close. "Thank God! I wish I had been there with you."

"Me, too. You could have revived my mother after she fainted."

Armond reared back, lifting his brow in question.

"You see," Callie began, "lots of times the baby isn't positioned right, so you can't tell, but there it was. Clear as the breeze."

Armond frowned. "What the hell are you talking about?"

"Our baby. They got a good shot at the genital area."

"And?"

"Our little guy was sporting his stuff proud as his daddy. You've got strong sperm, Armond Marceaux. You're the proud papa of the first-ever Gabriel son."

Armond stared at her a moment; then the straight-arrow special agent rolled to his naked back, pulling his wife atop him, and roared with laughter.

Epilogue

The party at Greenwood was in full swing when Zeus arrived. Joy Hennessy was throwing a belated wedding reception for Callie and Armond. Zeus grabbed a glass of wine, then wandered the room, searching for his hostess and the guests of honor. He found Joy first, her red hair bound up in a loose knot as she directed the placement of food.

"Zeke, I'm so glad you could make it." Joy gave him a brilliant smile. "Callie said she'd met you on the video shoot. Isn't that a strange coincidence? That you knew us both?"

"Yes, quite a coincidence." Zeus gave her a peck on the cheek. "You look happy, my dear."

"I am. Where's Harriet?"

"She's visiting home," he said, proud of his even tone.

"Where's home?"

Farther than you can imagine. "Greece."

"Really? I didn't realize she was Greek. Oh, wait, Mark will want to say hello to you."

As if conjured by his name, the magician joined his wife and laid an easy arm across her shoulders. He greeted Zeke with a handshake.

"Where's Harriet?" asked Mark.

"Greece. I'm hearing great things about your show." Zeus felt a bit fatherly toward these couples he'd united, and he followed their lives as best he could without the powers of Olympus to help. "That Elements Escape—fantastic."

"Thanks." Mark turned to Joy. "Dia says to tell you everything is fabulous, although she's never tasted curry that spicy."

Joy laughed. "That's because Callie made it. Her own reception and she's helped me make half of it."

"Callie likes being in the kitchen, just like you," Mark said with a tender touch to her chin that told Zeus all he needed to know about these two. "Do you suppose she knows how to—?" He whispered something to Joy that had her cheeks instantly fiery. She gave Zeus a mortified look.

He laughed. "I think I'll find Callie."

The guest list was an eclectic mix of people. Cops and special agents rubbed elbows with the New Orleans elite invited by the Gabriels. Greenwood's staff mingled with the varied mix of Callie's customers and friends and Armond's parents. Across the room, he saw Dion standing next to Lillian Gabriel, engaged in conversation with a tuxedoed circle of guests.

For a moment the two gods' eyes met. Dion had gotten him through those rough first hours and days after Hera had left, when his only thought was to drown himself in the amnesia of wine. It was Dion who'd brought him back to the living with the sardonic suggestion that slow suicide was not a fitting end for the king of the gods and if he was going to kill himself, he might try something with fireworks and lightning.

The suggestion had jolted him. Like Dion, Zeus had always grabbed life with both hands. Even without Hera, there were sweet moments in it, and he had his self-appointed task as matchmaker to fulfill.

After all, look how successful he'd been so far. Even without his powers, he'd think of ways to help.

Zeus lifted a glass of wine in thanks. Dion returned the salute, then turned his attention back to Lillian.

Zeus didn't know whether their affair would last, or go any further. Dion was too mercurial to settle long, but for the time, at least, he was not lonely. And Lillian Gabriel was a unique lady.

Mark's show was in Biloxi this weekend, and his crew added an exotic touch to the guest list. One leggy blonde captured his attention. Dia Trelawny, Mark's assistant and a known magician in her own right.

Zeus smiled fondly as he went over to her. Once they had shared a single, intimate kiss. All in the name of his higher purpose of matchmaking, of course. The fact that she was a descendant of Leda, the woman who had birthed him twins, had nothing to do with it. Nothing at all.

Would she remember him?

"Zeke Jupiter," Dia exclaimed, giving him her wide smile as soon as he reached her side. "Where's your friend Harriet?"

"Moved," he said shortly. "To Greece."

The smile got just a bit brighter, and more intimate. "That means you're here by yourself? You're free these days?"

"I came alone." Zeus smoothed the cuff of his shirt.

Apparently she remembered that kiss, too. When he put his mind to something, he was very good at it.

"I hear you've been very busy these days," Dia said. "Callie says you make her look good in those videos. Ever think of working on stage? I'm looking to start my own show. I could use a good lighting man."

The look she gave him was pure sex and invitation. For a time he could forget his loneliness in her bed. Zeus was so very tempted; then he shook his head. His unbridled lusts had ruled him once and had cost him dearly. He'd learned his lesson.

Besides, charming as Dia was, tempting as she was, she was not Hera. And Hera was the woman who still held his soul.

"The fireworks business is picking up. Mrs. Hunsacker keeps me chained to the office these days."

Dia took her dismissal with easy grace. "If you ever change your mind . . ." She gave him a kiss—not a Hollywood air kiss, but a real one—then ambled away, her hips swaying.

Sometimes, Zeus thought, he was a real fool.

Then he spied Callie and Armond, surrounded by friends. Armond shielded her from the jostling crowd, one hand resting protectively at the small of her back. As Zeus made his way over to them, he saw Armond whisper to one of the waiters, and a moment later a glass of ice water materialized for Callie.

"Hi, Zeke," Callie greeted him, giving him a charming smile. He must have a thing for women with nice smiles, Zeus realized.

"Is Harriet back from Greece?" Armond asked, shaking his hand.

"She's not coming back. She's moved there."

Callie laid a hand on his arm. "I'm sorry."

"Some things just don't work out." He patted her burgeoning belly. "How's the baby doing?"

"Kicking up a storm and keeping me awake nights."

Zeus eyed Armond from the corner of his eye, saw the glow of satisfaction about them both. He'd bet the baby wasn't the only thing keeping them awake nights. "How did your mother take the news?"

"Once she got over the shock of a masculine Gabriel—"

"—Marceaux," interjected Armond.

Callie waved a hand. "Whatever. It took another ultrasound before she'd accept the truth, but now that she's gotten over her shock, she's coming around."

"Excuse me, gentlemen," Lillian interrupted them. "If I may borrow my daughter a moment, there's a broadcasting executive Dion and I would like her to meet."

"Of course." Zeke executed a small bow and kissed her hand as she left, then turned back to Armond, who was staring at him with a curious look. "I heard you were back in New Orleans."

"I requested it, and after my casework against Titus, the request was granted." Armond toyed with the stem of the wineglass he held. "Something curious happened to me recently. I met a juggler and a whittler."

"Really? What made them curious?"

"I've learned to identify people in disguise. It's things like the shape of the ear or a characteristic gesture that give them away. They had the selfsame gestures as a third party I happen to know, a man with some curious ways, also. None of them looked alike, but I could have sworn they were the same person."

"Fancy that."

"Yeah, fancy that." Armond took a sip of his wine, still keeping his eye on Zeus. "Normally that kind of thing nags at me, forces to me to look for answers."

"Are you investigating?"

Armond shook his head. "The guy's basically good, and he did me a big favor. I decided to let him have his secrets, as long as he doesn't try any more tricks with me. Thought you might want to know that."

Zeus smiled to himself. Suspicious but fair, a worthy son of Ares. "Sounds like a fair deal, and I imagine he'll respect that. I wish you and Callie all the best, Armond. Congratulations to you both." Zeus patted him on the arm, then left, and his smile faded.

He was tired, tired of pretending everything was fine. It was easier with work or with strangers who didn't know about Harriet. At the doorway Zeus glanced back at Callie and Armond. They were talking, his head bent slightly over hers. He couldn't see their eyes, but the body language said it all. From the tender touch of his finger against her jaw to the blush in her cheeks as he whispered to her, those two were in love. They would last.

He had accomplished something good here, a worthy deed for the king of the gods. And it was time to move to his next couple.

But it sure had been a lot more fun with Hera.

Zeus sat in his presidential suite at Jupiter Fireworks, tossing darts at a sooty dartboard. Once, he had tossed lightning bolts. The dart hit the board, then dropped to the floor.

He was better with lightning bolts.

The intercom on his desk buzzed. "Mr. Jupiter?"

"Yes, Mrs. Hunsacker? More papers for me to sign? More crises to avert?" His efficient gem of a secretary hated to be reminded that there were certain tasks she did need her boss for.

"There's a woman here to see you. She says—"

A woman? "Send her in."

Zeus dropped his feet to the floor, then stood behind his desk. The full-length windows, with the Rocky Mountains behind him, provided a nice, presidential-looking backdrop.

The woman came in, and the darts dropped from his hand. *Hera?* Zeus rubbed his eyes. He'd gone through a period where every woman both reminded him of Hera and came up short in comparison, but he'd thought he was past that. He opened his eyes.

It *was* Hera.

Instead of her neat business suit, she wore a pair of trim jeans, an oversized sweater, and sandals. By the depths of Tartarus, she looked good. Smelled good, too. Was that almond?

"Hello, Zeus," she said hesitantly.

"What are you doing here?" That wasn't how he'd intended to say it, so harsh and unwelcoming, but— Well, maybe it was how he'd intended it. She'd left him, dammit. "Slumming?"

Her hands fisted on her waist. "You're not going to make this easy for me, are you?"

"Why should I?" He shook his head, trying to make sense of the confusion. "Make what easy for you? Why are you back?"

"I got exiled again."

"What?" His shoulders slumped. "Hera, I'm sorry for you."

"I'm not." She strode to face him across the littered expanse of his desk. "Meditation. Communing. Rules against doing this and going here. Peace, brother. I thought I'd go nuts."

Zeus gaped at her, totally lost now. "I thought you wanted that."

"Not when I've had the excitement of being with you." Her brown gaze met his. "Zeus, that place is boring."

He gave a crack of laughter. "I tried to tell you that."

"In my defense, I was young when we left. A very impressionable, idealistic age."

Zeus snorted. "My dear, you never were impressionable. You were always so strong-willed. It was one of the things I loved about you."

Hera grew very still. "Do you still love me? Before you answer, you should know that I love you. Very much. I regretted my choice before I'd even left."

"What took you so long to get back?" He wasn't quite ready to forgive her, although certain randy parts of him had already stirred with the promise of reconciliation.

"They wouldn't let me leave. They kept telling me all I needed was to calm myself, to let the peace inside, to empty myself of all jealousies and passions, and I would be one with them. Nobody understood when I insisted I liked passion and amusement."

Passion and amusement.

Once he had thought it would be enough. Then she had left, and he wouldn't go through that again.

Zeus forced himself to stay by the windows, not to leap across the desk for an embrace. "How did you get back?"

Hera fingered a stack of papers on his desk, not looking at him. "Remember you showed me how to make a 'screaming squirrel' firework?"

"Hera, you didn't?" Zeus's lips twitched with suppressed laughter. The screaming squirrel was a brilliant white light that shot around the sky with a high-pitched whine.

She nodded. "Half a dozen of them. Right after the ritual evening exhortations for harmony. It was taken as a sign of impending doom and caused a bit of chaos at first. No one hurt, just shook up."

"You can't go back?"

"Not even if they begged me." She looked at him

then. "When we were last together I was so sorry I didn't tell you my plans to leave. And sorrier that I didn't realize sooner that my place is at your side. I'm here to take it back. If you want me."

Zeus thought a moment. "So, D-alphus was boring."

Hera rolled her eyes. "Utterly."

"If I let you back, you'll promise to love, honor, obey?"

The old fire flashed in her eyes. "In your dreams, Zeus, my husband. I'll promise love through eternity, honor if you deserve it, and obey if I agree."

Zeus laughed. "Good, my wife! I need a woman like that."

"All I ask is your love back."

"That you already have. Are you still interested in doing a little matchmaking? We're two for two."

"Maybe in a day or two." She gave him a slow, inviting smile.

Yeah, he'd always liked woman with a smile that said something. "I thought a descendant of Semele—"

"That twit? Now Danaë, there was a woman of courage."

"We could always try for Leda."

"Alcmene."

"You chose last time. It's my turn."

Hera gave in with a grudging nod. "Your choice. But, later." She leaned across the desk to stroke his cheek. "I've missed you."

"And I've missed you." He reached to clasp her hands, but she evaded his grasp.

"Oh, wait, how could I have forgotten?" Zeus frowned as she fished around in the satchel at her shoulder. "There's another reason I can't go back. I don't think the Oracle is going to be too happy I stole these."

Stole? Upright Hera?

The Warrior

She held out her hand. On her palm were two rings. One with a gold lightning bolt. One with a misty cloud. The raw, fresh power in them glowed with a light that made the back of his eyes ache.

Hera picked up the lightning bolt ring and slipped it on his finger. "Welcome back, Zeus."

He put the other on her hand. "And to Hera."

They put their hands together, rings touching. Outside lightning crackled with delight and thunderclouds rolled in a joyous dance.

Zeus and Hera were ready for a new challenge.

THE TRICKSTER

KATHLEEN NANCE

Long after she's given up on his return, Matthew Mark Hennessy strolls back into Joy Taylor's life, bolder than Hermes when he stole Apollo's cattle. But Joy is no longer the girl who had so easily trusted him with her heart. An aspiring chef, she has no intention of being distracted by the fireworks the magician sparks in her. But with a kiss silkier than her custard cream, he melts away her defenses. And she knows the master showman has performed the greatest trick of all: setting her heart afire.

Mark has traveled to Louisiana to uncover the truth, not to rekindle an old passion. But Joy sets him sizzling. It is not her cooking that has him salivating, but the sway of her hips. And though magicians never divulge their secrets, Joy tempts him to confide his innermost desires. In a flash Mark realizes their passion is no illusion, but the magic of true love.

More Than Magic
Kathleen Nance

Darius is as beautiful, as mesmerizing, as dangerous as a man can be. His dark, star-kissed eyes promise exquisite joys, yet it is common knowledge he has no intention of taking a wife. Ever. Sex and sensuality will never ensnare Darius, for he is their master. But magic can. Knowledge of his true name will give a mortal woman power over the arrogant djinni, and an age-old enemy has carefully baited the trap. Alluring yet innocent, Isis Montgomery will snare his attention, and the spell she's been given will bind him to her. But who can control a force that is even more than magic?

__52299-3 $5.99 US/$6.99 CAN

THE PLEASURE MASTER

❧NINA BANGS❧

Stranded by the side of a New York highway on Christmas Eve, hairdresser Kathy Bartlett wishes herself somewhere warm and peaceful with a subservient male at her side. She finds herself transported all right, but to Scotland in 1542 with the last man she would have chosen.

With the face of a dark god or a fallen angel, and the reputation of being able to seduce any woman, Ian Ross is the kind of sexual expert Kathy avoids like the plague. So when she learns that the men in his family are competing to prove their prowess, she sprays hair mousse on his brothers' "love guns" and swears she will never succumb to the explosive attraction she feels for Ian. But as the competition heats up, neither Kathy nor Ian reckon the most powerful aphrodisiac of all: love.

___52445-7 $5.50 US/$6.50 CAN

Saddled
Delores Fossen

Getting a passionate man like Rio McCaine to do what she wants will be like breaking a stallion, Abbie realizes. It will take a lot of work. Easy enough to change her own appearance—to make herself seem more ladylike than perhaps she is, to present herself as the type of girl a man might want to marry—but to get Rio to do everything she wants, she'll have to resort to a lie. Or two. And if she wants to save her sister from the Apaches and keep her inheritance for her own, this half-Comanche gunslinger is the only answer. Still, while Abbie is relatively wily when it comes to getting what she wants, there are a few things that can throw her for a loop....Like what will happen when her handsome husband realizes he's been tricked? Abbie has a feeling it'll be like riding a bucking bronco—and part of her shivers in pleasure at the thought.

__52430-9 $4.99 US/$5.99 CAN